Real China

James Thomas

Order this book online at www.trafford.com
or email orders@trafford.com

Most Trafford titles are also available at major online book retailers.

Note for Librarians: A cataloguing record for this book is available from Library
and Archives Canada at www.collectionscanada.ca/amicus/index-e.html

Printed in Victoria, BC, Canada.

ISBN: 978-1-4251-7880-2 (sc)

ISBN: 978-1-4251-7881-9 (e-book)

*Our mission is to efficiently provide the world's finest, most comprehensive
book publishing service, enabling every author to experience success.
To find out how to publish your book, your way, and have it available
worldwide, visit us online at www.trafford.com*

Trafford rev. 8/19/2009

   www.trafford.com

North America & international
toll-free: 1 888 232 4444 (USA & Canada)
phone: 250 383 6864   fax: 812 355 4082

For Liang, Hannah, Kirsty, Rebecca and Xuan

Introduction

Whether travelling for leisure, on a brief business visit or coming to live and work, it is highly likely that the very first experience, when visiting China, will be something like this:

After arriving at the airport and being taken to the hotel to freshen up, your host will almost certainly take you for a meal, dinner or lunch, depending upon the time of day that you arrive. Since it will be important for the locals to impress you, the restaurant will be of reasonable quality with nice pleasant, probably cultural surroundings. As a first visit the food will be Chinese but benign, the strange stuff comes much later. At the entrance of the restaurant will be a tall pretty girl with snow white skin, long silky black hair and a smile that reveals almost perfect white teeth between fully swollen lips, coated in glossy scarlet-red lipstick. She will catch your eye and look at you as if you are the one of her dreams; you will notice the long traditional dress of red silk, splits on both sides that reach to the top the thigh (how else could she ride a bike?) a traditional Chinese figure-hugging *qipao* as it is called. She'll ask how many people and lead you to your table; as you follow behind you first notice the long shapely legs as they break through what seems the almost waist level side splits in her dress, your eyes will wander from the top of her delicate bony shoulders and then fall to her narrow waist before it widens to the full, perfectly rounded bottom. When she has shown you to the table, she'll quickly disappear and that will be the last you'll see of her until you exit the establishment where she'll give only a half smile and mutter an insincere '*man zou*' (mind how you go).

At your table, a more rounded, dumpy figure will appear, she'll be no more than five feet tall and stand over you whilst you select items from the menu, she'll do her best to persuade the host to buy the most expensive food. Her voice will be sharp and abrupt, her hair will be greasy and tied back and she'll try hard not to smile in case you think you might get something for free.

Meanwhile, an equally unattractive creature will splash Chinese tea from a chipped teapot into a chipped cup. She'll probably stare and will not say anything, you might say thank you but most likely your host will not, such niceties are not required. Looking around the place, you'll see many more of these drone-like figures, speaking loudly, almost shouting, at customers and colleagues alike.

Because patience is not a natural virtue in this most populous of lands, some small cold dishes will immediately be laid out in order to prevent the inevitable irritation of waiting too long for what was ordered. Unless the restaurant is up-market, it is probably not a good idea to eat them; they could have been salvaged from earlier tables or been stood around for days.

Eventually the food comes along, all in separate dishes, placed in the middle for all to share. The norm here is to order more than could possibly be eaten as this is the customary way to entertain. The food is likely to be very good, probably more salty and certainly oilier than you would expect, but tasty nonetheless.

I did not realise it at the time, but my first experience of China, just like yours will probably be, is symbolic of the country and its people. China is a veneer, a thin gloss which covers the reality. Whether you do business, travel, eat or virtually anything, things will always be different and often somewhat disappointing compared to your first impression. The beautiful girl with the pretty smile at the entrance contrasted with the almost rude and scruffy staff inside typifies what China is all about, nothing can be believed at face value, things are never what they seem.

Going into a restaurant is a simple example but it applies to almost every thing that is done be it business travel or leisure. When you see 'buy one get one free' the 'one' is usually a bottle of water or a pack of tissues. When you buy a bus ticket, you can end up sat in the aisle on a one-foot high plastic stool. Anything that seems good value almost certainly is not.

The Chinese seem incredibly insensitive at first glance and being politically correct in the sense that we know, only applies to the government. Shortly after 911, the Shanghai street markets were selling models of the now demolished Twin Towers with a Boeing 767 jet sticking half out of one of them, adjacent to the laughing bust of Bin Laden. All this was mounted on a polished wooden plinth to take prime position on the mantelpiece.

In the centre of the office complex where I worked, in Shenzhen, was an extremely attractive ornamental garden. I complained that they had not allowed for anywhere to sit, thinking it would be a nice place to eat lunch, 'If we did that everyone would sit there' came the reply.

It is a true statement that whilst China is changing rapidly, its population cannot keep-up, the deep seated beliefs haven't budged at all in the last twenty years of lightning transformation. Good manners, consideration and tolerance have yet to break into New China. The trouble is that every now and again, gritting ones teeth after somebody has yet again barged into you in the high street without saying sorry, it is easy to get an unexpected shock when somebody opens the door and then politely waves you through to the front of a queue.

It is always unfair to generalise, places like Beijing and Shanghai seem almost normal. It should also be said that the behaviour does tend to get worse as lands and towns further south are ventured.

This peaks at it worst when arriving in Hainan, that corrupt cheating little community that undeservingly resides on a potential tropical paradise. In Sanya, the main resort, they would not even take me in a normal licensed taxi to my hotel, preferring me to travel in an over-priced limousine.

All the taxi meters have been doctored, this is China's rip-off capital, I highly recommend that you fly straight over it and go on to Thailand for a well-earned seaside break. Paradoxically, even on this little den of deceit, I was touched once by unbelievable kindness at a roadside noodle stall where they were making fresh noodle soup. The soup was wonderful and I asked for a beer which they did not have and so one of the waiting staff cycled across the road to the nearest shop and bought one. The astonishing thing was that the total bill was fifteen yuan for two large bowls of beef noodles and a large bottle of beer, they had only charged me the same price as the shop for the beer and had not added any mark-up. I learned later that the people who operated the roadside stall were from Lanzhou, in North West Gansu province so my total suspicion of the Hainan native remained intact.

Staying on the beer theme, the local shop, close to my apartment building also delivers beer, twelve 640ml bottles at a time, any time of day or night for just 48 Yuan and he won't take the change if I give him a 50 Yuan note.

The point to be made is that whilst being constantly irritated and cheesed-off with the general rude behaviour, from time to time some people, particularly of limited means, will often show unexpected kindness. As tempting as it may be, being equally rude as some of the locals is not the way to behave whilst staying in China, except when you knowingly have been cheated but more of that later.

The theme here is not to put people off from going to China, on the contrary, but the idea behind this book is to give some preparation and education as to what the country is really like.

China seems to be approached internationally from four separate standpoints; firstly the sceptical one, who suspects a rip-off coming before it even surfaces, of which I fall into and am certainly in a minority. Secondly the corporate one where phrases like "ten per cent annual growth" and "1.3 billion consumers" induce the unsuspecting moneybags, that finance world stock markets, to invest heavily with the hope of huge returns. Thirdly there is the predominantly American angle that fears China as an emerging military power and furthermore blames the country for high oil prices. Finally there is the oriental-curiosity set who buy various paraphernalia with characters they cannot understand, practise *Tai Qi* (a kind of exercise that does not involve exercise) and read about *Feng Shui* (Something to do with pointing the bed north in order to get better orgasms).

I hope that perhaps the book gets read on the plane, on the way to a holiday or business meeting. The idea is to highlight all the traps and holes that I have fallen into, to watch for the dangers, to stay healthy and to trust nobody.

I have lived in Shanghai and Shenzhen, off and on over the past ten years and to be honest, I love the place and it's people but at times it has made me angry, disillusioned and frustrated. I have also had some of the best experiences of my life there and have enjoyed the company of many valuable friends but I have also been lied to and cheated frequently.

China is a complex mixture of contrasts, it has some of the poorest people in the world yet some of the richest, it has a communist government and a capitalist society, it has the meanest and rudest people you'll ever come across yet you will be touched often by the generosity and kindness. Most of all, the Chinese make me laugh, sometimes intentionally but more often without. In today's world, China has the most people, some of the most beautiful women, the daftest laws, the scariest roads and the smelliest toilets.

This book is not meant to be a travel guide but more an insight into its people, culture, laws, customs, and peculiarities. It is aimed at the business and leisure traveller alike and hopefully helps you to become China savvy, armed with the mental tools that took me many years of bad experiences to learn. It is not meant to be guide book along the lines of *Lonely Planet* although there are mentions of some of the places that you are likely to find yourself in and places to go that you won't find in such guides.

It does though tell you how to get around, what to do, what not to do, what to expect and what not to expect. It is not a comprehensive guide to the country, it only briefly covers those places that are most likely to be visited.

Hopefully, after ploughing through this text, the reader will have a detailed knowledge of Chinese culture *before* doing business or visiting on holiday and most importantly to recognise, understand and allow for the fact that the Chinese have a different set of values. If this can be well-anticipated then the visit, for whatever purpose, can be much more rewarding.

China is changing fast, really fast, although, as said before, the people are not. To see many of the sights and fascinating history is not so easy. The history gets harder and harder to find and the longer the visit is delayed, the more likely it will be a tour of urban centres and their high rise buildings, traffic congested streets and places like Shanghai which, has already become just another international city in the US skyscraper mould, not unlike New York or Chicago.

The book though does need to answer some of the following ten fundamental questions often a myth to all visitors and certainly were to me:

1. Why is a respirator a good idea when entering many Chinese toilets?
2. Why do the Chinese seem to produce so much phlegm?
3. Why do they then feel they need to decorate the pavement with it?
4. Why do they stare at foreigners so much as if they just stopped over on the way to Mars?
5. Why can they not figure out that it is easier to allow people to exit a lift or subway train before attempting to get in?
6. Why do they think that taking a back hander on virtually every deal is "Chinese Culture" and not theft?
7. Why are they one of the world's biggest savers yet receive one of the lowest interest rates?
8. Why do the Chinese copy everything rather than come up with their own brands and products?

9. Why do they constantly criticise the Japanese for doctoring their history books, when there is hardly a word of truth in their own?
10. Why does the only religion of any real importance come in 100 Yuan denominations?

These questions and many more will be answered and explained, read on!

A Note on Romanisation

There is, in this book, the use of some Chinese characters and the necessary Romanisation of them. Where ever possible I have used the *hanyu pinyin*[1] system, used throughout the mainland and also understood by pretty much anyone under the age of forty. It is greatly superior in consistency and pronunciation than any other used in Taiwan or Hong Kong and one credit to the Mao years.

So Beijing is always written as such, never as Peking; Canton is Guangzhou and I use Mao Zedong and Jiang Jieshi, not Mao Tse Tung and Chang Kai Shek respectively. One exception is Hong Kong, I do not use the pinyin Xiang Gang for obvious reasons.

---

[1] Literally 'Chinese language join sound'

The Main Chinese Festivals and Holidays

元旦 Yuan Dan，1st January

春节 Spring Festival or Chinese Lunar New Year. The first day of the Lunar Calendar, goes on for two weeks on the mainland

元宵节 Yuan Xiao Festival，the 15th day of Chinese Lunar New Year, also known as the lantern festival for the lantern displays, especially in the north.

三八妇女节 Women's day，8th of March

清明节 Qing Ming Festival，5th April Normally this is the time when people visit the graves of relatives, a compulsory pilgrimage for many.

五一劳动节 Labour day，1st May a week-long holiday

五四青年节 Youth day，4th May

六一儿童节 Children's day，1st June

七一建党 Communist Party day，1st July

八一建军节　Army day，1st August

十一国庆节　National Day，1st October anniversary of the founding of the Peoples' Republic, usually a week-long national holiday.

中秋节　Mid-Autumn or Moon Festival，8th month of the lunar calendar 15th . The time to give and eat moon cakes.

重阳节　Chong Yang Festival, 9th month of the lunar calendar 9th. Celebrated by eating sticky rice, wrapped in leaves.

Note: as elsewhere there is no Men's Day!
The Chinese have now cottoned on to Valentines Day, here it was invented to sell cards and flowers but in China it embarrasses young males into buying expensive gifts, which they can barely afford, for their indulgent girlfriends who can then show-off to their envious mates.

Contents

Chapter 1 - The Players 18
Chapter 2 – Culture 35
Chapter 3 – Food 64
Chapter 4 – Environmental Disaster 86
Chapter 5 - Love and Sex 101
Chapter 6 - Crime and Punishment 122
Chapter 7 – Corruption 133
Chapter 8 – Go Shopping 151
Chapter 9 - Language 165
Chapter 10 - A Quick History 174
Chapter 11 - Living and Working in China 219
Chapter 12 - Getting Around 261
Chapter 13 – Places Around China 280
Chapter 14 – It Could All End in Tears 314

Chapter 1 - The Players

As one grows older, the tendency to talk to oneself seems to increase exponentially, is it the onset of dementia or just that increasing life experience gives more subject matter to self-discuss or maybe with age comes the realisation that others just don't listen like they used to? I disguise this by turning it into a song or by singing to myself appropriate lines from other well-know verse. For example when I walk into a packed bar in Moscow, "Everyone is blonde and everyone is beautiful" as the Beautiful South would have put it, seems to sum-up up a brief spot of people watching. In China, walking down any street, Sting's *Englishman in New York* with the lines:

If "manners maketh man" as someone said
Then he's the hero of the day
It takes a man to suffer ignorance and smile
Be yourself no matter what they say

This is highly fitting to modern China, walking down the street people will crash into you with no apology, blow smoke in the face, spit out a lump of thick green phlegm, belch, cough and sneeze without covering their nose and mouth and stare in the most un-nerving manner. Everyone seems so rude by our standards and really it does not matter the status or social class, the rudeness and selfishness is a theme throughout.

Today's China could not be more different than rural United Kingdom; around the clock banging and crashing, over the top illuminated signs chasing each other up and down high-rise buildings and competing for brilliance; on top of that a sensory overload with the foul smells of pungent food, sulphur from factories, traffic fumes and unhygienic toilets. The rapid development of China in recent years has made it virtually everyday news, it will create the most dramatic series of events that shape the early twenty first century for all kinds of reasons from natural disasters to enormous trade deficits. Everyone who visits for work or leisure is going to be a (very small and insignificant) part of it.

The people behind the boom seem to fall into some very small groups. Because the overwhelming majority of Chinese simply go with the flow, due to years of communist programming, a few people stand out as the real drivers behind what is becoming an apparently unstoppable ship. Whether famous or infamous the businessman, the government official, their wives and the prostitute are the key to the nation. To the reader this is probably a ridiculous idea but take away any one of these essential actors and the system will break down.

The Businessman
Since "New China" is all about money and wealth creation, the businessman is an important cog in the country's wheel. The term is general and ranges from the chairman of a conglomerate to a one-man enterprise. The well known saying "it is not what you know but who you know" could never be truer than in China. So most businessmen put little effort into product knowledge just concentrate on securing useful contacts then milking them to death! Selling in China is very simple, if you are Chinese that is, meaning that the rules are uncomplicated although not necessarily the process.

The object is to befriend an important contact, this person may be an influential person in a government or a purchaser in a commercial company maybe a senior manager or technical 'expert' who specifies things. The next stage is to go through a series of entertainment rituals to build up a level of trust and confidence. The traditional way of doing this is to have dinner at an upmarket restaurant and order expensive dishes such as shark's fin, birds' nests and abalone. This is washed down with beer and some *baijiu*, a rice-based spirit that makes turpentine taste like barley water. After the meal they go to a KTV bar where they each select a girl, sit with her, talk with her, dance with her and take her back to the hotel and sleep with her. All paid for by the determined businessman.

Some customers relish in this and will absorb it endlessly, pretending that they are buying, just to lap up the entertainment. Where there are two or three companies going for the same business they will accept entertainment and favours from all suppliers even though some of them they have no intention of buying from. When the customer has some sort of confidence and trust in the supplier, he starts to open up and lets on the scale of the business and gives away secrets that will help to win the order when it comes to the 'fair' tendering process. Of course, in return, he expects around 10% to come back his way in a brown envelope stuffed with 100RMB notes.

For the customer there are great risks involved, if the supplier screws up the order the finger will point at him as to why he chose this particular vendor. For the salesman he has to balance the huge amounts that he spends on entertainment against the likely returns, if any. If the customer does buy a heap of crap like say the NHS computer then he or she can expect a knock on the door from the fraud squad, not that such a unit exists just a normal policeman. Having a job in procuring, or rather having the responsibility to make such decisions, is much sought after simply because everyone knows the salary is irrelevant, it is the graft that counts.

Businessmen, if that's what we should call them, are easy to spot in China. They tend to be overweight, smoke heavily, have bad teeth, ill-fitting suits or, more often than not, are wearing a t-shirt under the jacket, trousers at half-mast and never-been-cleaned pointed-toe slip-on black shoes. They always have little indicators to their wealth say a Rolex watch, a Bally belt and a full-featured mobile connected to their ear-hole via a blue-tooth plug. Showing-off is quite an important part of being Chinese so there must be something expensive, always on display; sometimes that might simply be an 18 year old pretty girl.

The Government Official

Look around any Chinese city and apart from the throat aching air quality and noise, the striking feature is the level of construction that is going on. It can be new high rises, hotels, roads, flyovers or urban railway schemes. Less obvious is the building of new hospitals and shiny plush local government offices. China is selling its manufactures worldwide, step by step, replacing or relegating other world manufacturing centres into insignificance. The government's cut of this, results in huge revenues due to the extremely high taxes that entrepreneurs have to pay. All this money has to be spent in order to provide growth, jobs and wealth for government officials. It works very simply, a particular government department is granted an annual budget for a set purpose and a small group of officials have the responsibility to spend it.

Spend it they must since they will get a generous kickback from the supplier and become rich themselves in the process. There is a substantial section on corruption later, but all companies operating in China, and especially those having long term business relationships with government officials, must send some of the profits back to the person or team of people that signed the deal.

Everyone is at it, if you ask a local person they will simply say that it is Chinese culture and see no wrong in it. If an official gets caught, then the opinion will be that he or she is a crook and needs to be imprisoned or shot (depending upon the amount). Of course most officials could be investigated and usually found guilty (by coerced confession) followed by a ten minute court hearing to have the sentence read-out. However, this only happens where they upset somebody higher up the chain or make the new found wealth so obvious that others start to point the finger. It must be said that not all public officials behave in this way but it is the norm not the exception.

So the system can be viewed from a simplistic perspective, the easiest way to riches is to be a crooked businessman or a corrupt official. Such is the worry of being left behind that many Chinese aspire to be one of the two, running their own business or being able to secure a decent job in a government enterprise that has a position of decision making or authority.

The Prostitute

It may sound strange to suggest that such ladies are an important part of this developing superpower however, the significance cannot be overlooked. Of course such women are a feature of every country but none more so than in China, and inconceivably considerably more than Thailand?

The Players

Geography has a lot to do with it, in round numbers we have 400 million relatively prosperous people living in the city which leaves 900 million poor, living in cramped conditions with less that 10 Yuan per day to survive on. So young women, often with an illegitimate child, leave the baby with their parents and head off to the city for a job, sending money home such that their parents and offspring can have a better life, attend school and so on. When they get to the city, they take jobs in the factories, restaurants and other boom industries only to find that the salary is higher than they received in the village however quickly negated by the increased living costs of the city. To save money they rent a room shared with two or three other girls, and suffer even worse living conditions than they had back home.

For the un-educated as these girls mostly are, restaurant and factory jobs go for 600 yuan per month only, that is only forty pounds. If reasonably pretty or attractive the earning potential is greatly enhanced. Sooner or later a friend or friend of a friend will tell them about the kind of jobs that are available in the city's nightlife. This will involve working in a bar, a KTV club, a massage joint or for some, though not so common, walking the streets.

The bars all have the same format like *Gongye Yi Lu* in *Shekou*, Shenzhen (the local expats call it chicken street) or *Tongren Lu* in Shanghai. A strip of bars where young girls watch the passing men and try to entice them in for a drink. The bars are over-lit with un-coordinating second-hand neon signs, bright in the darkness of night but dark and dingy in daylight. The girls wear cheap dresses, not particularly sexy or scruffy jeans with a low-cut bright red or similar top. The system is the same wherever, the girls flirt, kiss, hug and stroke their customer and persuade them to buy them drinks.

Real China

The drinks are usually 30 Yuan for the customer and double for the girl, as she gets a commission. Her salary is dependent to some extent upon how many drinks she can get out of her escort, he wants to drink slowly, she wants to drink fast, inevitably both get slowly drunk. Later in the evening, after the guy has had so much teasing from the little harlot that his trousers are showing a bulge of Eiffel Tower proportions, she will ask if it is OK to accompany him to his apartment or hotel. Of course this is at extra cost, the going rate is 500-1000 Yuan depending upon the city, but she will generally offer value for money, not that there is a *Which Guide* to such services although increasingly there are websites offering reviews on many girls, based on the experiences of past visitors.

They'll go back to the hotel, she'll ask him to wait while she takes a shower, before jumping into bed with the eager male. Normally condoms are worn but some girls, unaware of the dangers, will have sex without for more money. Some girls, if they like the man, will offer another *one* in the morning. Next day, after they have said their goodbyes and the bill has been paid, she will go home and sleep the whole day before returning to the bar for another evening's hard work on her next guy that cannot control his testosterone levels.

In a KTV establishment, the K stands for Karaoke, more preferred by the Chinese themselves, the system is a little different. Most frequented by our businessman and his clients as described above, and only after a long drawn-out meal with various rounds of drinking toasts or 'gan bei' so that upon arrival they are already half-cut and some may be seriously inebriated. The small group will be led into a private room, almost always in red velvet with crescent-shaped couches. A large TV with two microphones will be perched in the corner.

The Players

The 'mama' will discuss the package which almost always is a couple of bottles of whiskey, a fruit salad encased in a watermelon skin sculpture and a very large bucket of ice. Next, around 10 to 15 girls in long traditional silk *qipao* dresses are led into the room and each man picks one in turn, starting with the most important of course. Although seldom taller than five and half feet themselves, they will prefer tall skinny females with pale skin and big round eyes. I always slowly study each one from head to toe before I finally pick the one with big tits. Next comes the insufferable part, the microphone is passed around and each of the guys sings a melody in an attempted harmony with his new girlfriend. Bad singing voices are not easy on the ear but there is nothing worse than somebody who's tonal range is flatter than Norfolk but however thinks he is a reincarnation of Frank Sinatra; this applies to 99% of the Chinese male population. This over-confidence prompts them to sing at the top of their voice pulling highly emotional facial expressions whilst the remainder suffer in silence and, depending upon the seniority of the performer, will applaud enthusiastically with big Cheshire cat grins. The ladies will sing along, dance a bit but most importantly, prompt numerous toasts in order to get the bottles of whiskey per hour ratio up. At the end of the night, the friskier ones, who can hold their drink, may want to take one of the charming hostesses to a cheap hotel or anywhere private for further entertainment that does not involve singing. If not, the girls will expect a 100 Yuan tip on departure. The fee for a night of passion will vary depending upon the city and the class of the establishment, the cheaper ones will have correspondingly rough-looking women whilst the up-market ones will have seriously beautiful girls on the premises and the prices will reflect this. Contracts worth tens of millions of

RMB are normal and everyday in China, and so necessary expenditure on this kind of entertainment probably seems worth it.

The other type of prostitution is like any country probably and hidden behind the euphemistic system of massage. The Korean-style barber-come-knocking-shop is not so common. Massage joints are virtually on every street, the signs are seldom written in English, simply having the Chinese 足浴 (zuyu[1]) standing for foot massage; you may also see the reflexology foot-map on display as well. Some of these genuinely are foot-massage only and above board body massage but those that have VIP rooms are offering a fully sexual service as well. These places are cheaper than the bars and do include a full massage that ends with erotic stimulation in one form or another. On arrival, they take the client to the room where he can shower and change into the most ridiculous long baggy shorts, in some bright colour such as orange or yellow nylon with an elasticized waist, they fit all ages and sizes from 28" to 80". On top of this a robe is worn, similar colours and material as the shorts, normally washed into a thin frayed rag that would be better employed for washing the car. Sitting around for a while on the bed, the young lady will eventually come in, unlikely to speak any English however she knows the international sign language for shag and blow-job. She will be wearing a lab-technician's white overall and most likely be small and reasonably attractive. However, this five stone weakling has severe power in her fingertips and is able to cause excruciating pain all in the name of massage. She gets paid a set very low salary so the real money is made by selling extras, the extra being

---

[1] Literally footbath

her body. So whilst she is trained to apply traditional Chinese massage she also occasionally lets her hand accidentally on purpose slide up the shorts and brush the man's private regions. She'll do this more and more frequently until she is confident that a swelling is detectable, finally she'll pop the question. These places tend to offer sex at a lower rate than the bars and KTV places probably because there is no need to spend the whole night although some parlours will allow you to sleep there, if you arrive around midnight, thus almost becoming a cheap hotel with extras!

Most of these girls whether in the bar, KTV or massage joint are all looking to the day when a good-looking customer or more importantly a rich guy will come in and ask them out, it does not matter if he is married already. Surprisingly it happens quite frequently although the man is unlikely to be interested in her child, if she has one. Some wealthy men will even set-up a new home with her and keep his first wife completely ignorant of the affair as she will reside in a different city, the man effectively living two lives. It would not be uncommon for one of these nubile massage girls to openly ask if you'd ever considered a second wife.

Probably the most open display of prostitution I have ever seen is in the southern coastal city of Zhuhai. On any afternoon, in the main busy shopping street, extremely attractive young women, at least thirty of them, will walk up and down the high street mostly wearing sculpted jeans, ridiculously high heels and tits in your face low-cut tops. Their mission is to hand out name cards to as many males as possible, provided they are not accompanied by a lady of course. When the police arrive, these girls dart into shops like cockroaches running for cover under kitchen cabinets when the lights are turned-on. It is all a big show, I cannot believe that the police actually want to prevent it and are almost certainly well-paid for putting on their show of pretend entrapment. One can sit in any one of twenty or so little island bars that are also scattered down the middle of the road, and watch the display.

The Middle Class Woman

She is the bystander, wife of the businessman or mandarin, often exposed to sexual diseases passed on from her spouse. China has seen a bulging middle class develop in the past two decades, and the nuclear family of man, woman and child, often plus grandparents in a high-rise apartment, is common place in most cities. For the wife and mother she has a very different lifestyle to that of her parents. For a start she can drive a car around, she can afford to send the little one to school finance extra English lessons, and she need not do any house work because she will have a nanny or *ayi,* as they are called, to cook and clean, wash and iron. So what does she do? For one thing, retirement age for a woman seems to be around forty years only, it is very difficult to get a job past this age. Partly because the businessman likes to employ women he can screw on the side, not just ones to answer the phone, and partly because it keeps the unemployment figures low. Chinese companies are autocratic by nature, the boss decides everything and trusts no-one. Consequently middle-class mothers are slowly slipping into boredom. They go shopping of course, chat to other mothers about how their son or daughter is doing better than any other child but mostly they sit around, have their hair done, watch TV and maybe find a lover. Whatever happens she will strive to keep the family unit going in order to rear the following generation of entrepreneurs and government officials. If married to a business man she will have had to put up with the late nights coming home drunk, the smell of 'foreign' perfume and the increasing undesirability of his waistline. It is hard to imagine what copulating with a man with a beer belly is like but take it from me that making love to a woman with a fat tummy is like humping a beach ball so perhaps it is not too difficult to sympathise. He is usually far too drunk or tired to trouble her for a roll under the covers anyway so she becomes increasingly frustrated. She gets lots of sleep and exercise and reads about how foreigners have the wild passionate sex that she can only dream of. So her mind wanders and fantasizes about the love she thought she had married. It hardly becomes surprising then that married women having affairs is probably very common but seldom spoken about, in their eyes it simply does not happen. The evidence behind this I am afraid is personal but nonetheless convincing. When I sit at my desk and log into *Skype,* a service that allows computer to computer text and voice messaging over the internet for free, I am alarmed by how many times I am disturbed by Chinese females, usually 3-4 times per day. Some are twenty-somethings who want to have my babies, some want to sell me their wares but the overwhelming majority are married women who want to offer me an open goal during extra time. They have no idea what I look like, only that I am male and probably a Johnny Foreigner.

One of the most bizarre things happened to me on a flight from London to Beijing; during the night, when covered in blankets and the lights are dimmed, a middle-aged Chinese lady lay down across three vacant seats in the centre section of a Boeing 747, I was sat on the end. Over a period of maybe two hours she worked herself closer and closer to me, fishing around with her hand until she found mine and started to stroke it. After more passing time and participating in a kind of erotic handshake ritual she muttered a few words to which I responded. Delighted that I could communicate in her language, she went on to uncover my phone number and the name and location of the Beijing hotel I was to stay at. Later that evening, after arrival, she phoned me and suggested we meet, somewhat surprised I agreed and low and behold she was at the door one hour later. After two hours or so of having her wicked way with me, (I suffered greatly) it turned out she is a married lady and almost exactly fits the model above, frustrated with love and life and unable to be fulfilled by her husband. I am no spring chicken, a fifty year-old bloke for heavens sake! When they say "enjoy the flight" I usually mutter under my breath "yeah! Have fun at the dentist" but this time it took on a whole new meaning.

However, these frustrated middle-class ladies will not take any risks nor do anything to threaten the family home, she could not stand the shame and besides she enjoys the prosperity. Moreover, the single most important thing in her life is really the little god she gave birth to and the shrine called an apartment that she builds around him or her.

Of course there is a whole range of people in different occupations and life situations across Chinese cites including teachers, doctors, police, engineers, office workers and so on. But, these lifestyle pioneers, the first four, have more to do with the make-up of city life in New China than any other particular group.

If you are unlucky to need help from the police you will find them lazy, unhelpful and uninterested, unless there is some money in it for them or political pressure from above.

The Players

Teachers are virtually hidden, in schools and colleges up and down the country trying to turn everybody's little monster into a genius. Hospitals in China vary from good to downright dangerous and this likewise applies to the staff, it really does depend upon how much money you have.

The businessman, the official, their wives and the prostitute are the ones that are laying down the values of the new nation, so insidiously that nobody has stopped to think about it. Everybody wants to be a rich business man or powerful official, every woman wants to marry one and every young woman wants to meet one, even if it means selling herself to get there.

There is a lot of envy in China and so get-rich quick is the way forward, then it is your turn to show-off. Real China is about money, getting it as fast as possible and then showing to others that you have it. This leaves us to the 900 million others who are best described in Dickensian terms as "The Poor"

The Poor
Browsing gift shops in a tourist area of London, lifting up a model of Tower Bridge, turn it upside down and there it is 'Made in China'. When souvenirs of our capital city have to be made in the distant orient isn't there something wrong? Not for the country that produced them, world domination through manufacturing is the way, so the Chinese must be all rich and wealthy with a high standard of living right? Nothing of the sort, a few *are* making serious money, the rest are still destitute and poor.

This is where trouble lies ahead. To maintain stability in a country governed by one party in perpetuity, everybody has to be feeling good, expectations of better wealth and conditions must be felt by all, not just the thirty percent who live in the city. So for the seventy percent who have been left behind there is brewing anger and resentment. For a start these people are unlikely to be educated so they can easily become tools for the unscrupulous to lie and cheat to. Because these people are so far behind the elite, they jump at opportunities to become rich quickly themselves. The papers and television show examples of this daily. Just one example occurred in Chongqing where villagers were sold cars, only really fit for the scrap heap, however they came with lucrative taxi licenses. The licenses were fake and the vehicles worthless of course, but it is just typical of a scheme whereby sheer desperation to join the prosperous leaves the door open to being cheated on express wealth creation schemes.

Schools and Hospitals also want to make money such that they have priced themselves beyond the means of those in rural areas, even life-threatening conditions will not be treated until the money is handed over. An example case of this hit the news in 2007 where an elderly man took his very sick grandson to a rural hospital but the hospital would not treat the boy because of insufficient funds. The grandfather went back to the village, a thirty mile round trip, to get more money. Upon his return he was distraught to find that the child had died. Such stories are common place in a country where wealth dictates almost everything.

Rioting is now commonplace throughout the country primarily over land disputes. These disturbances are seldom reported outside of China but can be found in the local press and particularly in the Hong Kong papers when they occur in neighbouring Guangdong province in particular. The situation is almost the same in every case. Local officials have money that they want to spend on development projects and are determined to do so since, as explained before, their personal wealth depends upon it. They need to find land that they either don't need to pay a lot for or can have for free. This is usually on the edge of a city, where the urban transcends into rural and the area is mostly occupied by farmers whose small plot of land is their livelihood, and it is small, an allotment by our standards. Meanwhile back at city hall, plans are drawn-up to sell the land to developers and pay the farmer a pittance in compensation. The farmers have no resources to hire a decent lawyer who may also be paid off in any case and so the last resort is rioting.

Another shocking example was the discovery of slavery in Shanxi province in 2007. The English language *China Daily* reported that "nearly 1,000" children had been abducted and sold as slaves to work in the brick kilns of *hongtong*, *linyi* and *wanrong* counties. Most were abducted at railways stations all over the country although Zhengzhou was particularly notorious. The discovery was made by an under cover reporter who claimed that children were made to work in awful conditions up to fourteen hours per day. They got away with it, as usual, by having the police, local government officials as well as the kiln owners all being on the pay roll.

Every now and again a clampdown on these corrupt officials is announced but the police numbers are poor and those that are there can easily be bought. The poor villagers are then left to rioting and this is going on up and down the country on the edge of virtually every city from small to metropolis. It is not difficult to see how cities are simply spreading like an unstoppable cancer into the environment that surrounds them. Take Shanghai for example, the 70km distance from Pu Dong airport to the city boundary was miles of small farms just ten years ago, today it is a continuous spread of industrial and domestic buildings. Where did the farmers go? Hard to say but it is fair to surmise that in a city like Shanghai the displaced would have been far better compensated and more fairly treated than in most other areas.

There are many things that could grind the Chinese steamship to a halt; the West becomes sick of buying cheap low quality goods, crippling pollution, some virulent epidemic like SARS, stock market crash or just running out of money. Perhaps though the greatest danger is a peasants' revolt, a mass movement of the poor to overthrow the inequalities of the new unjust nation. We have to wait and see but little at this time appears to be in operation to stop a repeat Mao-style revolution except a build-up of the armed forces at a whopping 17% increase per year.

Chapter 2 – Culture

I don't like to use the word culture in the way it is often used, mainly to describe differences in regional behaviour. To me culture means arts, crafts and customs, often with religious origins, that are peculiar to particular races and societies. To some, we are considered cultured if we regularly attend the opera, which unfortunately counts me out although I did see Verdi's Aida at the Bolshoi once, which gets me off the hook at dinner parties and means I have something to talk about if I ever get stuck in a lift with Brian Sewell. Unfortunately I have very little idea of what it was about since it was all sung in Italian and the sub-titles were in Russian!

I did experience the Beijing Opera on one occasion and was somewhat disappointed, there was not much singing only a lot of female actresses shouting their high-pitched, glass breaking script. The music is almost totally percussional, crashing of drums, bashing of cymbals and not an art form that I would recommend, unless testing the latest drugs for headache relief.

What I mean by culture here is really the beliefs and values of Chinese society whether personal, family or in business. The Chinese, like all societies, behave in a manner that has a common consensus as to how they should, at large, behave. A lot of this goes way back to Confucianism upon which Chinese society was based for more than two millennia. The opinions of most citizens are polarised and almost impossible to change as if they are set in non-volatile ROM. It is really hard to have a decent debate with a sharing of different ideas and beliefs, everyone seems to agree on the same things and have the same opinions, at least publicly. I think a lot of this stems from the dreadful 'lose face' mountain that every foreigner has to overcome, nobody wants to be upstaged in an argument or embarrassed at getting their facts wrong so, everyone agrees. Ironically, the exception seems to be when arguing with a foreigner in a business meeting, even when they are proved to be wrong, they will not give-in and continue to push the same point to wear you down into submission. Finally the foreigner submits with something as ridiculous as 'Oh all right then, cheese really does come from the moon!'.

So really this section comes down to the behaviour of the people and how they react with you and each other, what makes them tick, what is important and what is not. For the business environment, I give a brief overview in a later chapter.

Manners Maketh Man?

At first one of the shocking things about coming to China is the sheer rudeness of the population at large. The numerous foreigners who report that the Chinese are polite, kind and friendly clearly never leave their 5 star hotel. They really are a rude and miserable lot as they go about their day to day life, pushing and shoving, loudly brewing up lumps of phlegm in the back of their throats before spitting it out, talking (shouting) with each other and interrupting impolitely. The word queue probably does not exist in the language and if it does it has fallen out of common use. Probably the first experience of this will be when you check-in for a domestic flight, correctly standing in the line, you'll be there all day as they push in front of you, often shoving their ticket into the hands of the check-in clerk in a slick split-second move before you even think about presenting yours. Of course the airline staff don't really care, nobody is there to maintain a degree of fairness. I observed a businessman angrily complain about this once at Dalian airport, the queue had become more of a maul, and the girl at the check-in desk replied 'it's nothing to do with me, I'm not the manager!'

In a lift, it never ceases to astonish me that so many people think they can rugby scrum their way into small cavity before the present occupants have had a chance to get out.

The same is true on the Shanghai subway. The trains are usually pretty full in any case but to exacerbate this, the instant that the sliding doors start to open, an almost violent scramble to get in is launched. They simply have not figured out that there will be more space if they wait a while for those who want to disembark be allowed to do so. Surprisingly and more recently Hong Kong has become infected with this behavioural madness. Shanghai people tend to think that they have some kind of superior status to other Chinese, a Shanghai ID card is to be coveted, but anyone observing the locals on the subway must conclude that they are not much more advanced than animals.

Spitting was supposed to have been a contributory factor in the rapid spread of SARS during the 2003 outbreak. It was noticeable during that time and shortly after that this nationwide practise had somewhat reduced. However, slowly but surely they are getting back into their old ways and a walk along many pavements encourages one to play a kind of hop scotch as you try to avoid stepping into the big green gobs. For the Olympics, this has been outlawed and instant fines are dished out to offenders. The fact that SARS occurred and spread so rapidly is not so surprising and I would imagine that other outbreaks such as the more recent bird flu will inevitably surface from time to time. So many people, living so close together, with little regard to basic hygiene is probably festering something new and maybe even more virulent than SARS.

Most people work and live in high rise buildings; that means at least 6 times a day, allowing for lunch, it is necessary to travel in a crowded elevator full of coughing and sneezing occupants who will not give a thought about placing a hand over the mouth, it is a major health hazard, I often risk passing out holding my breath whilst in these little disease dens.

I once saw a bus driver, the bus packed full of sitting and standing commuters, stop in the middle of the road, wind down the window, stick his head out and throw-up onto the carriageway; he then simply put the vehicle in gear and drove on.

The Chinese do not seem to be a very charitable lot. One of the best examples of this for the entire world to see, was broadcast on live television. It was the final of the Asian cup in Beijing and the highly partisan crowd had to watch their country convincingly defeated 3-1 by Japan. When Japan scored, the TV commentator remained silent, as if it did not happen, the crowd was quiet too, and I thought the sound channel on my TV was faulty. After the game, the stadium almost immediately emptied but those that were left had only remained to hiss and boo pantomime style, at the triumphant Japanese as they lifted the cup. It reminded me of the equally unsporting and miserable John Howard, Prime Minister of Australia, presenting the rugby World Cup to England's Martin Johnson. There were rumours too of fights and riots in Beijing following the match but it was not reported in the press nor shown on the TV so it is difficult to be sure what really happened.

Culture

Once, in a busy local bank, a very poor and heavily disabled, yet strangely cheerful old man wheeled himself into the queue. Most people looked upon him in disgust, sure he was dirty, he had no home, cannot work and stays alive, like so many other old folk, begging on street corners. Everyone kept pushing by him so that he remained at the back of the queue until finally a kind lady in front of me, who was also in line, allowed him to go to the front when it was her turn to pass to a vacant counter.

The man had come to change his collected coins into local currency, there are many Hong Kong people passing through Shenzhen so Hong Kong dollars are common and often accepted as valid tender. Most of this man's earnings were in that currency so he wanted to change it into RMB. The bank assistant refused and sent him away, complaining that his money was too dirty. The lady that had allowed him to the front complained angrily, but it was no use, the miserable woman working for the miserable bank (of China) would not budge. Later, outside the bank, I spoke to the lady who said that she had previously lived in England, remarking with a smile that she told the crippled old man that if he lived in the UK, he would have a comfortable warm shelter, money for food and an allowance for transport. She said the old man laughed and said that if that were the case in China, everybody would chop their legs off!

In a country where the ruling party labels itself as communist, the kind of system that is supposed to prevail, would be an egalitarian ideology with the poor, disabled and ambulant well looked after, at least one would imagine so. The reality of modern China is a system more like eighteenth century France, shortly before the revolution.

Real China

Losing Face

A Chinese trait that is mostly frustrating but sometimes amusing needs some explanation.

I have, on several occasions, brought Chinese customers to the UK for meetings, training or simply holidays (they were supposed to come for training but arrived with cameras and sunglasses rather than notebooks and pencils). On one occasion, I was travelling north with a certain Mr Chen and we stopped at the Milton Keynes service area for refreshment. I asked him to help himself to whatever he wanted. He watched me as I took one of those cafetierre-type coffee jugs and filled it up with hot water. Mr Chen then did the same, only not realising that there was coffee in the bottom, filled his up with Coca-Cola. With a fixed expression he drank all of his coffee flavoured cola, not wanting to look silly.

Another time I had just returned from Shanghai, landing at Heathrow, in the airport there are those moving walkways to assist the long distance between the gate and immigration. One Chinese man got on the one going the wrong way and, rather than get off and think that he would look silly, he continued to walk to the end, taking a very long time to reach it.

Again, at Heathrow, I picked up a Chinese customer and as I put his bags into my car I invited him to sit in the car and wait. After loading his heavy suitcases I closed the boot, opened the driver's door and was shocked to see the man in the driver's seat fast asleep. It took me ages to convince him that he was in the wrong seat because in the UK the steering wheel is on the right hand side. He did not want to move and admit to making a mistake, but I guess after a while he figured that we were going nowhere until he shifted.

Culture

None of these people wanted to admit that they had made a mistake, albeit a very simple one. In China they call it losing face.

One of the strangest and most difficult aspects to deal with, when handling the Chinese, is this 'lose face' issue. It really means do not get embarrassed, look stupid or be seen to make a mistake but practically it gives them a very large disadvantage when dealing with the outside world.

For a start, because of this deep fear of making a mistake, nobody wants to make a decision and certainly not do something bold where there is a possibility of failure.

There are Chinese entrepreneurs of course who have taken great risks and made a lot of money but for post people in most companies it can be a headache. If you are speaking to a group of people and ask 'is everything clear?' they will all say yes or nod their heads. If you then ask a question it becomes immediately apparent that you have spoken for the past two hours and they haven't understood a word. They will not ask a question for fear of looking stupid.

Sometimes, you will get a leader or manager who wants to look clever and earn respect from his subordinates by arguing with you on a particular issue. No matter how wrong he may be, and even if he knows it, he will argue and argue until you give in. To be proved wrong in front of his colleagues would be a major case of 'lose face.' The problem with this is that it does just not occur in meetings, it occurs in everyday life. Another example is when we were away on holiday, our landlord came into the apartment, used the phone, took a shower, put the air conditioning onto the arctic winter setting (it was August) and generally made himself at home. This was despite the fact that he promised us that we had the only set of keys.

Whilst I was ready to go around and confront him, the recommended course of action was to quietly change the locks, which we did. To confront him of his obvious misdeeds would be embarrassing and make life impossible for the future. However, when we finally moved out, he received the mother of all bollockings!

Given this it would seem highly likely that a convicted felon, sentenced for a crime that he or she did not commit, would never be reprieved no matter how strong the evidence that the conviction was wrong, the judiciary does not make mistakes.

On one occasion, the very rare event of a pardon and admission of a false conviction was widely publicised in March 2005. *She Xianglin* was released from prison after serving eleven years for the murder of his wife. This was in the city of Jingshan, a rural backwater in Hubei province.

He never should have gone to jail in the first place and at his original trial he was sentenced to death but the higher court sent the case back for a retrial as there was no evidence, only a confession extracted under police interrogation. The original court then, rather than admit they got it wrong, sentenced She to fifteen years in gaol. This lighter sentence although quite long ensured, under Chinese law, that the case would not go back to a higher court for review. This higher court did not bother to check as to the final outcome. She's wife had simply disappeared in 1994 and even though there were reports of sighting her in another place, the case was never reopened. In the end his wife was identified, she had ran-off and married another man, had a child and carried on her new life. Even then, the court would not admit its mistake and insisted that the estranged spouse had a DNA test; when this proved to be positive, they had no choice but to release the unfortunate Mr She.

Culture

Teng Xingshan was not so lucky, he was executed in 1989, despite pleas of innocence, for the murder of a lady by the name of Shi Xiarong in Hunan province. Many years later, in 2005 Shi, whom Teng was supposed to have been having an affair with, was arrested in Guizhou for drug trafficking.
In She Xianglin's case, he said that he was deprived of sleep and tortured for ten days until he finally admitted guilt. How many more innocent people have been put to death due to false confessions realized through torture will never be known, but even where severe mistakes are made, admission of them is rare.

The best government-level example of not losing face is the Taiwan issue. For commercial reasons only, virtually all western governments have signed-up to the 'one China' principle. However, it is seldom pointed out that China signed over the sovereignty to the Japanese in the early 20th century[1]. Taiwan became a real issue at the end of the civil war in 1949 when the losing Guomindang party, led by *Jiang Jieshi*, fled to Taiwan with most of the nation's gold.
The US stepped in and blocked the straights between the island and the mainland, preventing the communists' crossing. Taiwan then became the Republic of China and the mainland became the Peoples' Republic of China.
Ever since then there has been a stand-off, two Chinese nations doing their utmost to avoid losing face. In Beijing there is certainly, amongst the old school, a get even culture and in Taiwan something of an independence set.
The truth is that Taiwan is completely autonomous and is independent in everything but name. Beijing knows this but

---

[1] More information in Chapter 10

Real China

still maintains that it is part of China. Because of China's business importance, almost all of the major governments in the world agree to the 'One China' principle, at least publicly. The truth is that as long as Taiwan refuses to re-join the mainland, Beijing is losing face. China is increasing its arms spend by around 10-18% per year (depends which report you read). The USA openly criticizes this (often forgetting that it spends five times as much on defence as the Chinese). Most analysts believe that if China were to wage a conventional war upon Taiwan it would suffer great losses due to its inferior and outdated military hardware. In recent years China has been trying to correct this but export licenses from US and EU nations for military hardware intended for China, are becoming harder and harder to get; arms sales were banned following the Tiananmen Square incident in 1989.

In March 2005 China passed a law allowing it to legally attack Taiwan if it were to declare independence. At some time in the future, China will almost certainly issue Taiwan with an ultimatum along the lines join-up or else! Why does China care? It already has 1.3 billion people and some very big problems to deal with, why does it need another 20 million or so who really don't want to be part of the club? Very simple, to give up would be losing face, admitting that the Taiwanese can quite happily decide their own destiny.

Some knowledgeable Chinese have told me that the return of Hong Kong need not have happened; it was British officials who raised the issue. Over the years, the Chinese had not made any claims to Hong Kong since the island and Kowloon was British sovereign territory in any case, the 100 year lease only concerned the New Territories. The Chinese were simply going to allow the expiry of the lease to fade into the background, however the Thatcher government raised the issue much too publicly and the Chinese were forced to act.

The other big face-saving problem is the legendary Mao Ze Dong; his body lies preserved in Tiananmen Square, his large image is displayed outside the walls of the Forbidden City and his mug is on every single bank note. Millions of Chinese school kids are taught each year what a great man he was and how he made China what it is today. The reality is that he was a tyrant and a murderer, yet even today this cannot be admitted.

For anyone doing business in China, whether selling or buying, or even having a personal relationship the inability to admit to making a mistake, the avoidance of responsibility and arguing a point which is clearly wrong will be a constant source of frustration.

Humour
Surprisingly one does warm very quickly to the Chinese for their sense of humour, although they often appear to be miserable and downhearted, they do have the ability to laugh. Those of us who come from the British Isles have many qualities and many faults but perhaps one of our greatest assets is our pursuit of humour. Simply watch any foreign television channel or listen to any radio station and you will quickly be bored; back home you can always find something to laugh at, although it may have been repeated from 1975. The Chinese do have the same approach and socially most Chinese are good fun, they can see the funny side of most things and they will even laugh at themselves but there is a fine line between that and losing face so one has to be very careful.

Real China

Chinese TV has many comedy shows, as does the radio, British TV such as Mr Bean is extremely popular, it naturally helps that there is no language to understand. When you are in a meeting, if you can make them laugh, then you are going a long way to cementing a strong relationship.

In some ways the Chinese are a source of amusement for some of the daft things that they do. In the summer, particularly in the north, you will see men in business suits with their trousers rolled up to their knees, in Shanghai particularly, women (and often couples) go out shopping in their pyjamas. Many Chinese toilets are of the hole in the floor variety where you have to crouch down in order to deposit bodily waste; in the supermarkets you can buy a toilet seat mounted on a metal frame that can be positioned above the hole. This has been a major source of amusement to many ex-pats.

Just reading the papers one can find many amusing articles on things that go on around the country, probably not amusing for the person who you are reading about for often they involve a high degree of born-yesterday gullibility.

During the celebrations for the Lunar New Year it is customary to return home to one's family. Since China now has a very large population of migrant workers, there is a mass exodus that starts one or two weeks before the holiday and so train tickets are in great demand and often very hard to secure.

One gang in Guangzhou were standing outside the station and telling people, as they approached, that their train had crashed and would not now run. Being a charitable sort of bunch, they offered to buy their unused tickets at half price. Most ten years olds would not fall for that one but it seems that thousands did; of course the gang then re-sold the tickets at a much higher price.

Sometimes the stupidity can be tragic; an old couple were poisoned after using 'salt' they picked up in the street to flavour their food. Despite being taken to hospital for emergency treatment in Nanchong, (Sichuan Province), Mr Huang Haiyang died. His wife, Ma Zhengying was still receiving treatment, but was expected to survive. Tests revealed that the 'salt' they used was in fact nitrite.

Criminals can be even dumber; a would-be car-hijacker failed because he did not know how to drive, according to the Jilin City Evening News. After threatening a taxi driver at knife-point the young crook demanded he hand over his car. The frightened man did as he was told, but was puzzled when the robber failed to drive off. He managed to persuade the robber to give the car back, who tried his luck with another taxi. That attempt was equally unsuccessful. He was caught by a patrolling police officer and later admitted that he could not drive.

Another man, in Guangdong again, woke up with a snake wrapped around his body. Terrified he called his friend to help who then poured rice wine down the snake's throat. The snake, perhaps he was sleeping off a late night session, soon cleared off. Not remembering a thing, it's always scary to see who you wake up with. The reporter explained that this was probably because the snake wanted to keep warm. The next time you become encircled by a Python, not to worry, he's just giving you a cuddle.

It is easy to ready these kind of stories almost everyday and there is only a selection here, admittedly laughing at the misfortune of others.

Real China

A man withdrew 5,000 yuan (£330) from an ATM after finding somebody's card still in the machine. This is not surprising because Chinese ATMs do not automatically return the card, you must press the button to have it returned. The man guessed the correct PIN. This was in Zhengzou, Henan, the certain Mr Qi, was planning to withdraw his own money from the machine when he discovered that he could not insert his card. Then he realized the other card was already in the slot. Prompted by a sudden impulse, he randomly hit the number 1, as the PIN, six times. (Another silly fact, most Chinese choose 111111 or lucky 888888 for their pin)

To his amazement, the machine spat out the money. According to the paper, Qi's conscience caught up with him. He called the police and told them what had happened, and returned the money and the card. The card's owner turned out to be a woman who was in a hurry to get her sick child to a hospital or at least that is what it said in the paper.

A woman in Changsha, Hunan province read that music was good for the development of unborn babies so every day, during her pregnancy, she would sit down and play loud music with the loudspeaker pressed against her abdomen. The baby was born deaf.

In Wuhan, a police helpline was set-up (dial 110) whereby any citizen could ring up and get assistance. One man, who had worked all night, phoned the police to bring him some breakfast; the young on-duty official, named He Jinbao, took his instructions literally (as is common in China) and dutifully delivered the man's breakfast!

Bizarrely, a man in Shanghai was sentenced to six months in jail for causing injury to a corpse, according to the Wenhui Daily. On the evening of September 10, 2004, a trio named Zhang, Tan and Tu went out to steal some wire after a drinking session. Not knowing even how to wire a three pin plug, Tu received a fatal electric shock in the incident, whilst grabbing a live wire. Zhang's crime against the corpse was that he hid it in a small boat and sank it.

A variation on the 'Hell's Grannies' theme was amusingly reported in the ChongQing Evening News. Police officers in Chongqing Municipality "smashed" (my quotes) a larceny gang. But to their astonishment they found most of its members were senior citizens, with the oldest 85 and the leader Jiang Jingquan a very youthful 81. The ageing highwaymen raised no suspicions as they tottered around rural markets stealing clothes and shoes. A search by police led to their arrest in a rented room surrounded by their latest stash of booty.

Shanghai people have a reputation for being careful with their money so at what was described as an 'Egg Promotion' in a local supermarket, the papers said that a "human stampede" formed. The eggs were discounted from 3 yuan (20p) per 500 grams to 1.99 yuan (14p), with a limit of 2 kilograms per customer. Golden eggs perhaps? Long queues started forming in the early hours, long before opening time. Some customers were injured during the chaos and had to be taken to hospital, while the lucky ones only lost their shoes in the crush. Police had to be called to restore order.

A friend of mine, teaches English to kindergarten children at a school in Shenzhen; one day, she decided to take the kids into the park and give them a lesson there, explaining the different environment to them. Within twenty minutes a large crowd of people had gathered around the school children, all eager to get a free English lesson.

Real China

In Shanghai a company was selling 'magic pants' these were designed to cure erectile dysfunction; all the purchaser had to do was wear them and within days become a rock-hard super-stud but unfortunately it was a hoax. The fact that the power Y-fronts were pretty useless was not reported until one red-faced hopeful actually complained. The newspapers claimed that the company concerned had been selling about thirty thousand pounds worth each day to thousands of men frightened to complain.

I am not sure, but impotence may be a big problem in China, not just from this story but when I have taken customers to London for 'training', they often nip into a sex shop and ask for barrel or two of Viagra. It is also the most common fake drug on the market simply because people are too shy to complain.

The Chinese like their kids to be tall and will, rather stupidly give them all sorts of unsafe tonics or strap growth packs to their knees to spurt growth. In Shanghai a boy grew breasts instead of becoming taller; he started growing female breasts after he took a tonic that was supposed to make him a few centimetres bigger, instead of wearing larger trousers he now needs bigger shirts, or so it said in the Shanghai Evening Post. After being convinced he was not tall enough for his age, his mother was persuaded by a salesman, who passed himself off as a doctor, to buy a six-month supply of the tonic for 4,000 yuan (£260!). A few months later, the 15-year-old started growing breasts. But the phenomena stopped after he quit taking the tonic, the manufacturers of the product claimed that it does not contain any hormones. The paper did not say but one assumes that his modestly endowed mother finished off the bottle.

Culture

Often, the newspapers will print jokes usually at kindergarten level; here is an example from the joke section of the China Daily, they are always not very funny and never political or rude, not even in the double meaning sense.

Three men were discussing at a bar about coincidences. The first man said, ' my wife was reading a 'tale of two cities' and she gave birth to twins'.
'That's funny', the second man remarked, 'my wife was reading 'the three musketeers' and she gave birth to triplets'.
The third man shouted, 'Good God, I have to rush home!'
When asked what the problem was, he exclaimed, ' When I left the house, my wife was reading Ali baba and the forty Thieves'!!! (I didn't add the exclamations)

Superstition
Religion in China is not that strong, the main Chinese god comes in one hundred Yuan denominations. It always seems to follow that with an absence of religion there is always very strong superstition. For Moslems, superstition is blasphemy, for Chinese it is a way of life. Chinese New Year is the number one superstition event that involves the whole country. The whole concept of the celebration is to get lucky the following year and luck doesn't mean love, happiness or contentment, it means loads of money!
Happy New Year, Xin Nian Kuai Le, is sometimes heard at this time of the year but far more common is Gong Xi Fa Cai which in laymens' terms means hope you make some serious dosh next year.

Real China

Everywhere you go, you will see the character 福 (fu) which means rich. During the New Year festival, children are given little red envelopes filled with guess what? Money. So in order to get rich the following year, it is very important that you follow the signs of superstition around the time of the festival such as eat the right things, buy the correct items and get the timing right. For example, my friend's mother nearly killed her when she found out that she had cut her hair just after New Year; if you do this it is said that your brother will die. Buying new shoes at this time also seriously reduces your chance of a lottery win!

During New Year, the fu character is turned upside down because in Chinese upside down is *dao* and *dao* also means to arrive hence prosperity arrives. (I think it's bloody well daft too)

Another strange superstition is the number four; the best lucky number is 8. The number four in mandarin is 'si' which also means death so you will often go to buildings and find that there is no fourth floor. I received a discount on my mobile phone because I chose a number that ends in four. It is likely that obtaining one that ends in 888 is the desirability equivalent of having the number plate A1 in the UK.

Because of this daft obsession with superstition, the world will become fully aware as the 2008 Olympic games starts on the eighth day of the eighth month, and just for good measure the opening ceremony starts at 8pm – I kid you not. Who cares if athletes have to run in temperatures near 40 degrees combined with throat-gagging air, it has to be lucky!

The Chinese zodiac is also loaded with superstition as parents carefully chose when to conceive in order to give birth to a child in a 'lucky' year. There was a surge of births in 2004 because the year of the Monkey is considered to be very lucky, the previous year sheep and 2005, chicken, are not good years to be born in if you want to be eating off gold plates.

The year of the chicken, is a really bad year to get married, often known as the year of the widow. The dragon year, which last occurred in 2001 is a good year to have a baby boy and also name him Long or Long Long. Long means dragon in Chinese; so there are at least 50,000 or so infant boys, running around with the same name. In fact the famous movie star Jackie Chan's Chinese name is Long. Chinese names are the subject of a different topic altogether but they are generally based upon superstition or what their parents have in their mind when the child is named. Unlike western names, Chinese ones have a real meaning and are chosen as such.

The true meaning of western names is not considered these days, more what they sound like, although even we screw-up as Mrs and Mrs Pipe did when they named their son Duane. The problem is that so many Chinese people have the same name and with 1.3 billion it gets mighty confusing. Boys are often called Wen which means cultured and girls Hua or Qing meaning flower or young. What complicates the situation even more is that there are not that many family names around either, so looking for someone in the Beijing telephone directory must be like trying to find somebody called Mohammed in Saudi Arabia.

One of the most bizarre examples of superstition is in Shenzhen, beside the Hongli road, a major artery, are five or six tower blocks and an office complex all crimson red in colour. The buildings are striking such that they stand out like a live pig in a sausage factory. I asked how on earth planning permission could be given to such an eyesore. The story goes that when the site was first developed, they dug up a lot of human bones because previously it had been a burial site or graveyard. Since red is the colour to frighten away ghosts, red it had to be so the developer easily got permission to change the colour scheme. At night it is brightly illuminated – with red lights.

Little Emperors

In today's Chinese society, children are number one. In the early eighties a one child policy was introduced, in order to curb the population expansion. In the cities, almost everyone is limited to one child. However, now that the first generation of one-child families have matured, married and are starting to have children of their own, the law has been relaxed to enable couples who themselves were both only-children, to have two instead of one.

Whilst we in Europe have problems from an aging population due to better longevity, lower birth rates and so on, China is creating its own problem by enforcing the reduction in the number of children. Today there are nine workers for every retired person, by 2025 it will be four and by 2050 three; this is a demographic disaster. The sudden realisation of this is causing them to re-think and relax the law. However, if anyone has a child 'unlawfully' then the child cannot be registered, cannot go to school (except privately) and the parents could get a big fine. If working for the government, automatic dismissal is the penalty for flouting the one child law. Abortion rates are never published but they are sky-high due to the one per family ration book.

Of course, from the government's perspective, if a child is not registered it does not exist and so does not contribute to the population growth. In the countryside the one child law is much more difficult to control and there is also the preference for boys to work the land and keep the parents in their old age. Consequently there are a lot of unwanted baby girls. Many childless western couples come to China in order to adopt a baby girl; there are even instructions how to do this on the website of the Chinese Embassy in London. I have been to several hotels around the country and found groups of western couples with tiny new-born Chinese babies.

For those good law-abiding city folk, having a child is like giving birth to your own little God. Hong Kong Chinese, who enjoy making fun of their mainland cousins (for example, they used to call Jiang Zemin's private plane 'Air Force One') call them 'Little Emperors.'

In almost every way possible, these kids get what they want; the best food, smartest clothes and an expensive education. Many of them need not walk, their parents delight in supplying little electric bikes and cars. They hire an "ayi" a 24 hour nanny servant just in case Mummy can't cope with junior's every need and want.

Parents will suffer severe financial hardship in order to pay for their kid's education. Education has become the big issue, there is tremendous pressure on the children to perform well at school. Everything is exam based and is highly competitive, it really *does* matter which university they eventually attend and each year there are the ritual entry exams whereby the exam score is the only thing that counts. The whole education system is based upon passing exams. The trouble with this is that the kids become encyclopaedias, their heads stuffed with knowledge, but with little idea how to apply it or even find it a few years after graduation.

I have had numerous meetings with so many Chinese engineers who have doctor degrees and yet lack very simple understanding skills. Perhaps it is why China is brilliant at copying things yet pretty useless at creation, innovation and design. In fact several people have told me that that the first three to six months at university they learn military-style drill, marching here and there with a stiff back and probably miserable face.

A typical Chinese middle school will have 6000 pupils and around 100 kids per class. The school day will be from 8 am until 5pm and parents usually pay for additional lessons in the evening. A friend of mine has a 12 year old daughter who is busy learning English so as a favour I spend an hour with her on Saturday mornings with simple English conversation. The poor girl studies until 11.30 pm every night, on Saturday afternoons she has piano lessons, on Sundays more English. A whole generation of kids are basically being deprived of their childhood.

This isn't doing much to shape the national character though, a recent study of school kids found that 90 per cent of 12 to 16 year olds would bypass honesty for the sake of personal gain. This was conducted in ChongQing, a city where I have paradoxically found the people to be more honest than most. The hilarious commentary, quoted in the China Daily, had the nerve to say that most adults are shocked by this as 'the quality of honesty, has been long preserved by Chinese as one of their traditional core values'. (I must have been to a different China). The survey went on to discover some other startling (to them) facts about the Chinese youth, including the following:

In exchange for 'booties', 72.4% of the minor respondents would tell a lie.

Culture

If they detected a substandard food maker in the community where they lived, half of the students said they would do nothing, citing it as the duty of relative authorities, rather than theirs.

More than three-quarters would rather cheat in exams, if it could be hidden from monitors patrolling the examination room. Some admitted to providing a fake health report when applying for further study programs.

Some 64.5 percent don't arrive to appointments on time, and at school, 43.5 percent of the students said they have at least once given false excuses to skip school or PE lessons.

By far the most revealing fact is that when riding a bus nearly 60 percent of kids decline to offer their seats to the elderly, pregnant or disabled, complaining that 'we're tired too'.

Over 90 percent said they would not give a helping hand to school peers in trouble, saying that they should be helped by teachers.

This reflects a set of values, inherent in the people, it is not culture it is how people think and shows that the country is getting worse not better. These kids will grow up and be even more self-centred and corrupt than the generation before them. It is so often reported that core Asian values are to do things for the benefit of the majority at the expense of the individual, not so, China is a selfish society with even more selfish generations yet to come.

Real China

There is pressure though on a lot of kids, their parents suffer hardships in order to pay for the best schools and if the children fail exams or do not meet with the over ambitious expectations of their fathers and mothers, they feel great shame. Suicide amongst schoolchildren is on the rise.

Children are also very immature compared to their western contemporaries. They are not allowed out of the house on their own until they have finished school (age 18) they are sheltered from anything adult but benign television and they wear clothes with motifs and logos that a 5 year old would be seen with in the west.

Baby clothes are especially amusing, nappies are rare as most baby clothes have a huge hole in the ass so the baby can piss and crap like a farmyard muck spreader, anywhere he or she pleases. It must be like having a new puppy in the house. When the parents are out with their children and the kids need to go, they don't waste time looking for a toilet, anywhere will do. In upmarket shopping malls, Mothers will push their kids' bottoms into the lower roots and foliage of the nearest potted plant.

I was at the check-in queue for a flight once and a mother and baby were a little way in front of me. The baby had to go so the mother, rather than lose her place in the line, simply put the child down and allowed it to urinate from the convenient piss hole in the trousers, all over the smooth white tiled floor. She just left it there, would not dream of calling for the cleaners to mop it up. Five minutes later, a Taiwan businessman in hurry, wearing a crisp new suit, slipped on the mess and had his lower body soaked in the smelly yellow fluid, he must have wondered why his clients declined his offer of lunch.

Culture

One of the unfathomable and disturbing events of 2004, given the total dedication to these little gods that they have brought into the world, was the Anhui milk scandal. Ninety-seven people in local governments and supervision departments were held responsible for the April 2006 milk powder scandal. What happened was that a baby milk product was launched that was extremely cheap but not very nutritious. However, parents bought it and in several cases it resulted in infant death. As is usual in China, the scale of the fraud defies belief; an inspection team found 49 companies, one illegal producer and 3 substandard processors across 11 provinces, including Beijing and Shanghai, connected to inferior quality milk. A dozen of them were involved in the worst example in Fuyang (Anhui) resulting in the death of twelve babies. Hundreds of other infants suffered from what was reported as 'big head' disease, a medical complication stemming from malnutrition. The provincial government claimed that they would 'sternly punish individuals and officials involved'. Wait a minute, officials? It seems that government officials were also involved, my guess is for accepting backhanders for overlooking the need for rigorous testing that should have been in place for such products to be placed on the open market. On August 12 of that same year 54 Chinese substandard milk powder producers were shut down.

Quoting the China Daily 'Inspectors asked local governments and supervision departments to learn from the case and reinforce their sense of responsibility in order to safeguard people's health and life'. Fat chance, when there are fast bucks to made.

You have to wonder why the parents actually bought the stuff in the first place but in a way it is understandable This is a poor city in a poor province, people have to make their less than twenty yuan per day, go a long way. What's more, when the babies were obviously very sick and suffering a distressingly slow death, their families just did not have the money to take them to the doctor.

Staying with the subject of baby milk, in nearby Jiangsu province, a businessman set-up a team of wet-nurses under the slogan breast is best, he was renting out lactating women to busy mothers in order to feed their little wonder with the ultimate in baby milk. There was a local outcry over this and the man involved, a Mr Chen from Yangzhou, had to withdraw his advertising campaign. Technically he was not committing any offence but many people did not like the thought of 'human cows' and considered his business to be in bad taste. My request for fresh milk with my cornflakes was turned-down.

The practice of wet-nursing has always been common in China but normally only amongst family and friends, Mr Chen was the first man to see the opportunity for business. In western China, where civilisation has yet to reach, this kind of service is still employed by the very wealthy who use a servant to feed their offspring right up to when they start school; the last emperor, Pu Yi was famously known for being wet nursed by one or more of the concubines right into his teens.

Even the poorest people will do anything to make life better for their children or give them a head start, for example an old woman, again in Anhui, spends 4 hours per week picking up rubbish and selling it, she makes 300 yuan per month (£20) in order to pay for her granddaughter's education.

There are stories of kids murdering their parents because they cannot afford to send them to a good school. Schools in China are not free, the more you pay, the better the school, nice to know the good communist government (which laughingly describes itself as 'democratic with Chinese characteristics') is sticking to its principles. In the countryside there are very few schools compared with the city. Many children do not receive an education at all.

Even worse is the disgraceful *hukou* system, akin to the old apartheid South African pass laws. Chinese citizens all have identity cards and each ID card has the city of registration on it, if an ID card has Beijing on it for example then the holder has a hukou from that city and has the right of permanent residence coupled with the social and administrative benefits that come with it, for example education for the kids. ID cards issued in the prosperous cities are to be coveted; star prize is a Beijing ID, closely followed by Shanghai, Tianjin, Guangzhou and Shenzhen. If you are not born in one of these cities or even if you are and your parents are not, it is difficult to get the treasured hukou.

To get one you need to own a business or a reasonable amount of property. The bad news is for example, if you do not have say a Beijing ID but are living and working in the city, it will cost you a hell of a lot more to send your kids to school. Cities like Beijing and Shanghai, owe much to their existence and rapid development through the labours of big gangs of migrant workers. These workers cannot afford to send their kids to school because their wages are so low, often they are cheated and not paid at all. Their non-Beijing hukou means they have to pay substantially more (whilst p;aid substantially less) than the locals.

Real China

Premier Wen Jiabao is reported to have said, at a State Council meeting, that a nationwide probe would be launched at the end of 2004 to urge local governments and companies to pay all owed wages to rural migrant workers. The situation is said to be getting out of hand. One problem is that there are no employment contracts, these poor people cannot later sue for their low or unpaid wages. Less than 20 per cent of the total rural migrant workers have signed contracts with their employers. It was estimated that at the end of 2003, 17 billion Yuan (£1.1bn) was owed to migrant workers. There are supposed to be more than 100 million migrant workers in China and each year 13 million more farmers look for work in the city. This puts great strain on the education system and sadly these unfortunate exploited souls suffer. Despite the initiatives, nothing has changed, the economy is growing too fast to let controls get in the way.

According to the China Daily, there are 240,000 migrant worker's children in Beijing (so the real total is probably nearer to one million) and because they have no Beijing ID card, they are charged 50,000 Yuan per year for schooling, they only earn 1,000 (£60) per month, if they get paid at all. It is the sad reflection upon a society that holds the child in such high esteem, your own child that is, nobody else's. This makes the demography problem worse since only the elite are being educated and this reduces the number of wealth producing people even further, who in the future will pay taxes to support the old?

An extreme example of this is the city of Shenzhen, estimated to have a population of 10.7 million people yet more than nine million have no hukou. That means they have no right to education, social benefits and worse, if they need any kind of interaction with the government, they have to return to where they came from. So in reality you have just nine million workers and one million parasites that greatly benefit from the labours of the poor but offer them nothing in return.

On the whole, the Chinese are an incredibly selfish race; the big social issue is that the one-child and education system perpetuates the elitism of the spoilt brats. Fortune Magazine described them as the 'biggest me generation ever.'

Whilst the world watches China, rushes to invest with the force of an alpine avalanche and worries about missing the party, the real point is being missed. It seems highly likely that China will become the next superpower, one day its economy will overtake the US, it will build up its military and it will become 'developed.' The real scare perhaps is that today's Little Emperors will become self-centred big monsters that rule China and hold the rest of the world to ransom, potentially it is a frightening prospect and with far more sinister potential human rights violations than we criticise China mostly for today.

Chapter 3 – Food

It could be said that food is really a part of culture and I would go along with that but in China food is so important, such a critical part of society that it deserves a chapter all of its own.

There is perhaps no better way to go about describing the features of Chinese than with food, they take food even more seriously than the French and when in China no matter where you are and what time of day it is you can always smell it. Recently I was listening to '*Wake up with Wogan*' where the aforementioned said that the worst Peking Duck he ever ate was in Peking. It raises a smile but Peking Duck or Beijing *Kao Ya*, as the Chinese call it, is very different to our crispy duck pancakes that we eat in our local UK Chinese restaurant. In fact all the food in China is very different to what you eat in the UK, probably boiled rice is the same but they call it steamed rice, the difference is that in the UK, Chinese food seems eminently more palatable if highly limited in scope.

A friend of mine, who runs a Chinese Take-Away in Cornwall, told me how fussy many of his customers are, for example one guy asks for his beef and green pepper in black bean sauce "no green pepper and not spicy".

Strange as this may seem, I overheard a Swedish guy in the queue at MacDonald's on the M5 in Somerset asking for a Quarter Pounder without the meat! Why he didn't go somewhere else and buy a cheese sandwich?

The Chinese though, do not leave anything out, they munch through anything that isn't (immediately) poisonous. Nothing

Food

living, dead, animal or vegetable escapes the noisy munching of this seemingly ever-hungry people.

Chinese food does differ by region but there is such a large overlap that you can usually get most things in most restaurants in most towns. The food does split into four or five divisions; north-east (dong bei) which is mostly quite heavy and very salty in taste, Cantonese (Guangdong) which comprises virtually everything but tends to be lighter if very oily, Shanghai which again involves eating most things but can be very sweet and Sichuan which is very spicy but often oily too. Spicy food is also very popular in provinces such as Hubei, Henan and Hunan.

What is certain is that Chinese food will always have one particular kind of strong flavour that is either salty, sour, spicy or sweet. Almost for sure the Chinese have much less sensitive taste buds than we do, I am always telling them to go easy on the salt or chilli but they always say 'no taste'. I find that after a while, everything starts to taste the same and after a few weeks in the country I wake up in a cold sweat in the early hours of the morning, gasping for fish and chips or cheddar cheese.

Which ever type of food you go for, it is always eaten in the same way; several dishes are plonked onto a usually circular table and you eat what you like, with chopsticks. The Hong Kong government feels that their citizens are the dumbest around for certain, because every evening, at every commercial break, they play the same four adverts; one about crossing the road safely, one about stopping mosquito breeding (and avoiding dengue fever), one about keeping Hong Kong clean and finally the relevant one here an advert about using serving chopsticks as opposed to your own, so as not to spread germs.

Real China

It does not do any good, in China I have never, ever been to a restaurant where serving chopsticks have been provided, quite often your host will lick his chopsticks then pick up a piece of food, still moist from his saliva, and drop it onto your plate. He thinks he is being considerate, worried that you might go hungry because of the way you fumble with the chopsticks and clumsily drop food in the middle of the table attempting to get it from the centre to the mouth. The best way to avoid this charitable experience is to make sure you can use the damned things before you get to China or, and this is perfectly acceptable, ask for a spoon and fork.

It is normal for the host to order at least 3 times more food than you can possibly eat and the more people the better because then more dishes can be ordered. It is hard to believe that in the early sixties, the nation was starving. The Chinese also eat the most unnatural food. Much of it is vomit-inducing to most westerners, including snakes, dogs, cats and rats. They also combine flavours that should not normally be combined and then smother them in soy sauce or chilli oil so that it can't be tasted anyway.

This always prompts me to remember an old *Two Ronnies'* sketch where Ronnie Corbett approaches an ice-cream stand and enquires as to what flavours the stall keeper has, he responds in the way that only Ronnie Barker could by reeling off an almost endless list of ice-cream delights, in less than seven seconds. Corbett replies 'have you got smokey bacon?' Well in China, smokey bacon ice cream has yet to appear but you can get red bean, green bean, tarot, sesame or green tea ice cream, in fact you can even get green tea tooth paste. Dr Zeuss would be impressed too, you really *can* get green eggs and ham

Food

Usually, after eating more than your body normally allows and you can't wait to get back to the hotel and get out of your tight trousers, the host will ask what you want for your main food. Somewhat blown over by the question, you'll worryingly ponder was that the starter? What they mean is that the meal is usually finished with a bowl of rice or noodles, it is not so common to have a sweet desert.

Culturally, many tourist guides will tell you that it is rude to leave rice in your bowl, ignore it, it is about as contemporary as Englishmen wearing bowler hats and saying 'how do you do?'. Since much English is learnt form old books, many people will introduce themselves and repeat the now outdated aforementioned greeting and it must really confuse the Americans who have simplified it down to 'Hi!'

Almost everywhere in China it is unusual to drink wine, you may be served wine if you are eating for a special occasion or function but it is rare. Most likely they will serve tea before you start to eat and then beer during the meal; many women will ask for fruit juice or liquid yoghurt.

Local wine is of poor quality however much you pay, it is always harsh and slightly sour. Strong Chinese alcohol is usually made from rice and comes in varying strengths and price ranges. The most well-known brand is Maotai and can be very strong with around 55% alcohol, some others are even higher. The generic name for distilled rice alcohol is 'baijiu' which simply means white alcohol. Usually this is drunk 'gan bei' style which, contrary to common belief does not mean cheers, it means empty the glass dry (in one go). A gan bei session is usually a sort of macho ritual in which many Chinese guys like to drink themselves silly. Alas, they don't take alcohol well and quickly get bright red faces and either slump into a heap on the table or fall off of their chair.

Real China

Previously, at a dinner party in a very expensive Taibei, fish restaurant, the host ordered the most delicious mature red Bordeaux and, to my dismay, prompted several rounds of gan bei until the bottle was empty. He then repeated the exercise several times until we were drunk on an expensive luxury that we had hardly tasted!

In the summer of 2004 I attended two beer festivals, one in Dalian and the other in Tianjin. Now, as a lover of beer, this kind of festival should be one of the annual beverage highlights, many different kinds of world beers instead of the bland, sold everywhere types such as Qing Dao (Tsing Tao), Jinwei or Yan Jing. To my dismay, there were only five or six different beers there, even more shocking one of them was Budweiser; they would not even rinse their glasses with that stuff at a British beer festival.

However, there was an astonishing 200 or so food stores selling virtually everything from roast pigs and lamb kebabs to steamed bread and dumplings. It was the same format at both festival sites, only the Chinese could achieve this, a food tasting festival with a mixture of low-standard food stalls, advertised as a booze-up!

Actually beer is now so cheap, because the competition is high and almost cut-throat, a 640ml bottle can be purchased for less than 25 pence.

During 2005, beer wars were happening in Shenzhen between the market leader Qingdao and the local beer Jinwei (Kingway). Allegedly Qingdao people smashed-up Jinwei's offices and Jinwei people were reported to have wrecked some Qingdao delivery trucks, feelings run high in a market where every last bottle has to be sold in order to make a profit.

Food

Foreign brewers are trying to invest in China's beer market by setting up their own breweries or buying out local ones. They almost certainly jump in with both feet with the '1.3 billion customers' slogan tattooed on the inside of their eyelids but forget to recognise that China already has too many bland, yellow, gassy beers that sell for next to nothing and so there is little chance of making serious money.

There is a really disturbing trend of foreign multi-nationals buying out local Chinese breweries; Harbin beer was recently taken over by Budweiser (why do they add rice?) brewer Anheuser Busch after a drawn out take over battle with rivals SAB Miller. Heinekin have been in take over talks with Kingway in Shenzhen and even the biggest local beer Tsing Tao has been buying stakes in other breweries around the country. Ultimately what will happen is the market will fall into the hands of a few large corporations, the supply will be controlled, the quality will go down (as if it could get worse) and the price will go up. Sounds just like the UK!

There has been a lot of concern as to what actually goes into Chinese beer, Kingway have gone out of their way to put on their cans and bottles the message, '不添加甲醛' (which means no added formaldehyde) because it is rumoured that many beers in China actually *do* contain the stuff. Formaldehyde is a preservative that is also carcinogenic. The rumour amongst expats in Shenzhen, and I cannot verify this, is that Kingway also contains rohypnol the so-called 'date rape' drug and is banned in the USA. There is certainly something not natural about Kingway, it gives me a headache, just one bottle, whereas three or four pints of Tsing Tao have no such effect. Kingway does marginally taste better however.

Real China

Some foods are common all over China such as noodles, rice and dumplings described in the next section. Noodles are usually fresh and really do taste mush better than the dried ones we are used to and often served in soup. They may be chipped from a large block of dough (*dao shao mian*) straight into an oily, salty or spicy gruel or the chef can be seen stretching a very long piece of white dough then smashing it against the worktop, as he does, the long thick dough breaks up into just as long but multi stranded noodles.

Chinese breakfast is dreadful, particularly in small hotels where everything seems to be bean curd in solid, liquid or crispy form; you are unlikely to get a cup of coffee and a fried egg is delivered to your table, covered in soy sauce.

In general, the food is clean and safe, not that the cooks are particularly clean, just that cooking is normally done at very high temperatures, boiling or frying, and this kills most of the bugs. Most Chinese kitchens are nothing less than filthy, they just never clean them; years of grime and decayed food provide a healthy environment for rats and cockroaches but not humans. I have seen so many restaurants where a peek into the kitchen shows years of fat splashes up and down the walls surrounding a single gas burner heating a huge wok. Often the kitchen is too small to prepare food so many restaurants peel the vegetables and cut the meat, on the pavement outside. The dirty dishes get passed out the window to someone with a large bowl who washes them in the back alley, in cold water.

At the start of a meal, you are likely to be given some cold dish while you wait for the main meal, this could be peanuts, chicken feet or pickled vegetables; don't eat them, they could have been around for weeks and any left over get given to the next customer. For all you know, each 'hors d'erve' could have been subject to the foraging of three hundred chopsticks. Please try to avoid raw fish, it is asking for trouble, in Foshan, Guangdong province, more than one million people were infected with liver flukes (a parasite that causes hepatitis) from eating raw fish, according to the *Hong Kong South China Morning Post*. (Dec 04).

Sometimes unscrupulous western companies take advantage of the slack regulations, a good example was the General Mills company with their Haagen Daz brand. They were using a small apartment in Shenzhen to manufacture their ice-cream cakes to service their five retail outlets in the city. It seems that 'a citizen' shopped them to the local health authority who upon inspection closed the place down, firstly because the factory, if you could call it that, was illegal and secondly it did not meet the hygiene regulations. The main issue though was that the address on their hygiene certificate had changed hence it was only reason for operating illegally despite the poor environment. The most likely explanation is that the local Chinese manager found much cheaper premises to make the desserts and pocketed the difference. The parent company with its inattentive executives, who only care about the 'bottom line', probably saw no reason to check.

Dong Bei food, as the name implies, comes from the north-east, it includes the three Manchurian provinces of Heilongjiang, Jilin and Liaoning as well as Hebei and the great metropolises of Beijing and Tianjin. This part of the country, especially the far north has very cold dry winters when nothing grows. Much of the food therefore, is harvested in the summer and preserved for consumption during the winter. You will not find any exotic fruits from this region and so they mostly eat a range of root vegetables that can be kept and consumed throughout the winter, not unlike our turnips and potatoes.

Also very common from this region is corn or sweet corn and products made from it such as 'xiao mi' (little rice) basically tiny yellow grains in a watery and bland soup. Bread is also much more common here than in the rest of China particularly 'man tou' which is a large steamed bread of wheat or corn flour. The king of meats in this region is pork and just about every part is eaten.

I once had dinner with a group of locals in Changchun where the table centre-piece was a pig's head, just a pig's head; the most important member around the table had the privilege of prising the eyeballs out with his chopstick and allowing it to slide down the throat, without chewing. The rest of the head, skull aside was just a large lump of fat.

Aubergines or egg plants are very common here, often stewed in a delicious if oily sauce. Meat is always salty and tends to be pork as said before. Many vegetables are pickled and served as a cold dish, usually before the main dishes arrive. A common dish, popular with the locals is pork bones that have been stewed such that the meat is ready to drop-off, served up on a large platter; the restaurant equips its hungry diners with plastic gloves so that the meat can be picked up with the hands and eaten medieval style.

My favourite, although you get them everywhere in China but sadly not in the UK, is dumplings. Dumplings come as two main types; jaozi which are boiled or sometimes fried and baozi which are steamed. They are made simply from flour and water, formed into a circular dough and filled with virtually anything. The dough is then folded and pinched along the edge like miniature Cornish pasties before they are cooked in boiling water or steamed in baskets. Because they are small, they cook very quickly. Dumplings are the most common food for the northern Chinese to eat on (Chinese) New Year's Eve. Especially delicious are cha'r shao bao, (roast pork steamed) dumplings, others are filled with vegetables, egg or shrimps, often a mixture of two or more.

In Hong Kong, where dumplings come under the general heading 'Dim Sum,' (点心 *dian xin* in mandarin) they often use rice flour to make pink, translucent shrimp dumplings, however dumplings are definitely northern fare.

It is normal to dip your dumplings into some sauce, usually this is a mixture of soy sauce and vinegar or sometimes it is chilli; personally I don't bother it spoils the delicate taste of the dumplings. For the Chinese, the delicate taste buds didn't get passed down through the generations, they need a shock to get them salivating. Some dumplings maybe sweet and contain red bean paste or sesame paste, you dip these in a kind of custard like sickly, sticky cream.

A high fat diet seems quite normal in the north, eating thick slices of pork fat is an everyday fare. A colleague of mine told me that one of her favourites is duck's blood soup, it conjures an awful image in the mind but in reality it is simply chunks of dried blood floating in a salty liquid, I suppose not much different to black pudding, nonetheless it would go down well in Transylvania.

One speciality, reported to be served in a Haerbin restaurant, is human afterbirth. Apparently a restaurant has made a deal with the local hospital to serve it, usually stewed or in dumplings (with soy sauce of course). Customers are able to inspect the health certificate before they eat it and check that it is disease free. According to the highly censored English language newspaper the China Daily, 10% of Chinese people have Hepatitis B so it might be worth giving the sweet and sour afterbirth a miss.

The most famous of all north east food is of course Peking Duck, the trouble is, as Terry Wogan found out, is that it is very different to that which is served in the UK. The duck is of course roasted, as the name implies, but not until it is crispy as we are used to. The skin is removed and it is the skin only that is served with pancakes, spring onions, cucumber, and plum sauce. The skin tends to be very fatty and nowhere near as nice as you get in your local Chinese restaurant back home. The rest of the duck, including the head and feet is served in various ways with rice, vegetables or noodles, in fact anything that takes your fancy. Upon the very first visit to Beijing, almost certainly your host or tour group will take you to one of these 'Kao Ya' (roast duck) establishments but you are likely to be disappointed, "crispy aromatic duck" won't be served.

Perhaps the weirdest restaurant of all in Beijing, *Guolizhuang* situated on the shores of xihu (west lake), it specialises in serving up the genitals of male animals, a speciality penis diner. No animal seems (eunuchs are now rare thank god!) to have been spared the nightmarish though of having its pleasure stick roasted and dipped in chilli sauce. The animal's todgers on offer include dogs, horses, donkeys, yaks, oxen in fact anything well endowed enough to get stuck into. Men go for the testicles to as they believe it will boost their manhood, women are advised against this due to the hormones. I guess it can only be a matter of time before steaming hot turds, garnished with coriander, become an expensive delicacy, no doubt Panda's will be the healthiest.

Food

Shanghai food or really any food that comes from the east of China tends to be sweet. Here it is much more likely to get sweet and sour fish (never sweet and sour pork or chicken balls) than anywhere else. Most fish comes from the river in China and is probably farmed, moving around the countryside, small scale stagnant fish pools can be seen. The popular way to serve fish is with spring onions, ginger and soy sauce, all steamed together.

The Shanghai-nese also like to eat the hairy crab which comes out of the surrounding lakes. These tend to be quite expensive and the dish is most popular during the autumn months; they can be seen in restaurants, quite small and green, bound up with vine leaves and just sitting there, still alive, waiting to be dropped into boiling water. The preference is always for the female crab and these command a higher price because inside, they are usually full of eggs. It is easy to spot the difference, if you look underneath the little creature the shell of the female at the rear has a wide vee marking that comes from the back almost to the front. It is very common in this area to be served chicken feet as an appetiser.

Snake can be easily found in Shanghai, on the menu as opposed to the streets. A complete waste of time, it has less taste than chicken and has bones like fish – an inexcusable consumption of scarce creatures. The skin also is very rubbery and unless it is deep fried to a crisp, it is chewy and almost inedible.

As the people of Shanghai get richer and richer, their taste for food gets more and more bizarre. They are following the Hong Kong lead of eating disgracefully expensive delicacies that are only eaten because of the price and the status that implies. The rarer the animal is, the higher the price. Included in the list are shark's fin, abalone, birds nests and turtles.

Real China

More common folk will eat a lot of bean curd or *doufu* as it is called; this can be hot, cold, in chilli, with noodles and even fermented. Fermented bean curd has a really pungent smell, not unlike sweaty feet, becomes black in colour and yet, surprisingly, tastes fine.

Another strange one is black chicken soup, a watery soup that is made from chickens with, strangely enough, black skin; the Chinese tell me that it is really healthy. In fact they are always telling me how certain foods are really healthy. Best to ignore comments like this, if they were right they would be living for 200 years or more.

Sichuan food is hot and spicy and it does not matter what the dish is, it cannot be tasted anyway because there is so much chilli that the mouth quickly becomes numb and tingling with pain. Worse still, next morning, it burns your ass on the way out!

I actually like spicy food, a lamb madras goes down well, but in Sichuan, after a couple of mouthfuls, it is just unbearable. The most common dish is a thick oily bubbling soup that is made of oil and chillies, usually with the insides or the spare parts as I like to call it, of a pig. Submerged in the bright orange-coloured oil. It maybe to some peoples liking but to dip chopsticks into this big bowl of bright red, noxious oil and pull out a piece of stomach that is both rubbery and hairy and is enough to make Desperate Dan turn vegetarian.

The other weird dish is again a large bowl filled with tiny hot fiery red chillies dry this time, not in oil. On a ratio of about ten to one, chilli to chicken pieces, the pot is explored with ones chopsticks until a tiny piece of meat is secured. This is also too hot to contemplate and the chicken is always on the bone. In China, where chicken is eaten, it is never separated from the bone so great care needs to be taken when biting into a large piece of breast meat, the result may be a splinter in the roof of the mouth. One of the few dishes that does not serve chicken on the bone is *gongbao jiding* (宫保鸡丁) in Hong Kong they call it Kungpo chicken but it is not the same. It is a spicy, but not too spicy, dish of chicken bits (literally nails) red peppers and cashew nuts.

For some reason rabbit is popular in Sichuan, naturally with lots of chilli, just browse a local supermarket and it will quickly be discovered that deep fried rabbit's head is a popular snack.

One of the peculiarities of eating in Guangdong is the pre-meal ritual where the first half cup of tea is used to rinse the bowl, plate, chopsticks and teacup. This is then tipped into a larger glass bowl which the waiting staff will come and collect, the next cup of tea is for drinking. Recently in Guangzhou, a certain Ms Huang sued the restaurant for throwing away her false teeth, she had put them in a tea cup to soak before the meal and the waitress came along and tipped the first cup of tea away, unaware of the lady's dentures, and re-filled the cup. Nobody seemed to notice her gnashers floating in the large glass, waste-tea bowl at the centre of the table!

Guangdong or Cantonese cuisine, as *we* call it, is easily the best but also can easily be the worst. This is the place to get sea food such as shrimps, prawns, crayfish, lobster, sea fish, scallops and all the '*fruits de mer*.' The flavours tend to be more subtle but the odd Chef will add a bucket of salt and a vat of oil if he so pleases and then it is impossible to taste anything.

Prawns are usually steamed and served in their shells, they should be peeled (many don't bother), dip them in soy sauce and vinegar, and gulp them down. Sauté scallops, served on the shell, with garlic and a little oil are also worth trying. Sea cucumbers or slugs are common fare too, an awful sensation in the mouth but the taste is acceptable if not desirable. It is fascinating watching Chinese people eat fish, their mouths are a complete and highly efficient filleting factory; they take a large piece of fish, chew away for several seconds and the bones are automatically ejected from the corners of the mouth, evolutionarily perfect!

Sea-food in China can be excellent and superb value for money; I was disturbed by a recent TV programme whereby Rick Stein was praising the merits of Corsican seafood, he then said "Sea food will cost you an arm and a leg in Corsica!" Have you ever eaten in *his* Padstow sea-food restaurant? No! I can't afford to either.

When it comes to food, the big problem with the people of Guangdong is that they will eat anything. Just go to a large sea-food restaurant in Guangzhou (Canton) and take a look at the food they have in the tanks, it might be a disquieting experience. They will have what could be expected of course, lots of different fish, crabs, other crustaceans and prawns but they will also have live chickens, ducks, dogs, rats, mice, rabbits, snakes and a large assortment of bugs and insects.

The SARS epidemic, which started somewhere in Guangdong, was consensually thought to have originated from humans living in close quarters will many different types of animals. The government has since stopped the Cantonese from eating rats in case that was also the cause. More recently, the blame has been laid on eating civets, a member of the cat family, not unlike our pine martin in appearance. It is reported that 70% of civets carry the SARS virus, these used to be a delicacy in Guangdong.

In Guangdong, to eat anything that is totally abnormal, disgusting or downright stupid is considered a delicacy. Clearly there is something wrong. One thing that does please is the wide selection of vegetables and fruit that are available, perhaps because of the warm and humid climate. Many of them will not have reached the British Isles, particularly the enormous variety of green vegetables, wild mushrooms and peculiarities like lotus root. This is the sweet root of the lily flower that looks radish-like and white with holes in like Swiss cheese. *Ku gua*, a bright green vegetable with a strong bitter taste and *jiu cai*, something between an onion and a leek with a deep pungent smell that stinks the house out when it is fresh.

Guangdong has lovely fruits too, *huo long gua* (sometimes called dragon fruit) is a bright pink fruit, the size of a drinking mug with a sweet white flesh that is speckled with black, poppy-like seeds. The most famous Guangdong fruit of all, comes in a short season during the spring. Fresh lychee (*li zhi*) the taste has no comparison to the tinned type that can be bought in the local Chinese back home. What cannot be found in China, is a Chinese Take-away! Although in reality food can be, and often is, taken away from any restaurant.

Another means of eating that is especially popular in Guangdong, but common all over China, is hot pot or *huo guo*. Very simple, sit at the table and in the middle is a big pot of bubbling liquid into which various fresh foods be it meat, seafood or vegetable are dipped and pulled out when they are cooked. It comes with a free facial sauna as part of the process. Beneficially, this way of eating is extremely hygienic, the chopsticks are constantly sterilised in boiling water or sometimes oil.

Chinese eating habits are diagonally opposite to our own, they do everything we were told not to do when we were kids. Noodles are slurped and hoovered-up, sounding like a small child finishing her milkshake hastily through a drinking straw. Splashing everywhere; they seldom eat with their mouth closed and often talk and chew at the same time with food residue sliding down the corners of the mouth. They also talk, or rather, shout their dinner conversation such that there should be a health warning on the level of noise pollution in every restaurant. If they receive a call on their mobile phone, they shout even louder.

Usually Chinese restaurants are very large and can accommodate hundreds, sometimes thousands, of people. here it can be more deafening than in the old days at a Black Sabbath concert. If a restaurant is quiet, with very few people (heaven to me) the Chinese will walk on by, thinking the food is poor; many restaurateurs position their customers by the window so it always looks full. The food tastes the same wherever you go and if the restaurant is quiet, chances are the service is better anyway so opt for the latter, don't go with the crowd. Some restaurants will even pay unemployed people to sit outside and pretend to be waiting for a table in order to attract more customers. This is a place where seeing is *not* believing.

One thing though, in all of the big cities, a MacDonald's or KFC can always be found and increasingly other chains such as TGI Fridays but the prices in most restaurants that serve western food tends to be higher than would be anticipated.

Food

An interesting detour, highly recommended on any visit to China, completely free, is to visit a supermarket. These places are always big and crowded but well worth a look. For a start there are more vegetables than I had ever thought possible, especially green ones. The fruit consists of types very similar to the ones that we have but much more variety and some that are unrecognisable.

These large stores tend to have a great deal more variety, for example there will be one 20 meter chest freezer dedicated to dumplings. For certain though, fruit and vegetables do have more taste then we are used to, I imagine because pesticides and fertilizers are too expensive for most farmers. Cucumber is a very good example, ours are smooth, about 12 inches long with an almost sculpted look and feel, and have about the same taste as a glass of water. In China they are irregular in shape, but regular enough to identify them as a cucumber, have knobbly skin and taste very good indeed. Be warned though food needs to be washed thoroughly because human excrement is cheaper than manure. The Chinese do not yet have a team of genetic engineers creating designer fruit that is ornamental, rather than nutritious, for the likes of Tesco and Sainsbury; they are though, growing GM rice.

The climax of the supermarket visit will be the fish counter, even Jacques Cousteau would find species that he had not previously come across, many are from the river, live and still in tanks swimming around but most sea fish have expired and are laid out on ice. Take a look at the live crabs and lobsters, live turtles and live frogs in addition to many kinds of live bugs, perhaps best to omit the details.

These unfortunate creatures must know they are on the menu, I once saw a crab tear its way out of the shopping bag of a man in front at the check-out queue. It sped across the floor, and hid under a shelving unit.

It should now come as no surprise that supermarkets sell live poultry. In a Shanghai restaurant, a lady came in for lunch carrying her shopping, including a live chicken, clucking away from inside her plastic supermarket carrier bag.

The market here responds to the need to buy food in large quantities, rice in ten kilo bags and eggs at a couple of kilos at a time. What does not make sense is that the stores only have small baskets with which to do the shopping, although they supply trolleys to carry the basket' they haven't figured out that if they had bigger shopping carts, people might actually buy more groceries. Part of the problem is that like housing, supermarkets have more vertical space than horizontal and tend to be on more than one floor.

When a foreigner goes to his or her local supermarket, it creates an interesting focal point for the locals to dwell on. They take time out to pause and carefully examine the contents of the 'laowai's' basket as (s)he browses amongst the cans of salt, oil and sugar, flavoured with the odd vegetable or piece of meat. Even worse, upon arriving at the check-out, the girl will have no problem in asking 'what are you buying this for?' or simply comment 'you drink a lot of milk!' It's a bit like Asda handing out AA cards (I don't mean the car people) at the checkout given the trolley loads of booze us Brits buy these days.

Many people have said that the food is very healthy and you can eats lots of it without getting fat. I strongly disagree with this; firstly the food contains far too much saturated fat be it in added oils or simply meat that is predominantly fatty tissue. Secondly, vegetables tend to be cooked to death, removing the nutrients by first boiling them, followed by stir frying in a large oil-soaked wok! Thirdly, a potentially serious health issue is the astounding amount of salt that is consumed, it is added to everything to the point where the taste is nothing *but* salt.

The number one killer in China is stroke, a result of high blood pressure, compounded by high salt consumption. Virtually all doctors and dieticians agree that a diet rich in sugar, saturated fats and high salt content is a sure way to an early grave though diabetes, coronary heart disease or stroke, especially when combined with smoking.

With this dreadful diet, rising wealth and sheer ignorance about what is good for them, obesity is now a problem in China; the papers report that 'a dramatic rise in obesity is sweeping the nation'. The government puts it down to a by product of strong economic performance and increasing prosperity. This of course probably has a lot to do with it, nobody has to survive on a bowl of rice per day anymore, well at least in the cities.

A survey jointly released by the Ministry of Health and the State Statistics Bureau in October 2004 reported that, in China's big cities, 30 per cent of the total population is now overweight, compared with 21 per cent in 1992.

It is suggested that the average Beijing burgher consumes a staggering 83 grams of vegetable oil per day compared with 25 grams as the recommended daily maximum. According to a recent report by the Earth Policy Institute, a Washington-based environmental research group, China's meat consumption last year amounted to 64 million tons, nearly doubling since the 1980s. The government agencies concerned with health are actually quoted as saying 'The explosive increase of greasy foods being consumed has changed the look of Chinese who once were more accustomed to lean diets'. This is true, westerners can carry a *little* extra weight and still look fine, the Chinese cannot, they appear round, dumpy and Mongol-like with only just a few extra pounds.

Blame also falls upon the longer working hours meaning that people are more likely to turn to fast foods and eat out, where they cannot control the ingredients that are put into the food, instead of cooking at home.

To complicate the situation, the yearning for quick weight control solutions has brought in a booming market of dubious products that may do further harm to people's health.

Of course now there is a big opportunity to push fake drugs that claim to reduce weight, burn off fat and increase metabolic rates. With a fledgling consumer protection regime, there is a very good chance that some of these drugs could do serious harm by burning off necessary fats and oils.

With not much in the way of a foods and drugs administration regulatory body, these companies promoting their quick fix solutions can virtually get away with murder. The daily TV adverts are farcical. Rub-on lotions to burn away fat, pills that sprout instant swollen breasts and creams that dissolve birth marks and scars. Even sports shoes that make you grow taller!

Without proper regulation, people will always be hooked, just like buying a lottery ticket seems an easy way to get rich, taking a pill or applying some ointment, seems an easy way to get thin and so people go for it.

It is important to state here that the food in Taiwan and Hong Kong has much less fat, sugar and salt and is therefore much healthier than that consumed by their mainland cousins. It is highly noticeable in the people too.

Food

Finally on the subject of food, I thought that I had tried just about everything in China but one day, at lunch in the central city of Wuhan, I was served '*chou yu*' which literally means smelly fish. I tried it and it tasted fine but after enquiring as to where it got its name from, the explanation that followed threw me sideways. They simply wait until the fish has gone-off, has become pungently smelly and then cook it! It seems superfluous to say that for me, lunch ended abruptly at that point.

Chapter 4 – Environmental Disaster

There have been two pieces of technology that one could argue should never have been introduced into China, one is the mobile phone and the other is the motor car. Both technologies have enabled the population to reach new heights of vulgarity and, in the case of the car, bring extreme danger with it.

In a country where the average office worker's salary is around £200 per month, splashing out on a mobile phone for the same sort of value is quite normal. Virtually everyone who is employed has a mobile phone and spends a significant chunk of their normal life speaking on it.

The Chinese are noisy anyway, in normal everyday life, they speak about 6dB louder (four times) than an average Englishman (and 3dB louder than an average American!). On a mobile phone this easily doubles again and I am convinced that the further way the distant caller is, the louder they think they have to speak in order to be heard. The really dumb thing is, to make life even more unpleasant, they enable reception virtually everywhere including subway trains and even in lifts. More worrying they leave the damned things on when flying, easy to deduce because a few thousand feet above the runway, the text message signals start to beep.

As the reader may have guessed, I am not a big fan of what they call the *shouji* [1], (the popular name for a mobile) personally I almost feel embarrassed to answer it when it rings in a public place, feeling highly reluctant to speak loud enough for the person on the other end to hear. However, in a

---

[1] literally hand machine

meeting in China, no matter how important the visitor and how far he or she may have travelled to be there, if the mobile rings it will get answered, and it will ring many times. It could be argued that this is just another example of poor manners by our standards, no matter it is perfectly normal behaviour by theirs.

The ring-tones are usually silly if not ridiculous, like 'Jingle Bells' or 'We Wish You a Merry Christmas' on a thirty five degree mid-July day. The 'Marseillaise' can be heard on any street corner but 'God Save The Queen' has yet to catch on.

Along with the love of the pocket phone comes the need to have the latest model and the corresponding desire for thieves to steal it. Showing off with a large colour display, MP3 loudspeaker, high resolution camera and multi-coloured press-on cover comes naturally. So those who want to steal one, do not need to be particularly devious in order to do so.

There was a lovely example of the dependence on the mobile in a newspaper article. It described how the authorities in Henan City University had decided to switch off the electricity supply between 7 and 9pm in order to save costs. There was little mention of how this might make life difficult for students now forced to do their homework in the dark, instead the bright reporter thought it more important to declare that the seriously inconvenienced pupils now had to recharge their phones, clandestinely, in the classroom.

The Motor Car

In his buck-the-trend book, *The Coming Collapse of China*, Gordon Chang suggests that at some stage in the future there will be a kind of catastrophic breakdown of the country. There are various arguments for this but the main two are the banking system and a social unrest situation that may boil over into nationwide riots and lawlessness. I talk later about the banking system from the perspective as a customer. In the conclusion, report worrying and increasingly violent incidences of rioting that occur at various times up and down the country.

The doomsday prediction is China will eventually come to a standstill because its development is and continues to be at the expense of great harm to the environment. A major contributor to that will be the motor car as its multiplication in numbers choke both the city centre streets and the nearby unfortunate residents. In future centuries, historians will look back and describe how the twentieth century's rise of the auto almost destroyed civilisation. Perhaps that it is a bit strong but we seem to have consumed most of the Earth's carbon resources in the less than 200 years yet the planet has been around for several million.

If it were possible to accurately add-up the number of deaths caused by the four-wheeled monster, it most certainly far outweighs that which occurred in the second world-war[1]. For some reason we do not seriously question its presence and investment in vehicles and roads continue to perpetuate its existence.

It is quite bizarre really that in most Asian countries drug dealers, if caught, usually receive the death penalty. Drugs are not a good thing, we all agree, but how many people actually die from drug abuse? Not that many in the overall (cause of death) league tables, yet anyone who visits the Chinese-majority pseudo democratic dictatorship, entitled the Republic of Singapore can scan the authorised newspaper and read how

---

[1]   30 million in the UK according to the Cardiff Road Safety Centre

young people, with their whole life before them, are frequently killed in car accidents.

Singapore ruthlessly hangs drug dealers many times per year, always without remorse and never shows mercy. In fact according to Amnesty International, Singapore has the highest execution rate in the world, as a proportion of population*.

A first time visitor to Earth from some higher civilisation somewhere in the universe might ask why don't they hang their car dealers, they kill far more people? In Singapore the government is the real dealer. Cars attract very high taxes, the end price is probably three times higher than UK; the locals say buy one for yourself and two for the government. The real problem for the government in China is that in order to sustain its one party state existence and authority, the vast majority must feel that things are getting better and quality of life improves almost day by day. Owning a car is part of this feel-good factor, so whilst they know the harm that is being caused, curbing the car numbers will be a problem for their popularity.

The very first time when I visited China in 1998, there were bicycles everywhere, even in Shanghai, now it is cars and even in the supposedly poorer cities, motors dominate. China is the great automotive market for the world's manufacturers and most of them already have plants there. Now every city dweller aspires to have a motor car and the banks, probably under government direction, are more than happy to lend them the money to do so.

'SINGAPORE The death penalty: A hidden toll of executions' (15 Jan 2004) From 1994 to 1999 there were 13.57 executions per million population, almost three times as many as Saudi Arabia who came in second. China was fifth with 2.01 per million (reported).

Real China

In 2003, vehicle sales were 4.4 million units, the figure for 2004 just topped 5 million and in 2005 it was 5.76 million. That is about a 13.6% increase year on year. Interestingly, and this is what everyone who rushes to China to get rich does not expect, profit margins have dived. Typical returns per vehicle have dropped from 35% to 5% in just a few years. Shenzhen now has more cars than Hong Kong. I know there are a lot of bikes to replace but this kind of growth is frightening.

The economy seems to average growth around ten per cent each year so the figure for autos is especially strong. It is not difficult to see why Volkswagen, General Motors, Ford, Honda, Nissan, Toyota and more recently BMW have built large manufacturing plants already. Even worse, they are not shipping so many fuel efficient, one litre hatchbacks, it is 2.5 litre V sixes all the way and China does not have strict pollution controls like the USA, Europe and Japan so the manufacturers don't bother with expensive add-ons such as catalytic converters that might just reduce the pollution a bit. What makes this especially criminal is the fact that cars were, until the market became so competitive, selling for maybe 30% more than they would in Europe.

Almost every city now is choked with traffic, Beijing is probably the worst, and the pollution levels go off the scale. The delightful singer songwriter Katie Melua caused a stir amongst Radio 4 listeners when she suggested in her hit single *9 Million Bicycles in Beijing* that we are "12 million light years from the edge" astronomers disputing her aspersions. Ironically the nine million bicycles have gone and it seems now that there are nine million cars!

The weather in China, especially during the winter, tends to be very dry and seldom windy so the pollution levels get dangerously high. This is compounded by the fact that many northern cities have combined heat and power systems; that is the power stations, as a by-product of cooling the coal-fired steam turbines, produce hot water that is pumped around the city to heat the houses. For this to work properly, the power stations must be located close to the population centres meaning even more localised pollution. To deal with this issue means a complete re-structuring of the current ethos, it means reducing the number of vehicles not increasing them and it means switching to cleaner fuels. It is frequently reported that China brings two new coal-fired power stations online per week.

I don't know where the data for this come from but let's do a simple calculation: Assume each unit household or business consumes electricity at a rate of $2kW$[1] (on the high side). China probably has 800 million of these so needs 1.6 million MW. With economic growth at 15% a year best case and homes coming on line who have no power, lets say the annual growth is 30%. So they need 480,000 MW additional capacity each year. A typical coal-fired power station produces 8,000 MW so China needs 60 new ones each year and therefore it is probably a good guess that 1-2 new power stations are needed each week!

Moving away from coal will be extremely difficult since the country is so rich in this resource and China already has an insatiable thirst for oil. In the latter part of 2004, when the oil price surged to more than fifty dollars per barrel (seems cheap now), the monotonous news channel CNN, the channel that thinks, judging by its coverage, that all of its viewers are Americans who spend most of their life gambling on the stock

---

[1] For the non-technical $1kW = 1000$, $1MW = 1000,000$ and $1GW = 1,000,000,000$. W of course means Watts.

market, repeatedly reported that the reason for the rising oil price was due to the huge demand for fuels in China. It never occurred to them that the USA, who use per person twice as much oil as we do in Europe, have been pissing the stuff away for the last fifty years! Annoyingly, in most hotels all over Asia, the foreign 'news' channel that is most likely to be beamed into the average hotel room, will be the ever bland and parochial CNN. Frustratingly, when the hotel decides to offer a breath of fresh air, in the guise of BBC World, the UK will hardly be mentioned.

Just consider for a minute, as described earlier, a generally self-centred, ill-mannered and ignorant nation like the Peoples' Republic, it follows that when they get to hide behind the wheel of anything with an engine, the result is carnage.

For a start the road system has few rules or if it does, few people pay any attention to them. Driver training is brief and poor and anyway, there is no need to bother, just go out and buy a driving license from your local forger. Although to get a genuine driving license, a theory test is required, the road test is issued by the driving school! I did my theory test in Guangzhou, around one hundred people at a time sit behind computers and answer the multi-choice questions in a set time. Because I am a foreigner, I was entitled to the help of a translator. Of course she had done it many times and simply told me all the answers.

There are no government driving examiners, the fox in charge of the chickens situation is that private driving instructors not only teach but also examine their students! Some simply exchange a wad of crumpled notes for a pass certificate.

Environmental Disaster

A person I spoke to on a plane from China, who lives in the UK, gets forged UK driving licenses sent over each year so he does not need to take the test which he would certainly fail.

A local Chinese newspaper in London's Chinatown, almost a law unto itself, advertises these. The very same also advertises a service for residence visas by opening a company in the UK (costing about £25) as a fast-track means for Chinese people to remain in the UK once they get here.

The accident statistics in China are frightening but inconsistent, for example in the year of 2004 there were 107,000 road traffic deaths and a further 500,000 more were injured. This is an increase of 2.4% and 2.7% respectively. In 2006 there were 80,000 road deaths and 400,000 injuries. Both sets of data came from the China Daily! The Chinese statistics are the official ones, it is highly likely that the true rate is far higher. The best way to look at it is that China has 2 per cent of the world's vehicles yet 15 per cent of the road deaths.

Most of the accidents are occurring in and around the cities on the east coast where car ownership is high. The 800 million or so farmers tend not to own cars; in fact around the countryside, it is rare to see a tractor

Walking around the country, it is really not that surprising that the accident rate is so high; people behind the wheels of cars behave no differently and with no less care than if they were walking on the street. The same pushing in and rudeness prevails. Bus drivers are one of the worst for driving too fast and ignoring traffic signals, especially red lights. Bus drivers in Shenzhen are paid 800 yuan per month, the rest of their salary depends on how many passengers they pick up hence they speed around the city, dangerously and recklessly fighting with other 50-seat buses for customers.

Real China

In Shenzhen, the accident rate *has* been reduced by putting barriers between alternate carriageways in order to stop dangerous overtaking and driving on the wrong side of the road. Almost every traffic signal now has a camera installed.

The motor car has now become king in China, the Shanghai government recently banned bicycles from the city centre because they were getting in the way of traffic, however they hurriedly reversed the law due to public outcry and considerable international embarrassment.

As a pedestrian, crossing the road is a frightening experience, for a start drivers ignore the road signs and traffic lights, crossings might as well not be there, and the worst thing of all is that when there is a controlled pedestrian crossing, with a green light for foot soldiers, drivers turning right simply plough through the crowds on the crossing.

The average Chinese driver is rude, arrogant, impatient and downright dangerous. Even crossing a one way street requires you to look both ways because there will always be some daft bugger driving the wrong way.

The most common victims are of course children, 40 children every day are killed on China's roads. Often the victims are the poor migrant workers who come into the big cities to find work and have no concept of road safety; they are frequently mowed down by fast traffic because they misjudge the speed of vehicles, look the wrong way or simply do not expect the dangerous and idiotic behaviour of Chinese drivers.

The Chinese police have a very limited number dedicated to road traffic and so most drivers get away with what is no less than dangerous driving, on a daily basis. Every day the papers report about a road accident in the local metropolis and the comment is always that we must learn to cross the road more safely. It makes one want to scream out loud "shit! you need to have decent road safety laws and have the common sense to enforce them"

It's a bit like those debates on American TV where they discuss why people are so easily tempted to use their hand gun, whilst nobody asks the question, why do they have them in the first place?

The arrogance, stupidity and sheer bloody mindedness was exemplified just outside my home in Shenzhen recently; they changed the road scheme such that a one-way street had its direction reversed. The local authorities put up lots of warning signs and new traffic lights, it was very clear.

However, the vast majority of drivers, who were used to using that road, continued to use it as normal, driving the wrong way down a one way street. Within an hour, on the first day, there was a serious collision and this continued for about a week or so, not a blue uniform in sight. The locals finally decided to obey the signs, not because they were causing a danger to others, but because they were likely to get hurt themselves.

Yet sadly, every Chinese person aspires to own a car, it is the ultimate status symbol, a major part of your showing-off Chinese persona.

The aforesaid is of course hypocritical for certain, we cannot go without blame ourselves, the BBC show 'Top Gear' is beamed worldwide. Jeremy Clarkson and friends describe, with boyish *Scalectrix* enthusiasm, how fast a car goes and how much horsepower it has, in a totally irresponsible way. If the speed limit is 70 miles per hour, why is it legal to sell a car that can travel at 130 miles per hour? The Germans are far the best at setting these double standards, espousing their eco-friendliness yet have motorways *sans* speed limits. Even

Real China

worse, if this book sells well, I'll be straight off to my nearest Porsche dealer

According to the World Bank, China's pollution problems are likely to have an affect on its ability to produce food for its 1.3 billion. It seems that the layers of noxious gases in the atmosphere are filtering the suns rays to the extent that crops have difficulty photosynthesising. The concern is that China may yet again have difficulty in feeding itself. It also follows that the water supply is greatly affected as the pollutants run off the land and contaminate rivers and lakes.

The long term health effects are probably a time bomb ticking away until the whole thing explodes into a toxic mess. Heavy smoking, poor air quality and high dust levels are a certain fast-acting carcinogenic mix. The car is not the only problem and by no means the most serious but it is just adding more instability to the already fragile environment.

The ice cold winters in the north east consume large amounts of coal but from a supply point of view, this is one resource of which China has plenty. However, with inefficient stoves, central heating burners and progressive industrial activity the end product is smog-choked cities.

When visiting any population centre during the winter, it can sometimes be difficult to see other buildings across the road, the air has that awful toxic, throat gagging coal dust smell to it and the natural need to frequently sneeze or cough splatters of black particles onto a handkerchief.

As the energy needs are ramped-up year on year, the government is fortunate that it does not need to consult the population when it plans, and then rapidly implements, new power stations. For example Shenzhen has two nuclear power stations and there are plans for a third.

Environmental Disaster

The newspapers often report that polluting industries have been closed down or moved out of the city but this is unlikely to be true. These old, inefficient 'smokers' employ a lot of people, high unemployment or rather much higher than it is, could lead to civil unrest and instability.

In the Panyu district of Guangzhou, there is a decorating materials factory which produces so much pollution that eighty per cent of the school teachers take regular sick leave due to respiratory diseases such as chronic rhinitis. Anyone visiting the area cannot help to notice the leaves on the trees appear to have been 'dyed white.'

It is not difficult to figure out that another issue is noise pollution; the government planners really do not give a damn where they place their highways, flyovers and busy junctions. At a school in Baiyun district of Guangzhou it was reported that the teachers (all 800 of them!) had to use microphones and amplifiers in class in order to be heard. The article did not mention whether or not the kids actually learn anything or if they go home each night with thumping great headaches.

Not reported at all inside the country, in April 2005 villagers in Huaxi, a town in Zhejiang province went on the rampage, rioting over a local chemical factory that was producing life-threatening levels of toxic waste (two women were reported to have died). The anger was so great that the people took over the town, whilst the police ran away in fear.

In November 2004, there was an air show at the coastal city of Zhuhai, which is just across the water from Macao. By the sea, in a warm and humid tropical climate, the air quality should be reasonable yet the flying displays were cancelled due to poor visibility brought on by the chronic air pollution.

Beijing is said to be moving more than 130 polluting enterprises out of the city, reportedly it has already moved

Real China

200 factories in the past 20 years. This may or may not be true but it does prompt the question how on earth could they award the Olympic Games to a city where the air quality is so poor? Not to mention the chronic traffic problem's other affect, difficulty in crossing the road safely. Of course it is highly naive to suggest that the air quality will be anything less than perfect for the Olympics. This is still an authoritarian communist country, they will simply ban cars and close factories a month or so before the games, the air quality will be on a par with the Scottish Highlands.

If anything destroys 'New China' and its rampant growth to riches, it will be the way it had to cripple the environment to get there. The motor car will be a significant player. Beijing had 564,000 vehicles in 1993, today it has 2.35 million, the prediction is for it to have 3.8 million by 2010 and 5 million by 2020, effectively every urban family will have a car.

Of course, this represents the big hope for faltering foreign auto manufacturers such as General Motors who see the 'great' Chinese market where their future car sales will be. Despite the growth statistics and the market potential of 1.3 billion consumers, there may only be 300,000 or so who have the resources to buy a car. Only 300,000! I can't believe I just wrote that? That's the population of the United States.

From the perspective of a typical western auto maker; used to unions, social contracts, holidays and sick pay, China must look like a dream. It has low wages with no legal minimum (or rather there is but it is not enforced), no unions, limited holidays, long working hours and a highly compliant workforce.

On the other hand, a car is for most people, three years salary so this represents something of a paradox. At the moment, most vehicles are for domestic consumption only, but it is

Environmental Disaster

only a matter of time before shipping overseas becomes normal. It won't be long before the 'quality German ultimate driving machine' that everyone (except me it seems) wants to own, is made in China.

It would be very hard for us in the West to criticise the Chinese for their automobile love-affair since we started and perpetuated it in the first place. Environmental hypocrisy is a world disease. One of the most irritating practises now found in most hotels, started by the ever-green Germans, is the request to save the environment by not having the towels and bedding changed daily. We all know that the real reason is to lower the hotel's laundry costs and meanwhile there is a gas-guzzling, carbon splurging 5 litre 4x4 in the parking space marked 'General Manager'.

The point is that we have disgracefull double standards when it comes to the environment, it should be of little wonder that the Chinese don't really care either. It is equally shameful when governments, particularly the US and EU complain about the trade imbalance with China when so many western companies have closed their local manufacturing plants, fired the workers, and set up in the middle country. All in the name of lower costs and higher margins.

Interestingly re-cycling is not an issue in the people's capitalist republic, mainly because the very poorest people will scour the streets looking for rubbish, collect it and take it to where it can be re-cycled. They don't do this for free of course, they earn a few jiao (tuppence) per twenty kilos or so. We would turn our heads in disgust to see the very scruffy, unwashed and usually very elderly peasants as they struggle with what looks like a hundred weight of rubbish bearing down on their Quasimodo-like backs.

Real China

I believe I could solve the rubbish problem in the UK almost overnight; since the vast majority of it comes from supermarket (over) packaging, the law should make it compulsory to return the cornflake packets, cellophane wrappers and yoghurt pots to Tesco et al. The local authority would then collect it from these monster stores, on the periphery of our towns and cities, a few times per week.

If the garbage is recyclable, the local authority does it for free, if it is not then the supermarket has to pay for its disposal. This master-plan would ensure that our mega outlets would both reduce the amount of packing and where packaging is necessary, make sure that it is recyclable. They would all squeal about the costs and reduce their contributions to the Tory party but in the long run it would save them money on all that unnecessary, wasteful and costly packaging.

For China though, as long as it maintains its shameful disparity between rich and poor, by maintaining 700 million or so desperate peasants, there will be no shortage of people to collect the refuse.

Chapter 5 - Love and Sex

Say one thing and do another is common throughout the world but the Chinese are the masters. Nowhere is this more obvious in the national make-up than the areas of love and sex.

They like to think that they have very high moral values when compared with the west and the US particularly, and so sex is hardly ever talked about publicly, in the media and certainly not within the family.

There is great censorship within the media, sexual topics are hardly ever mentioned in news coverage or in the papers. You won't see any bare breasts on the TV and there is no page three to ogle at. When Wei Hui launched her novel *Shanghai Baby* about the sexual adventures of a slightly promiscuous young lady in the city, it was immediately banned.

The stunning beautiful former ballet dancer Tang Jiali had her book of artistic nude poses banned (still easy to see her undraped form though, plug her name into Google images and well, you know the rest)

The internet is heavily censored; traffic going to and from the country is channelled through just a few hubs. Trying to access websites out of China is very slow because of this. Amusingly it is referred to as the Great *Fire*wall of China. No figures are published, but there must be thousands of security people whose job it is to monitor the Internet and block undesirable addresses or URLs. This system is not just for pornography of course, but also (if not mainly) for controlling political information and restricting the truth; sites like the BBC News are also blocked, rumoured to be un-blocked in

2008 probably because the Chinese are pissed with CNN over their constant Tibet coverage.

In fact, local Chinese are not allowed to subscribe to foreign satellite broadcasts such as the BBC and CNN, they can only be seen in hotels; even then, news reports about Taiwan or China are often blacked out.

During February 2005 the BBC recorded a special Question Time edition from Shanghai, it was chaired by David Dimbleby and had a couple of Chinese officials plus Chris Patten and (David) Tang Wang Cheung, the man who thinks we should all wear mandarin suits instead of shirt and tie. The programme was not screened in China even though it was incredibly bland and despite Chris Patten standing behind the Beijing authorities, in a sycophantic manner, with comments like 'everyone believes in the One China principle[1].'

At the time the government had just announced their anti-succession law which gives them the right to attack Taiwan if the latter declares independence and so it should have been a fascinating debate.

It was shown in the country only on *BBC World* and it was only censored once when there was a question about human rights, but the whole thing was disappointing due its impotent and unrevealing content.

For most people, this censorship continues at home, in the family, and at school. There are no sex education lessons at school and so children go from coveted babies, still wrapped

[1] The One-China Principle means the re-unification of Taiwan with the mainland. The Chinese press always report that foreign dignitaries supposedly sign-up when they visit Beijing. To his credit Chris Patten, whilst serving as the last governor of Hong Kong, drove a single-minded plan to organise the then British colony into a democracy prior to handover. He did this to the dissatisfaction of the Chinese and British governments plus various colleagues and industrialists with their self-centred business interests.

in cotton wool at 18, straight into adulthood without any training. The first thing the vast majority of China's female teenagers know about menstruation is when they get the shock of what seems to be unnatural bleeding. The following is a typical but not uncommon example of a story in a local newspaper:

A couple from Jingguan city, in Guangdong province had been trying for a baby for 12 months without success, so they went to the doctor to see if there was anything physically wrong with them. The doctor found that the wife was still a virgin and, after a quick brief on the facts of life, sent them on their way. What is not clear is what they actually *were* doing in order to get pregnant?

Such stories are common but not surprising since nobody told them what to do; they couldn't learn from their peers or school and certainly could not get so much as a hint from the TV. They daren't ask friends or relatives and it must have taken great courage to consult the doctor.

The authorities do seem to be becoming worried about the lack of sex knowledge when it comes to adolescents. It seems to have only just dawned on them that university students might be tempted to have sex with each other.

In July 2004 a survey was launched to try and find out just how much of this was going on and then decide whether to leave it be or organise some proper sex education. Forms were handed out to universities up and down the country, those few students who did actually get the forms, being Chinese, asked how much they'd get paid to fill it in! Most students however never saw it because many of the university authorities, being highly educated and forward thinking, decided that the form would make the majority of their students *start* to think about sex! (Is that not what it was meant to do?).

Reportedly some university boffins were shocked to see phrases like 'pre-marital sex' and 'contraception' so they must have dropped dead on the spot when they read blowjob! Other universities said the survey would disturb students' minds and give them sexual fantasies. In fact the survey was very sensible, asking about sexual activity, their knowledge of others' activity and their awareness of sexually transmitted infections. The survey was anonymous but those few forms that were returned showed that most students gained their sexual knowledge from sadly, pornography.

In Shenzhen a 'sex cafe' has recently opened, the idea is that as well as going for a cup of coffee, young people can also get advice on sex. This is nothing like a seedy backstreet Soho establishment. The cafe is set-up so that young people can borrow books related to sex and follow addresses of websites giving advice on sexual health. It is a non-profit place, set-up by the local government, many people will not go there for fear of embarrassment but it is perhaps a good initiative in a country ignorant of most things, in particular sex.

A big worry in Shenzhen, when compared with other cities, is its high percentage of females of child bearing age. This comes in at 44.98 per cent of the registered population, significantly higher than that of Beijing at 30.36 per cent, Tianjin at 29.78, Shanghai at 29.47 and 23.81 in Guangzhou. An almost unique statistic is that over 53 per cent of the floating population, which makes up some 83 per cent of the city's total population, are young females. The government seems to think that this is a serious threat to sexual health. The cafe also hands out free condoms.

To be fair most Asians have a much more reserved *public* face to sex than westerners; anyone who 'accidentally' stumbles across the porn channel in a Japanese hotel, will notice that

Love and Sex

the interesting bits have been pixelated or made fuzzy. In Hong Kong they actually publish the names of censored blue movies. This is a tremendous public service, its really nice to know that the police have checked which ones are worth watching! You can go into a video store and say 'reach under the desk and get me a copy *Japanese Girls Get Creamed Part 3!*' (I didn't make that up, it was actually named in the government's banned list and published in the *South China Morning Post*).

Prostitution is also banned in China and most other Asian countries although it goes on everywhere. In China it is quite strictly enforced but anyone who runs a KTV (karaoke) establishment or massage parlour can easily make sure the local police are well rewarded, financially or otherwise, for looking the other way.

The euphemistically called working girls are everywhere; in most cities, walking into a bar, especially if a male Caucasian, it becomes just a matter of time before a girl makes eye contact and smoothly slips into the seat beside. Some girls will come straight out with it, "do you want a massage?"

The more careful ones will say that they are trying to learn English. Don't be fooled both introductions mean do you want a shag and how much will you pay me?

Depending upon the city or location, she will offer to stay the night and expect a financial reward the following day. The price is really determined by the place, Beijing and Shanghai being the most expensive with the amount diminishing the less developed the city is. In Shanghai it is probably cheaper to fly to Bangkok for the weekend, pay for hotels, flights, two girls a night and still get change from what you might have paid there.

Sometimes it is so blatant as to be almost unreal. In the city of Changchun, in the North East, there is a hotel called the Swiss Bell (Hua Yuan in Chinese); on the second floor of this hotel is a bar which really is a full scale knocking shop. The girls in there will come over unannounced and talk, drink, play pool and even dance for no charge. For 300 Yuan they will be happy to spend the night. Surprisingly the hotel itself is four star, clean, smart, has good food and is inexpensive.

One is highly likely to receive a phone call in almost any hotel room at 11pm or so offering a massage. In Shenzhen some girls will hang around in the street outside the major hotels. The sub-district of Shekou, where many foreigners reside, is crawling with these girls, often hanging around in the streets as well as what the ex-pats call the 'Chicken Street' bar area.

In Hangzhou, I stayed at the Zhi Jiang hotel, the room phone rang so much that I could not get to sleep so I unplugged it from the wall. Five minutes later a girl knocked on the door, she was not to be so easily deterred. One of our team that was tempted caught a nasty dose of gonorrhoea, which serves as a danger sign to all.

Because the police automatically assume that girls carrying condoms are prostitutes, most girls don't carry them. Sometimes it gets really out of hand and so the authorities have to be seen to be doing something about it. Punishments can be harsh.

In the south coastal city of Zhuhai, two Chinese defendants were sentenced to life in prison during December 2003 for organizing a sex orgy involving more than 200 Japanese tourists. The case is alleged to have sparked public outrage across China. Twelve other defendants were sentenced to prison terms ranging from two to 15 years. The story goes on

Love and Sex

to report that Police have asked Interpol to help find three Japanese suspected of soliciting prostitutes for the orgy. The Chinese it seems were particularly offended and could not resist pointing out that the party in September of that year, coincided with the 72nd anniversary of the start of Japan's occupation of China during World War II. It was as if to say that this group of horny Japs only did it to make a political point; That's it, they were thinking about the war!

The people were named and the Zhuhai Intermediate People's Court sentenced *Ye Xiang*, assistant to the general manager of Zhuhai International Convention Centre (where the orgy took place) and *Ming Zhu* to life in prison. Almost certainly the general manager shopped him to save his own neck. The penalties did not stop there either, the hotel's deputy sales manager *Liu Xuejing* was sentenced to 15 years and another defendant, *Zhang Junying*, was sentenced to 12 years.

Ten others received between two and 10 years in prison. They include hotel staff, night club bosses, pimps, prostitutes and the employees of a local Japanese-funded company.

Earlier media reports had said that as many as 400 Japanese men and 500 Chinese prostitutes had sex at the Zhuhai hotel over the three-day period. It sounds like it was the 'Mother of all Parties;' the hotel has since been renamed.

The newspapers also said that 'the case has raised great concern at home and abroad.' In actual fact it was not widely reported outside of China. Apparently the prostitutes had come from many night clubs in Zhuhai and Shenzhen and were paid between 800 yuan (US$96) and 1,800 yuan (US$216) a night. The penalties are certainly harsh by our standards but only 20 years earlier the death sentence was frequently handed out for wife swapping or even nude photography.

Real China

The statistics on sexually transmitted diseases (STDs), that were released to the press, for Guangdong province, for the year 2004 makes worrying reading; there had been a 24% increase in the numbers treated, slightly more men than women. At the end of that year Guangdong had treated 1.26 million patients out of a total population of 110 million, this is just one province. It was reported that 20% of these people worked in KTV lounges and bars in Shenzhen, Zhuhai and Dongguan.

The absolutely astonishing figure, that passed without comment, is that 70% of the people treated for STDs were married. So much for the faithful, family-oriented Chinese and their superior moral values. In fact one fifth of all sexually transmitted diseases occur in Guangdong province, Shanghai on the other hand, brags that their residents 'lead the country' in the use of condoms.

The papers also report that condom sales reach a peak on Valentine's Day; a bunch of flowers, nice dinner, box of chocolates and a well deserved bonk!

Previously, before couples were to get married, they would have to undertake a compulsory medical examination to see if all was well. This was done under the pretext of minimising birth defects, although perhaps more likely incest because in village communities, it was common at one stage. This law was scrapped in 2003 but it hit the news again in 2005 when Heilongjiang province reintroduced it. Reading between the lines to see what is really going on, the article in the *China Daily* had a pre-amble on syphilis and how it disfigures unborn babies. Before the tests were stopped, the last year of data in 2002 shows that nine per cent of those tested had contagious or sexually transmitted diseases.

Love and Sex

Run that by me again, nearly one in ten young people have some kind of venereal disease? The mind boggling thing about remarks like this is the way they are reported without comment or discussion. Just imagine if a story like this hit the papers in the UK, there would be around the clock media coverage, ministerial resignations and probably a *Newsnight Special*. Even worse, since compulsory testing was stopped, the number of babies born with congenital diseases has doubled.

The Chinese press and people alike will be proud to tell you that they have a superior set of moral values when compared to the West but the truth is, instead of being chaste until wedlock, they are a highly promiscuous lot and the absent or poor standards of sexual education compounds the problem because most young people do not protect themselves.

Interestingly for the don't-talk-about-sex nation, the biggest exporters of sex toys and marital aids are located in China. The biggest of all, interestingly called 'Loves Shop' is located in the eastern province of Zhejiang in the city of Wenzhou. The company started as a joint venture with the Japanese and did have a tough time getting a license but now it is the biggest of its kind in China, probably the world. At their scruffy headquarters where four Chinese guys sit in a darkened room answering the phone and taking orders. They all cough and shout down the phone, flick cigarette ash on the floor and sip hot water; it is a typical Chinese enterprise. The showroom next door is filled with just about every kind of sex toy that could be imagined.

For ladies there are the usual range of vibrating dildos, clitoral stimulators and crotch-less panties. The colours are amazing and Mr Zhong advises me that the vibrators with the flashing lights and sophisticated control panel are for the Japanese market. On the other hand he says, the Americans just need on or off!

For men there are many different types and colours of inflatable dolls as well as what can best be described as a piece of artificial female torso like something from a horror film, cut off just below the buttocks and not venturing much beyond the waist. It comes complete with the appropriate orifices and abnormally long and straight pubic hair; must be like shagging a molehill. These 'girls' have their apertures extremely well oiled and vibrate like the engine of a forty tonne articulated lorry when idling. Apparently they ship them by the container load to Tokyo.

Nowadays similar products can be found in certain UK high street shops like *Ann Summers* for thirty pounds a go, the ex-factory price is only three or four.

According to the China Sex Health Commission, quoted in the China Daily on the 1st August 2005, sales of sex products within China exceeded 100 billion yuan (US$12.33 billion) in 2003, a number that is expected to grow by 30 percent annually. How on earth do they come up with figures like that? The population is, we are told, 1.3 billion, so each man, woman and child spent $12 on a sex toy. They may have an insatiable libido but with statistics like this, one tends to dismiss all government data with a pinch of salt.

For certain though, Chinese attitudes towards sex are changing, their minds are beginning to open up; for the older generation this could only be due to what they see as the harmful invasion of Western culture.

In Guangzhou, for the second year running, a 'Sex Festival' was held in November 2004. Models were there displaying lingerie (not the see-thru stuff, and if it was they had body stockings on underneath) and sex toys were exhibited.

Love and Sex

The excuse was that this was to educate locals about sex culture and sexually transmitted diseases, including AIDS, in a bid to 'promote sex education and enhance people's sexual health,'
'Knowledge of, and access to, products such as condoms can help minimize possible harm to teenagers who might have sex, as they might be exposed to the threats of venereal diseases and AIDS,' was the quote of one of the organisers. Of course the real function was to sell erotic products under the mask of AIDS prevention. Importantly, (or amusingly) Doctors and counsellors were on hand to answer questions about sexual issues and marriage problems.
It is not clear how great the AIDS epidemic is in China, since the real figures are not reported. It was only recently that the government admitted that they had a problem at all. To admit that the Chinese have an AIDS problem is to admit that the highly moral population have casual sex - that must have really hurt.
For some reason, AIDS is a particularly acute problem in the central province of Henan and also Yunan in the south-west. Almost certainly, because these two areas were a bit sloppy with their blood supply. It is quite normal for poor people especially, to sell blood donations to mobile blood banks. Many of these blood banks operate illegally and sell blood to hospitals at a profit, there is a healthy (bad choice of adjectives) market in the stuff. This has been blamed for the high level of HIV/ AIDS in Henan.
The issue was ignored and carried on for many years throughout the 1990s until what we have today is an epidemic that the government has only recently admitted to. Thousands of farmers in places such as Henan and Shanxi Province, relied on selling their blood to illegal blood banks in order to

earn extra cash and lift themselves just above the breadline. Many of those who took part in the practice have since been diagnosed with HIV/AIDS.

A survey carried out in 2003 by Henan provincial health authority, of the 280,000 people identified as having used the illegal blood banks in the early 1990s, 25,000 have tested HIV positive, getting on for 10% and probably a gross underestimate. They claim that the government is now supervising these blood donations and collections, but for a decade the illegal practice went on unchecked. They now claim that voluntarily donated blood accounts for more than 80 per cent of all clinical consumption, so twenty per cent is still dodgy? Upon receiving a blood transfusion, there is still a twenty per cent change of receiving HIV infected blood.

Although Henan is a hotspot, the numbers of AIDS and HIV cases are generally, across the country, on the increase. When a foreigner comes to China for work, he or she will be tested for AIDS prior to the granting of a work permit.

For the overseas traveller coming to China, there will certainly be plenty of opportunities for love and sex, there is no need to take illegal call-girls. China is probably only second to Thailand in the league table of least difficulty to find a local girlfriend. This is in sharp contrast to the birth ratio of 117 boys to 100 girls according to the 2000 census. This imbalance is not noticeable in the cities, in fact it may be the other way around. There is much more of a problem in rural areas where a son is desired and baby girls may be left to die or given away to foreign families for adoption. In the cities, where it really does not matter any more, except for traditional purposes, the balance between the sexes is normal.

Love and Sex

In cities like Shenzhen, the opposite is true! Shenzhen is one of those migrant cities where many people come to find work. Most of these people are young women, often college graduates, young, pretty, slim and looking for a man. In Shenzhen, sexy girls are everywhere, they easily outnumber men.

During those heavy times when the brain relocates to the trousers, coming to China or almost anywhere in Asia is a delight to the eyes leaving behind the western world of crop-tops, hipster jeans and a big roll of fat in between, gets left behind.

The girls are usually very slim, have a small frame and gently curving bodies; everything is in proportion. A typical Chinese girl is around five feet to five feet four inches tall although they tend to be smaller in the south and taller in the north. In some ways they are like models, the skin is soft and covers the bones to exactly the right depth; the stomach is always very flat, the kind of shape that jeans were made for. Breasts tend to be small but the nipples are very large, sometimes it looks as if they are fighting to pierce the bra that contains them.

Ideally the hair is long and straight, falling down the back persuading your eyes to gaze downwards towards the bottom. Sadly more and more local girls, ignore this characteristic and beautiful feature, dye their hair orange (the net result of blonde colour on a jet black base) and get it permed. Chinese men like girls to be very slim, almost unhealthily skinny, but the real attraction for them is white skin, the whiter the better. Big eyes are plus feature, to the extent that many girls have surgery on their eyelids. Seldom does it look right. The power of international media with tiles like *Vogue*, *Elle* and *Cosmopolitan* have made it out here, to the extent that these girls, who have their own special oriental beauty, try so hard to make themselves look like western women. The bleached blond hair, which actually comes out orange as said before, and their growing dependence upon cosmetic surgery, are the tell-tale signs.

Getting a sun-tan though is a serious drawback to their chances in the love stakes so women will often be seen walking around with umbrellas and avoiding the sun wherever possible.

There is a difference between the north and south as well, not just the height and build but in the faces. When we think of the Chinese race and their appearance, our thoughts are drawn to the eyes more than anything, Prince Philip insultingly called them 'slitty', but the real difference is that the shape of the skull is very different. Both front and back are much flatter, there is no bulging cranium and deep eye sockets and the nose is broad at the bridge.

In the North they tend to have flatter faces than their southern relatives. However, unlike Koreans and Japanese, Chinese women have longer legs so they look much more in proportion.

This may be a simplistic view but certainly Koreans and Japanese spend a serious amount of their time sitting cross-legged on the floor both at mealtimes and recreationally, what's more they have been doing so for centuries. Surely the evolutionary process is going to respond and bless them with short legs in order to make the mealtime ritual more comfortable?

For a westerner, having to sit on the floor for a couple of hours at a formal East Asian dinner is a severely uncomfortable affair. The legs go numb in combination with the pins and needles feeling, it is necessary to keep fidgeting and, because of the long thigh bone, it is impossible to get close enough to the snotty little table and therefore frequently drop noodles and other greasy tit-bits into the lap. I have been to some dinners in Japan where they offer diners an undersized kimono that just about covers the midriff. Uncomfortably sat, next to the little table, a traditionally attired lady juxtaposes herself and glides various morsels into the mouth then washes it down with copious amounts of sake. This hostess, getting closer and closer as the night wears on, seems politely amused as various bits of flesh pop out of the ill-fitting garment at regular intervals during the meal. This kind of entertainment in Japan is extremely expensive but I would rather they took me to a more comfortable environment where the ladies were more sexy than motherly, this was most certainly not a whore house.

Nudity is very rare and on the whole, girls dress modestly; every now and again a very short mini-skirted beauty will walk by but most girls dress without drawing attraction to the obvious areas of male attention. Even though this may be the case it does not mean that they do not want to show a little bit more. In Xi'an, college girls have to book weeks ahead in order to secure an artistic nude photo session, it is not clear whom they show or sell the pictures too.

Artists and photographers claim that it is very difficult to find good female nude models, the reason given is because they shyly tend to hide their faces during a session. Perhaps it is more to do with the fact that for one hour's work they earn between fifteen and one hundred Yuan (£1 and £6.70) for still life and photography respectively.

A nude beach, claimed to be China's first (August 2004), was created in Lin'an City, Zhejiang. The beach sparked a lot of controversy; supporters said nude swimming helped humans stay in touch with nature, opponents argued the move would erode community morals, nudity should be strictly reserved for massage joints.

The inspiration to establish a nude swimming area supposedly came from the beach management after eight female university students took off their clothes and swam naked, he obviously wanted too see a lot more. 'Although shocked initially.' (just like Sid James in *'Carry on Camping'*) They decided to capitalize on the incident and quickly put up boards saying 'Nude Swimming Area,' one for men and one for women. The signs have been regularly torn down by objectors ever since.

A colleague of mine, a fiery red-haired Irishmen, after more than one or two drinks will happily entertain the bar-set and describe many of his intimate experiences with the local girls. He once described how the ladies are shocked when they see him naked, not for his oversized beer-belly, but for the fact that (to use his words) he has "matching carpet and curtains".

A patient accused a hospital of infringing her privacy after she noticed a camera lens in the ceiling of an examination room of the gynaecological department. Such an incident in a developed country would be outrageous and treated as a criminal offence but in good old China, it was reported in a way that suggested it was a sensible thing to do. The response from the hospital was that it was put there to prevent allegations of illegal conduct by the staff. Incredibly, the Fuzhou hospital involved, claimed that it had every right to install such a device, going on to argue that the videos were securely kept so as not to infringe personal privacy (and then sold off as pornography by an unscrupulous hospital warden no doubt).

In my modest experience of three relationships with Chinese women, the third one harmonious to this day, all have been very different to previous experiences with Western ladies.
It is perhaps unfair to generalise but it seems even women in their thirties are very sexually naïve. They have all been incredibly affectionate, loving and tactile and in both sexual and non-sexual situations, all seem fascinated with the male penis; they just cannot leave it alone.
They treat it with the same dedication as a young boy with a new video console, a kind of toy. Sometimes they fiddle, with lovemaking on their mind, but most of the time they seem to be fully satisfied with squeezing and tugging away, often too hard, until the owner of the poor 'bishop' starts to feel sore. At first it is a novelty but after a while it becomes a chore. I have discussed this with a few friends who also have a long-term Chinese partner and they complain (or not complain) of exactly the same thing. Education did not teach young women to do this but when they get into a relationship, it seems to be pure instinct in the way dogs sniff each others bums.
It would irresponsible though not to give a warning to take extreme care. For most foreign men who come to China, it is just a matter of time before they take a local girlfriend but many of these girls like to have three or four boyfriends at the same time, many are disloyal and sleep around. If shelling out for this book has one benefit it should be that nobody has unprotected sex in this country.
It may be that you could get lucky and meet a chaste virgin but it is increasingly unlikely. For some reason, it seems that most mixed relationships are Western male and Chinese girl, seldom the other way around. But it does happen, I did have friends in Shanghai where an English lady was happily

married to a Chinese man, nowhere near as common as the other way around.

These less than chaste nymphs will not hesitate in going to the hospital and get their hymen re-attached before they marry the true man of their dreams.

Sexism is alive and well, being politically correct hasn't got here yet (although PC with respect to government is well ordered). My local supermarket has a range of household cleaning utensils; brushes, mops etc that are sold under the brand name *Good Wife*! A brand of toothpaste named *Darley* in roman script has on its packaging a stereotypical picture of a black man with a big white smile, the Chinese name for this particular brand is 黑人牙膏 which literally translated means "black man toothpaste".

It is perfectly normal to advertise for staff that are male, female and even specify whether they are married or not, with or without children and even of a certain age. For young and pretty girls, the chances of employment are much higher. Sleeping with the boss is quite normal in order to secure chances of advancement and sexual harassment goes on unreported. Strangely though, in most households, women control the finances. They tend to monitor the cash, give their husband an allowance and settle all the bills.

Women tend not to have the same dress sense as other Asians, as such it is very easy to tell the difference between a woman from China as opposed to Hong Kong, Taiwan or Singapore. There is no golden rule, just a combination of things, going bra-less is almost unheard of and tops and bottoms tend not to match that well, stripy tops and check trousers are not unusual.

They often wear the ankle length stockings or pop-socks with high heels and a skirt, it's the biggest turn-off ever. They never wear thongs or G-strings (in case you are wondering how I know, most trousers have a heavy panty line), all the more surprising because weren't they invented in Asia by Sumo wrestlers? Many girls wear a thin white dress or trousers with black knickers or their clothes are embarrassingly see-through in the sunlight. It would be easy to market a brand of white trousers annotated across the bum with 'I swapped pants with granny' the irony is, given the ignorance yet desire for the English language, they would probably sell quite well.

I once saw a five year old boy in the supermarket with a Macdonald's T-shirt, slightly modified, the golden arches had become phallic shaped and the slogan was "I'm fucking it".

Young Chinese women are extremely vain, narcissistic is a better word; as soon as they are in sight of any reflective surface, a quick dash is made towards it to check themselves out, admiringly re-touching the make-up, stroking their own hair and renewing their true love of the self on an hourly basis.

Most disappointing of all is that Chinese women don't seem to age that well; once they pass mid-thirties, they appear to go downhill rapidly. An attractive Western woman, who looks after herself these days, will be desirable right into her early fifties, in China that would be extremely rare.

To fathom out why is unclear, whether they just lose the urge to be beautiful after they have given birth or whether there really are biological differences. Getting old and becoming fat are to some extent mutually inclusive but oriental females do not carry weight very well. They become very thick around the middle and flat around the bottom, almost as if the fat gets siphoned off and re-positioned to create a very unattractive and unwomanly shape. By contrast Western women seem to enlarge through bigger bottoms, arms and thighs but maintain if not accentuate the essentially female form.

Men seem to dress in dark greys and browns, like their ladies, it is usually easy to spot someone from the mainland in a crowd of Asian Orientals. The shoes are dreadful, almost like a uniform, black leather slip-ons, narrow with a square toe and always dusty or dirty never cleaned since they were new. In the summer, the trousers get rolled up to the knees and the shirt to just below the chest exposing a swollen white belly. It is not uncommon to see a man in a full suit only to be offset by a pair of white trainers. Men seem to age better apart from the unwillingness to clean their teeth, a full smile from somebody in their middle age reveals a mixture of black and grey decay with the odd flash of off-white.

Businessmen dress only to show-off, recognisable by their accessories and trinkets rather than crisp apparel. They will have a Rolex watch on display just above a hand with dirty and grotesquely long fingernails, a Bally belt holding in a an engorged midriff that the jacket can't cover any more and Dior sunglasses pitched just above a smug smile that reveals teeth like the inside walls of my Granny's coal bunker.

Returning to the women, on a typical day, it is commonplace to see and hear women, as well as men, preparing what one pictures as a green congealed and sticky lump of phlegm in the back of the throat before noisily blasting it out onto the footpath. I therefore think that any hesitation can be forgiven for fearing that I might get some of that when it comes to a situation of passionate kissing.

Finally, it really is something of an enigma as to why there are so many simply gorgeous women in their mid-twenties yet virtually none in their mid-forties. Fortunately it isn't necessary to lose too much sleep worrying about it, the good

Love and Sex

news is that unlike when I am in England, a twenty five year-old would not even give me a second glance, in China they love me!

Chapter 6 - Crime and Punishment

China gets a bashing internationally for many things but the number one issue, from which Western governments preach, is human rights. The Chinese, perhaps justifiably, argue that this is a case of people living in glass houses throwing stones. This section does not cover the human rights arguments and discussions since there are many books, documents and websites on the subject. However, it is worth looking at the kind of crime that goes on in this gigantic nation today and the punishments that are handed out. A point well worth making though is that even if there is a human rights problem in China, most Chinese don't think that way and there is a general consensus of approval (in the cities at least) on the way the country is governed at present.

The reader should be warned that most of the data comes from the government unchecked, so it is extremely difficult to know whether or not the statistics are correct. A recommended perspective to take is that really bad statistics are probably much worse and the good ones are viewed through rose coloured spectacles.

The main issue is capital punishment, the alarming frequency of its use and the wide number of crimes for which it is handed out. Not surprisingly, I am firmly opposed to capital punishment. There is no need here to waste text on the arguments for and against but the majority of statistics tend to show that there is no positive correlation between handing out the death penalty and reducing crime, in fact often the reverse is the case. Proponents of the ultimate penalty are simply motivated by vengeance. For the state to be able to take the life of another human being is repulsive and sickening and any nation that carries this out cannot remotely consider itself to be civilised, in fact it is downright medieval. The United States is included in that comment, where criminals, usually black, illiterate or retarded, serve half a life time of pointless appeals before their final day is decided by the state.

The subjects here have a different set of values, most Chinese believe that criminals should be shot and not just for murder, for a whole range of crimes that were last punishable by death in Britain, during the early 19th Century.

In China the death penalty may be applied for all sorts of crimes, 68 in total, that not only includes murder but also smuggling, organising prostitution, kidnapping, rape, corruption, drug trafficking, counterfeiting, firearms offences, armed robbery, theft of infrastructure, theft of artefacts and many more. Often the trials are brief and sentences are carried out the same day. The following was printed in the China Daily (21 Aug 2004) and is particularly disturbing:

Three con-artists in Beijing were sentenced to death in Beijing Friday after being convicted of illegally obtaining 100 million yuan (US$12 million) by fraud.

After the trial, the three defendants, Zu Feng, Sun Liang and Sun Liansheng, were escorted to the ground for immediate execution.

The three defendants, working in cooperation with two others, stole 160 million yuan (US$19.3 million) from 1997 to 2001 by creating false seals and counterfeiting transfer accounts, financial certificates and loan formalities.

According to court investigation, Zu Feng and his accomplices enticed, through the middleman, Beijing-based Capital Iron and Steel Company Ltd. to deposit 100 million yuan (US$12 million) in the Beijing Cuiwei lu Branch of the

Real China

Shanghai Pudong Development Bank in April and May of 2001.
Then they obtained the application form and blank transfer check provided by Huang Xiaoqin, a accomplice working in the bank. The check was made with a false seal. In this way, they withdrew 70 million yuan (US$8.4 million) of bank loans to be provided to a real estate company in Beijing.
Zu Feng and his accomplices were also convicted of nine other accounts of fraud from 1997 to 2000.

The abhorrent reality is that judgement was made and the convicted were then immediately taken away and shot, no post analysis and no appeals. This was in Beijing, a city that has been awarded the highly civilised Olympic Games!

Most executions are carried out in the open air on a plot of land designated for that purpose. There is somewhere allocated in every city. The unfortunate victims have their hands secured behind their backs, are told to kneel then shot in the back of the head.
Notoriously for China, before an execution, the condemned are taken to a public place, for example a railway station or public square. Their names and crimes are read out in front of a gathering crowd, they will have a sign hung around their neck with their names and wrong-doings described. Next, the unfortunates are driven away to the killing grounds and immediately shot.
Being an efficient lot, in order to save time and effort, they like to execute people in batches, in other words wait until they have ten or twelve and then take them all to the station, organise the press and TV cameras, read out the crimes then take them away and bang, its all over. I have heard the

immediate family has to pay for the bullet but this has probably ceased, the cost would be less that ten pence.

Until very recently, executions were held publicly, often at sporting venues such as football stadiums. This article was on the Amnesty International website and describes and event as recent as 1999:

In a bizarre holiday celebration several hundred schoolchildren were taken to watch six men being sentenced to death at a public sentencing rally, according to a Chinese internet report.

'The Chinese government regularly 'celebrates' national holidays by executing large numbers of criminals,' said Ingrid Massage, Asia director at Amnesty International. 'This year, the Mid-Autumn Festival falls in the same week as China's National Day on Friday 1 October 1999 and there has been a surge of executions.'

The schoolchildren were part of an audience of 2,500 people. Held in a gymnasium in Changsha, capital of central Hunan province, the sentencing rally was timed to coincide with the Mid-Autumn Festival on 27 September. The six men were then taken to an execution ground and shot, according to the report on the 'Tom' web portal.

Pictured wearing their school uniforms, the children are described as elementary and middle school students, between the ages of six and seventeen. They heard the details of the convicts' crimes read out in public -- including murder, assault and kidnapping -- and then witnessed the criminals being sentenced to death.

Taking children out of school to attend sentencing rallies appears to contravene the Convention on the Rights of the Child, ratified by China in 1992. This states that education should be directed at the 'development of respect for human rights and fundamental freedoms'.

Real China

The six men in Hunan are among at least 100 people executed in recent days in China.
Both in law and practice, China's criminal justice system does not currently offer fair trials under international legal standards. This is particularly alarming in criminal cases where the death penalty is passed. Confessions may be extorted through torture, access to lawyers is limited and the appeal system is fractured and decentralised. Amnesty International opposes the death penalty in all circumstances and is calling on China to halt all executions immediately with a view to abolishing the death penalty in law.

The article does make a very good and accurate point that holiday time is often when China clears out its 'death-rows.' There are three major holiday seasons; the long New Year or Spring Festival, the first of May Labour Day or Golden Week and the week following National Day on the first of October. Just before these holidays, any prisoners that are sentenced to death, will meet their unfortunate end. It means that probably thousands of people up and down the country are legally put to death in batches three times a year. One can only guess as to why they do this unless it is simply so that the people, who are responsible for guarding and feeding the condemned, may also go on holiday.

The point about brief court cases must be true, as I have witnessed the comings and goings of a real court building. In 2007 I was working in the southern city of Guangzhou (Canton), just opposite the courthouse. In a typical day five or six coach loads of defendants would come and go. One can easily deduce that court appearances were very very brief. It seems that the overwhelming majority have already confessed to their crimes, arguably torture assisted, before they meet the judges with their grim faces and military uniforms.

More recently there has been a growing trend of putting people to death by lethal injection. In fact they have to execute so many people and the demand is so high that they have a fleet of execution vans, made in Nanjing. It is uncertain how it works but it seems that the condemned are driven from the court or prison to the crematorium and either killed on the way or immediately after arrival.

Sometimes, the papers will inform us about a wave of executions, particularly if it covers a subject that the government thinks has national and international acceptance, a good example is drugs.

In June 2004 dozens of drug dealers were sentenced to death in a series of drug-related criminal cases across China to coincide with the forthcoming International Day Against Drug Abuse and Illicit Trafficking.

In south-western Yunnan province, Tan Minglin and three other people convicted of smuggling or selling five tons (yes, five tons!) of drugs, including heroin and ephedrine, were executed after having all their belongings confiscated.

Chinese drug trafficker Ji Xinmi (C) had his verdict announced during public sentencing outside a railway station in Guangzhou, Guangdong Province, June 24, 2004. Appropriately Ji was sentenced to death for smuggling drugs on the railway in southern China.

South China's Guangdong province 'intelligently' cracked a series of such drug- related criminal cases. Li Qingyuan was sentenced to death while his colleague Lu Guowu was sentenced a two-year stay of execution with all his property confiscated. Tan Zhong'an, another accomplice, was given a seven-year jail term and fined 10,000 yuan (US$1,200) by a local court in Shenzhen.

Four more drug-related suspects, including Liu Shenming, Ma Guoli, Wang Jianwei and Ye Yuezhen, were also executed respectively by courts in Fanyu, Huadu, Conghua districts, as well as a development zone of Guangzhou.

Another Chen Xue'an and three other suspects accused of illegally purchasing 60 kg of drugs by raising over four million yuan (US$481,000) were sentenced to death in Wenzhou city of east China's Zhejiang province.

In Hangzhou, capital city of the province, a total of 17 suspects were declared guilty of smuggling drugs and sentenced to death on the same day, the newspapers also informed us that two of these people were AIDS/HIV carriers as if to say that the executions had a double benefit.

According to the Ministry of Public Security, China cracked a total of 546,900 drug-related criminal cases in the past five years from 1998 to 2003, seizing a total of 51.03 tons of heroin and uprooting 427 hectares of opium poppy.

Statistics show that 235,600 criminal suspects were arrested for producing, trafficking and selling drugs over the past five year period. It has to be assumed that most of these people were put to death, the numbers are frightening.

The government goes on to say that its strike-hard policies of creating narcotics control units in combating drug-related crimes and its highly-effective measures and substantial efforts of the related units in localities across China have paid off in the war on the drug-related criminal cases.

China claims to have an anti-drug police force of about 17,000 members, and its central government has said it has input more than 600 million yuan (US$72.55 million) for drug control efforts over the past five years.

Despite all this, from time to time fledgling instances of some kind of debate about tightening up controls on the use of capital punishment are occurring. Currently courts are normally chaired by a panel of three judges, there is no jury. After a brief trial, these three will decide on the defendant's fate. The sentence will then be passed to a higher court, still at provincial level, for upholding any decision. At present the Supreme People's Court, the highest one, does not review death sentences although there are calls for it to do so, consequently sentencing is inconsistent, from province to province.

The Chinese will always quickly point out that supposedly developed countries such as Japan and the USA still use the death penalty but they never add the caveat that this is only for murder, or 'murder one' as the Americans like to call it.

Many academics now publicly say that the death penalty should not be used for non-violent crimes yet at the same time the government is also carrying out its strike hard policy on corruption.

Other officials simply say that the death penalty should remain but only the highest court can have the authority to uphold the decisions.

Before 1997 people could even be executed for hooliganism and petty theft but as each year passes there are signs of a mellowing in attitude. In China clemency is sometimes shown whereas this never happens for example in much overlooked and supposedly 'civilised' Singapore. Often in China death sentences are suspended for two years so that the offender can save his or her own life by serving two years gaol with good behaviour. If successful, the sentence is then commuted to life imprisonment and life is exactly what it means. There are some quite vocal abolitionists, for example Qiu Xinglong, dean of Xiangtan University's School of Law in Hunan Province he is quoted as saying

"The most popular argument death penalty advocators stick to is that the brutal punishment deters crimes, but there is no scientific evidence proving the crime rate is relevant to the existence of the death penalty".

For those that make the decisions though, the death penalty does deter crime or at least that is how they justify their value system that says criminals, even those that have committed lesser crimes than murder, *deserve* to die. Capital punishment in both China and the USA falls outside the definition of human rights, yet the right to live is the most fundamental one of all.

There is an even more sinister side to all this and in a land where money is valued more than anything, it is the most worrying theory of all. That executions are carried out in order to make money; their organs are used for transplant patients who often travel from overseas, mostly emigrant Chinese. There is much documented evidence of this.

Falun Gong is a political group that poses as a religious sect, accused by the Beijing government of taking over the peoples' rational minds and is therefore ruthlessly banned in China.

They describe the case of 56-year-old Ms. Zhao Chunying who was arrested and tortured to death by police. The photos are published on their website. On April 23, 2003, she was detained by Chinese police for posting a story on the Internet about torture she had previously suffered in police custody. Less than a month later, she was dead and photographs taken by her family indicate her death was horrifyingly brutal. After repeated demands from her family, the Jixi City Procurator-ate conducted a post mortem on Zhao's remains. The autopsy revealed a large knife wound to the head, four broken ribs and numerous black and purple bruises indicating a violent beating. On November 15, 2003, the Heilongjiang Judicature Appraisal Committee carried out a second post mortem on Zhao's remains. In addition to the findings of the first autopsy, the second autopsy discovered a fractured skull but also revealed that the heart, spleen, pancreas and other internal organs were missing.

It is estimated that 90% of the transplant organs come from executed prisoners. One doctor coolly put it that when a patient has the option of dying relatively peacefully under anaesthetic on an operating table or the stress of a bullet in the back of the head, he tends to take the former option.

With the assistance of a translator, Wang Guoqi, a former doctor at a Chinese People's Liberation Army hospital, who left China in the Spring of 2000 and fled to the United States, testified: "My work required me to remove skin and corneas from the corpses of over one hundred executed prisoners, and on a couple of occasions, victims of intentionally botched executions. It is with deep regret and remorse for my actions that I stand here today testifying against the practices of organ and tissue sales from death row prisoners.'

Dr. Wang Guoqi, was formerly a doctor with the Peoples Liberation Army before he went to the US and claimed asylum in 2000, he gave a shocking report of events in China. He detailed one incident in October 1995, in Hebei Province that he said has "tortured his conscience ever since". This was when a prisoner did not die after receiving the execution shot to the head. Dr. Wang and other burn surgeons were ordered to harvest skin off of the half-dead and convulsing prisoner, his kidneys were extracted immediately by three other doctors. Inside the ambulance they began to remove the skin, but due to an angry growing crowd outside, they left the job half-done and the not quite dead corpse was thrown in a plastic bag and onto the flatbed of a crematorium truck. Dr. Wang admitted, "Whatever impact I have made in the lives of burn victims and transplant patients does not excuse the unethical and immoral manner of extracting organs in the first place".

Chapter 7 – Corruption

To say that China is corrupt is like saying Sir Richard Branson is self-employed, it does not begin to explain the scale of the situation.

Having done business in China for many years now, I have only ever done one deal whereby the customer did *not* ask for some kind of kickback. It is virtually impossible to do a deal without something like this going on. The customer would never ask for this money from a Western supplier, it is the local representatives that have to allow for this in their profit margins.

It is probably fair to say that almost all transactions in developing countries involve a certain amount of money on the table and a large brown envelope under it. The so-called scandal of BAe Systems giving commission to their Saudi Arabian customer is perfectly normal in the scope of international business deals. For the Americans to complain about it is the ultimate hypocrisy, they know damned well that they would have done the exactly the same thing had they won the contract.

Whilst this kind of behaviour is familiar and irritating on a day to day basis, nationally it is crippling the country and as the economy grows, so does the corruption. The government has had a policy of "strike hard" on corruption by regularly handing down capital sentences for the worst offenders but even so, each year the problem gets worse.

The government should not be too surprised and must account for most of the blame, it has set-up a legislative environment and set of rules where it is easy to be corrupt and easy to get very rich by less than honest means.

Real China

The problem is complex in some ways but straightforward in others; the complexity comes from a deep-seated value system that lying and cheating is basically acceptable, the real crime is getting caught. It will take generations before that is weeded out of the mind-set.

The system of values that we are used to in Northern Europe gives a majority situation of trustworthiness and honesty. It sounds a shocking thing to say but most Chinese, given the chance, will be dishonest. The straightforward way to reduce the problem is simply to have clear and watertight tendering, reporting and purchasing procedures, enforceable by law.

What happens is that as China grows, it has to build infrastructure on a grand scale so an increasing number of capital intensive projects are launched each year.

For the nation it means new roads, schools, hospitals, apartment buildings and public transport projects. For the people who make the decisions it means 5-10%

Money is put aside and each province manages its own process of putting these large projects into action. The contracts are awarded at a price much higher than they should be, and the surplus cash is kept by the officials who are involved in the procurement.

Unless the funding is managed from Beijing, there are no formal tendering rules, the purchaser decides whom to place the contract with and what the value should be. There is no requirement to get maximum value for money, only to get the job done. In most cases the official(s) will get away with it if he (often she) is smart enough in selecting a competent supplier so that at least the project is completed on schedule and at an *apparently* fair price.

Another common means of graft is for the large state owned enterprises, mostly who are losing money (either due to bad performance or corrupt managers, invariably both), through bank loans. When these SOEs are in trouble, it could result in very high unemployment, which the government can ill-afford. High unemployment leads to social unrest which in turn affects the government's power base so this has to be avoided.

Very simply, it works like this, the company needs cash mostly not for new ventures but just to pay the bills. The manager then trots along to the local bank and organises a new loan. The bank official willingly complies, without any irritating details such as analysing business plans. The banker is naturally delighted since some of the money will make its way into his personal piggy bank.

Frequently family members work in the bank too so the constant supply of dodgy money will never run out. The only problem is that some of them get silly, very greedy and then get caught. They start driving around in large Mercedes, buy several properties and adorn themselves with expensive jewellery; any disgruntled worker who has been wronged in the past will then not hesitate to tip off the authorities.

It does not end there, a further complication is that the outsiders who come in to investigate are also corrupt, taking pay-offs from the very crooks they are supposed to bring to justice in the first place, and so the cycle goes on. Some officials also plan for a quick escape if they ever do get caught, sending their wife and child in advance for overseas study.

Recently the government introduced a law whereby it has to approve all applications for communist party members' families to live and study overseas. Even though, the numbers of prosecutions amounts to tens of thousands each year and as

China grows so does the number of corruption cases, the problem seems to get worse not better.

The following are just a few examples of the scale and diversity of corruption in China. Most were reported in the papers in order to serve as an example, in almost all cases they refer to people who have very high positions in provincial governments, people who see millions of dollars pass through each year but just cannot resist diverting a chunk into their own personal coffers.

In October 2003 Mr Li Yushu, former vice-mayor of Leshan in South West China's Sichuan Province, was executed after being convicted of abusing his authority to take bribes valued at 8.9 million yuan (£590,000). Li was accused of illegally accepting the cash from 1996 to 2001 by abusing his power and position as vice-mayor, the head of the communications bureau, the head of a communications development company, and the chief of construction of a bridge in Leshan. At an intermediate people's court in early 2002, Li was sentenced to death and deprived of political rights for life (what was left of it), and had his assets confiscated. Li appealed the decision to the provincial higher people's court, which rejected the appeal and upheld the ruling, and reported the case to the supreme people's court for approval. Li's family would almost certainly have suffered greatly too, probably had all their possessions confiscated.

April 2004: Liu Changgui, former vice governor of the South-Western province of Guizhou, was sentenced to eleven years in gaol on charges of taking bribes and owning a huge amount of property he could not account for. The sentence was handed down by the Intermediate People's Court of Zunyi

City at the first trial held in 'one morning.' Liu, 58, was a technical school graduate and 'had not received higher education' (they put that in as if it explains his dishonesty). He served as acting mayor and mayor of Guiyang city, the provincial capital between 1994 and 1997, and was elected vice governor of Guizhou in 1997. He was arrested in April 2003 on charges of bribery. The court verdict said Liu accepted bribes amounting to 1.34 million yuan (£89,000) between 1995 and 2000 from two local companies and he owned another 1.7 million yuan (£113,000) of personal property he could not account for. The court also ruled that 300,000 yuan (£20,000) of Liu's personal property be confiscated. The point here being that Liu did not receive a death sentence, the threshold for this, which is of course never publicised, seems to be around one million US dollars.

It is not just officials that are at it either, for example in October 2004; Feng Ji, CCTV film and TV department's former deputy director, was sentenced to 11 years in jail for taking bribes. Feng was the second figure at CCTV found guilty of corruption following Zhao An, a former CCTV director. In August 2003, Feng was accused of accepting 600,000 yuan (£40,000) for bribes from a television producer in Heilongjiang Province and a former employee of the Haiyun Film and TV Programs Studio in Hainan Province. In November 1998, Feng was approached by a man called Zhao, a television producer in Heilongjiang Province, who produced the TV series *Blood Times* but he had failed to sell it. Zhao deposited 100,000 yuan in a bank account under the name of Feng, hoping Feng would use his influence at CCTV to buy the series.

Real China

Quite often families use their positions in different organisations to embezzle cash with relative ease, again from October 2004: Yi Yang, the daughter-in-law of Liu Fangren, former Party secretary of Southwest China's Guizhou Province, was sentenced to 15 years imprisonment in Zunyi. Yi was convicted of accepting bribes of more than 5 million yuan (£330,000) through her father-in-law's position. She was also deprived of her political rights for 5 years (what are they anyway? Free speech? Right to vote?) by the Zunyi Intermediate People's Court. Yi used to work at the Guizhou Branch of Industrial and Commercial Bank of China in Guiyang, the provincial capital. With the help of her father-in-law, Yi registered and established Guiyang Yangda Industrial Co Ltd after she quit her job at the bank in June 1997 and then became the director of the company.

In 1999, Yi successfully helped a Beijing investment company purchase 33 million shares in Guizhou Zhongtian Group, a State-owned enterprise, after she sought help from her father-in-law. With the involvement of Yi's father-in-law, the shares of Guizhou Zhongtian Group changed hands at 2.41 yuan (16p) per share, much lower than their market value. In return, Yi took bribes worth more than 5 million yuan on four occasions between June 1999 and the end of 2000 from Liu Zhiyuan, general manager of the Beijing investment company. Liu Zhiyuan spent only 79.53 million yuan (£5.3m) to purchase Guizhou Zhongtian Group, a profitable local State-owned firm. An investigation revealed that the State suffered a serious economic loss due to the illegal purchase. Yi and her father-in-law shared the massive bribes between themselves. It was reported that Yi's punishment was reduced because she confessed after she was arrested. And she has returned all the bribes she accepted, the official said. Moreover, Yi was merely an accomplice, while her father-in-law Liu Fangren played a decisive role in the sale of Guizhou Zhongtian Group. Yi has decided to appeal to a higher court. Yi's father-in-law Liu Fangren had been found guilty of taking bribes and sentenced to life imprisonment in June earlier that year.

Frequently financial criminals receive the ultimate penalty; in September 2004 the Supreme People's Court approved the death sentence by two local intermediate people's courts to "four severe financial criminals". Wang Liming and Wang Xiang, former staff members at sub-branches of the China Construction Bank in Zhengzhou (Henan Province), together with jobless Miao Ping, were found to have forged bank bills to illegally obtain cash. Liang Shihan, a bank clerk who used to work at the Hainan branch of the Bank of China, was also convicted of accepting massive bribes.

By using forged bank transfer accounts and postal orders, Wang Liming colluded with Miao Ping and several other defendants to swindle 28.4 million yuan (£1.9m) of deposits from the sub-branch where Wang worked as an official, Shen said. More than 20 million yuan (£1.3m) of the money could not be retrieved.

In an unrelated case, Wang Xiang, a staff member at another sub-branch of the China Construction Bank in Zhengzhou, embezzled 40 million yuan (£2.7m) of deposits by using false bills, 20 million was never recovered.

In Guangdong, Liang Shihan, an official with the Zhuhai branch of the Bank of China, was convicted of making 31 letters of credit worth of £24m for suspect Zhou Qiang who thus far has escaped capture. Zhou later used eight of the

Real China

letters, causing a loss of £5.43m. In return, Zhou gave Liang £367,000. The four were executed on the 14th September.

Sentences though seem to be inconsistent, in February 2004 a top county official was executed in China's Guangxi Zhuang Autonomous Region for bribery and abuse of power. Wan Ruizhong was a former Communist Party secretary of the region's Nandan County and was convicted of taking bribes and abusing his power. He was executed following approval by the Supreme People's Court.

He was also convicted of plotting to cover up a mine accident that killed 81 miners in July 2001. The deaths occurred when the county's Lajiapo mine, under Wan's direct jurisdiction, flooded on the 17th July 2001. Investigation of the accident led to the exposure of Wan and other corrupt officials in the county. He was also sentenced to the confiscation of his personal property of 500,000 yuan (about £33,000), and his illegal income of 2.68 million yuan (£178,000) has been turned over to the national treasury.

People who have embezzled more than Wan, have received lighter sentences. The papers reported that the day before Wan's execution, Yan Zhihua, another prefectural official, was sentenced to one year in prison with a two-year reprieve for his role in the cover-up. It was reported also, without being specific that other officials responsible for mine accidents in the area have been sentenced to death, 10 years or 13 years in prison for their roles in similar cover-ups.

On the 12th February 2004, Wang Huaizhong, former vice-governor of East China's Anhui Province, was executed after being sentenced to death the previous December for taking bribes. The papers said that he was put to death by lethal injection. It is rare and also unusual for them to state the method used. Also unusually, he was allowed to meet with his family before the execution. Wang's penalty was approved by the Supreme People's Court after losing an appeal for a lighter penalty in January, at the Shandong Provincial Higher People's Court.

Wang was executed for taking bribes valued at 5.17 million yuan (£344,000) from 1994 to 2001, and possessing 4.8 million yuan (£320,000) that he could not account for. He was tried in Jinan, Shandong Province, instead of Anhui it was reported, in order to prevent possible collusion between Wang and other related local officials. It was also claimed Wang was the third senior corrupt official at the provincial or ministerial level to be sentenced to death since 1978. The previous two were Hu Changqing, former vice-governor of Jiangxi Province and Cheng Kejie, governor of South China's Guangxi Zhuang Autonomous Region, both executed in 2000. The reason that Wang's punishment was so severe was because as well as taking bribes, he also extorted bribes on four separate occasions.

Not unusually, some of the bribes taken by Wang were used to obstruct investigations by relevant authorities into his own corrupt actions. The paper then went on to report that all of Wang's personal property was confiscated and he was also "deprived of his political rights for life".

Critics have openly pointed out that Wang's case again revealed the inadequacies of the Party's power and supervision systems, which have enabled such a corrupt official as Wang to be promoted all the way from the grass roots.

Apparently Wang established his career step by step by faking growth figures of the local economy and launching what they called "image projects". For example, when Wang was head of Fuyang in Anhui Province in the 1990s, he inflated the local growth rate to 22 per cent, against the actual 4.7 per cent, according to the papers, this resulted in billion-yuan economic losses for the city. The news media did not explain the link between the statistics and the losses.

What does appear to be strange about Wang's case and others that are mentioned here is if these people were *deputy* directors or governors, what happened to the top man? Surely he was also involved, it is inconceivable that so much cash could be stolen without the boss knowing? Did he close a blind eye or did he do a deal and shop his sub-ordinate? My bet is on the latter but the truth will never be known, the freedom of information act is a few centuries away.

By now, it should come as no surprise that even the tax man is crooked. Li Zhen, former director of the State Taxation Bureau of Hebei Province in north China, was executed in November 2003 for taking very large bribes and embezzling public funds. He took advantage of his position as a government official, received payoffs of more than 8.148 million yuan (£540,000) and 'misappropriated' public funds (it never said how) totalling 29.67 million yuan (£1.5m), of which 2.7 million yuan made its way into his own pocket. Over 416,000 US dollars of illicit money was confiscated from Li's home after he was arrested on the 30th March 2000. The Intermediate Court sentenced Li to death at the first trial on Aug. 30, 2002. Li appealed to the Provincial Higher People's Court, but this was rejected the previous month. The Supreme People's Court then examined the case and upheld the original death sentence.

Corruption

A lot of the financial criminals escape overseas, initially they get their families out of the country. The usual reason or excuse rather, being overseas study, then they plan their own exit. According to government figures, they had extradited 71 corrupt fugitives from overseas since 1998. A significant problem they have with extradition is that a large number of foreign governments will not extradite to China because it uses the death penalty so readily. In fact China only has extradition agreements with nineteen countries, most of these are poor developing ones where most of the rich crooks wouldn't want to live in any case, so it is not that difficult to find a secure new home.

This is particularly true in the case of Lai Changxing, Time Magazine called him 'China's most wanted man,' he allegedly masterminded the biggest fraud case in the history of the People's Republic. Through the Fujian coastal port of Xiamen (Amoy), he is said to have shipped cars, cigarettes, alcohol in fact anything requiring import duty and VAT. The items were then sold on the open market at much reduced prices whilst the paid-off provincial government either played an active part or closed a blind eye.

At the main trial in July 2001 fourteen people, including the mayor of Xiamen, were convicted and executed; since then two hundred more have been tried out of a total of nearly six hundred people involved. The tax evaded was estimated to be 1.9 billion pounds which pays for a lot of schools and hospitals. Lai fled to Canada where he claimed asylum, the Canadians will not extradite him because he will face the bullet, despite assurances previously from premier Zhu Rongji and now president Hu Jintao (I would not believe them either) to the contrary.

Real China

Statistics are yet again published without debate, newspapers reported in 2005 that around 4000 officials had escaped the country with an incredible 35 billion pounds since 2000. Maths was never my strong point but a quick calculation, five years is 1800 days or so meaning a whopping that's 20 million pounds in round numbers, each day since 2000, has left the country in the hands of dodgy fleeing officials. The Great Train Robbery was scrumping apples in comparison. How on earth can a country survive with this kind of rotten corruption, seemingly at every level of every organisation be it private or government?

When they quote various officials who have opinions on such matters, they always completely miss the point, and say the problem is due to not having enough negotiators with the foreign language skills necessary to ensure that their 'fugitives' as they like to call them, return to justice. The problem is they just don't have the controls in place to stop the theft in the first place.

In September 2004, the trial opened regarding a couple that had fled to Thailand in 1996 after having embezzled substantial sums. It was reported as 'China's biggest ever corruption case' (haven't we heard that before?)

The trial was in Zhongshan, a relatively small city (two or three million people only) in Guangdong. The accused were the Chens, allegedly having 'misappropriated' funds of about thirty million pounds (after a while you stop getting shocked by the numbers involved). Chen Manxiong, was previously a manager of the Zhongshan Industrial Development Co and his wife Chen Qiuyuan was the company's lawyer.

The newspapers said that the court had yet to pass rule on the case, but the two have already admitted their guilt. It seems that the Chens were fanatical gamblers and lost a large amount of public funds in the casinos of Macao. To repay their heavy gambling debts, the couple conspired with (you've guessed already) two officials in charge of the lending department at the Zhongshan Branch of Bank of China and loaned the money in 48 separate cases between 1993 and 1995. They claimed that the two bank officials, Feng and Chi, were jailed (highly unlikely given the sums involved) in the previous year.

The Chens managed to escape to Thailand (with a million or so in their pockets) before the scandal was exposed in June 1995. Later they changed their names and bought false passports before being caught by Thai police and jailed for being illegal immigrants, they were extradited from Thailand in 2000.

I followed the case but it was after some considerable time that the sentences were released. Mr Chen received life and his wife ten years but bizarrely, and this could only have been part of the extradition deal, they were returned to Thailand to first serve their ten year sentences there for flouting immigration rules and using fake passports.

It goes without saying that the police are also corrupt and tend to take part in the cover-ups, receiving payments to ensure that they find no offences committed from a person that they have been instructed to investigate.

In Guangzhou one police officer was sentenced to death, he was Zhang Linsheng, head of the traffic department, receiving around half a million dollars in shares for his wife from a company that he had awarded a contract to. Another policeman, head of the vice division, got life imprisonment for privately selling off the porn on his own website that he had confiscated in various raids, probably on www.nickedporn.com.cn!

When I started to do some research for this book on corruption, pouring through the newspapers and cutting out the clips, I ended up with so much material and so much information that the whole thing started to become a book on corruption. I could go on and on citing examples, reporting sentences until the reader becomes bored with the numbers and sums involved. Just one case of this kind would be talked about for years if it were to happen in the UK. In China an Enron occurs each week! Every three months or so, new statistics are released. The pattern is the same; various banks lend money to companies, the person who approves the loan and the lender conspire and the money ends up in their individual savings accounts. Around one person at senior level in the provinces is uncovered each month, many more are never caught. Embezzlement of public funds was detected in fifty five different ministries at central government level; money that is collected and should go into the treasury seldom gets there, it just fills the pockets of the officials that collect it. Sooner or later this has to implode and destroy the ruling party, putting the offenders to death seems to be a poor deterrent, the problem gets worse.

One final case though, worthy of mention, concerns the notorious Zheng Xiaoyu. He was head of China's Drug and Food Safety Agency. Over a period of years he took bribes for approving drugs for general market use which had not been properly tested and some were in fact potentially lethal. The papers reported that at least ten deaths were caused by these sub-standard medicines. Zheng was convicted in May 2007, lost an appeal and then executed the following month. The

Corruption

English language *China Daily* incredibly reported "Zheng's death sentence was unusually heavy even for China."

Finally, this section is best rounded up with a letter that was published in the China Daily, in English, so that us foreigners of which there are 200,000 or so living in China (70,000 of them are in Shanghai for some reason), appreciate Chinese values.
It shows the admission that China is corrupt (or maybe just a little bit) and holding the country back but also how they like to divert attention from this by almost blaming the USA and printing nonsense about it. This hate-inciting letter was (proudly) published in the China Daily which means it has full consensus in government circles.

"Corruption the worst enemy
Corruption is the worst enemy of the PRC; and corruption is even a worse enemy to the People's Republic of China than the great Satan, the USA. Corruption drags the performance of the Chinese economy down by 40%; if corruption is cleaned up China can power along at twice the present speed and reduce the American lead by half. China is today a competitor of the USA and China will catch up to the Americans by year 2020. I believe that China can even do better by two times our present performance if we can weed out corruption. When Singapore became an independent nation their Minister Mentor Mr Lee Kuan Yew, devoted his first few years to the elimination, and today Singapore is well known the world over as a clean government.
I argue that mere 'police action' is not the best solution. I believe that the best solution is a combination of police action combined with a serious indoctrination of CHINESE ETHICS. The main thrust, I believe is still a good education in

CONFUCIAN ETHICS. Our schools must indoctrinate our children in the confucian virtue TO BE A GOOD MAN; the foundation of all confucian education. China needs to return to the good ole days of our great Mao Tze Tung, when all Chinese people were honest and good Chinese patriots. Today too many of our Chinese officials are corrupt and this problem is the 'brake' to slow China down.

A VIRTUOUS SOCIETY IS A GREAT AND POWERFUL SOCIETY. America (USA)today is a very corrupt society and their leaders only seek to enrich themselves and leave their poor to become more poor. The USA of today is beginning to unravel and their well constructed American myth that the USA is RICH is beginning to show cracks ! Today the USA is becoming poorer for all the citizens; and only a handful of their elite are becoming richer and richer. This will begin to accelerate until eventually the USA becomes a two tier society like MOST MALAY SOCIETY; a small handful of elites who are rich and the mass of society living from hand to mouth. AMERICA WILL CRUMBLE IN THIS MANNER.

China is well placed to be better than the USA because we can imbibe into our society values that our fore-fathers lived by, THE CONFUCIAN ETHICS. For the USA it is already too late but for China we are at the crest of our ascent to the top as the world's superpower and we have the right amount of time to be the best.

SHOOT CORRUPT OFFICIALS AND CHINA WILL BE GREAT !

For a start he gets one thing right that corruption is a great enemy of China but since just about every man, woman and dog participates, given half the chance, eradication is not an easy task.

Labelling the USA as 'Satan' is quite typical, when ever China is under pressure on any international issue, it cites examples of similar instances, whatever that may be, in the United States.

I could not agree more that changing the system of values is a pre-requisite to defeating corruption but that can hardly be called the ethics of their forefathers who not only suffered brutal empires but also lived in corrupt a system of privilege and dictatorship. Chairman Mao himself, under his communist regime, set-up his own system of a richly advantaged few and a mass of starving poor. Confucianism with its strict order of hierarchy and subjugation of women particularly, is completely at odds with Mao's *preached* communism.

He charges the USA with a transgression of the rich getting richer and the poor getting poorer yet this is exactly what is happening in China today, to an obscene degree.

It all ends with mob-cheering, foot-of-the-gallows stuff, that goes down well across the land yet solves nothing; shoot the perpetrators and all will be well.

If they really want to stop corruption then simply organise a system of controls and audits so that funds are monitored closely and stealing from the state or whatever cannot happen in the first place. They would argue that they do this but unfortunately the trifling level of auditing that does occur usually involves corrupt officials.

Putting too much real effort, as opposed to headline rhetoric, into anti-corruption legislation could of course be too much of a hurdle for the people who legislate. They may very simply want some of the action themselves and therefore would be unlikely to make it too difficult to set up a nice little retirement nest egg for themselves, if and whenever they get the chance.

Real China

They even cheat foreign and fellow Chinese countries such as Singapore with the famous Suzhou Business Park. The Singapore government invested heavily in land, real estate and services only to find out that another, local Chinese park, had been authorised with much lower rents and probably bank loans that were never repaid.. Subsequently the Singapore Government never got much return on its investment and in the end sold back to the Chinese at an undisclosed (no doubt incurring heavy losses) price.

Chapter 8 – Go Shopping

Some light relief! It is worth dedicating a chapter to shopping because in China the shopping experience is both unique and varied, most people on any kind of visit will take time out to go shopping.

For the locals, browsing the streets and malls is the number one pastime, they do not appear to buy that much but the main shopping roads, indoor plazas and centres are always crowded. In the baking hot humid summer, many people just go out to their local supermarket to get some cool air and relax in the air-conditioned environment, not being able to afford to switch it on at home. Their small apartments are unbearably hot due to poor insulation and ventilation so why not spend the evenings in the local superstore, relax and watch the world go by in relative comfort?

Except in the up-market designer outlets, it is a fair bet that at some stage bargaining will come into play, there are noticeably two ways of doing this, the polite way and the Chinese way.

The typical foreign tourist will see something they like and ask the price, since it is seldom marked. The vendor will look the potential buyer up and down then make a guess as to what they can afford. The reply will, depending on the nerve and greed level to be applied, be at least twice if not three times the going rate. A disadvantage will be smiling and showing particular interest in the product, it will definitely keep the numbers high. Offering substantially less is normal until the point where the shopkeeper gives in and sells it at an equally beneficial level. This is still likely to be much higher than a local would pay, as said before, cheating the foreigner is considered a god-given right in this country.

The Chinese method of barter is very different, they tend to look at something, cast a very mean eye over it, ask how much then, looking quite disgusted, throw it back down and walk away. Usually the assistant will shout out a lower price, but the highly skilled shopper slowly walks away pretending not to notice, as the frustrated seller keeps lowering the price, screaming down the aisles at the top of her voice. Eventually the price does not fall any further and the buyer, if really interested, will return looking severely annoyed. The goods will be picked-up again with a highly investigative look before shoving the cash firmly into the sales assistant's hand. No smiles, hardly a word is spoken, no please, not much chance of a thank you, the money is handed over and the goods are sold.

When browsing any commercial centre, particularly clothes shops, don't rush in! hang around for a while and take a good look at what other people are buying and see what price they are paying. In general the quality in China is poor and the production costs are very low so it is madness to be paying too much for virtually anything. Also bear in mind that warranties are not worth the paper they are printed on and exchanges are rare.

A very good example of a Chinese shopping trap is 'Woman's World' or Nu Ren Shi Jie on Shenzhen's busy main shopping street Hua Qiang Bei Lu. Shenzhen is just over the border from Hong Kong and massive savings can be made when comparing like for like with that of the former British colony.

This is a huge indoor mall on five floors with lots of different, but privately rented, shopping stalls. All are selling reasonable quality clothes at highly discounted prices, but, beware they have no problem ripping off the 'Laowai'. These are the kind of shops where no prices are displayed, they simply look at the potential mug of a customer before deciding what price to charge, well-dressed people get charged higher prices. However, with a bit of care and hard searching some really good clothing items can be had at rock-bottom prices. All sorts of apparel are for sale from overcoats to underwear, shoes and handbags plus various accessories; often with either strange Chinese brands or slightly mis-copied western ones. In general, it would be a mistake to pay more than fifty yuan for anything here, the locals don't, so why should you?

Mirrors are deliberately concave so that when you slip into that expensive glittery cocktail dress, wishing you'd passed on the apple pie and cream at lunch, do not be too surprised at how slim you look. Even if the clothes that *are* tried on give you all the charm or an over-filled refuse sack, the shop assistants will disingenuously describe how gorgeous the customer looks.

In the larger glitzy shopping emporia there is little difference from those to be found in Europe or the USA except that the prices, for the same thing that could be purchased back home, tend to be more expensive not cheaper. Some things though are a lot cheaper in China, one example is radio controlled toys. There are many on offer, some are humungous and include cars, ships, planes and even helicopters. It is worth pointing out that using these in the UK could be breaking the law as there may be an issue with the actual frequency that they operate on, it is most likely to be different from those that are licensed back home. However, most people seem not to care. MP3 players appear to be considerably cheaper but take a look at websites such as eBay and note typical prices before travelling, many Hong Kong individuals and companies sell these kinds of China-sourced things very cheaply and will mail internationally. A lot will be fakes of course.

When out and about, it is essential to always be on your look-out for being cheated, practices that may seem alien to you are common place in China. A friend of mine went shopping in the busy border complex of Luo Hu at the Hong Kong / Shenzhen crossing. He went to buy a pair of golf shoes and tried the ideal pair on in a small shop. The shoes, size 42, were a little bit tight so he asked to try a size 43. Obligingly, the assistant took the shoes away, returning a few minutes later, and handed the *larger* size shoes to my friend. The assistant, while absent from the room, had removed the insoles to make the footwear feel more roomy and used a biro to modify the size from 42 to 43!

This shopping complex that stands out in front immediately after crossing the border to China from Hong Kong, is a paradise for people who want to buy cheap souvenirs and novelties to take home.

It is probably the biggest single centre of fake goods in the whole of China and if the authorities really were serious about stopping the counterfeit trade they would have closed it years ago. It is also shark infested with wise traders, pickpockets and handbag thieves. Take a look at a watch counter and suddenly the assistant will whip out a couple of fake Rolexes or '*lolex*' as they call them. They can be had for less than ten pounds, they usually work fine and are impressive copies but the jewels soon fall out and the gold plate peels off. There are no warranties at this place, everything has to be checked extensively before purchase and then if it fails the next day it's too bad.

Go Shopping

In this complex young wise men and women will approach you from every shop door, every alley way and even in the toilets. They want to sell fake DVDs, fake handbags, fake Ipods, uncomfortable massages and a table at lunch!
Beware of special promotions like 'buy one, get one free' the one can be anything they like; I bought a DVD machine thinking I would get a second at no charge but the *one* that came free was a bottle of water!
There are a great number of fake goods around, some are clever and some are obviously not right. Sometimes they get it ridiculously and often amusingly wrong; there is a common brand of 'Polo' footwear that comes in a box with a union jack on it. The very same national flag can often been seen on a jumper or t-shirt with the letters 'USA' underneath. Although fake brands are strictly disallowed, it goes on everywhere and is near impossible to control. Virtually in every market and mall there will be fakes on display. Fake goods can even be picked-up in Wal-Mart, the US multi-national that has 64 stores in China, seems to have no problems selling suspect clothes with cloned logos from famous brands. To be fair, Wal-Mart is in everything but name, a Chinese supermarket - in the way it is managed, the products it sells and, in my opinion, lousy service it delivers. My guess is that its US executives have provided the funds and not a lot else, reportedly profits have been hard to come by in the early years of trading.
Some fake goods can be dangerous, a friend bought some expensively branded sun block, in what appeared to be an up-market department store, after thirty minutes of solar exposure we all had faces resembling prize tomatoes.
Often logos are copied and modified very slightly, for example I was looking at a girl wearing a pair of jeans (no

surprise there) with what looked like the 'Levi's' label on the back. It was almost identical except that the usual picture of a pair of denims being stretched between two horses was, on close inspection, being torn between two tanks. We have to take the point though that if manufacturers really want to get their brand recognized, stick it where it is bound to be stared at, on a woman's bottom.

Chinese fashion companies are particularly expert at cheating their own people, in all shopping areas brands will be on offer with some ill-created western name and Paris-London-New York written beneath. It seems that most people are easily fooled, being 'western' means that they can of course charge higher prices. Another friend of mine, a fashion designer, worked at a clothes manufacturer in the southern city of DongGuan and every item destined for the domestic market had 'Made In Italy' stamped on it.

Putting some message on in English is also a common technique used when pushing the otherwise mundane skirt or sweater. The problem is that often the words are meaningless, the grammar is awful or in extreme cases it is just a random list of characters. I saw a most un-sexy middle aged woman in Beijing wearing a gold jumper with the word SEEX embroidered across her chest, she clearly did not know what it was supposed to say and even if she did would fail to recognize that it was spelt wrong in any case.

One of the more amusing brands is 'Titi' they market young women's fashions; either the creators are very clever or very ignorant of reality because of the slogans that are embroidered onto the chest of their blouses, t-shirts and pullovers. They have the basic 'Titi', and then there is 'Love Titi' and my favourite 'I think about Titi since 1986', which could be when the entrepreneur responsible reached puberty. Whether or not the word is intentional, the shop assistants have no idea whatsoever of the associated meaning.

Sales are as common as they are at MFI, but often they have hiked the price in the first place. The discount signs require some quick maths, when '8.5 折' is displayed, it means 15% discount, in other words it's a bit like calculating percentages only this time subtract from 10 and multiply by 10. Frequently, in a sale, they won't allow prospective buyers to try anything on, the thought process is 'if I am taking a risk selling at a discount, you should take the risk as to whether it fits or not'! Someone I know wanted to buy a skirt in a sale and was prevented from trying it on before buying, so she nipped home and brought one of her own snug fitting skirts hanging in her wardrobe, in order to measure against. The match was perfect so she made the purchase but the shop assistant was furious, as if she had been cheated, such are the obscure minds of this unfathomable nation.

One of the most common items of copied merchandise is DVD movies. These are available on the street for around ten Yuan in Beijing or Shanghai and as low as five in Shenzhen. They are of variable quality but have become better over time. When it costs only 30 pence for the latest Hollywood release, it seems remarkable value for money, and perhaps understandable that the film industry gets very upset. On an average purchase of say twenty disks, around two or three will not play so the gamble is a sure bet. The very recent ones are usually of poor video and audio quality because somebody has just sat in the cinema with a video camera and copied the film. Some of them have been stolen and copied, they are issues of the promotional DVDs that the big film companies have released to film critics, of whom some it seems have no problem with selling them on. These are easy to spot as a message keeps coming up on the screen to inform the viewer that it is not for sale.

Understandably the movie industry is quite upset by this and puts great pressure, at the highest level, to stop the practice. In most cases the fakes are not on general display but ambling through the various shopping streets up and down the country, there will be a frequent approach by a scruffy local who whispers 'DVD' in the ear. If interested, they will lead the way to somewhere close-by to view their collection, this is usually a stairwell in a building or a small alleyway, normally it is safe and not a robbery trick.

If tempted, it is strongly advised that these are only bought for personal use, if resold or imported into the UK then a criminal offence is committed and will lead to prosecution.

In April 2004, an American (could only be with a name like this) Randolph Hobson Guthrie III was sentenced to thirty months in a Chinese gaol for selling DVDs on eBay and another website called '3 Dollar DVD'. He lived in Shanghai and was sending large quantities of the copies back to the USA. He was marketing them for three dollars each and buying them at a guess for around 80 cents. Since it was illegal, he did not pay any taxes so his profits were high. According to the Chinese press, he had sold $840,000 worth so was well on the way to getting seriously rich before his luck ran out. It did not say how he was caught but probably US customs traced the source back to Shanghai, where he lived.

It is true to say that buying a few for personal use will not bring any trouble but loading the suitcase with plans to sell them back home will get you into serious mire.

The same goes for antiquities and fossils, there have been reports of westerners getting fined or gaoled for taking antiques and in one case, a fossilized dinosaur egg out of the country so beware, it is illegal to do this.

Incredibly I was stopped at the border between China and Hong Kong with a small pot that I had paid a few pounds for. I was accused of exporting what they described as 'Cultural Relics' I was let go but the goods were confiscated; the worry is that had I bought several then I would have been before a judge as a trafficker and in China the assumption is guilt unless innocence is proven and frequently confession through torture.

Software is also very easy to buy, with copies of normally very expensive programmes such as Microsoft Office, Autocad, Photoshop and other supposedly protected utilities. Photoshop should be banned in China it has got to the point where virtually every picture from magazines to bill boards has been doctored or *photoshopped* (one of those new verbs like 'to text') to the point where seeing is definitely not believing.

Ripping off intellectual property is not confined to the scruffy man in the street, I once purchased a PC for the office from a reputable dealer. It came with full warranty, a manual and back-up support. However it did not take long to discover that the installed Windows XP was a copy version. I complained and was told, 'You've clearly never bought a computer in China before, they all come with non-genuine Windows'

The warranty system is also highly suspect, even in seemingly creditable stores there will never be a full-year guarantee and there are very few consumer rights. It is stressful but necessary, when sold shoddy goods, the only way to either get your money back or a receive a replacement is to go back to the store where the item was bought, ideally at a busy time and start a row with the shop, causing a scene so that in the interest of not upsetting the other potential customers they quickly give in and comply with the valid complaint. It is distressing and we could all do without it but this is one example of what the media likes to call typical Chinese culture, it is what my Granny would have called 'daylight robbery'. I would totally ignore books like *Lonely Planet* that advise keeping calm, smiling and politely complaining. It is utter rubbish, they will think you are a complete fool; look angry, raise your voice and make threatening remarks – the only method that works.

Most transactions are carried out in cash. They have a weird system to prevent their staff pilfering the till. When something is purchased from a store, the money is never paid to the assistant, he or she will write out a ticket which is then taken to a cash till. The item is paid for and the receipt is returned to the assistant where the goods are finally handed over. Probably, this system is designed so that as few people as possible handle money. Most shop assistants will earn between 1000 and 1500 yuan per month (between seventy and one hundred pounds) so running off with the day's takings must be very tempting.

A good reason for the cash culture is that goods have a 17% VAT rate across the board and, unlike businesses in the UK, the shops cannot reclaim it. It is not surprising therefore that they like to deal in hard readies. It is normal to ask for an official receipt or *fapiao*, the shops buy these in various denominations, like currency, from the government. That way they cannot avoid paying tax. In order to encourage restaurant patrons in particular, to ask for a receipt, the government has put a scratch-off area on the newer ones whereby if lucky, the odds are about a billion to one, up to 1000 Yuan in cash can be won.

Go Shopping

All money that goes through banks is controlled so shopkeepers are very careful not to use their business bank accounts, rather their personal ones for the running of their enterprises. The more upmarket shops will take the local bank cards for transactions, these are similar to Switch, some will take Visa and MasterCard but it is necessary to check first as sometimes they only take credit cards issued by local banks.

A common and irritating feature of a visit to a commercial district is the prevalence of beggars. Whilst some are genuine, unusually some are well-dressed, well-fed and very crafty not typical vagrants. Frequently old people, who hang around on street corners and jab their empty bowl into the ribs of passers by, almost like its a duty to give them some money. They seem to feel that they do not have to go through the annoying formality of saying please. Some of these highwaymen are extremely persistent. Spotting a foreigner is like finding the end of a rainbow, their heads twitch and home-in like a meercat and the face twists in anticipation of potential ecstasy from easy spoils.

Some individuals will go to unhealthily extreme lengths in order to earn money from begging. There was one lady who each Saturday lay on the floor of a busy shopping street with a baby in one arm and the upper torso and other hand half way inside an overturned litter bin scooping up apparently discarded rice. As ever, things are never what they appear to be at first, she had put the rice there in the first place. When I first saw it I was shocked, perhaps disgusted but feeling intense pity. Then I saw her virtually every week, in the same place at the same time, eating rice from an identical container that she wanted passers by to believe had been thrown away. Although it is a trick, there must be easier and less drastic methods of fooling the busy shoppers.

Real China

Why do this? It has a lot to do with religion and belief in the great Chinese God *Lord Banknote* these apparently desperate people can easily pick-up three thousand Yuan per month; a typical shop worker gets around fifteen hundred so it seems worth the extra effort to blacken the face, jump into some scruffy old clothes and hang around outside expensive restaurants and wait for the coins to drop. A fair number of the elderly are cared for in homes but they soon check-out and go back to the street. The newspapers often report that these conspicuous vagrants are entitled to care and food at many local hostels, however they prefer to go out and beg.

The most upsetting types of begging includes the use of small children, sometimes late into the night. Often, the children are more persistent than their parents or guardians, they'll grip tightly onto the leg of a passer-by like a randy dog until they give-in and donate some cash. Much worse, sometimes severely disabled children are used, often they have limbs missing and are deliberately made to look dirty and desperate, their guardians drop them off in a town centre early in the morning and collect them later that day after many hours of crawling along the pavements with an outstretched hand grasping an empty bowl, it is a wretched sight, most people pretend they are not there and the children themselves never get proper care from their 'guardians'. Upon seeing these kind of inhuman, degrading and upsetting sights, it is difficult to know what to do. My local colleagues advise that giving money just encourages them when there are support organisations and facilities for such people. If this is so, the question begs why the police do not prosecute the offenders, especially the so called parents and carers of these poor children?

Go Shopping

For certain the disabled kids have been abandoned by the adults who brought them into the world and left to the mercy of unscrupulous and crooked orphanage charities. The ones that allow these desperate youngsters to be begging bait are the same ones that get prosecuted frequently for baby trading.

Out and about in the town, sooner or later the need to visit a toilet will arise. Chinese toilets have the most shockingly foul smell ever; it is a mixture of human waste and whatever potent chemicals they use to clean them, not that they are ever very clean.

Paper is not normally available, it is necessary to keep your own supply handy. Once when out, with what I thought was a respectable lady, in Guangzhou a few years ago, she needed to visit the lavatory and so popped into a nice hotel on the street front, a few minutes later she emerged with an almost complete toilet roll stuffed into her now bulging handbag. So this simple example explains why premises, commercial or government, never leave anything for the public to take as they need, otherwise they simply steal the lot.

A Chinese friend of mine runs a small office with five employees, very cosy, almost like a family, yet he locks the tea and coffee in his drawer because he just cannot trust even his friends and leave it out to be used as required.

Since transvestism doesn't appeal, I don't get to check out what happens in the ladies toilet but I always used to wonder why the men's urinals always have a large pool of the yellow smelly stuff underneath them; all became clear when I saw a man poised about three feet back from the wall, trousers dropped to his mid thigh, projecting his pee like an ornamental fountain, almost like a schoolboy piss up the wall competition.

Real China

Since the WC is best described as a fume chamber and when the need arises to dispense with that one cup of coffee too many, either practise at holding your breath for the two minutes or so necessary, longer if you're partial to chicken vindaloo, or wait and visit a hotel or upmarket shopping mall. It is sometimes necessary to buy a cup of coffee just so there is a chance to get rid of the last one.

Chapter 9 - Language

This is not the book to teach the Chinese language but as a foreigner to whom languages do not come easy and who has struggled with Chinese for many years, it seems like a good idea to explain the basics of Chinese and hopefully put across some of the fundamentals and quirks of what to us is an alien tongue.

Firstly the language spoken in the mainland is Mandarin or what they call *putonghua* which means common speech. It is not Cantonese, this is only useful in Guangdong (Canton) province but even there, everybody also speaks Mandarin so forget about impressing the owner of your take-away back home, learning this would be a great waste of effort as it is mostly useless in China.

Sociology is not my field but it seems clear from learning the language that has the most speakers in the world, that language and culture are very closely related. In China there is a population that is noisy, rude and abrupt by our standards, extremely vague and invariably situations materialise where the first impression is completely different to the reality.

From the first point, Chinese is spoken very loudly, more so than any other language I have heard, in fact it is closer to shouting. Secondly, it is rude in the sense that please is seldom used in everyday speech and thank you is certainly not used as frequently as we would expect. It is abrupt in the sense that requests are spoken in the simplest terms possible, for example we might say 'please could I have a cup of coffee' they would say 'wǒ yào yī bēi kāfēi' which directly translates to 'I want one cup coffee'. When embarking on the first steps to learn the language, the impression is that it is very easy, all of the verbs are simple and do not change whether the subject is singular, first, second or third person. There are no tenses, adverbs or so called aspect markers are generally used. There are no articles and very few prepositions, what could be simpler? The problem comes when it is desired to put more than a few words together, then the grammar, word order and introduction of words here and there to give some kind of indication to the meaning make the language terribly complicated. For example you cannot join two sentences together with a simple 'and' or 'but' conjunctions are very involved and often used in pairs. As is always the case with anything to do with China, what seems straightforward at the outset turns out to be the opposite and much more complicated than need be.

The Chinese of course write with their own character set but fortunately there is a Romanisation system, known as *pinyin,* that helps a great deal in the pronunciation but has the side effect of delaying greatly the decision to learn the characters. The pinyin system was created in 1958 and became an international standard in the early eighties, replacing the incomprehensible Wade-Giles system. It is only used on the mainland, not in Hong Kong or Taiwan, although it has recently been introduced in Singapore. The Wade-Giles method is still used in Taiwan but it is a very strange system that is used both inconsistently and unreliably. For example road signs in Taiwan Romanise 中 (*zhong* = middle) as chung, jung or chong depending how they feel. This never happens on the mainland.

In order to explain pinyin, it is necessary to understand the general structure of the language. Chinese is monosyllabic, that is each character is a single syllable sound. In order to

Language

generate these syllables the sounds are constructed from initials and finals. There are 21 beginning sounds called initials and 39 ending sounds called finals, so for example take the word for car which is *chē*   the ch is the initial, a bit like ch in cheese and ē is the final that sounds a bit like ugh, so the pronunciation is a sort of *ch-ugh* sound, said distinctively but as one syllable, easy eh?

In fact not every final can be used with every initial but we still end up with around 500 sounds. Some of these sounds are extremely difficult to pronounce for those who's first language is English, the sounds such as *shi, chi, zhi, cai,* have no equivalent and there is a need to ram the tongue uncomfortably into various positions within the mouth cavity in order to get them right.

If that weren't complicated enough, because Chinese is composed of relatively few monosyllabic words, the spoken vocabulary is multiplied by the addition of tones. Each sound can be said with four different tones or five if the unstressed one is included. The so-called first tone has a flat but high sound, the second starts low but rises to the same level as the first, the third starts low, falls further then rises and the fourth tone starts high and falls low very fast.

The most common example of this, used in virtually every basic Chinese book is 'ma'; mā   (妈) with the first tone means mother, with the second tone má (麻) it means hemp or flax, with the third tone mǎ (马) it means horse and with the fourth tone mà (骂) it means curse or swear and finally the toneless ma (吗) appears at the end of a sentence or clause to indicate that a question is being asked.

The other feature of the language, both vague and confusing, is the tendency to over-use the more common sound and tone combinations. For example shì, with the fourth tone, can be (是) the verb to be, or it can be (事) matter or affair, or (市) city, or (室) room, or (示) notify/ show and in fact the list goes on[1]. The real problem is that so many words sound exactly the same that the language learner must listen extremely carefully in order to fully understand the context before you having a clue as to what is going on. For me, after two years of part time study I could hardly understand a sentence, with German it took two years to become fluent! It would be extremely difficult to understand a book or even a letter written in pinyin because so many words have the same sound, fortunately the characters are all different, with a few exceptions, and so if you do make an effort to learn the written language then the spoken becomes easier, in fact I think that although the pinyin system helps tremendously with initial pronunciation, depending upon it for too long, delays real fluency with the language and actually hinders progress.

The characters themselves are not as confusing as they look at first sight. They originated as pictograms and through the centuries have evolved as they appear today. In mainland China, they use the so-called simplified set; having been introduced to aid literacy during the communist period. In both Taiwan and Hong Kong, the traditional system is still in use. Many of the two character sets are in fact very similar but some are radically different such that it would be difficult to guess. For example the character for dragon in simplified form is 龙, in traditional it is 龍 and the sound is '*lóng*', second tone. Many people seem to feel that the simplified

---

[1] Note that the character is always different but since it is not possible to see the words coming out of someone's mouth, it doesn't help in conversational Chinese.

form has taken the true meaning away from the original pictogram from which it was derived. A good example of this is the word for horse, changing from 馬 under the traditional system to 马 in simplified form. The horse seems to have lost its legs.

Surprisingly, the characters are not as difficult to learn as one might at first think, although there may be two thousand or so in common everyday use, they are all in fact formed from around one hundred or so basic strokes or characters that are combined to form more complex ones. Look at another example, 想 which means to think and is pronounced *xiǎng* with the third tone. The character comprises three other characters, namely 木 *mù* which means wood, 目 *mù* which means eye and 心 *xīn* which means heart. So the Chinese think with their eyes, heart and a piece of wood, which explains a lot, but perhaps early civilisations actually believed that. Notice that the characters are always squashed or stretched so that they fit into a perfect square, school children spend a significant amount of time practising their handwriting, initially on squared paper.

Chinese is also written in a specific way, or what is referred to as stroke order. Each character is made from a number of strokes and you must write them in the prescribed order. The reason for this is because, up until recently, Chinese was written with a brush, painting in the wrong order or direction could blur the meaning. Take rén 人 which means people of person and then rù 入 which means enter, the difference is very subtle but if written in the correct order, distinguishing between the two is simple. Typing on a computer is very easy, modern entry methods allow entering the word in pinyin and then selecting the correct character from a list.

Real China

Although these learning tools help a great deal, it must be stressed that the true meaning from the Romanisation or pinyin is seldom clear, the character is necessary because so many have the same sound but completely different meanings. Often, especially when two or more characters are combined, meanings are nothing like that which would be expected, take for example xiǎo xīn 小心, the characters mean small heart but the true meaning is *careful!* míng bái 明白 these characters mean bright white but the true meaning is the verb *to understand.*

Returning to the issue of the relationship between language and culture, the Chinese will seldom lapse into understating anything and so it follows that the most over-used character just happens to be 大 *dà,* which means big. And so moving around the country there will be big hotels and big bridges and big museums, I have never, ever seen a small hotel labelled as such even if it is not much more than a guesthouse. I once pointed this out to my Chinese colleagues and they simply fell about laughing, it seemed quite ridiculous to them that you would actually call your little guest house a small hotel. "people wouldn't stay there". The Chinese language version of the guide book for the British Museum is entitled 英国大博物馆, *yīngguódàbówùguǎn* British *Big* Museum.

It soon becomes obvious that the characters themselves, whether road signs, advertising or simple notices are often written in huge proportions, usually red in colour and strung from almost every building. This is very much a hangover from the Cultural Revolution era when nationalist and socialist mottoes were pasted high on every telegraph pole, bridge and building up and down the country.

Language

The language though is interesting in the sense that when the ability to read characters emerges, things start to fall into place. Beijing is two characters *bĕi* 北 third tone, which means north and *jīng* 京 first tone, which means capital. So therefore Beijing means just that, north capital. We used to call it Peking but Beijing is using the pinyin system and now seems to be universally adopted in preference. Nánjīng means south capital (previously Nanking) and Tokyo in Chinese is dōngjīng which means east capital. The characters for Japan, rìbĕn 日本 do mean rising sun and the characters for China zhōngguó 中国 mean middle country or kingdom, the old name for China. The characters for the U.K. are yīngguó 英国, which directly translates to brave country and which I kind of like whereas the USA is mĕiguó 美国 whose direct meaning is beautiful country. When they named the latter, there was no wall-to-wall concrete and endless streets of fast food outlets, motels and gas stations.

Whilst I could not resist the temptation to directly translate names as I have done here, strictly speaking it is wrong, to the Chinese they are just names. There is a village on the edge of Dartmoor in West Devon called Crapstone but the rumours that it is named after Mick Jagger are completely untrue.

Accents vary across the country but the northern pronunciation is very different from the southern one, in the north they tend to speak with their tongue permanently lodged into the roof of their mouth and put a Farmer Giles-like *argh* sound at the end of most words. Conversely the southerners seem to talk though their teeth. The best advice is to spend early studies on getting the pronunciation right, practise with a natural speaker until the tones and the sounds come out just as the locals would say them. Failure to get this right will mean that native speakers will simply not understand or even refuse to try, resulting in constant frustration and anger. Everywhere where Chinese is spoken on the mainland, the flow of words is constantly interrupted by the sound 'neige' (nàge) 那个 it sounds, to the untrained ear, like they are saying *nigger* and must be extremely disconcerting for black people. In fact it means *that* but in speech is really equivalent to our pausing with umm every now and again, a kind of nervous must say something when the correct word does not come immediately to mind. We shouldn't complain, I here so many British people slip a verbal *fucking* into almost every sentence. At the Guangzhou end of the guǎngshēn expressway there is an electronic voice that says, after you've paid the toll *pīngān yīlù* meaning continue safely but I am sure it says *pīngān mílù* which means get lost safely!

A constant source of amusement to natural English speakers will be what has become known as *Chinglish*. This is where the Chinese translate to English using only the dictionary or some third rate website that uses a look-up table for instant interpretation. It results in various signs and notices that are meaningless as well as a steady source of humour for foreigners.
Outside my apartment in Shanghai was a notice that read 'The rat medicine is put on the green stuff, please order your children not to eat it' A hotel in Tianjin was advertising 'Commoness rooms' at a standard price and 'Luxuriousness rooms' at a 'fat price' To cure the pain of an internal flight, the first thing I do when I get on an airline is scour the in-flight magazine for prime examples, it never ceases to surprise that even expensive quality publications do not bother to check the English text. A headline the English

Language

language paper *Shenzhen Daily* read 'Thais beat bird flu with passports for cocks'. Does that mean you need to drop your trousers at immigration and how do they think you catch it in the first place? I can just here the official asking "How come it's much bigger in the photo?" Disabled people will be upset to see that they are entitled to park in spaces for the "deformed"

The situation is further complicated by the fact that their dictionaries are based on pre-war versions, having not been modernised or updated so words that have gone out of circulation back home can pop-up unexpectedly in China. When I decided *not* to bid on a project for the usual reasons of unachievable specifications, low profit and corrupt tendering procedure I received a complaining fax entitled "Your Caprice" which I ashamedly had to look-up. In addition to the presence of London smog, bowler hats and umbrellas, they still think we walk around saying 'how do you do'?

Just a small tip, when learning Chinese, it is a good idea not to inform any local business partners because they always arrogantly think the *laowai* (as they call us foreigners, in Hong Kong Caucasians are colloquially known as ghosts) does not have the slightest idea what they are talking about and will openly talk about him or her, good or bad, in their presence. To understand what is really going on, without them knowing, is an extremely useful trump card. They will be flattered and amused when you say *Nǐhǎo* (hello) or *xièxie* (thank you) but start to put a few sentences together and they'll shit themselves!

Chapter 10 - A Quick History

It could be argued that more things happened in the twentieth century that changed the lives of ordinary people than at any time in the history of the world. Technological achievement brought fast transport, health care, sanitation, computers, television, radio and the internet. Notoriously it brought two world wars, nuclear bombs and mass environmental change. It was also the hundred years of the great exterminators, leaders who excelled in the murder of their own and other people. There was Adolf Hitler, Joseph Stalin and, the most notorious of all, Mao Ze Dong. There were several more in division two, mass murder occurred in Iraq, Cambodia, Rwanda and the Balkans but not on the same scale as that committed by these three monsters.

The Guinness Book of Records describes Chairman Mao as holding the record of killing the most people (they forgot to mention the motor car) yet oddly his preserved body lies for all to see and, or so it appears, respect in a corner of Tianmen Square. However, before looking at Mao, it is worth summarising the mostly dynastic period before he appeared as the leader of the world's most populous nation.

China has a very long royal history where virtually nothing changed for more than two thousand years, even new technology was hardly introduced at all during this period, save some radical inventions, it stopped altogether after 1430. It was only during the twentieth century that upheaving events and technological change happened in China, partly due to the influence of external powers. Because of this, the concentration here is on what happened during the past hundred and fifty years but one has to go back to the start and fill in a bit of the information that today's China has forgotten.

The importance of having some historical knowledge of the world about us cannot be overestimated. It should be on the national curriculum, as significant as mathematics and language skills, knowledge of history leads to an appreciation, understanding and empathy for all sorts of world issues. For example, in Israel, due to the ultra-orthodox grip that strangles the country, children are not taught that the land previously belonged to the Palestinians, the Jews have only been there in numbers since 1948. Even worse, most British people do not know that the UK played a pivotal role in creating the mess that resulted from it.

Perhaps if we had all been taught the history of Northern Ireland, like Cromwell's massacres and territorial carve-up, the situation there would have been resolved years ago.

A visit to China can be enhanced and better understood with just an elementary knowledge of the history that led to where the nation stands today and so this section aims to do just that, whizzing through 200 years in just a few pages. Sadly most Chinese people are ignorant of their own history, as a direct consequence of government policy, so sensitivity is called for when discussing this topic with the natives.

Most of China's recorded history is of a series of repetitive dynasties under the Confucian system of leaders and followers. The ruling dynasty would comprise an emperor, an army and a relatively small number of officials to administer quite a large territory. The common peasants would work the land and usually be governed provincially or county by county. The emperor also had a large pool of concubines so that he got to shag somebody different every night. The justification being that it was a necessary custom in order for the emperor, almost God, to sire a male heir. Chairman Mao reportedly only had four or five nymphs, poor chap.

Early China was much smaller than it is today, centred around the middle of the current chicken-shaped map. The capital city would also change with each dynasty as they set up their base in different parts of the country probably depending upon where their trusted army and pool of followers were concentrated. Some of the dynasties lasted for hundreds of years, other for just a few decades. In common with all of the dynasties the rulers were ruthless and cruel, a Chinese tradition that carried on towards the end of the twentieth century and some would argue to this very day.

The best place to start is with the Qin dynasty and the emperor Qin Shi Huang, he was the creator of all those terracotta soldiers and horses near Xi'an. This dynasty is important because it is the first one that created anything like China as a nation. In 221BC Qin Shi Huang subjugated several other central provinces (as they are today) and formed a territory of approximately sixty per cent of what we now know as China.

The Qin created a system of bureaucracy, enforced by terror, with laws and customs. Confucian critics were quickly put to death. The capital was XianYang, near Xi'an in the North-West Sha'anxi province. The foundations of the Great Wall were built during this period. In fact the Great Wall was built over several dynasties right up until the 17th century Ming period but the Qin created this fortress firstly on their northern border by linking several walls in different provinces. The Great Wall stretches incredibly from Heilongjiang in the north east all the way to Gansu in the far west. Qin Shi Huang could be considered to be the very first emperor in the sense that he founded the dynastic trend that continued for two thousand years.

Soon after Qin died in 210 BC, there were revolts and the Han dynasty emerged as the ruling authority four years later. The capital was Chang An, modern day Xi'an, and the new dynasty adopted much of the administrative order created by the Qin. However, the Confucian system was more reverently adhered to and conscientious scholars were given high posts in the civil service. One of China's four "great" inventions, paper and also porcelain were invented during this time.[1]

The important point to note about the Han is that most ethnic Chinese today are of the Han race. The Han extended their territory to the far west right into modern XinJiang province to ensure that they had a safe passage for their goods to middle Asia and Arabia beyond. This route is famously known as the Silk Road and explains why camels can still be seen in Xi'an. The Han ruled for three hundred years or so but had collapsed into a warlord anarchy by the year AD 220. No strong successor emerged and so a period of tribalism prevailed until the LuoYang-based (in Henan) Jin dynasty restored order and unity.

The Jin reigned from 265 to 420 but were forced to establish a new base at NanJing in about 317 after successive invasions from barbarians. The last one hundred years or so of the Jin was a period of increasing fragmentation and more tribalism lasting right up until the year 589 although in the sixth

---

[1] Most historians have a problem with this, the Egyptians invented paper and had a highly developed writing system long before the Chinese however all Chinese will tell you that paper was one of their 'great four' inventions (the compass, gunpowder and wheelbarrow were the other three)

century further technological advances were made, most notably the invention of gunpowder.

During this time Buddhism grew rapidly. It is well worth taking time out to visit LuoYang, close to Zhengzhou in Henan, where considerable evidence of this can be seen.

The *Long Men Shi Ku* (Dragon Gate Caves) Grottoes are a series of caves and recesses that line the bank of the Li River for about 2 miles. There are more than one hundred thousand Buddhist images varying from a few inches tall to ten feet or more, carved into the rocks. It is an amazing site in terms of the number and variety. Many were vandalised during the Cultural Revolution but the whole area is still marked as a World Heritage site. The site was inaugurated by the Wei Dynasty which had a small territory in the North between the times of the Han and Jin, it was later added to greatly during the Tang period.

China was briefly re-unified by the Sui dynasty from 589 to 617 a reign similar to that of the Qin, brutal and ruthless with forced labour and various military campaigns. The Sui did though miraculously complete the Grand Canal (*da yun he*), an astonishing achievement like the Great Wall, it is still in use today and runs almost 1800km from Beijing in the north to HangZhou on the east coast. The Sui collapsed after much quarrelling and in-fighting with the usual round of murders and shaky loyalties.

The Tang Dynasty came next, the Chinese themselves generally consider this to be the glory period of their history. It lasted almost 300 years from the year 618 to 907. The territory was expanded from its base at Chang An and contacts were developed with India and the middle east. Literature and arts flourished as did Buddhism. Under the

A Quick History

Tang, block printing was developed and this enabled widespread education. Examinations were set such that the most talented and educated people were drawn into the civil service which beneficially diminished the powers of warlords because influence was earned through ability rather than force. This system carried right on into the Qing period. There are a few legends that are always highlighted in Chinese history, the first is the poet Li Bai who lived from 701 until 762 and seems to have a special place in the hearts of today's Chinese. For various reasons he travelled around the country for most of his life and it seems frequently drunk himself silly, in fact many of his poems were about alcohol, below is an example:

Bringing in the Wine

See how the Yellow River's water moves out of heaven.
Entering the ocean, never to return.
See how lovely locks in bright mirrors in high chambers,
Though silken-black at morning, have changed by night to snow.
... Oh, let a man of spirit venture where he pleases
And never tip his golden cup empty toward the moon!
Since heaven gave the talent, let it be employed!
Spin a thousand of pieces of silver, all of them come back!
Cook a sheep, kill a cow, whet the appetite,
And make me, of three hundred bowls, one long drink!
... To the old master, Tsen, And the young scholar, Tan-chiu,
Bring in the wine! Let your cups never rest!
Let me sing you a song! Let your ears attend!
What are bell and drum, rare dishes and treasure?
Let me be forever drunk and never come to reason!
Sober men of olden days and sages are forgotten,

Real China

And only the great drinkers are famous for all time.
... Prince Chen paid at a banquet in the Palace of Perfection
Ten thousand coins for a cask of wine, with many a laugh and
quip.
Why say, my host, that your money is gone?
Go and buy wine and we'll drink it together!
My flower-dappled horse, My furs worth a thousand,
Hand them to the boy to exchange for good wine,
And we'll drown away the woes of ten thousand generation!

In fact his death was supposed to be alcohol related since, according to folklore, he drowned attempting to rake the moon out of the river.

Another story which is forced down the visitors throat, both in Xi'an and at the Forbidden City in Beijing, is that of Yang Gui Fei (719-756). She was a concubine of the Tang emperor Xuan Zong, alleged to have been exceptionally beautiful, although plump by today's standards as the Tang liked them that way, they should visit the UK today! Apparently the emperor was so mesmerized and head over heels in love with her that he neglected his official duties to the point where the country was becoming unstable. The solution was that the offending princess had to be killed and so reluctantly Xuan Zong was ordered to end the life of his beloved. The story is immortalised in a long poem by Bai Juyi. The story was also put onto film by Mizoguchi Kenji in 1955 called princess Yang Kwei Fei. What is astonishing about Chinese history is not that there are stories like this, but rather that there are so few.

The Tang started to lose their grip on power after a military defeat by the Arabs at the Talas river battle in north west

A Quick History

India in 751, previously the Tang had been more or less invincible. Over the next hundred years or so the dynasty steadily denigrated following power struggles, interior rebellions and economic exploitation. (sounds like the recent Tory Party) The eventual result was that the country became increasingly vulnerable to northern invaders. China then fragmented into different kingdoms and dynasties, lasting for around fifty years until it was next unified under the Song dynasty founded in 960 remaining in power until 1279.

There were two phases of the Song period, the Northern which continued until 1127 and then the Southern. The Northern faded because they were unable to rebel the invaders from the north who had become increasingly powerful.

The Song built cities which became major centres of trade and culture, they developed a bureaucratic system of accountable civilian masters, further enhancing the emperors' power. The Song also discarded Buddhism and went back to the Confucian value system of obedience to one's superior as in subject to master, wife to husband and so on.

The notable philosopher of this time was Zhu Xi who's promotion of the Confucian ideology during the period, carried right on into the 19th century and to a some extent contributed to China's stunted development.

Unfortunately for the Song, one of the greatest powers the world had ever seen, the Mongols rose at this time, with their vast empire they had conquered northern Asia, including parts of China, Arabia and some of Europe.

This was the age of Genghis Khan (1167-1227) and it was he who started the erosion of the southern Song people. It was completed by Kublai Khan, Genghis' grandson, who established the first non-Han dynasty under the name Yuan. Very quickly the country was colonised and the traditional

Real China

Han race were discriminated against both socially and economically, even top scholars were sent to do menial tasks in distant parts of the empire. What did happen though was that the Yuan quickly adopted the Chinese dynastic system. It seems that young Kubla found it hard to overlook the benefits of a system where the country provides several hundred of its prettiest girls strictly for the emperor's sole pleasure.

The Mongols installed their capital in *Dadu*, which is modern day Beijing, and were responsible for some cultural development, introducing music from the west, drama and novels.

Advancement in printing and porcelain continued and they were careful to guard against famine by building a network of granaries throughout the country. At this time, Islam was first introduced into China through interaction with Middle Eastern countries from trade across the silk road. It was around this period that Marco Polo visited China and told his story of life there, to the amazement of the people back home. Contact with the west was encouraged and scientific developments from there were introduced into China such as hydraulic engineering. It enabled the Grand Canal to be completely overhauled and improved. The Yuan also introduced western food crops and their new methods of preparation.

Looking back throughout history at different times and in various places, many regimes have fallen because of internal struggles which weakened them to the point where they could be taken over easily.

Even in modern day politics, the Labour party became virtually un-electable in the eighties due to its internal strife as has happened more recently to the Conservatives. With increasing squabbles, the Yuan became ripe for a takeover.

A peasant and former monk called Zhu Yuan Zhang formed a rebel army initially centred at Nanjing, before moving north, gaining numbers and support as it went. With a lot of death and destruction, detail omitted here, they eventually took Beijing to establish the Ming dynasty. Thus the country had been re-established as Han Chinese and the new Ming dynasty ruled the nation from 1368 until 1644. Not stopping there, the Ming armies also took back a lot of the South-East Asian territories from the Mongols including Vietnam however repeated wars against the Mongols was a feature of their reign, the former powers were never fully defeated.

The early Ming period was particularly well known for its maritime expeditions around the world, it reached its height under the third emperor, Zhu De. It was he who moved the capital from Nanjing to Beijing and built the Forbidden City. Zhu De had an expansionist policy of co-opting nations into what is best described as a kind of commonwealth. There was very little warring and conquering, rather nations joined China through trade, gifts and bribery. Foreign diplomats would be taken to Beijing and lavished with banquets, luxuries and dozens of concubines. The system remains to day only now it is brown envelopes and KTV bars.

Zhu De's most famous explorer was Zheng He (1371-1435), a Ming eunuch who built more than 1600 ships and, many historians believe, discovered America seventy years before Columbus. His fleets are said to have sailed around the world to Europe, Africa, Australia and Asia with ships that were exceptionally large for the times, some were 475 feet long compare that with Columbus' Santa Maria at a mere 75 feet. The problem is that many of the records of Zheng He's achievements were destroyed and so what he really achieved is uncertain. There is though, quite a lot of circumstantial evidence for example Asian-looking tribes in Africa and South America. There are also unexplained wrecks, probably of his fleet, in the Caribbean. Zheng He's exploits are described in the Book *1421: The Year China Discovered the World* by Gavin Menzies. This is quite a remarkable book because Menzies looks at world history through the eyes of a skilled navigator (he is a retired RN Captain) analysing the oceans and their currents. From this perspective he travelled the earth seeking evidence to prove his theory. Since he is effectively re-writing what has been conventional thought for five hundred years, his manuscript has not been received warmly from many historians.

The last recorded voyage of the Ming pioneers seems to be in 1433, after that they suddenly stopped. There is no real reason why this happened, but the school of thought is that the Ming had elevated themselves to what they believed to be a perfect society whereby they no longer needed foreign goods, technology or influence. The National Palace Museum in Taipei, which is far better in every sense to any I have seen on the mainland, guides you through the dynastic and technological history of China and parallels this with that of the west. What is striking is that Chinese technology was way ahead until the mid-fifteenth century when it suddenly stopped whilst the west leapt on to discover electricity, steam and the birth of the industrial revolution. The later Ming and Qing had a lot to answer for.

The Ming were gradually worn down by wars with the Mongols and defending coastal cities from the Japanese until eventually they were defeated by the North Eastern people from what we often call Manchuria, derived from its Japanese name. Today, in Chinese, it is simply called *Dong Bei Qu* (north-east district) and it includes the provinces of Liaoning, Heilongjiang and Jilin. The Manchus, although strictly speaking not Han Chinese, had adopted the customs long before they took Beijing in 1644 to establish the Qing which was to be the last imperial dynasty, lasting until 1911.

The Qing were suspicious of the Han and excluded them from high office, they also prevented inter-marriage and prevented them from migrating to the Manchu homeland. The Chinese peasants were also ordered to grow the long plaited pig-tail which fills our minds as the epitome of this period. The Confucian system of subject and master prevailed. Following the successful subjugation of the Chinese, the Manchus looked beyond their borders and annexed territories such as Tibet, Outer Mongolia and Taiwan. So for the first hundred years or so, their position looked unassailable but their downfall would come from a long way away, principally the new empires of the west, British, French, Russian, American and German.

The final fifty or sixty years of the Qing period is arguably the most interesting because it is the period that was dominated by the Empress Dowager or Ci Xi as the Chinese know her. She started life as a second class concubine but it seems that she won the emperor's heart when it was her first-time turn for a royal rogering. The story goes that she was carried to his bedside by a eunuch, naked, wrapped only in a blanket and laid at the foot of the bed. What goes on behind closed doors is private to the people involved but she must have done something very special to impress her master that night so much so that she immediately became his favourite. Nobody can be sure what she did but it is odds-on that this was China's first blow-job.

She also had the emperor's first son and of course that means she became the mother of the heir, and therefore had special importance and power. Some believe that she actually had a daughter and went out on the streets of Beijing, beyond the walls of the Forbidden City, and swapped her for a boy. The reason behind this supposition is that later in life, when her 'son' (later the Emperor *Tong Zhi)* came of age and could therefore govern independently of his mother, she allegedly poisoned him in order to maintain power for herself.

In fact her life was full of selecting heirs that were very young so that she could always 'guide' them and later, when they reached maturity, she would have them done away with. Whatever you believe, she was a nasty piece of work, surrounded by her eunuchs, she would command the execution of friends and relatives without hesitation. Her stubbornness and desire to hang on to the dynastic way of life and reject technology and modernisation made China a garden of rich pickings for the new foreign powers who came to trade. Chinese historians blame Ci Xi for the collapse and humiliation of dynastic China and the great suffering that came with it.

Throughout the nineteenth century, the Qing protected its traditional way of life, but the population was now growing, it had reached more than 300 million and so work and land was badly needed for these people. There was widespread dissatisfaction amongst the population yet to suggest anything other than the imperial way of life, where China was the centre of the world, would amount to heresy and severe punishments would result. Not only were the Chinese now centuries behind in technology but also in their social structures, government and administration. They remained cruel, barbaric and vindictive towards their own people. This time also saw the emergence of new bandit groups such as the Triads from the south and the White Lotus sect from the north.

The Portuguese were the first to establish a foothold in China with their settlement at Macao, they were soon followed by the Spanish, the French and the British.

When these foreign powers came to trade in China, the Qing saw them as their inferiors and expected the visitors to kowtow to the Emperor, which they indignantly refused to do. This was to ignite an already explosive situation from their unwelcome visits.

The Russian were treated better because China needed security on their long northern borders. Generally though, foreign trade was less than agreeable. The Chinese believed that Western products were inferior and had no need of them so they restricted all trade to the port of Guangzhou (Canton) and only through a handful of licensed channels. Despite this Poitiers style approach, trade levels blossomed.

There was now considerable demand for tea, silks and spices in the west and this gave the British especially, a large trade deficit with China and so they looked for exports and turned to opium and raw cotton, exported from British India and imported mostly through Guangzhou.

The Qing had outlawed opium some time ago, but there were always plenty of corrupt officials and illegal traders to allow sales to flourish, they dispatched a commissioner Li Zexu to the south with the task of stopping the trade. Li confiscated opium stocks, detained all the foreign nationals and destroyed twenty thousand chests of illegal British opium. The British soon responded and sent a fleet to attack, the result was what became known as The Opium War and the Chinese were humiliated in defeat, something of a shock as they believed that they were invincible. The Chinese were forced to sign the Treaty of Nanjing, in 1842. The treaty was signed aboard a Royal Navy ship, the Cornwallis and most importantly Hong Kong was ceded to Britain in perpetuity. British citizens were to be allowed to reside, without interference at Guangzhou, Shanghai, Amoy (Xiamen), Ningbo and FuZhou. The Chinese also had to pay six million dollars for the opium that was destroyed and a further three million for unpaid debts. In addition the system of allowing trade though a limited number of channels had to be abolished. British subjects could trade in the designated ports however they wished. Even more humiliating was that the Chinese had to pay the sum of twelve million dollars to cover British expenses during the war. There were other conditions such as the release of all British subjects in detention and of any Chinese who were locked-up for their part in the trade with the foreign powers. To say this was one-sided is an understatement and events like this still linger on in some Chinese minds today, it contributes to their desire to show the world that they are once a more superior race.

The Opium War was not the end of the squabbles, more and more foreigners came to China for a piece of the action.

During the mid-nineteenth century, China's problems were compounded by natural calamities of unprecedented proportions, including droughts, famines, and floods. Government neglect of public works was in part responsible for this and many other disasters, but the self indulgent Qing administration did little to relieve the widespread misery that resulted. South China had been the last area to yield to the Qing conquerors and the first to be exposed to Western

A Quick History

influence. It provided a likely setting for the largest uprising in modern Chinese history - the Taiping Rebellion.

The Taiping rebels were led by *Hong Xiuquan* a village teacher and unsuccessful imperial examination candidate. Hong formulated an ideology combining the ideals of pre-Confucian utopianism with Protestant beliefs. He soon had a following in the thousands who were heavily anti-Qing and anti-establishment. Quickly raising an army he set-off to take over the country. In 1851 Hong Xiuquan's militia launched an uprising in Guizhou Province, where they proclaimed the Heavenly Kingdom of Great Peace (*Taiping Tianguo*) with Hong as the King. The new order was to reconstitute a legendary ancient state in which the peasantry owned and worked the land. They outlawed slavery, concubines, arranged marriage, opium smoking, foot-binding, judicial torture, and the worship of idols. The Taiping weren't just a military threat to Qing stability but their rejection of Confucian morals, which were the backbone of society at that time, citing the potential end of the imperial system. Its advocacy of radical social reforms alienated the Han Chinese scholar-gentry class.

At one stage the Taiping had captured Nanjing and had driven as far north as Tianjin but were driven back having failed to consolidate their positions. Characteristically the movement's leaders found themselves in a net of internal feuds, defections, and corruption. Additionally, British and French forces, being more willing to deal with the weak Qing administration than contend with the uncertainties of a Taiping regime, came to the assistance of the imperial army. Leading the British army at that time was General Gordon the very same who was famously massacred in Khartoum then ruthlessly avenged by Kitchener a decade or so later. Before the Chinese army succeeded in crushing the revolt, however, 14 years had passed, and well over 30 million people had died in the struggle. The Taiping were finally defeated at Nanjing, Hong was captured and of course executed but it did set the scene for other rebellions albeit on a much smaller scale. There came the Nian rebellion in the north, Muslim rebellion in the south and a very powerful Han-race army, based in Hunan, had emerged under general Zeng Guofan. All this was chipping away at the Qing's authority. Our General Gordon became there after popularly known as 'Chinese Gordon.'

The Opium War shocked the Chinese into a limited degree of modernisation. Western technologies were studied, new schools set-up and attempts to adopt foreign means of industrialised production in shipping, for example, were carried out. In the meantime, the Qing had a continual internal conflict, fearing simultaneous dynastic decline. From a few forward thinkers, the *Tongzhi* Restoration was introduced, although named after the Emperor Tongzhi (1862-74), it was really engineered by the young emperor's mother, Ci Xi. The whole system was a farce, allowing a little bit of modernisation here and there but at the same time strengthening the dynasty. This was an example of typical propaganda that carries on today with the present one party state. The government absurdly describes itself as 'democratic with Chinese characteristics'.

At least the penny had dropped that China did need modernising and this 'Self Strengthening Movement' as it became known, tasked a group of scholars and administrators to update communications, transport, agriculture, medicine, the military and education. The ruling Qing had no plans for political changes, as had happened in the west, and so changes were thwarted by bureaucracy and corruption. Because of this, the aftermath of the Taiping and a rigid Confucian order, the movement failed.

For the foreign powers, Russia had the first go at carving up some territory. By the 1850s, they had invaded the Heilong Jiang river valley of Manchuria, having been earlier ejected from there under the Treaty of Nerchinsk. In 1860 Russian diplomats secured the secession of all of Manchuria north of the Heilong River and east of the Wusuli River (Ussuri). After 1860, many more foreign successions took place. There was a whole series of ports up and down the country that were effectively foreign enclaves under which the Qing had no jurisdiction, each port was somewhat menacingly reinforced by warships anchored in the bay. The British had *WeiHa*i, in the North East and the Germans *QingDao*[1] further south. This helps to explain why QingDao beer (TsingTao) is one of the oldest beers in China. It was of course widely copied and now almost every brewery in China makes a gassy yellow liquid they call beer, just like most of Germany.

Whilst all this was going on, foreign powers also started to pick off the surrounding territories which had come under Chinese suzerainty and had been a Qing ego boost. France colonized Cochin China, as southern Vietnam was then called, and by 1864 established a protectorate over Cambodia.

---

[1] Following the murder of two German missionaries in 1897 the Germans occupied all of Shandong province until the beginning of WW1. A sore point at the time since Confucius was born there in 551BC.

Real China

Following a victorious war against China in 1884-85, France also took Annam, which is the central part of Vietnam. Britain gained control over Burma. Russia penetrated into Chinese Turkestan (the modern-day Xinjiang-Uyghur Autonomous Region). Japan, having emerged from its century-and-a-half-long seclusion and having gone through its own modernization movement, defeated China in the war of 1894-95. The Treaty of Shimonoseki forced China to cede Taiwan and the Penghu Islands to Japan, pay a huge indemnity, permit the establishment of Japanese industries in four treaty ports, and recognize Japanese hegemony over Korea. In 1898 the British acquired a ninety-nine-year lease over the so-called New Territories of Kowloon, which increased the size of their Hong Kong colony. There was no real need for Britain to sign a lease at that time, they could simply have added the New Territories to its existing sovereignty over Hong Kong. This oversight meant that in the 1997, the end of the lease saw the loss of Hong Kong as a whole.

Britain, Japan, Russia, Germany, France, and Belgium each gained spheres of influence in China. The United States, which had not acquired any territorial cessions, proposed in 1899 that there be an 'open door' policy in China, whereby all foreign countries would have equal duties and privileges in all treaty ports within and outside the various spheres of influence. All but Russia agreed to the United States overture.

The Chinese were being outclassed and humiliated by superior technology and know-how. In 1898, the young Emperor Guang Xu ordered many changes to the system both socially and institutionally. He had listened to a group of forward thinking scholars who had convinced him that China needed to change and modernise giving the example of its Japanese rival. To enable the innovation and technological progression, institutional changes would have to be put in place. The proposed reforms covered a wide range of areas including a clamp-down on corruption (where have we heard that before?) re-introducing the civil service examination scheme, changes in government structure, legal systems and postal services. Modernisation priorities would be in defence, agriculture, medicine and mining. They even suggested sending students abroad to learn the new technologies.

From the old guard, there was great opposition to these changes, led by Ci Xi, they engineered a coup and took over the government once again. The emperor was confined to the Summer Palace where he died in 1908, believed to have been poisoned by Ci Xi, who famously copped it only one day later, also probably poisoned. Before they debatably got to her, she had six of the advocates of reform executed others escaped by managing to flee the country.

At the turn of the century, an underground movement surfaced, which had clandestine support from the government and known as the Righteous and Harmonious Boxers, (*YiHeQuan*) better known as the Boxer Revolution. This group, yet again, without mercy or compassion, went on the rampage murdering missionaries, Chinese Christians and other foreign-influenced groups. In June 1900 they had sufficient power and numbers to attack the foreign legations in Beijing who had to hold on for weeks under siege from these ferocious barbarians. If the Boxers captured a foreigner, he or she would be subjected to the most excruciatingly painful and slow death. They would be tied up and wounded in several places on the body. The gaping flesh would be left open and untreated. Eventually the injuries would become infected or insects would lay eggs and their larva feed on the lesions until the victim slowly died. Another common method was slow strangulation whereby people would be supported underneath their heads with the feet above the floor. The head then carries the full weight of the body and the neck slowly stretches to the point of asphyxiation over a period of days.

The Qing declared war on the foreign powers who quickly responded, taking Tianjin and marching onto Beijing. Once again, the Qing were humiliated. Under the protocol of 1901 they were ordered to pay reparations and allow access to certain territories for each national group. The execution of ten Boxer leaders was also ordered. During the conflict the British had burned down the Summer Palace since this was dear to Ci Xi (something the Chinese like to remind me of every now and again). Much worse was what the Chinese did to themselves, they completely destroyed their own library of historical manuscripts and artefacts thus thousand of years of historical records in China were lost forever. It would have been like us burning the Anglo-Saxon Chronicles, documents treasured for more than 1500 years.

After this some reforms were put into place and some modernisation along the Japanese role model was followed. Most significantly new armies were formed both centrally and provincially which actually caused severe problems in later decades after the Qing collapsed.

The final implode of more than two millennia of dynastic and imperial traditions though came not from abroad but from within. The striking thing about Chinese history is that looking previously through the centuries, right back to the BC period there are only a handful of Chinese who did anything of note. Qin Shi Huang, the first emperor, Li Bai the drunken poet, Zheng He the amazing explorer and then you finally get to Dr Sun Yat Sen (or Sun Zhongshan in pinyin). Most famous Chinese were notorious rather than glorious; there is no Chaucer or Shakespeare, no Newton or Faraday, no Wellington, Drake or Nelson and certainly no leader that remotely encroaches upon Churchill. Sun is credited with the overthrow of the Qing and forming the Republic of China. His mausoleum is a marble statuette come coffin at the top of a long steep climb at the summit of fresh green hills overlooking the polluted atmosphere above NanJing. It is almost a Chinese pilgrimage to go there, irrespective of whether they come from the mainland or Taiwan.

Sun had spent much time abroad, mostly in Japan, and his ideas rapidly gained popularity at home but especially with the overseas Chinese community. Sun promulgated his "Three Principles of the People" which were nationalism, democracy and livelihood. The nationalism principle was to overthrow the Qing and end the spheres of foreign influence upon the country. Democracy was how Sun described his goal of having an elected republican style government and the third principle was of a socialist ideology. At the time, following the Bolshevik revolution in Russia, socialism was gaining popular support around the world, many scholars were promoting the misquoted Marxist ideals. Sun's new country would follow a similar model.

The republican revolution started on the 10th October 1911 in Wuchang, now a suburb of Wuhan. It quickly spread across the country and after a month or so fifteen of the twenty four provinces had declared independence from the Qing. On the 12th February 1912 the last emperor *Pu Yi*, who was still a boy, abdicated. On March the 10th, *Yuan Shikai,* having done a deal with Sun, and of whom nothing is ever spoken, was sworn in as the first president of the Republic of China, in Beijing.

What followed next was what historians describe as a period of warlordism. Sun did not really achieve the peace and stability that had been promised because the Qing had set up so many provincial armies. The individual governors and generals, often thousands of miles from Beijing, began to flex their muscles for power and to add territory to their sphere of influence. The result was almost three decades of anarchy. Sun died in 1925 and after a bout of infighting was succeeded by Chang Kai Shek (or *Jiang Jieshi* using the pinyin system). Very different to Sun, he also came from Guangzhou, but was a military man who was trained in Russia and used his armed force to sustain his Guomindang government. Chang set up his capital in NanJing and united most of the country although due to warring provincial governors, skirmishes were still commonplace.

Enter Mao Ze Dong (Mao Tse Tung).
Mao was born in the village of ShaoShan, south west of Changsha in south-central Hunan province. He was the son of a farmer and had two younger brothers plus a sister. His father, by the standards of the time, was a well-off peasant and rice farmer who owned more land than normal such that he unusually needed to employ additional labour to work the fields. Mao was close to his Mother but despised his father. Hunan is along way from Beijing and so the demise of the Qing dynasty did not influence their daily lives and his Confucian upbringing continued uninterrupted. He was though keen to become educated and studied hard in as much as anyone could in those times. At the age of 14 his father bought him a wife, six years older as was customary and she

moved into the family home. She was called Miss Luo but Mao rejected the arranged marriage and always claimed that he never slept with her. It is uncertain what happened to Miss Luo, whether she was simply passed on to the next brother or whether she became his father's concubine is uncertain but his mother left several years later so it is easy to draw conclusions. Mao later left for Beijing and worked in a library where he was able to read many political texts. Mao also wrote poetry, supposedly of very high quality but when translated some of the art form is lost.

As time passed, Mao began to develop a political mind, fuelled by the increasing Soviet influence at that time. He edited a daily newspaper in Changsha (the provincial capital of Hunan) and became furious when the governor later censored his reporting and the right to free speech. Mao was to later ruthlessly and hypocritically control the media when he was to rule the country with an iron fist . At that time Hunan was governed feudally by its warlord master, backed with a fairly severe penal system that saw weekly beheadings in the square at Changsha. Mao eventually joined the then socialist Guomindang [1] which had a communist wing, although still led by Chang. Eventually Mao and his colleagues broke away and formed a separate Bolshevik-like group, leading Chang to respond by putting a price on Mao's head.

The period from late twenties to the mid-thirties was a period of guerilla warfare. The Soviets still backed Chang's government and urged Mao to reconciliate but only because they saw the Japanese as the main threat and only a united China could ward them off. At that time, Mao's followers

---

[1] The GuoMinDang or nationalist party continues to exist and is the main opposition in Taiwan.

Real China

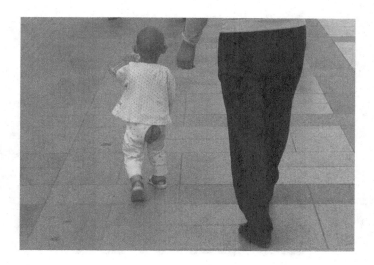

Above: Infant 'muck spreader' pants out for a walk in Beijing (photo B.Lunn). Below: Changchun, power station electrifies, heats and pollutes the city. A typical urban Chinese view.

A Quick History

Above: Mao's "capitalist roader" Deng Xiao Ping, the man who started it all, looks over the city he encouraged to make money on his 1992 Southern Tour (Shenzhen) from the peak of Lotus Mountain Park. Below: A warning to the poor that they will be fined 500Yuan for stealing the rubbish.

Real China

Above: A busy street in Macau such is the worry of fake drugs. Below: A typical market selling Chinese souvenirs can be found in any city.

A Quick History

Above: Shenzhen Garden City, the arrowed buildings on the right are coloured red to frighten away the ghosts. Below: *Jinwei* beer, trying to convince us that it does not contain formaldehyde.

Real China

Above: Luo Hu Commercial centre at the Shenzhen Hong Kong Border, probably the world's biggest fake goods mall. Below: Tiananmen square with Heaven Gate in the distance.

A Quick History

Above: The beautiful Yangshuo scenery, as seen on the 20 Yuan note. Below: Farmers preparing their dinner in the river.

Above: Cormorants used to catch fish on the Li river. Below: The *Qin Shihuang* terracotta soldiers near Xi'an, to date they have not even dug half of them out.

A Quick History

Above: The beautiful *xichong* beach near Shenzhen. Below: The Chinese female, slim petite, curvy and long black hair. It is no surprise that so many foreigners get hooked.

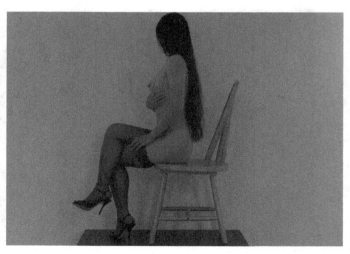

Real China

The traditional *qipao* dress with splits to assist riding a bike

206

numbered a few hundred thousand, mostly poorly armed peasants whereas Chang's army had several million soldiers with the latest fighting hardware. Mao's communists occupied the border areas of Jiangxi, Hunan and Fujian provinces, only attacking where they thought they could win and retreating when they thought they could not. What really emerged for the first time was Mao's skill as a brilliant military general. His vision towards revolution was to mobilize the millions of peasants to overthrow the government and for China to become a free socialist state. He suffered personal tragedy also during these times, Mao's sister Mao Zehong was captured and executed by the Guomindang in 1930, his youngest brother was killed fighting for the communists in Jiangxi just 29 years old and his other brother died fighting warlords later, in 1943.

Eventually Chang's forces with their superior weaponry and numbers were closing in on Mao's communist militia. Somehow, they had to escape and that is exactly what they did in what is famously known as The Long March. The concept was to travel north and meet up with other communist forces therefore standing a better chance of survival and maybe even victory. The Long March was a treacherous journey across some of the most difficult terrain in western China from Jiangxi, through parts of Hunan, Guangdong, Guangxi, Guizhou, Sichuan, Qinghai, Gansu and finally to Sha'anxi. Along the way they suffered frequent attacks and ambushes from Chang's forces. Starvation and exhaustion cost the lives of many. For Mao, the Long March was the time when he emerged as the dominant leader of the communists and this would assure him of the presidency if they were to ever take power. The march took a year to complete, starting in October 1934 and reaching Sha'anxi in the same month of the following year, they had covered an estimate 4,960 miles. There were many defections, deaths and dissentions but they eventually settled in Yannan, north of Xi'an, which became their new base. In Qinghai they met and joined forces with another army leader, who later relinquished his men and power to Mao. The cross-country trek had a devastating effect on the communists' numbers, reducing from an estimated 300,000 right down to less than 40,000.

Bizarrely, in 1936, Chang was captured by the communists on a visit to Xi'an[1] but he was later released, probably the result of pressure from Stalin who wanted a united China to fight the Japanese.

Despite Stalin's wishes, the now highly aggressive Japanese neighbours moved into the northeast, quickly advanced down the country and took the capital, Nanjing, on the 13th December 1937. Chang fled and set up a new base in the west at ChongQing.

At this time, one of the most disgusting acts in the history of mankind took place. In what is now known as the 'Rape of Nanking' (from Iris Chang's famous book) occurred. The Imperial Japanese army went on the rampage, without explanation or justification. It was just widespread murder, rape, carnage and destruction. Estimates of the numbers who died vary but the average is around 300,000, tortured, burned, decapitated in the most horrific way, in under three weeks. The incident remains today a constant source of disagreement and mistrust between Japan and China as one side plays the

---

[1] Known as the Xi'an incident

numbers down and the other plays them up. Whatever the true number, it did happen and it was an atrocity that compares with humanity's worst. Today you can visit the museum in Nanjing, 'Memorial Hall for Compatriot Victims of the Japanese Military's Nanking Massacre'. It is a somber place that tells the story of what happened; it includes photos, poignant statues and mass graves of the victims. It does though end with a message of peace and hope for the future and does not seem to condone retaliation in any way. News stories of the World War 2 holocaust, commonly make the headlines today but in the West the Nanjing story is seldom told.

It is probably a fair point that the Japanese invasion of China fuelled the communist cause as it was they whose numbers now started to increase to fight off the invaders, meanwhile Chang was intransigent. Mao attacked the new enemy with his peasant fighters, using the same guerilla tactics he had used to pick off the Guomingdang's weaker forces earlier. For most of the time the communists had to sit out World War 2 and wait for its conclusion before they were able to re-commence the civil war in 1946.

Following the conclusion of WW2, Mao's army had swollen to millions and he now had the upper hand being just a matter of time before he marched into Beijing. The Peoples Republic of China was declared on October 1st 1949 with Beijing the new capital and Mao as head of state and chairman of the party.

Chang escaped to Taiwan along with his lieutenants, devoted followers and most of the country's wealth including gold. US warships moved into position, preventing the communists from pursuing him there. Chang remained in power in Taiwan until his death in 1975.

Mao had won the war through motivation and enlistment of the peasant masses, rather than through any military technology, frustratingly even when they captured the Guomindang's aircraft, there was nobody to fly them. He was to later tease visiting diplomats that it was the Japanese who really brought him to power as his numbers only rapidly increased in order to fend off the Nippon invaders. The last emperor, Puyi, had been installed as head of Japan's puppet government in Manchuria which was dissolved following their surrender, he later joined the communist party congress in China having an afterwards uneventful life until he died in 1967.

The problem for Mao and his close followers was to rebuild China from war, starvation, destruction and disease. Initially all was well and during the early fifties China had a strong stable government probably for the first time in more than two hundred years. Over time power got the better of him and he experimented with some fairly radical policies that led to great suffering amongst the population including hunger, torture and execution.

The first disaster was in 1959 with the introduction of The Great Leap Forward, the idea was to increase China's steel output beyond that of the UK (a leader at that time) and to dramatically intensify agricultural production, using China's vast supply of cheap labour. Virtually the whole nation became steel producers, building a furnace in their back yard and melting down everything metal. On the farm, ridiculously high and unachievable yield targets were set for rice and other crops. Because most peasants were instructed to make steel, there was no time to grow crops and since nobody wanted to

A Quick History

admit to underperforming and disappoint their masters, remarkably high crop yields were reported, even higher than the daft targets that had been set in the first place. Therefore the government thought all was well and things were going to plan. That was until the winter of 1960 when the country ran out of food. It is estimated that around 40 million died of starvation. Even worse, many growers were murdered for allegedly profiteering from the misfortune through selling food at higher prices elsewhere (a common feature of food shortages that also happened during the French Revolution and the Irish potato famine)

There were other mad-cap schemes, such as the killing of sparrows because they were believed to be eating the crops, people would stand on their rooftops waving white sheets to prevent the birds from landing until they dropped from the sky, dead from exhaustion. It is very noticeable even today how few birds there are in China, the early morning song is seldom heard, hardly surprising since at the time most Chinese did not know the difference between a sparrow and a turkey. Today's over-population was yet another Mao-led policy of encouraging procreation in order to increase the supply of young men to work the land, it did not dawn on him that they needed feeding as well.

The most sinister off all threats though came with the Cultural Revolution, it simply destroyed the country. Earlier, in 1956, Mao had launched the Hundred Flowers campaign where an open forum was set-up for people to openly discuss and, where appropriate, criticize government policy. The pleasantly encouraged dissenters came out of the shadows but were immediately cracked down upon hard. From then on they kept their mouths shut but it was just a sample of what was to come a decade later.

Real China

The Cultural Revolution started in 1966, initiated from a poster on the wall in a Beijing university warning about subversives within. It was picked up by Jiang Qing (Mao's last official wife) and got the Chairman's attention. Very quickly a campaign of inquisition started prompting the formation of the Red Guards who were to root out so-called 'Capitalist Roaders' from the country. It was a period of disaster and chaos as the Red Guard numbers multiplied and lawlessly held their own trials, instant judgment followed by summary execution or imprisonment.

Everybody was expected to carry the 'Little Red Book' listing quotations from Chairman Mao and the leader himself was (self) elevated to God-like status. The vast majority of the victims were innocent, some had even been honoured as martyrs during the war against the Guomindang. It was a time when families turned against each other, children were expected to report on their parents, students on their teachers. Many families were shipped off to rural areas, especially educated folk, to work on farms and in special factories. Millions died, many more were tortured or imprisoned; a whole generation passed without an education. The revolution went on in a chaotic way until late 1969 and then slowly order started to recover with the Cultural Revolution ending with Mao's death in 1976.

During this time, no one was spared suspicion or humiliation. Mao's closest and most trusted allies at the top were also purged. The greatest tragedy was that of Liu Shaoqi, once modeled as Mao's successor he fell out of favour during the Cultural Revolution and was imprisoned a sick man, neglected and died in gaol. Liu's number two, Deng Xiao Ping was shipped off to an engine factory in Jiangxi. The prime minister, Zhou Enlai survived unscathed during the turbulent period.

Some excelled and those who were particularly diligent in carrying out Mao's orders were the so called Gang of Four, Jiang Qing, Wang Hongwen, Yao Wenyuan and Zhang Chunqiao. Following Mao's death in September 1976, the four were arrested and bizarrely blamed totally for the Cultural Revolution. They were tried in 1981, Jiang and Zhang received death sentences that were later commuted to life imprisonment. Wang and Yao were sentenced to twenty years. Jiang Qing killed herself in prison in 1991, Wang died of cancer in 1992, Zhang was released later and died in Shanghai in 2005, Yao was released and died in December of the same year.

When Zou Enlai died in early 1976 there was a public outcry of grief, even today he is held in high esteem amongst the Chinese. He was with Mao from the early days of the communist cause right up until his death. He only survived so long at the top because he almost uniquely never questioned Mao. When Mao died there was not so much grief, maybe people had finally had enough, however his body is preserved in state in the corner of Tiananmen square and today one can file past and pay respects the world's greatest murderer, most Chinese do.

Philip Short's book 'Mao, A Life' is an exhaustive and well balanced biography that covers much more than just his political life. He explains that Mao's responsibility for all the deaths come under three or four distinct periods, the first being in the early thirties, when fighting the GMD government, a series of witch hunts against his own army to root out communist non-believers through torture and murder.

The same thing was repeated at Yannan and then later with ferocity during the Cultural Revolution. The other deaths, by far the most, were due to his starvation causing policies such as the Great Leap Forward. There are wildly differing estimates as to how many actually did die, thirty million on the low side and sixty million on the high. The Guiness Book of Records under its section 'Crime, Mass Killing' puts Mao in first place ahead of Stalin and Hitler in second and third respectively.

It is difficult to understand why through the media of book, television and film we are constantly reminded of only one of the twentieth century horrors, the tragedy of the four million Jews. Why do we hardly ever discuss the Rape of Nanjing, WW2's sacrifice made by twenty four million Russians and Mao's forty million dead Chinese, the time for Spielberg et al, through popular film media, is long overdue in making the world aware of this?

Mao also had a prolific family life. His first marriage to miss Luo was unconsummated but his second to Yang Kaihui resulted in three children; one son died aged four, the eldest Anying died in the Korean war, aged 29 and the daughter Anqing is still alive. Yang herself was beheaded, along with Mao's sister in Changsha, as an act of revenge following Mao's assault on the city.

His third wife, He Zizhen, followed Mao around during the revolutionary decade before the Japanese moved in, even accompanying Mao whilst pregnant on the Long March. They had five children, four of them were either lost, abandoned or died as infants. However, their daughter Li Min survived and is still alive. He Zizhen died in 1984, at the age of 75, astonishing considering what she went through.

A Quick History

Finally the notorious fourth wife, Jiang Qing, only bore one daughter, Li Na, who is still living somewhere in China. After her, Mao had enough of marriage, preferring a bed full of teenagers in his later years rather than any serious commitment. Jiang though remained his 'wife' until Mao's death, although they did not have an intimate relationship for the best part of twenty years. She died, committing suicide in prison in 1991.

After Mao had died, there was a brief power struggle and Deng Xiao Ping emerged as party leader. He quickly showed what Mao had suspected all along that he really *was* a capitalist roader since it is he who started China's graduation from communist hell to the free market economy that it is today. Deng famously went on a southern tour in 1992 where he is supposed to have said that making money is actually a good thing as well as encouraging capitalist practices. He solved food shortages by allowing farmers to sell their excess produce (after selling their allocated quota at fixed price to the government) on the open market. Today China seems to have too much food and wastes a lot of it. He retired towards the end of 1992 and was succeeded by Jiang Zemin. Perhaps justifiably, Deng has been labeled as the man who improved the lives of the most people in the shortest space of time in the history of mankind.

The blot on his copy book was the Tiananmen Square incident of 1989 where thousands of students gathered in June of that year, demanding democracy. Often called the June the 4th Massacre, the demonstrations started peacefully a month earlier, demanding better government accountability and the reduction of corruption. On the 20th May, martial law was declared and on the 2nd and 3rd of June the army moved in. On the 4th, tanks and troops advanced to disperse the protestors, many were killed, either shot or squashed by the tanks. Following this there was widespread persecution of students and their families, even one of my friend's family in Tianjin, sixty miles away, were called upon by the police to check that the then teenage children were not at the rally. The incident drew widespread criticism from around the globe, foreign investment either pulled out or was cancelled and tourism stopped. It took China a decade to recover politically. How many were killed is uncertain, the estimate is between one and seven thousand and definitely thousands more were injured. Although China is today effectively capitalist it still has a one-party dictatorial government with a strong and growing army and powerful police force. Open criticism will still lead perpetrators to torture, gaol or worse.

Taiwan
It is worth taking a quick look at the history of Taiwan since China's claims to the island are not that conclusive. The Portuguese named it Formosa Island meaning beautiful as they sailed by in the sixteenth century. It was not originally occupied by Chinese but by ethnic aboriginal tribes that were first colonized by the Dutch East India Company in 1642. They were later ousted by a Ming warrior Zheng Chenggong in 1662. This was towards the end of the Ming period and later the island was surrendered to the Qing in 1683. By this time, the Han invaders, mostly from Fujian, had mixed with the local aboriginals, intermarried and produced offspring.
In 1887 the Qing formally made Taiwan a separate Chinese province.
Previously, in 1871, a Japanese ship had been wrecked on the southern tip of the island and all its inhabitants were killed.

A Quick History

Japan pushed the Qing government for compensation which was refused on account of Taiwan being outside of their jurisdiction. The Japanese then launched several attacks resulting in much bloodshed. Following the 1894/5 Sino-Japanese war, mostly over Korea, the Qing were heavily defeated and Taiwan was ceded to Japan under the Treaty of Shimonoseki in May 1895. The population of the island rejected this and declared itself a republic but this was quickly put down by their new masters. At the time of the transfer of sovereignty from China to Japan, Taiwan was still about 55 per cent aboriginal in terms of territory. The island became increasingly integrated as part of Japan, with many business, structural and administrative procedures adopted and introduced. Taiwan people had to swear allegiance to the Japanese emperor and learn the language. Even today, Japanese is commonly spoken as a second language, particularly amongst older people. During the 1930s, Taiwan became progressively integrated as part of Japan itself, the governor one *Chen Yi*, although Chinese, was educated in Japan.

The real contention came after the Second World War because during the Cairo Conference in 1943, the intention was declared to hand Taiwan back to the Republic of China (then under Chang Kai Shek's Guomindang government) following Japan's surrender. However, the wording and legitimacy has been questioned and as such many claim that Taiwan need not be ceded to any other nation. The Peoples Republic of China claimed that Taiwan ceased to be a legal entity in 1949 and is part of the PRC. The situation as to Taiwan's true sovereignty was most certainly not clear-cut following Japanese surrender. There are some facts that need to be borne in mind: firstly it was never originally part of

Real China

China; secondly, when it was, it was taken by force and
thirdly it was wholly ceded to Japan by the Chinese in 1895.
Unfortunately today, because China is the great market upon
which future wealth will be based (or so many believe) the
tendency is to brown-nose the PRC government and rubber
stamp the 'One China' philosophy.

After the war, Chen Yi was now reporting to Chang's GMD
government, having returned to Nanjing. What followed
shortly afterwards is known as the 228 incident where an
uprising against the new Chinese government was brutally
suppressed by Chen, who's reputation was now as a highly
corrupt official, with support from the ROC army. It is
believed that Chen's troops executed three to four thousand
people up and down the island. The event is still remembered
today and there is a memorial close to the presidential offices
in the capital Tabei. Interestingly, as rhetoric and hostile
missile positioning from the mainland over 'one China'
intensified following the re-election of pro-independent *Chen
Shuibian*, more than one million Taiwanese participated in a
rally where they joined hands from the north to southern tips
of the island, a distance of some 500 kilometers. It was called
the 228 Hand-in-Hand rally.
Taiwan is still a highly charged issue. Many believe that one
day China will invade, it has not happened previously because
of Taiwan's superior American defence technology and
capability and so the Chinese could not win without suffering
very heavy losses. Today Chinese military spending is at a
level that will reverse the odds, in just a few years. Unusually
for an Asian nation, Taiwan is one of the very few territories
that does not publicise hatred of the Japanese and as a
consequence has excellent relations.

Chapter 11 - Living and Working in China

Whenever somebody makes their first visit or comes to China to work or tour, there is one simple piece of advice that should be heeded; assume that everyone is crooked unless they prove otherwise. Some might say that this is a deeply racist remark but that would be to miss the point completely, it has nothing to do with judging people by their appearance, ancestry or colour the issue is with behaviour.

The Chinese simply have a different set of values that says cheating and defrauding is great, if able to get away with it, and shameful if caught. Discussing this with locals comes with the usual answer, it's a different culture. Again not true, Britain is a multi-cultural society and on the whole the benefits are far greater than the woes but there is a standard set of basic values that we all adhere to, irrespective of race, colour or religious origin. The (mainland) Chinese simply do not have the same beliefs as we do. It took me five or six years of visiting, touring, trading and living to understand this fully, virtually every 'friend' has constantly lied to me and frequently cheated me. As said in the introduction, the aim of this book is to help prepare the new arrival, for this value shock. Jumping off the plane, starting a new job and residing in a thirty storey high-rise is tough enough but doing so in China is nothing less than distressing, no language skills, alien food and looks from the natives like you've just landed from Mars; trying not to look dead amongst a flock of vultures is the name of the game. Never forget, nothing is ever what it first seems.

Real China

China has very sensibly opened its doors to foreign investment. Many foreign companies have put sizeable amounts of cash into manufacturing plants up and down the country, all are household names back in the west. Other organizations, particularly the fashion businesses, source their designer goods from China and sell them at rip-off prices in the high street. The straightforward reason is an endless supply of compliant workers, gladly over-exerting themselves for very long hours. No industrial unrest, strikes or union membership, poor standards of safety, low comfort and non-existent benefits.

When selling into China, over-excited pioneers gasp and jump-in with glee at the market of 1.3 billion people forgetting that 800 million of them could not afford an ice-cream. The great danger and most common mistake is to over-estimate the potential market size and then end up with disappointing sales figures and poor returns on investment.

Government statistics tend to be either conflicting or untrue, take for example the growth figures released in July 2005. The gross domestic product was reported as being $812bn, a year on year growth figure of 9.5%, as reported in the Chinese press with lots of governmental self congratulation. However, at the same time, the investment in fixed assets had risen to $353.7bn with an annual growth figure of 25.4%. No need to be an economist just apply some simple maths, the GDP has grown in round numbers by $70bn in one year, and of that the fixed asset investment had risen by $72bn. Subtracting the fixed assets which includes roads, buildings, infrastructure and so on, from the total growth the economy actually contracted by $2bn. Either the figures are completely wrong or China's economic miracle is mostly achieved through Government spending, not by economic activity.

Living and Working in China

Worth noting that expenditure on fixed assets is just over half the nation's GDP, unheard of anywhere else in the world, so is this wrong or did somebody release the statistics forgetting that one or two readers might be able to use a pocket calculator. The government periodically talks about how the fixed-asset expenditure is too high but based on this data, if it were to be reduced; the economy would probably slip into severe depression. The point to be made is that yes, China is growing like the clappers but *your* market may be a lot smaller market than you might think.

There are many business books on China, how to do business with the Chinese and corporate strategies for the Chinese market and so on, there is no point to cover that kind of ground here, most are written from a CEO's perspective and have little meaning to Joe Average. Much more interesting, and almost universally overlooked, is to go through the day to day stuff of actually surviving in a place like this. Some arrive as an English teacher, others may come for a short term contract and increasingly more expect to settle here long term. Whichever it is to be, at first it will not be easy.
I am able to report on two experiences of moving here, once to set-up a factory and another to set-up a representative office. The business investment rules keep changing and become easier and less expensive with time. The issues with living in China have perpetuated without alteration.

To work legally, a working visa is essential. This really has to be obtained inside China but a tourist or business visa is required to get here in the first place. For many unfortunates who come to teach English, especially in the south where it is easy to hop over the Hong Kong border and renew a tourist visa, the employer will go to great lengths NOT to secure an employment visa. This is because they have to fill out a lot of forms and pay tax on the salaries that they subscribe. Most teachers in Shenzhen, for example, are working illegally. Worryingly, one day there will be a clampdown from the government and these people will probably be deported and receive a heavy fine. It is not really their fault, they would happily get a working visa, if only their employer would legally sponsor them.

The visa procedure changes all the time but the core elements are as follows, assuming first arrival in China is with a non-working visa. The first step is to register with the police, if in a hotel they will do it automatically but if renting an apartment or staying with friends, it is a must. The employer should apply for a work permit for their foreign staff and submit it with a complicated form, a passport copy and a health certificate.

To get the health certificate, the new arrival has to attend a designated hospital and have an examination which takes about three hours passing around the various departments, stopping for a quick check at each one. The medical costs about 400 yuan and a passport sized photo needs to be brought to stick onto the examination details that are filled-in, doctor after doctor. The examination is mostly thorough, in addition to the usual height, weight, pulse rate and blood pressure is a look at the teeth, an eye test, an electrocardiograph, a chest x-ray and a blood test.

All this is to disguise their primary Dracula-like intentions of getting some blood. For what they are really after is a test-tube of the red stuff to check for syphilis, HIV or AIDS. The Chinese interpreted the phrase blood bank a bit too literally. The patient walks up to a glass screened counter, just like the bank or post office, and passes the arm, sleeved rolled-up, through the slot in the glass where a white-coated nurse on the other side stabs deep into the vein and extracts about a quarter pint of blood. She then withdraws her hypodermic weapon, whilst the now injured forearm leaks like a newly discovered oil well. She mops up the spillage, secures with a dressing and presses it firmly against the now very sore limb.

What is best described as the blood pressure stall is a bit of a circus, as the physician pumps up the mercury column, the wide-open door invites a small group of unashamedly curious Chinese outpatients to gape at Johnny Foreigner undergoing the examination. Meanwhile hospital staff walk in and out, the phone rings and tannoy broadcasts interrupt the process continuously. I shudder to think how many turn-up when a female undergoes a cervical smear.

The medical form is four pages long and in addition to the core tests required, has tick boxes for spleen, liver, kidneys, gall bladder, lungs, skin, hair and many more; the doctor ticks most of them after only recording the blood pressure. The hospital is though very clean and the doctors and nurses are well presented but most of the equipment is dated. It was here I found out that this particular hospital is where the health declaration forms, that are filled-in at the border, are checked. This had me a little disconcerted as I had been falsely filling-in these irritating little bits of jobfillers for years, expecting to be told that I must have made a mistake with my passport number as according to their database of health declarations it belongs to Mickey Mouse.

When the work permit is finally granted, they send a little hardback book[1] with name, personal details and photo. This is then taken to the PSB or public security bureau (Mao's Spanish Inquisition) for a searching interview. They ask some very basic questions about education history (anyone like me who did not go to Oxford or Cambridge, in Chinese eyes, must be thoroughly stupid), how many previous visits to China, occupation and what makes you so stark raving mad that you want to live in China. They are then supposed to visit the workplace declared and check that the truth was being told and the business is not a security threat, in my case they never did.

Finally, all these documents are taken down to the visa office and they hand-glue the working visa into what always seems the last blank page in the passport. At the visa office they have a nice little scam going whereby they reject the passport picture that you brought with you, even if David Bailey took it, and charge an exorbitant fee for them to take a new one. The total charge is 700 Yuan or so. The whole process from arrival to legal working status, takes two to three months although there are efforts to simplify and speed everything up, it varies from city to city.

One should not be surprised that they charge tax way before the work permit is received, no doubt taking advice from Gordon Brown. It is mandatory as soon as the job commences, whether or not the work permit is in place, to register at the tax office. The tax level is not that high. To give an example, it would be about fifty pounds per month on an

---

[1] Some cities are now beginning to omit this stage, simply adding the visa page to the passport.

in-country monthly salary of say eight hundred pounds. If caught avoiding tax, the fine will be in the thousands.

Arriving in China in order to set-up an office must be done before the work permit applications are submitted, although they will keep extending a normal visa until that is complete. There is lots of detail on how to do this at the Chinese Embassy website but the simplest method of having a presence in China is to have a representative office, it is inexpensive and easy to accomplish. There are plenty of agents around who will do this for you but they will charge an excessive fee, the government now allows foreign firms to do it themselves. The down side of a representative office is that trading with local companies is not allowed, the money must change hands between the overseas parent and a local company that is authorised to deal with foreign banks and enterprises, unfortunately surprisingly few are. The rep office merely provides pre and post sales support. This kind of set-up is ideal when marketing relatively high value, small quantity equipment. Taxes are paid on the total costs, since there is no local revenue. Employing Chinese staff legally will result in an extra 35% in social costs to be paid directly to the government.

The second method that allows trade with Chinese companies and consumers is to have a wholly owned subsidiary which requires a minimum investment of $100,000 (it keeps changing so please check). There are excellent tax benefits particularly if the business is high tech or a lot of what is manufactured in China will be exported.

The third and most dangerous option is to enter a joint venture with a local Chinese company. It works like this: they have a plant with old technology, inefficient workforce and outdated production methods. The unsuspecting foreigner comes along and invests some money, advises the management and receives shares in the company. In the first place the shares are probably worthless, in order to make the venture worthwhile products manufactured in say Europe would then be transferred to the new (old) factory in China. Financial control under these arrangements is near impossible unless the new foreign investor is allowed to introduce new staff. The new funds simply line the pockets of the local management. There is hardly a successful joint venture in the country, there are so many ways to get burnt and few means to profit from such an arrangement. Big organizations such as Volkswagen started off this way but nowadays have full control. In the early days this was the preferred option but now it is as rare as a Japanese apology.

Even the big multi-nationals get this badly wrong; Pepsi Cola set up a joint venture with Sichuan Radio, Film and Television Industrial Development Company (in itself a bizarre partner to make tooth-rotting brown fizzy drinks) forming Sichuan Pepsi. Very soon the car park was full of Mercedes, the locals were residing in new luxury apartments and gambling trips to the Macao casinos were frequent. Pepsi US blamed Sichuan Pepsi for siphoning off the money by reporting in their financial accounts, an outrageous allocation for advertising. Pepsi US decided to recover some of the losses by hiking the cost of the licensed drink formulae (recipe for cola). The case then went to court of which the outcome is still pending but it seems the venture failed badly, The parts of the transcript that appeared in the newspapers reported Sichuan Pepsi were accused of repeatedly breaking contracts and in their defence claimed that this was inevitable because Pepsi US were spying on them. This translates to me

as "how dare you try to catch us going about our God-given right to pilfer your funds and copy your products."
More recently, the Royal Bank of Scotland has taken a 15% stake in the Bank of China. Why don't they give the money to charity and save themselves the pain they'll go through as their funds bleed away? No doubt the conclusions drawn in the boardroom was "there's 10% per annum growth in China with 1.3 billion people, we gotta be there". Gordon Chang argues convincingly that virtually all Chinese banks are insolvent with bad debts, propped up by central government funds.

Employing Chinese staff is a real bundle of fun; initially I assumed that the desire to work for a foreign enterprise was because of the higher salary, in fact most companies pay the same, remember they have only set-up in the first place because of the cheap labour!
The main reason Chinese think working for an overseas enterprise is so attractive is because of the assumption that it is easy to get some illicit cash. Essentially foreign employers assume that their staff are honest whereas Chinese employers know most of them are potential crooks. For example we employed a new administrator, sweet and innocent looking young woman who came across as naïve yet willing to work hard. She was sent out to get a quote for printing some brochures, the price came back at 10,000 yuan. I asked a friend to get a quote for the same job from the same company, the price was 8,000 yuan. On almost day one she had decided that she had the right to her twenty per cent. She was horrified to find out that we had checked, in the west she would have been fired but in China the replacement would be yet another

crook, possibly even more greedy, so a good bollocking and the knowledge that we were onto her solved the problem.

This kind of thing goes on everyday in China, most western foreign companies, certainly at first, cannot imagine that it happens so extensively. For every transaction, the buyer and seller get something on the side, it is how they operate and how they think. The opportunity is that Western companies innocently bat without gloves and so the chances are they can get away with a lot more, and usually do.

The Beijing office of the Swiss company that I worked for always asked for commission for their 'distributor' on every order. This was a representative office and so the payments for goods sold was directly to Switzerland. The commissions therefore had to be transferred back to Beijing. The locals convinced their Swiss masters that the only method of completing this transaction would be through a private bank account. The straight and humour-less Swiss, being the most naïve nation on earth, complied without question. Some of this money no doubt had to be paid to the customer but the rest, numbering tens of thousands of dollars, was pocketed by their Chinese employees. It used to make me furious, and one of the reasons I left, so much of the UK factory margin for which I received frequent complaints for being too low, was being illegally frittered away by our own Chinese employees.

Hiring a female can be a real eye opener, for a start they know that if they are pretty they have a better chance to get the job, hence their CV always arrives with a sexy or arty photograph. On the day of the interview, even if good looking, the attire will be inappropriate, jeans, mis-matching outfits and never a suit. There will have been no research about the job, very little knowledge of what she wants to do just a straight focus on the remuneration, despite this most of the girls do have college degrees, otherwise they would be cleaners, waitresses or even pretty KTV hostesses.

Questions are almost always answered with a yes or no and if you try to be clever by saying something like, 'tell me about your last job' there will either be a long silence or 'I was a secretary'. One girl told me the reason that she wanted to work for a foreign company was in order to have an easy life! Another, who desperately wanted to be a *xiao mi* (the Chinese euphemism for a secretary that sleeps with the boss for small favours such as luxury travel, nice hotels and a new wardrobe) made it quite obvious that was her intention. 'I think I am very good at traveling with the boss and making the business trip relaxing and without the stress' looking me straight in the eye so that I was under no illusion as to the real meaning.

When hiring technical people, never believe the CV, it is best to set an exam to test what they really know. Even PhDs, if genuine, are not the result of independent research but more parrot fashion learning. Besides their certificate is probably fake just like the thousands of companies that advertise ISO 9000 certification. There is a man at the end of our road, who cooks roast lamb skewers from a wheelbarrow; he has a sign that says "ISO 9000 Approved".

It has to be understood that setting a time for an interview is a vague target, the candidate will either turn-up late, won't turn up at all (no phone call to apologize) or, more rarely, make an appearance hour early. Sometimes it is a day late and the excuse will be "the job I really wanted, I didn't get so I came here today instead". But then no different to booking a Cornish plumber, he will arrive a day late and feel that the desperate customer, with no central heating, should be grateful he came at all.

Whoever the employee is, it must be understood that they will operate not in the way that would normally be anticipated, but in a way that can benefit them personally. They are not interested in long term gain, only short term cash; they do not want a career, have no loyalty and will jump to the next job for 50 yuan more per week, without hesitation. Having said that, the jobs market is not good so currently the employer has most of the power.

Chinese employers treat their staff with similar contempt and justly most do not deserve any loyalty. A friend of mine worked in China on a six-month fashion design contract, she was shocked at how the workers slave at the factory from nine in the morning until eight at night with a only brief lunch break. The place is *literally* a sweatshop because no air conditioning is provided in the south's long sticky and humid summer. The workers get no holiday pay, no sick benefits and no overtime. If extra production is needed, they must work longer hours, if they don't they get fired. After three months, my friend was asked to hand over her passport as they wanted to extend her work permit for a year, in actual fact they cancelled it, having got enough of her creative designs, and she had to leave the country in ten days.

As I travel into work on the bus each morning, as do millions of other people in each city, everyday, it is difficult not to notice that seldom will I see somebody under forty, in fact under thirty seems rare. OK, it is fair to say that professional people are now more likely to drive to work, but the startling hard fact is that most people over forty do not have a job. What they do during the day and where they go is hard to tell. There is no unemployment benefit, somewhere time is passing them by, cast aside because of age and appearance rather than capability. The official line of unemployment at only 5 per cent cannot be remotely correct, it must be nearer thirty, the true statistic could be so shocking as to threaten the very existence of the ruling party.

People hang around outside of my apartment building and every other city dwelling, every morning, looking for casual jobs, others sort through the rubbish. When hiring casual staff they do everything possible to look busy yet not to finish the work. Perhaps understandable because when they do, they know they are out of job.

Glancing over CVs, it seems hard to believe that the typical ambition of a graduate female, with a university degree, is to be a secretary. Few companies invest in training schemes for their employees. Graduates do not embark on an accelerated career path, it simply means that a university degree assures them of a job in a reasonable environment rather than building high rise apartment blocks, going down coal mines or cleaning the streets. What China needs (as well as the UK) are colleges that train skilled workers and craftsmen, bricklayers, carpenters, electricians, plumbers and so on. In that way the nation has a valuable resource and the people involved can earn a decent income and work at something they enjoy and that is within their capabilities.

If you are a company that sells products in China through distributors or agents and have no presence in the country yourself, then it can become very difficult. In China education is weak, knowledge is poor but when they have information, they have power and so guard it carefully. That means that when a question is asked, the response will be a pack of lies, requesting a business forecast is not worth the effort, that means commitment and embarrassment if they get it wrong.

Real China

They will always report that the customer is very greedy and wants lots of what they call 'under the table money', this is the number one method to cajole the foreign principle into paying even more commission. It will never go to the customer, they always negotiate this to a minimum.

When you visit though, they will treat you like a king, nice restaurants, KTV bars and sometimes a free shag but beware, entertaining is one of the few skills they have. The overwhelming majority of potential customers will be happy to allow eager suppliers to entertain them without the slightest intention of buying. They offer warm invitations to come and present products in order to receive lavish treatment and luxury extras that they can hardly afford. Others will be intent solely on stealing designs and ideas then give it their mates to deliver on the cheap. A French architect I know suffers greatly from this kind of skullduggery. In order to get a contract, he must offer conceptual designs of buildings and gardens. Despite agreements and warnings, his creations get passed on to third rate local contractor to realize the conception.

One customer I had the displeasure to deal with in Xi'an, a certain Mr Tong, was a master at milking suppliers for all they were worth. He agreed an order with us for two million US dollars but delayed signing the contract for almost one year. He just turned-up once a fortnight with some excuse for a meeting so that he could continue his leisure activity that he knew would stop once the contract was signed, my employer seemed to be financing his sex life. That was bad enough but what made it ten times worse was that he had privately done a deal with our own Chinese employee in the Beijing office who kept the whole thing perpetuating.

Tim Clissold in his recent, almost incredible book *Mr China*, describes a catalogue of situations where he lost millions of investors' money through dealing with corrupt local joint ventures and outright crooks masquerading as businessmen. The stories range from managers who won't be fired, through others who copy and set-up competitive enterprises down the road to daylight robbers who abscond overseas with the cash.

The customers also have no idea of basic manners and decency, not giving a damn how they mess their suppliers around. I went to a bid-meeting for a tender that we had proposed to a Nanchang based organization called Hongdu Aviation. They decided to hold the meeting in tropical beachside Sanya on Hainan Island. It was during the weekend and I flew down there with my briefcase, proposal and sun cream. I arrived for the presentation in the hotel at the invited time, correct room and date yet felt very uneasy, wondering why the room was empty. A few minutes later, a nervously stuttering young girl eased her head around the door and told me that the meeting had been postponed because they (the customer) wanted to watch football on the telly!

Formal meeting rooms all follow the same design; normally there is a very large and wide highly polished table, enough seating for maybe 12 to 20 people. The middle of the table has a trough which is filled with plants and flowers such that the people opposite are obscured. Not unlike peering around foliage in the jungle to see who is speaking at any particular time.

Tenders are a farce in general, I once received a tender from a Guangdong company and saw that it was word for word written around a competitor's products so, knowing we had very little chance other than to make an offer that could not be refused, the bid price I put in was very low. At the meeting where the various sealed offers were opened, (one company arrived twenty seconds late and was disqualified) the prices of the three bidders were chalked on the board. Now, the international (as in everywhere except China) concept of a tender is that the cheapest bidder, who complies with the requirements, should be awarded the contract.

In this case they disingenuously stated that no company was compliant and would not be drawn to explain their reasoning. Because of this, they said, they wanted all bidders to make a new offer. Of course it was just a trick to give the company that they really wanted to buy from, (and receive their pre-agreed kickbacks) a second chance to win the bid. As it happened, we got the business because the preferred supplier could not lower his price *and* be able to afford customer commissions. Ultimately we won the contract and did not need to stuff some brown envelopes.

If you do want to sell products in China, do not bother if you have a lot of international competition because the final price you sell at will make it near impossible to make money. With a unique product you can make serious money.

Be careful with the military too, the EU and USA have an arms embargo on China and that includes so called dual-use technology. If you meet customers in a hotel and they do not give name cards then almost certainly it is a military end user.

Somewhere to Live
There are many reasons to find a home, a short-term job or contract, a teaching position, setting up a new factory or transfer from another office. Finding a home can be stressful, time consuming and bewildering although there is a large stock of rented places to choose from. If you work for a large

multi-national, probably best to skip this bit as the Personnel, or pretentiously named Human Resource department, does everything required, just falling short of wiping your arse. For the rest of us, finding an abode is a pain in the aforementioned noun.

The Chinese character for home is 家, pronounced jiā, which comprises two parts, the little bit on the top depicts a roof and the larger part underneath is a pig, nothing was ever created more apt it's a pigsty! That is exactly what most houses are. The vast majority of city folk live in an apartment, within a tower block, grouped in fours or fives with usually five or six flats on each of its twenty to thirty floors. So on an average of three people per dwelling, a typical apartment complex will house two thousand or so people.

It is almost inevitable that a house rental is organised through an agent. These people make UK estate agents look like Salvation Army workers. They always want to palm you off with what they want to dispose of not what you want. They will at first invite you to view some dustbin that would be unfit for a dog. They then do this continuously until the point where you get so pissed-off you give-up and walk away then suddenly hey-presto! They wants to show something habitable.

The problem is that unless the Chinese can afford a cleaner or a house maid, they just don't bother to clean. The layers of dust, dirty toilets and a disgusting kitchen come as a shock and not something that can be imagined at home. The best option is to rent a brand new one which at least will have a clean kitchen and bathroom.

The kitchens are always very small, older ones have grease smears and splashes all up the walls, your shoes will stick to the floor and as you move across the tiny space, cockroaches will dart for cover under the fridge. The kitchen units are much lower than we would be used to, the sink is an ideal height to piss in but gives a severe backache when it's time to wash-up (dishwashers are unheard of). The cooker will have one or two burners, almost always gas, and no oven; ovens are rare many people confuse them with UV sterilisers that are sometimes fitted beneath the hob. Gas is cheap, electricity is expensive so virtually all kitchens are equipped for the former. Even the water heater will be gas and often only in the shower, the kitchen commonly has only cold water. The fridge will be filthy if not new, months of decaying food stuck to every groove and orifice it is no wonder that they have problems with cockroaches. Cockroach beetles are in fact a serious problem, they get everywhere, they seem to be pretty smart too, only coming out when it is dark and dashing for cover when the light is switched on. In Shenzhen, they have big ones, up to two inches long that fly and land on you! Part of the problem is the lack of hygiene and inability to clean the kitchen, that compounded with an awful lot of people in a small space. Some Chinese are so sloppy they cannot be bothered to use the dustbin and just throw their waste food out of the window of their twentieth floor (or whatever) apartment. The issue with this is that bits of food and other domestic degradables get lodged on various surfaces and ledges as they make their way south, creating a nice little food store and breeding ground for the dreaded bugs.

The drains smell no matter how much bleach gets squirted down there, mostly because of the lack of plumbing skills, if one peers beneath any sink or waste device, the absence of an S-bend to isolate the drain smells from the plug hole immediately explains the awful pong.

There is usually no space for a washing machine in the kitchen so this lives on the balcony where the washing is also hung out to dry. Domestically made washing machines are cold-fill only and they do not heat the water. To compensate for this, detergents are loaded with bleach, greatly shortening the life of the average designer-filled wardrobe; it is a good idea to hand-wash valuable items.

If the toilet is not new, it will never have been cleaned, although generally the bathrooms are not *too* bad. It is best to keep the bathroom window open because the water heater may not have been well serviced and carbon monoxide poisoning is common, along with the occasional explosion. With the window open your neighbour may delight in the odd glimpse of your bare bum, but at least you live. I like to give them a full frontal, it's nice to make my Asian hosts a little envious. Bedrooms are simple, usually wooden floored, as carpets are uncommon. The bed itself will be larger than you might expect but hard, and I don't just mean firm I mean like concrete. Most apartments will have air conditioners fitted but if you live in the south there will not be any heaters, even though early December until mid-March you need them as apartments are poorly insulated and the temperature can drop to five or six degrees at night.

A rented apartment, almost always furnished, is likely to be reasonably well equipped with a TV, DVD, Microwave and other comforts. You'll need to buy all your soft furnishings, a water machine plus kitchen crockery, cutlery and cooking utensils unless some kind Westerner was there before and left some behind but even if he did, the landlord is likely to have kept it for himself.

It is normal to sign for a one year rental contract although you may be able to negotiate six months at slightly higher cost.

Real China

You will need to pay two months rent as deposit which may need a bit of a fight to get back, plus you normally pay half the agents fees, the landlord pays the remainder.

The buildings themselves are fine when they are new but the quality of construction is so poor that they soon look tired and shabby after just a few years. These towers go up very quickly, essentially a steel frame covered in concrete, as such few rooms have load bearing walls, so the first thing that happens when anyone moves into a second hand, or sometimes new, apartment is the internal walls all get hammered down. Since at least one apartment, in any given tower, changes hands each month and noise transmits through the structure unimpeded, peace and quiet is a remote possibility.

One of the biggest issues will be the lift, usually there aren't enough, often very slow and annoyingly other people maybe running businesses from the building such that they jam the thing with their home-manufactured, usually copied, produce.

Apartment living at the best of times is tough but with the Chinese it can be a nightmare. As stated above when people move in, the first thing they do is knock the walls down and re-arrange it to their own tastes, but they don't wait until you are out to work, shit no, they wait until you go to bed! Or so it seems. Constant banging, anytime of the day or night, maybe they are all frustrated drummers or maybe they need the re-assuring sound of a hammer but it will drive you nuts. The neighbour will without doubt have a karaoke machine at home, and when he gets a few friends around to play, he will open the door and turn up the sound level just so *you* can enjoy him singing too. You could of course opt for one of the plush Western compounds which have no Chinese, only expatriate families from the Western or Antipodean world but they cost three or four times as much, running into several thousand US dollars per month.

China is also exceptionally dusty, it is horrifying at how quickly the house gets coated in grime, not a little but in terms of a millimetre or so and it only takes just a few days, worse still we have to breathe it. The cause is a mixture, it could be due to the construction around the place, high levels of pollutant suspended particles or it could be the lack of rain to wash it all away. In Shanghai, if we left the apartment widows open, the white net curtains would become black in just a day or two. Going away for a couple of weeks vacation in the summer, leaves the apartment at the mercy of the high humidity and means that you return to a wardrobe full of mouldy clothes and shoes. Since carpets are not so common in homes, vacuum cleaners are naturally rare so the daily cleaning ritual is like going back to the old days using simply a mop and brush.

Security is usually and necessarily very good in Chinese apartment buildings, most apartments have two entrance doors, an inner wooden covered double locking steel door and an outer Alcatraz prison type steel bar door, with ornate Chinese characteristics. There will be guards at the entrance 24 hours per day with either key or smartcard entry, CCTV in the lifts and for visitors there will be a video phone to your home from the lobby area. All this makes it very difficult to inconspicuously sneak a dolly bird home when the wife is out of town.

Some foreigners actually buy their apartment but I would suggest it is an extremely risky thing to do. You need to look at the contract very carefully and that means employing a bilingual lawyer who is not in bed with the builder – a tall order. It is true that prices are rising in China, they have even introduced a capital gains tax to prevent speculation, but the locals like to buy a new house, not an old one so they are difficult to sell at a profit as the value reduces with age, not increases like the UK and other western countries. The other issue is that there is no such thing as freehold, the government owns all the land, you lease it for seventy five years or less. If at some stage the government does decide to knock your building down and build yet another six lane highway, too bad, they won't consult the owners, just go ahead and do it, paying whatever compensation *they* decide.

The prime example of this is the Three Gorges Dam, on the Chang Jiang (Yangtze River) downstream from Chongqing in one of the most beautiful scenic areas of China, they decided to build the biggest hydro electric power station on earth. It involves building a dam which in turn means flooding the valley. Around 1.1 million people have had to be compulsorily re-housed, that's like moving Birmingham! No public consultation, no enquiry, no environmental impact assessment. Once the government decides, it happens without delay.

Apartments come unfinished, that is bare concrete walls, no plumbing, no electrics and no kitchen or bathroom so it is necessary to budget the extra perhaps even double to kit it out. If you buy a duplex apartment you don't even get the stairs! The banks will eagerly lend 80% of the value at about 5.5% interest so financing it is not a problem. You really do need to know what you are doing though, consider that you buy a nice place on the 24th floor with grand views over the city, admiring the lights at night, then one day the lift fails, the contract has no provision for long term maintenance and your neighbours refuse to cough-up their share of the repair costs? Those on the lower floors will probably suffer some inconvenience and use the stairs rather than shell out for elevator repairs.

The Bank
The banks are not easy to deal with, they have complicated rules and regulations tied to a totally inflexible approach that creates some of the most irritating bureaucracy imaginable.
On the other hand, opening an account is surprisingly easy, you simply need an address (it can be your work or even somebody else's), a phone number (this also need not be yours and could be a pay as you go mobile) and your passport. You fill out a form and receive a bank card on the spot. Pin numbers are six digit not four as elsewhere and it is impossible to go overdrawn, the bank won't allow it.
Transferring money from overseas is simple, it follows international banking laws but if for example you transfer two thousand pounds from the UK to China, it will stay in your Chinese bank account as pounds. To convert it to local currency, it is necessary to go to the bank and fill out a form, even though you are registered there, show your passport and so on. After about one hour, the foreign currency will be converted to Yuan and you may make a withdrawal. Chinese bank cards are now accepted all over the country for direct payment of goods and services but in most cases not for air tickets. UK banks charge a lot of money to transfer funds to a foreign account, in the order of twenty five pounds. There are other cheaper methods such as *Western Union* or *Moneybookers*, with the latter, the transfer took much longer than promised and after a long period of ignoring my complaint, I referred the case to the Financial Ombudsman and was awarded compensation.

Real China

The first Chinese bank account that I opened was in 2001, it was at the branch of the Guangdong Development bank in Shanghai, it sticks in my mind because in order to transfer money to another account (to pay my rent) I had to withdraw the cash then go to a different counter and pay the money into my landlord's account, even though we both held bank accounts at the same branch. Things have changed in that short time, today internet banking is quite straightforward, but again you need to fill out yet another form and show the passport. Some banks have not figured out that foreigners might use internet banking, so often the space to fill in the name is only big enough for three characters. If your are a bit of a toff with several patronymics and a double-barrel surname forget it! The internet banking though is currently only in Chinese script so if you cannot read this then it will be very difficult to use. In the past year or so, new ATMs have been rolled out with both languages displayed, and can be used for deposits and withdrawals.

The Chinese still have a great love of cash which becomes evident sitting in the bank, waiting for your number to be called just like at the supermarket delicatessen, and watch the constant stream of people come in and out with briefcases overloaded with 100 yuan notes. Small electronic machines that count notes are readily available and many people have them at home. The love of cash also keeps the tax man away and is an essential part of giving or receiving bribes.

Business banking is extremely rigid, the government restricts how much cash you can take from your business account in any one month, simply to cut down on the number of cash transactions as tax departments have direct access to business and probably private bank accounts.

All banks offer the same kind of service so it makes little sense to shop around, interest is less than one half per cent and as a foreigner, if you want a credit card, you'll need to fund a large deposit or own property in order to use it.

Hospitals
I am not too qualified to comment here, as I have only been for my 'foreigner compulsory medical' but most people tell me they are not great institutions. The quality varies greatly from establishment to establishment, depending upon funding, staff levels, service and its geographical location. The best hospitals are in Beijing and Shanghai, they become poorer and poorer the further away from the large urban centres you get.
Most Chinese people worry about their medical care too, some travel from all over the country, just to see a Beijing consultant. The system works that they queue the day before they want the appointment and buy a ticket for around ten yuan to see the doctor the following day. The trouble is that the system is abused, many touts simply line-up to get tickets, then sell them on to peasants for one hundred yuan a time.
There has been a recent explosion of medical services on offer, particularly cosmetic. The usual face lifts, boob jobs and magical treatments that defy science. There are strange potent drugs that have the same effect as colonic irrigation, the TV advert shows a cartoon of little workmen inside the colon chipping away at what looks like brown rocks (instead of old turds) with a pneumatic drill. They always show the product being endorsed by what they say is a Western doctor, switching the camera to a bald bloke in white coat, to add credibility.

In January 2006 there was a big fuss over a hospital in Jiangsu which the government closed because nine out of ten cataract patients eventually had to have their eyeball removed.

Reports of people still becoming infected with HIV from blood transfusions are widespread.

Dentists vary from good and expensive to crude. Some have the latest machines and instruments from the likes of Siemens, others have pre-war yellowed and rusty hardware. In many cities, dentists are often in the high street and have a shop window front that same as any common store. Passers-by with nothing better to do stop and stare at some poor devil being worked on. In many respects they are no different to our miserable system whereby the dentist likes to inform you that fillings you've had for years and give no trouble, need replacing.

The thing to remember though is that all medical and dental treatment has to be paid for on the spot, including drugs, nothing is free.

Take the Weather with You

It is worth mentioning the weather in China because it is horrible! There are brief periods of comfortable warm weather but essentially there are pollution compounded long cold winters, a month of spring as we know it, baking hot summers and a brief autumn.

The winter is very dry with hardly any rain in the north and central areas accompanied by a lot of very cold temperatures. Mid-day in Beijing will be below freezing whereas in the far north such as Haerbin, temperatures of minus thirty are common, it is so cold that the air actually hurts the face when out and about, the nose becomes very stiff and uncomfortable as the moisture inside freezes. The ground becomes compacted ice and cars drive noisily and manoeuvre over what seems to be a complete city of speed bumps. In the far north-east it stays below freezing from October through to March but many cities including Changchun and especially Haerbin use the opportunity to boost tourism by displaying huge ice sculptures. They are made from ice bricks, some look like the CS Lewis' Snow Queen castle in Narnia and many have lights inside the ice so the whole display is quite spectacular after dark, when the temperature has, of course, dropped even ten degrees further.

The North West, Beijing and much of surrounding Hebei province suffer from the most appalling sand storms, where visibility drops to a few yards and it becomes dangerous to walk the streets. The sandstorms have been caused by decades of soil erosion due to over cultivation in the great northern plains of Inner-Mongolia and deforestation in Qinghai. Farmers have removed virtually all of the trees in favour of marketable crops but at the same time they took away the resistance to the wind that drives the sand particles east during the winter gales. Each year these sand storms have become worse and very dangerous to go out in them.

Northern buildings tend to be well heated so it is comfortable to remain inside. Because the winter is so dry, and windy days are not commonplace like they are back home, the pollution hangs around and builds up to such high levels that buildings across the street become grey silhouettes. Atmospheric inversion is common where the pollution is trapped by a layer of warm air above the ground level cold air, breathing feels uncomfortable.

Real China

In the south, the winter is brief and not very severe, the lowest temperature maybe five degrees in Guangdong but southern buildings seldom have any heating, compounded by very poor insulation, they become freezing cold to work in. Nanchang, the Jiangxi capital, has a brand new airport with no heating, causing instant haemorrhoids as you plonk your bum onto the shiny steel seating. In Shanghai, most hotels will not turn the heating on until December. The winter in the South only lasts from December through to early March and seems to be at its worst during the Chinese New Year holiday. Few people buy heaters, they just sit at home in their overcoats. Several people have told me that they don't take a shower in the winter as it is too cold! During this time I tend to leave a space of a few yards between us. The south retains it's humidity during the winter, the bathroom will still be wet at night from the morning shower and I have seen, this is absolutely true, a cloud in my living room.

During the summer, the temperature reaches a searing heat, Beijing and much of the central area of China suffers from temperatures in the low forties Celsius. Again, without a day or two of rain, the pollution quickly builds and reduces visibility. In the south, it is not so hot, maybe thirty five degrees maximum but the humidity becomes the problem. A short five minute walk and your clothes will be saturated, sit in a chair and feel your legs, bottom and back stick to the surfaces and moisten your clothes. At home you rush for the shower, removing your shirt which is wet across the shoulders, sticking to the moist skin as you peel it off. The waistband of your trousers or skirt will certainly be moist as it makes close contact with the body, underwear has absorbed sweat from between the legs. The whole day feels uncomfortable and the air conditioning systems are set quite high simply because

246

China's power system cannot cope with the demand. It is distinctly noticeable how, as you cross the border from Shenzhen to Hong Kong, the temperature indoors drops a few degrees on the Hong Kong side.

As many people long for the warmer climate of the Mediterranean, the summer heat in China is not the slightest bit as desirable. Personally I like our cold, damp British weather, in the winter you can always wear warm clothes to keep cosy but in the blistering heat and humidity it is impossible to keep cool, you would still sweat buckets even if you were to sit around stark naked.

Most Chinese people do not use their air conditioning except in the most extreme weather, they open all the windows and sit in their lounge in great discomfort as the moisture bubbles to the surface of the body like squeezing a wet sponge. Failing that, they go to a shopping centre from the time they finish work until they get kicked out, sitting around in the cooled air. Electricity is expensive, not much cheaper than the UK so people tend not to use energy hungry air conditioners, they buy a fan and sit next to it on full blast, blows the pollution even further up the nose.

The summer also gives rise to the most spectacular thunderstorms, I often watch in amazement from the twenty fourth floor of my apartment block as the storm approaches and every few seconds a streak of lightning comes down and strikes each tower block in turn. It is like something out of Star Wars, as if a spaceship were above the clouds, repeatedly zapping targets on the ground. With the thunder and lightning comes torrential rainstorms leading to roads that turn to rivers within a few minutes and widespread flooding. Floods are a serious problem all over China when the heavy rains come in June and July, the lower levels of the huge arterial rivers become reservoirs as the water runs down from the western mountainous regions. In the baking Chinese summer, the heat and humidity cannot be escaped.

After living in China, I will never, ever complain about the weather back home again. I miss the crisp green vegetation, the clarity of the atmosphere, the fresh feeling of the wind, the lunchtime beer garden at the local pub, the smell of the rain, hailstones stinging the ears, wearing a coat in August; weather just doesn't get any better!

Getting Married

It could happen that if you come here for a while, you just might meet someone, fall in love and want to get married. There will be no shortage of slim young beauties, with soft skin, sweet smiles and a near desperate desire to wed you. Like everything else in this great nation, marriage is easily done but you need to follow some basic procedures and spend some money. There are some very strange ideas and beliefs about the steps that have to be taken so it is worth putting a few lines here to give an idea of how it works. If you plan to marry in China, to a Chinese national then you need to have stayed in China twenty one days prior to the marriage. When you arrive you must register with the British Consulate who will ask you to swear an affidavit, just like back home, that you can legally marry. The notice is displayed at the consulate for twenty one days before a Certificate of No Impediment is issued in both English and Chinese. The Consulate, always onto a nice little earner, will charge you more than 1000 yuan for this. You can then, following a medical exam to check that you and your Chinese bride are not into incest (more money) and finally apply for a marriage certificate with the Chinese authorities. There is no ceremony, you just fill in a form. The marriage certificate will be in Chinese but you can get an authenticated translation, that is legal in the UK, at the British Consulate, to which they delight in charging some more of your hard-earned cash. If you get married in the UK then your fiancée, if divorced, will need a certified translation of the divorce certificate. If you want your new spouse to settle with you in the UK then you need to apply for a settlement visa, serious money to the Consulate now, more than 2,000 Yuan but check it goes up faster than house prices. For a fiancée this will be valid for six months, (working is not permitted) within which time you should get married. Following marriage, whether or not a fiancée visa was applied for, a twelve month visa will be issued which allows employment and then, after the expiry of this, permanent right to residence will be granted. UK citizenship can be applied for after three years from the date of legally entering the UK provided your spouse has spent a certain amount of time in the UK during this period, not robbed any banks or cheated the taxman and can pass an English language test. The rules are very clearly laid out and the Foreign Office makes it very unambiguous what documents they need; if you have the right ones, the procedure is straightforward, non-judgemental and fair. Once in the UK, your new Chinese partner will have to apply for visas at the Home Office in Croydon, again the procedures are clear, fair, efficient and well administered. They do exactly what they say they will do in their documentation. It is very important though that you always check the websites of the Foreign Office and Home Office before applying (www.fco.gov.uk and www.homeoffice.gov.uk respectively) because the rules, forms and fees change regularly (upwards).

When you apply for a settlement visa for your fiancée in China, at the British Consulate, (there are four of these, Beijing, Shanghai, Guangzhou and Chongqing) it is likely that you will have a lengthy interview. They are trying to check if you really are an intimate couple and whether or not there is some kind of financial arrangement and the marriage is only to enable passage to the UK. So you have to provide evidence of the relationship such as phone calls, letters or emails. It is likely in any normal relationship that anything written may be somewhat personal, intimate or even explicit but that will only help your case not harm it. The Consulate will carefully check everything out so approval for the visa can take up to three months.

Looking at it the other way, marriage to a Chinese national does not give you automatic right to abode in China and there is no such thing as a marriage or fiancée visa in China. Also, if your partner actually takes out British citizenship then he or she must give up their status as a Chinese citizen and apply for a visa to visit their own country. I get sick of hearing complaints about British immigration rules and regulations but the truth is that our system is clear, unbiased, non-racial and probably the fairest in the world.

Health
The American composer Eubie Blake, when he reached the age of 100 said 'If I'd known I was going to live this long, I would have taken better care of myself'. Somebody else said that 'money is the most envied but least enjoyed, health is the most enjoyed but least envied'.

Living and Working in China

There is a good point to be made here that looking after yourself and staying in good health should be the number one priority, even though the reason to live in China may be to make money and have a good time. China is full of health hazards, far more than we have back home so it follows that special care is taken.

The Chinese themselves do not seem to worry too much about their health, they only talk about money and the character for good fortune 福(fú) is displayed in almost every public place, you will never see the sign for health 健康(jiàn kāng)! It is generally accepted that they eat far too much, even dangerous, levels of salt, oil and saturated fats. Smoking and its associated diseases are at near epidemic proportions as are diabetes and stroke, the main killer. This does not seem to bother them too much. However they do get scared when there are some well publicised disease outbreaks such as SARS, when they were frightened to leave the house. Once, after my regular Saturday morning session of teaching English to a friend's twelve year old daughter, I asked her if she would like to have some lunch in KFC, just across the road. Normally KFC or McDonalds is a real treat to most kids in China but this time she stared at me for a while, brewed a worryingly stern expression and said 'No, I am afraid of Sudan 1'. (A health scare on a chilli powder additive that made the headlines in 2005)

The first danger, as you will tend to have three meals per day, is that you cannot assume that restaurants are clean. In addition, Chinese eating habits are such that several people share the same food, probing in and out with their chopsticks so that germs and bugs are easily spread. Hong Kong television, almost every night, advises people to use serving chopsticks or spoons, that is you use one pair to pick up the food and put it on your plate and another pair to put it into your mouth. This is extremely good advice. In Japan it is extremely bad manners to allow the chopsticks to touch your mouth, not so in China.

Sea-food is common in China and widely enjoyed yet they have some of the most polluted rivers, lakes and shores in the world; eating shell fish is asking for trouble, especially uncooked types such as oysters. Never, ever be tempted to eat sushi or sashimi, the Chinese do not have the same hygiene standards as the Japanese. Shrimps and prawns are usually fine because they have been reared in a tank and never got to see what the deep blue sea was all about.

It is difficult to know what meat you are eating and where it has come from but generally go for beef or lamb where possible as this seems to have the least risk. Food that is boiled or steamed will also generally be safe. Many restaurants now have the kitchens viewable from the eating area where you see spotlessly clean chefs wearing masks and gloves. Hygiene has become a marketing tool rather than a bare necessity. It is normal to hang meat for some time before eating, this is especially true with roast duck and is generally fine but be especially careful with chicken, smell it, look carefully at the colour and texture before eating.

One of the good things about *huǒ guō* or hotpot is that you have a ready supply of hot boiling liquid which should mean a trouble free meal as the food, chopsticks and other utensils will be constantly sterilised.

I have known many people personally who have picked-up quite worrying ailments from food in China. One friend contracted hepatitis A, a direct result of poor hygiene. Two other colleagues both suffered from stomach parasites at different times in different restaurants. Another colleague picked up a serious throat infection that had an almost diphtheria effect of closing his throat such that he could hardly breath. The latter case, the doctor advised, was caused by drinking beer from a dirty bottle. There is a trend in Asia and increasingly in the UK too, of serving beer especially, straight out of the bottle. If you think about it, this practise is extremely unhygienic, for a start the bottles, unlike drinking glasses are never washed or sterilised. What is worse is that you have no idea where they have been stored and for how long. In a cellar for example, they tend to get dusty and could possibly have been urinated on by rats or mice, it is a real possibility. The rule is always ask for a glass, never accept a drink from a can or bottle and that goes for anywhere not just China.

Hepatitis can easily be vaccinated against and as a minimum, inoculation for tetanus, diphtheria, typhoid and polio should also be up to date. Chinese children have an extensive vaccination programme that includes the aforementioned plus meningitis, mumps, measles, rubella and uticaria (nettle rash, no idea why this is included as most city dwellers will never see one).

If you do suffer from some kind of parasite then you are most likely to notice through changes in bowel movements and stool consistency although when returning home, the jet-lag will also affect this for five or six days. If in any doubt see your doctor immediately.

Malaria is not a problem in most of China, although it is possible in the tropical border areas with Vietnam and India and also in and around Hainan. Of more concern is dengue fever, especially in the south. Dengue is a mosquito borne virus, unlike malaria (which is a parasite), and causes flu-like symptoms in its victim. Just like the common cold, there is no real treatment except to drink plenty of fluids and rest, perhaps take aspirin or similar to relieve the headache, but you should take medical advice as the diagnosis can only be confirmed with a blood test. Dengue hemorrhagic fever is a severe, complication of dengue fever that is extremely serious and often leads to death. The extent to which you suffer depends to a great extent on your general health and level of immunity. You get dengue fever from the bite of an infected *aedes albopictus* mosquito, (its written on the side) it spreads the disease by biting infected people then passing it on to an uninfected victim. The main control of this insect seems to be through destroying breeding sites. The television service in Hong Kong constantly warns you about this. One of the pieces of advice you get when looking into this is to avoid heavily populated areas which in China is virtually impossible. According to the WHO though, it seldom causes death.

Mosquitos are a constant pest, one bite that is not felt followed by an hour of itching and scratching. The females *only* bite, they need the blood to lay their eggs which they do in still water. Water containers and especially those containing plants are the mosquito equivalent of a maternity ward. Just leave some water unchanged for about five days, look closely and observe the tiny mosquito larvae swimming around. When visiting a garden centre, and these are springing up all over the country, cover up all the bare skin otherwise you will be like a naked virgin walking into a football stadium full of vampires.

The first half of the year 2003 was dominated by news of SARS (Severe Acute Respiratory Syndrome), a new kind of killer flu that started in Guangdong in southern China, thought to be a bug that jumped species from animal to human. It was contagious mainly due to poor hygiene, you were unlikely to get it from breathing the same air, much more likely from tiny droplets if someone infected sneezed or coughed directly at you. Unusual about SARS was that the bug could survive on a surface for some time, it was believed to have been transmitted in Hong Kong by an infected person who pressed a lift button which in turn was pressed by several others who later either sucked their thumb or picked their nose, so always wash your hands before picking your nose; they should teach school kids that idea.

The frightening thing about SARS was that it was transmitted globally in a matter of weeks; there were severe cases in Canada, as well as Asia. Because the disease was not fully understood at first and how it was being communicated, many medical staff were also infected, in fact the man who identified the disease, Dr Carlo Urbani an expert on communicable diseases, died himself of it in Vietnam. SARS was contained through quarantine and travel restriction, after nine months the all-clear was given.

It was though an event that terrified the populations of various nations; Beijing, one of the worst hit areas, virtually closed down and people stayed indoors. In Hong Kong, bars and clubs were empty, few ventured out. Airlines were only half full, many flights were cancelled and many staff lost their job.

It seems that the principle means of insuring against the disease was basic hygiene, avoiding other people's body fluids and that includes the Chinese dining model. Equally important is the constant washing of the hands. Part of normal day to day life means touching various surfaces that have been touched, coughed-on or sneezed-on by infected people. Many Chinese toilets do not have soap so it is good idea to take some anti-bacterial wipes with you.

Diseases, and more worryingly new diseases, seem to be a feature of our changing world, people living in close proximity, global travel and frequent holidays means rapid spread of new bacteria and viruses. In China in 2005, pig disease erupted, that is a variant that was contracted by humans. The human death toll from a pig-borne epidemic in Sichuan Province had reached 31 by the 28th July, according to the Chinese Ministry of Health. Reported were 152 cases of pig streptococosis II. The epidemic broke out in late June in cities and counties including Ziyang, Jianyang , Lezhi County and Zizhong in Neijiang County. All the patients had direct contact with ill or dead pigs.

The greatest worry or all, when it comes to new contagious diseases, for which there is no antidote, is avian or bird flu. This disease has suffered epidemics in South East Asian countries particularly, and can cause rapid deaths of the birds infected. What is worrying is that the current strain is particularly severe, killing an infected bird on the same day as contraction. It can affect all birds but seems to be particularly virulent in poultry such as chickens and turkeys. The flu can jump from infected birds to human beings via direct contact or through their droppings.

It seems to be as infectious as foot and mouth was in the UK a few years ago. It easily spreads from farm to farm through infected cages and materials and from the clothing and footwear of the workers. It appears to be spread from country to country via migratory waterfowl; duck and geese are either unaffected by the virus or have very mild symptoms but they do acts as carriers, spreading it to chickens when they come into contact with them.

Living and Working in China

The great worry with bird flu is that firstly there have been an increasing number of epidemics in Asian countries in recent years including Taiwan, Vietnam, China, Thailand and Hong Kong. Secondly there have been the rise of cases, hitherto unheard of, involving human infections and thirdly, perhaps most worrying, the fatality rate among humans is far greater than that of SARS.

Control seems to be most effective by rapidly destroying infected birds; this was highly successful in Korea, Japan and the Netherlands where outbreaks have occurred in the past few years.

The Chinese had a particularly severe outbreak in November 2005 in which a large number of chickens were infected and substantially more destroyed. This mostly affected the north eastern Liaoning province but cases popped up nationwide. Shortly after this, the government announced a plan to vaccinate 14 billion birds, an amazing target, footing up to eighty per cent of the cost. It is claimed that three humans contracted the disease and died. However, an article in *New Scientist* written by a Japanese virologist named Masato Tashiro, claims that the actual number of human deaths from bird flu, the H5N1 virus, is more like three hundred. The Chinese refute this and deny any cover-up, the fact that the scientist involved is Japanese must have really got up the government's nose.

There is no cure for this disease, nor any totally effective vaccination. The good news is that you are unlikely to get it unless you come into contact with live poultry or its droppings. Many restaurants and some supermarkets, especially in Guangdong, sell live poultry. There does seem to be no worries from eating infected chicken or eggs, provided it has been well cooked, although when a local outbreak occurs, chicken and eggs seem to disappear from the menus immediately.

Another health hazard, that would not be thought possible back home, is the constant threat of fake foods and poisons. These include fake eggs (I know, hard to believe) fake baby milk which we have heard about and the use of industrial products instead of the proper ones. For example, three people were arrested for selling industrial salt to a school in Shanghai, this was in turn fed to the kids who became very sick. You have no control over what goes into restaurant food so each time a judgement has to be made as to whether the place is safe or not, in most cases it is, the Chinese natural gullibility seems to make them far more vulnerable to food scams.

Medical insurance is relatively inexpensive in China, less than a quarter of what we would pay so if you are on a budget, take a policy out locally as those bought overseas are extremely dear. If you need to see a doctor, there is no general practitioner scheme as we have in the UK, you just turn up at a hospital, tell them the symptoms and a doctor will treat you on the spot. It will cost around 50 yuan for the consultation plus the medicines. If you need antibiotics, it will normally be directly administered via a drip there and then, you will not get a prescription that you take to a pharmacy. Some doctors are good, others give silly advice, one told me that I had liver problems just from looking at my hand, another advised my mother-in-law, a diabetic, not to eat fruit because there is too much sugar. The British Diabetic Society recommends that diabetics especially eat fruit because the sugar is absorbed slowly, rather than the usual shock of several grams of highly refined sucrose consumed in a typical Chinese meal.

Living and Working in China

Hospitals, like almost everything here, have become big businesses, the main focus now is to make money, promoting health is secondary. So doctors and hospitals offer and sell treatment that the patient does not need, have more expensive VIP consultations (pay more get seen quicker) and offer an extensive array of cosmetic surgery as standard. A more worrying trend is to cut corners with medicines, when Guangzhou hospitals bought cheaper medicine from the No2 Qiqihar Pharmaceutical Company, they did not know that they would be killing their patients. Stories like this are in the papers and on the news almost every day.

The Chinese have now become besotted with their own appearance and TV adverts for various creams and lotions to get rid of birthmarks and give the average adolescent girl a pair of super-tits go on unimpeded but I was shocked to read that the incidence of breast cancer in China is rising rapidly. It is fair to think that this is normal since it is a problem in developed nations with their fatty diets. The difference though is that in China, the problem is with twenty-five to thirty-five year olds, not post menopausal women as seems to be the more familiar situation. Could it be that these young women, their hearts set on a pair of juicy whoppers under their t-shirt, are plastering on the hormone creams and in the process doing themselves undue harm? One day the truth will come out but for now I can only speculate and check out young women's breasts wherever possible.

It may be a good idea, if you are spending some time in China, to take a multi-vitamin each day because avoiding certain foods, as one does in China, may mean that you have some nutritional deficiencies. I also take fish oil tablets because I simply do not trust the seafood, having seen the water that it comes out of.

The final point, which I have made before, is to stress that the greatest danger to health in China is the motor car; it kills more than one hundred thousand each year, almost a million are injured. It is always much safer to take the bus!

Chapter 12 - Getting Around

Moving around the city in which you live will be relatively easy, you can walk, take a bus or taxi and increasingly an underground railway.

Walking can be interesting because of what you see, smell and feel but the pavements will be uneven, crossing the road dangerous and avoiding other people and bikes a hazard. The terrain tends to be flat in most places so it is hard to find elevations to get a good view of the city. Different smells come from every doorway, somebody is always cooking in this country. Pretty girls will stand in the doorway of almost every restaurant beckoning you to come inside and sample their fare.

People will stare at you wherever you go and you will here '*loă wài*' rudely uttered or they just point at you and stare unbrokenly. I often respond by stopping and giving a perplexed look as I scan them up and down. Imagine walking around London pointing at every non-Caucasian and shouting 'foreigner'! Kids will approach you and say hello or worse their parents will push them to say hello and practise some English, it probably bothers the French a great deal as the Chinese assume that every foreigner's first language is English.

If you really want to walk around the countryside then you need to take a plane to one of the mountainous regions and get herded around with the local tourists. Most cities do have public parks but again they tend to be crowded.

When you do walk about, wear shoes with a decent tread on the soles, this is because most cities, that have their pavements laid, are covered in smooth, slippery tiles. In the wet it is really easy to have a nasty accident, even worse in Shanghai, many slopes into the Metro stations use these tiles and the city suffers from considerable rainfall.

The Chinese cannot walk in a straight line, if you walk in a predictable and direct way, constant direction and speed you bet your life that somebody will crash into you by walking obliquely across your path and what's more they will blame you for the collision! Once this happened on a staircase, I was descending steadily downwards, parallel to the sides when someone came quickly from behind my right shoulder, cutting diagonally across me close enough to trip over my left foot. The stupid woman then got up and from her tumble and started to swear at me!

Buses in China are terrific, they are cheap, plentiful and a pickpockets delight. I throw in the latter point as many people lose mobile phones and wallets on the bus due to the crowded nature of the thing, the noise and vibration makes it difficult to notice what is going on. I have spotted first hand an organised attempt to steal passengers' phones or wallets as they board, when their attention is momentarily diverted.

A typical bus ride in China will cost between one and three yuan and there is no need to wait very long, one will come along every few minutes. For payment, most buses have a raised tin-can next to the driver where you throw in your cash, others have a conductor, for the former you need the exact change. Many drivers, for some strange reason are female, when you see a five foot tall, skinny little woman driver it beggars belief as to how she handles all the heavy controls as most are manual transmission, not automatic.

The biggest problem is that all the bus signs, timetables and stop information is in Chinese, the staff will not speak English either so if you have a regular route from your home to place of work you quickly identify the correct bus and stick to it whereas if you want to explore, using the bus network, it would be impossible without being able to read and speak Chinese. Some foreigners I have met, use a trial and error system, taking a different bus everyday until they find the best one that suits their purpose, there must be an easier way and worse you suffer an expensive taxi ride to get to where you really wanted to go in the first place!

There are several types of bus, the large air conditioned type, the large non-air-conditioned type and the 20 seat minibus. The minibuses seem to be able to stop anywhere and deviate from their routes, often they wait until they fill-up before they depart, placing little plastic stools in the aisles so they can cram even more passengers in, no matter how unsafe it may be. The drivers of these vehicles are simply fruitcakes with a death wish and I never use them. Shenzhen banned minibuses from the city in 2007, the only problem being the out of work drivers were given jobs on the large buses. Their driving habits never changed they just became an order of magnitude more dangerous.

China has too many taxis, but it keeps the fares low and means you can actually find one when it is raining. The service varies from city to city, Shanghai is easily the best but Beijing, on account of the Olympic Games is fast catching up. The starting fee also varies greatly from city to city, Shenzhen has the highest at 12.5 yuan and Wuhan is the lowest I have seen at 3 yuan. After the first two kilometres, the fee is charged at between 1.3 and 2.6 yuan per km, again depending upon the city. Different cities have different regulatory taxi regimes and this determines what crooked practices the drivers can get away with. From Shenyang airport to visit a customer I was charged 140 yuan but the return journey on the meter was just 45 yuan. The life of a taxi driver is hard and so he or she is always looking for a bonus. In may cities, they do not want to use the meter, rather charge you a rip-off fare, but in the more advanced ones you could complain and they would lose their job. A good tip, if you have a camera phone (try buying one without a camera), is to photograph the driver's nameplate, always clearly displayed, it ensures that you win the arguments. In Shanghai, Beijing, Guangzhou and more recently Shenzhen, the system is well regulated and there should be few problems. However, they will try to take you the long way around or if the journey is too short, pretend they do not know where your requested destination is. Recently a colleague of mine in Shenzhen was in a taxi that stopped half way between his home and the city, because the traffic in the city was bad. The driver refused to go any further but complied in the end after his license number was noted. Very few drivers speak English so you must be able to tell them where to go or else get a Chinese speaker to write it down for you. The cars themselves vary in quality from very old Chinese made Citroen copies to brand new Audi A4s. I never understand why the firm that makes London Taxis does not market out here, they're crying out for them. Mostly they have a steel frame between you and the driver as protection for the latter. The pre-recorded announcement tells you to wear your seat belt but they are seldom fitted, so if you are unlucky enough to be involved in a crash, an instant broken neck is highly likely as your head bashes into the metal barrier between you and the driver.

Driving standards are poor, changing lanes without indication, screaming through red lights, speeding in built-up areas and driving on pavements. The poor old pedestrian, is always the one to suffer as the big cities become choked with vehicles and the ego infested idiots who drive them. I think the Chinese actually believe their own propaganda because when I complain about the way in which traffic has priority over the pedestrian, the answer comes back "there are so many people, that's why".

When paying the driver, it is essential to get into the habit of asking for a receipt, that way if ever something is lost, you have a record of time, date and taxi number. It is not necessary to tip the driver, locals never do, although some try to keep the change unless you ask for it.

Knowledge of local geography is not a strongpoint, drivers know most of the major hotels and large roads but if you need to go somewhere different then be prepared to give directions or find it on the map and point it out to the driver, although there is no guarantee that he will be able to read the map. Some of them also get extremely agitated if it turns out that a foreigner knows the way better than them.

The final warning on taxis is never, ever take an unlicensed one, the risks of kidnapping are too high, so many Hong Kong businessmen have disappeared in Guangdong, having taken unlicensed taxis.

Trains

There are many unpleasant experiences to be had in China but none much worse than a visit to the railway station. In fact the trains themselves are quite good and in my experience run slowly but on time.

The first problem for foreigners is that most railway stations do not have any English language signs so it is very difficult to know where you are going if you can't read the characters. The second problem is that nobody speaks English either so basic things like buying a ticket or catching the right train is a big headache. In some ways, coming from the UK, it is a real nerve to criticise anyone else's railways and what makes the Chinese network so horrible yet so successful is that they shift millions upon millions of people everyday. To be fair, railway stations anywhere are not nice places; at Paddington for example, they make you stand in the freezing cold staring at the departure board until the platform number of your train is displayed ten minutes before departure, only then you can dash for a seat, hardly civilised.

In China the stations themselves are usually very large buildings with large squares at the front. There are several different types of ticket offices depending upon class, day of travel and destination. Train departures and arrivals are clearly displayed but in Chinese. Some stations have a window with a sign that says 'English Speaking Interpreter' but you normally will see this only in the main tourist areas. Quite often queuing up for a ticket itself is irritating as people try to push by you and even though your body may be in front of theirs, they wrangle their arm around in order to push their crumpled banknote into the attendants serving aperture, a split second before you do. I tend to queue up with my arms in a sort of butterfly position to maximise my body width, if they persist in poking their head through a quick garrotte will be a strong deterrent.

On most trains, there are two types of seats the so called hard and soft seats yīng zùo （硬座）and rǔan zùo（软座）respectively. This is a direct translation from the Chinese language but means first and second class accordingly. You are most likely to take a train for up to three hours, anything more, then flying becomes preferable. Trains are very cheap, a single to Nanjing from Shanghai, first class will be around 100 Yuan for a three hour journey.

There are sleeper trains for long distance travel, I once took one of these from ChangChun to Beijing when snowed in at the airport. At the station, which was cold, dark and populated by beggars and touts, all of the tickets had been sold. They had been bought out by wise-guy opportunists who took their chance as soon as news of the airport's closure hit town.

They of course then sold them on at a profit to newly arriving passengers, making their way from the closed airport.

The beds are a bit on the short side, very narrow and three-high a bit like the accommodation on a submarine I imagine. Fearing theft, I slept with my briefcase as a pillow, when I woke-up a mid-twenties scruffy young woman was transfixed, staring at me just a few inches from my head as if I had been beamed down from a space ship, it felt like I had.

You can get tickets from your hotel to save you the bother of translation and inconvenience of the ticket line but you will pay a premium. When you finally get your ticket, look at it carefully, it will tell you the carriage and seat number, only on short distance trains are you not allocated a seat. Most importantly it will tell you your train number so that you get on the right train. I am not sure of the system used but it seems that trains that are prefixed with T tend to be faster and more luxurious, some start with N which means they are not so good and those with no alpha prefix, just a number, have no soft seat accommodation, stop at virtually every hamlet and village on the way, are very cheap and mostly used by farmers complete with their pigs, goats and chickens.

The next bundle of fun is progressing to the waiting room, some major stations such as Shanghai have a separate waiting room for soft seat passengers but this is uncommon. Firstly they x-ray your bags, just like at the airport although personnel metal detectors are not used. You then pass through to the waiting room. The waiting rooms are enormous, usually one will be designated for maybe one or two train-loads, they accommodate at least five hundred people in long rows of front to back facing seats. The trains are heavily used by migrant workers and you will find the waiting areas packed with these people, all their personal belongings, wife, child and even parents. They always look poor, wearing old clothes, dirty necks and unhealthily thin almost as Dickens described the orphanage kids in *Oliver Twist*. These people seem mesmerised by the presence of foreigners, if you open your notebook computer the shock will be too much, their first sighting of a laowai *and* a computer, all in the same day. In the run up to Chinese New Year these peasant workers will hang around outside stations for days waiting for the chance of a cheap fare home.

Your train number should be clearly displayed and sign posted or if not it will be announced by a guard through a megaphone, so loud and distorted as to be unintelligible even to fluent Chinese speakers. In this case look at other people with the same ticket and follow them. Boarding usually occurs about ten minutes before departure when you are told to go to the appropriate platform and board the train. An attendant will be there to check your ticket, usually she has a white cap and gloves, and wears a close tailored blue uniform of flared tunic and trousers that really hug the bottom well. These women tend to be more mature but more friendly than their airline equivalents, smiling and content, adding to the way that their tight uniform highlights their curves.

Once on the train, they will be up and down throughout the journey selling all kinds of snacks and tit bits. If you ask for coffee, she'll give you a paper cup and a sachet of *Nescafe* instant coffee, the kind that comes with dried milk and too much sugar all in one. This is quickly followed by the flask lady who fills your cup with boiling water but there is nothing to stir it with so you end up with a weak coffee-like drink (like they have in America) for the first half followed by a cup of sludge for the remainder, better to order tea.

The trains are very clean, soft seats tend to be more like second class back home although leg room is reduced, hard seats are designed to be uncomfortable firstly because they squeeze too many people onto a seat and secondly because the seats are very upright as if your doctor has designed them for back patients. Making them even more uncomfortable is the very short cushion that gives very little thigh support, on a long journey you have to regularly stand up and move around.

When you leave the train, it is the usual mad rush to exit the carriage followed by the slow crawl to the station gate, keep your ticket handy because it is likely to be checked again before being allowed to exit the station and fight through the wall of taxi touts.

The final bit of advice when travelling by train is to watch your valuables at all times, public transport is a thieves' paradise, drop off to sleep by all means but only holding onto your bag.

The other point worth mentioning is that if you attempt to take a train during or just either side of the New Year holiday there will be so much pushing and shoving through the crowds that I seriously advise against it unless you are an experienced and talented prop forward.

I have travelled by train quite a lot and can honestly say that every train has run on time and never has a train been cancelled, they do not seem bothered by leaves on the line or 'the wrong kind of snow'. After passing through the station and onto the train itself, it is relatively pleasant and pain-free. Train crashes are rare although there was a worrying accident in August 2005 when a train en-route from Xi'an to Changchun ran into the back of a freighter. Six people were killed, the cause was due to signal failure. Not the type we are used to caused by years of neglect, no this time somebody earlier that day had pinched the electric cables.

On the same day, I read that somebody had been stealing manhole covers in Shenzhen (I assume to sell as scrap metal), six were stolen in one street and a lady was seriously injured falling down an uncovered orifice.

Aeroplanes

In my first job in China, I was based in Shanghai but had to cover the whole country. That meant that I had to use planes like normal people use buses, so I am something of an authority when it comes to suffering at the hands of Chinese airlines.

China is dominated by three large carriers, Air China, China Southern and China Eastern. They are based in Beijing, Guangzhou and Shanghai respectively. On top of that there are many smaller airlines including Shanghai Airlines, Shandong Airlines, Xiamen Airlines, Hainan Airlines, SiChuan Airlines and Shenzhen Airlines. In 2003 they had a bit of a reorganisation and a couple of the large airlines were swallowed-up by their bigger brothers, namely North West, based in Xi'an, joined Eastern and Northern, based in Shenyang, joined Southern. New in 2005 was a low cost airline Spring Airlines out of Shanghai that offers fares to places you have never heard of, and never likely to want to go, for around 200 yuan.

Getting Around

In general, Chinese airlines are equally poor in pretty much every respect although Shenzhen airlines pokes it nose above the rest with its wider leather seats, more leg room and sexy cabin crew with their surgically fixed smiles.

Buying tickets is at best confusing as there is a weird discount structure and the fact that you have to pay in cash means you have to be *loadsamoney* to get by. Increasingly airlines have what they call an e-ticket system, you can pay on-line with your (Chinese) bank card and print out a reservation number. However in many cases, when you get to the airport, this must be exchanged for a proper receipt before you can check-in and get a boarding card. It is handy though if starting from outside of the country and want to book domestic tickets before you arrive, sadly only a very few airports can cope with it but things change fast.

When you get to the airport, and there are two types; old, dark and brown or new, bright and silver. The latter thinks it gives them a license to charge nearly five pounds for a cup of coffee (even BAA haven't tried that one), otherwise not a lot of difference they are all very poor by our standards. (I wrote this before the opening of Heathrow's Terminal 5!)

On a domestic flight there is no need to check in more than one hour before departure, in fact many airports will not let you check in early in any case. You get the usual brawl of pushers, queue jumpers and phlegm throwers in the check-in queue of course but it is usually not too much hassle. You need a photo ID and can request a seat to which they agree and put you somewhere else anyway. The bags are usually x-rayed directly behind the desk so the current wave of extreme Islamic nutters have little time to escape. The Chinese do not like to check their bag in, they are terrified that the airline will lose it, consequently they struggle with three or four oversize bags through security and onto the plane.

When boarding the plane, there is always a big fuss as they struggle to get too many heavy and bulky hand bags into the lockers. Sometimes the planes are pushing off of the stand and commencing taxi while this kafuffle is still going on. At holiday times such as the lunar New Year when the mass exodus from the cities to the villages begins, the areas between the seats are absolutely stuffed with belongings, usually presents to take home to their family; at this point the airlines just forget the safety rules and give up trying to get everything put away where it would not impede a fast escape. And so legs, feet and arms everywhere are resting on large bulky attire in these checked plastic holdalls that seem common all over China.

I am always astonished to see the Chinese rush to the insurance counter at the airport and buy life insurance for their trip, as if the only likely way to get killed is on an aeroplane yet the nutcase of a taxi driver, weaving in and out of fast moving heavy traffic, that took them to the airport was much more of a death threat.

On domestic flights in China, you cannot take alcohol or any liquid in your hand luggage, no matter how small the quantity. If you transfer from an international to a domestic flight and do not put the duty free scotch, you bought back at Heathrow, into your check-in bag, they will confiscate it.

The reason for this, now confirmed by the news agency Xinhua, is that when a China Northern flight from Beijing to Dalian crashed on the 7th May 2002 killing all 112 people on board, the blame was rumoured to be put on alcohol. The story told internally is that one passenger, who had just found out that he had terminal cancer, went into the toilets with some high spirit alcohol, doused the surroundings and set light to it, causing an explosion and crash into the sea. The man, a Mr *Zhang Pilin* (who had terminal cancer) immediately came under suspicion because he had taken out seven insurance policies immediately before the flight that would have netted his family around one million yuan. It goes without saying that the policies never paid out.

If you change your flight, you must get the ticket changed because when you go through security, for reasons that I have never been able to fathom, they check your ID, boarding pass *and* ticket. If none of these match, they will send you back. You will need to be especially careful because if the name on the passport for example is Michael but you are commonly known as Mike, conceivably tickets could be booked in the name of the latter and, as surnames always come first in China, it is easy to see why this could be a problem.

Nowadays, Chinese airlines use modern Boeing or Airbus jets, there seem to be no more of the old Tupelev Russian bombers converted to airliners around any more. (There are still plenty in Russia however) Every now and then though, it is possible to spot one of these planes, especially at airports like Changchun which is also used by the military.

The security briefings over the years have not changed very much, often they miss them out and even worse they are still going on when the wheels of the plane leave the ground. The flight from Shanghai to Xi'an which was operated by China North West, but has since been absorbed by China Eastern (although only the colours have changed), broadcasts the safety demonstration from small LCD monitors. This is fine except the subtitles are in Chinese and the soundtrack is simultaneously given in Japanese and English such that both are unintelligible.

The latest trend is in-flight exercises, after the meal is served and everything has been collected, the cabin crew will stand in the aisles at equal intervals and direct the stretching and shaking movements whilst most of the passengers start to wave their hands around in the air, punch imaginary balloons and thump their feet on the floor. Meanwhile I bury my head into a book, pretending not to notice what is going on.

On international flights, China Eastern does not let the process of landing get in the way of selling the duty free, the minor disadvantage of the cabin crew being thrown over the nearest passenger as the plane wheels crash down seems acceptable.

Sichuan Airlines advises its passengers to remove their watch before using the safety slide (in addition to the high heeled shoes) so it is fair to assume it must be made of rice paper.

The trouble is that one has to ponder over whether the same blatant disregard to the safety rules is applied by the maintenance technicians.

For certain, Chinese airlines take greater risks than would be allowed on international flights: A friend of mine boarded a plane at Dalian in July 2004, there were severe thunderstorms at the time and many delays. The flight was full and after an hour or so of sitting on the tarmac, the pilot announced that the plane was overweight and he was not responsible if an accident occurred. They then asked everyone to get off the plane and identify their baggage so that those who did not want to take the risk could leave the flight. A few passengers did this, the bags were re-packed and the plane took off for what turned out to be an uneventful flight.

On another Air China flight from Tianjin, the plane started to speed along the runway in order to take off but then suddenly stopped and we were all thrown forward with our seatbelts almost cutting our bodies in two. The pilot had aborted the takeoff then slowly taxied back to the terminal. Meanwhile there was no information given whatsoever as everyone was pressing the call buttons, attracting the cabin crew and angrily interrogating them as to what was going on. The only reply was that the pilot was too busy to say. Half an hour later we departed without further event and three hours later, just before landing in Shenzhen, the captain informed us that there was a technical problem earlier.

In recent months I have come to avoid Air China like party political broadcasts, every flight that I have taken has been severely delayed and either no information was provided, "the aircraft is delayed due to the delay" they broadcast in two languages, or just a plain pack of lies like delay due to the weather when no other airline from the same airport has any difficulty departing on time.

I do not have a lot of good things to say about Chinese airlines, the service is extremely poor, the food is worse than in a five yuan per dish restaurant. Delays are common, without explanation, and if the flight is not full they will cancel it. The airports are sparse with their cold uncomfortable steel-seat waiting areas, where shops exist the produce, whether gifts, food or beverages, are very overpriced. The new international terminal in Beijing challenges this argument but it was especially built for the Olympics so some showing-off was required.

With the exception of Shenzhen Airlines, the crew are pretty but miserable and rude, planes are cramped and increasingly overcrowded. Each day more and more people fly in China and more and more flights are added every year, the skies are getting as busy as the cabins and it does make one worry as to whether the safety systems are keeping up with the traffic growth, I hope I am wrong but I fear the worst.

It seems to be stating the obvious, but many western tourist groups that I bump into and chat with over breakfast, seldom realise that China is a big place and even a short holiday will involve lots of internal air travel, it is not a pleasant experience, perhaps there is no way that it could be with so many people.

Hotels
Unlike many other locations in Asia, China does not have a low-cost hotel or guest house sector to cater to foreign travellers on a budget. Normally, as a minimum, you will have to stay in a three star hotel or greater.

Three star hotels are nonetheless quite large establishments with reasonable sized rooms, restaurants and other facilities. They do not normally have a western restaurant, you need to go to a four star for that, so coffee at breakfast will be unlikely. A three star hotel can cost 150-200 in a poor city and as high as 500 in Shanghai. One thing they all share in common, is a heavily stained carpet; I have no idea what the typical Chinese businessman does, seems like a ritual to mess up the hotel-room like a seventies rock and roller.

Four or five star hotels tend to be cleaner and newer, with better facilities but everything comes at a price.

Checking in usually takes a long time as they analyse your passport, copy its details down onto a form and get you to sign it. They do take credit cards and will always ask for one as a deposit or an amount of cash approximately double the going room rate when checking in.

A porter will be dieing to take your bags because he expects a tip from westerners; locals never, ever give tips. It is probably fair not to since most hotels have a 10% service charge added to the bill.

Once in the room, you will quickly become irritated by the number of people who keep knocking on the door, checking the bathroom, checking the minibar, turning down the bed, almost any excuse they can think of. It feels like a case of "there's a lao wai in room 2207, go and check her out"

Late evening, there is a fair chance that a female will call the room and ask if you need a massage, the first time this happened to me, I naïvely said no thanks its too late, not knowing what the lady was really trying to sell.

There will be complementary tea, sometimes coffee, and either a thermos flask of hot water or a small kettle. Somewhere will be an inventory of the room with the prices of everything in case you are tempted to steal one of the worn and frayed towels or chipped china tea-cups. When you check-out, they will carefully check the room before they let you go.

Hotels are often noisy with all sorts of banging, drilling, loud TVs and a small party always in the adjacent room.

Most now have a KTV lounge which they think is the ultimate in good entertainment but this is really not my scene, even if I could sing.

Virtually all hotels in China operate their own prostitution service; I never really understood this until I sat down one day and figured it all out. In the majority of hotel rooms will be a card offering massage services, either visit their 'health' centre on a given floor or have someone come to your room.

Real China

There will also very likely be a warning not to accept offers from cold calls to your room.

On one of my very first trips to China, after a long flight and a very stiff neck that later went south, I ordered the in-room massage, it was a bargain advertised at 80 yuan for 2 hours. About five minutes later, a girl comes to the room wearing tight jeans and a T-shirt, this surprised me a bit as I had expected a lady in a white coat with a kit of equipment like oils and towels. We talked a while and she asked me to lay down on the bed face down with only a towel covering my buttocks, while she started to stroke my back, she waited a whole thirty seconds before she suggested *nǐ yào bù yào zuò ài?* Which crudely means would you like a shag? Somewhat surprised I replied that I only wanted a massage and that my neck and shoulders were very tired. She gently moved her hands around my neck, across my shoulders and then slowly down my back until the tips of her fingers were at the top half of my bottom, slightly under the towel. Next she moved behind me and quite firmly pushed my legs apart as she shuffled between them. Now her hands were moving up and down my legs and, each stroke getting closer and closer to my groin slipping her paws from top to inside and brushing with my testicles.

Then without warning she asked me to turn over, removed the towel and only concentrated her efforts directly onto what was by now an enlarged member. As she did this, she kept attempting to negotiate a price for full sex, I gave-in eventually and after much wrangling settled for 500 yuan.

She then removed her jeans, exposing the most un-sexy pair of *Bridget Jones* style briefs I have ever seen, large, grey, washed-to-death nylon. Fortunately she removed them just as fast revealing a black but very straight thicket, not the short and curlies that I was used to. Maybe the American who came up with the term 'beaver' had been to China first. The T-shirt then came off underneath a pink bra that did not match the grey panties, a size too small as her breasts were pouring over the top and sides like the head on a frothy beer. She took this off and was now fully naked. Not a pretty girl but not ugly either, her body was very slim and curvy, pure white skin and a soft round bottom. Her breasts were large, very large in fact, but they did not droop, they appeared to stay in place as if the bra was unnecessary.

Breasts are a funny thing, men only think about what they look and feel like; women use them as sex tools and like to show partial glimpses of them in their choice of clothing yet their real purpose is to feed babies. As far as baby feeders go, these were a pair of luxury restaurants. Her nipples were large, fully erect, each one the size of the top third of my little finger, their dark brown colour contrasted heavily against the skin that was as white as a freshly distempered ceiling. I would guess that she was no more than 20 years old.

At this point she dashed to the bathroom and showered before returning to the bedroom to earn the money that she had really come for all along. The lesson to be learned here is that if you order a massage in your room, it means that you want sex, not a massage. In a country where prostitution is illegal, it seems either shocking or encouraging, depending upon your perspective, that virtually all hotels offer this kind of service.

Chapter 13 – Places Around China

This book is not really meant to be a tourist guide, more a medium to educate those as to the essential knowledge required to visit, work or live in China. However, things are not the same in different parts of the country, so it is worth spending a little bit of time on some of the main places that are likely to be visited, equally for work or pleasure. If you come as a teacher then you could end up almost anywhere and it would not be easy to cover all of the possibilities but, surprisingly for such a large country, the basic values of cheating and lying don't change. What is clear is that the two big cities, where most foreigners end up, are Beijing and Shanghai. It will be easiest to assimilate to life in these places because English is more widely spoken, quality standards in almost every aspect of everyday life from schools to restaurants are higher and it will be far easier to find those comfort items that you miss from back home. The downside is that the cost of living in these places is much more expensive than anywhere else, often more than our own green and pleasant land.

The following is a précis of some of the more popular cities in China and what you can see and do when you get there.

Shanghai
Shanghai is a big city, a really big city, it has a population of around 20 million people, plus a migrant worker population of a couple of million more. The previous top figures in the Chinese Government, namely president Jiang Zemin and prime minister Zhu Rongji were both Shanghai men. It has given the city, over the past two decades, an unprecedented

amount of funding and development. The underlying strategy, that they do not admit to, is to make Shanghai *the* world city with what they think is the biggest and best of everything. No doubt one day, Shanghai will have the tallest buildings, (the recent completion of Taipei 101 must have really waved the red flag at them) the most elaborate architecture and the desire to be a city to compete with London, New York or Tokyo. Everywhere you go in Shanghai there are new developments of apartments, offices and government buildings. Very recently, a team from Shanghai went to see the London Eye so that they can build one too, it will be bigger of course. The 'Shanghai Star' will be 170m in diameter, 35m bigger than the Ferris wheel on the bank of the Thames. It will be completed in 2008 and sit next to the Huangpu river. The current Chinese way of thinking is to have the best and biggest of everything and be a real challenger to the United States' widely thought of unbeatable position.

The Chinese government does not care how much money it costs to get there either and so sod the poor, they can't waste valuable funds on the 800,000 or so who earn a few dollars per week. China has an extreme capitalism now that would make Karl Marx shudder in disbelief, nothing gets in the way of making money and improving China's *perceived* position in the world. Nowhere in China is this unashamed extravagance more in evidence than in Shanghai.

As I said earlier, Shanghai is divided by a wide river, the *Huang Pu Jiang* 黄浦江. The river separates *Pu Dong* and *Pu Xi* and there are many river crossings between the two areas. At the centre of the city is the Bund or *Waitan* in Chinese. It is one of the world's most impressive city water fronts, desperately trying, but failing, to upscale Victoria Harbour in Hong Kong. On the Puxi side of Waitan are many old colonial buildings and former custom houses in French, British or American architectural styles. On the Pu Dong side are the shiny new financial skyscrapers including the *Jin Mao* tower that houses the Hyatt hotel as well as the more dominant sputnik-like Oriental Pearl TV tower. This area of Pu Dong is known as *Liu Jia Zui*. You can go to the top of the TV tower in a lift that feels like a rocket but the queues are probably quite long and if the pollution level is normal, not much to see when you get there.

Shanghai is now a common destination for Chinese tourists. You can also go to the top of the Jin Mao tower but the coffee bar at the top asks for an entrance fee. If it has been raining the view is great but most days the pollution is so thick that there is little to see except that pink haze.

There are two main shopping streets in Shanghai, the first is *NanJing Xi Lu* (Lu means street or road) which runs in a straight line west from Wai Tan, the other is *Huai Hai Zhong Lu* which is not so far from this and tends to have more up-market shops. If you like big malls then head to *Xu Jia Hui* where there are several in a small area. For markets, the most common is *Xiang Yang* (recently closed) which is at the far end of Huai Hai Zhong Lu, in the direction of Xu Jia Hui. Here you can by all kinds of mostly fake designer goods from around 300 or so market stalls, it is a magnet for foreigners. The traders, who previously had market stalls, now walk the main street selling their illegal wares.

I am always amused when I listen to many people who have visited China for the first time or when I read their reported words in newspapers. They often say how warm friendly and kind the Chinese are and what a lovely place it is and how they want to return. Maybe these people never left their hotel rooms or maybe they just didn't know they were being ripped-off. It is pre-programmed into most Chinese hawkers to cheat you and whenever you go to one of these markets you can bet that you will be paying double the going rate, just because it is 20% cheaper than you get back home does not mean to say that you have a bargain. These people are ruthless and cunning and generally think of foreigners as stupid. If you are with a Chinese guide, I will guarantee you 100% that they are on a commission. Shanghai people are famous for being the meanest in the country, they don't like to put their hand into their pocket and when they see a foreigner they will always, always charge a higher price. I lived in Shanghai for 2 years and I seldom went to Xiang Yang market, I just don't like dealing with crooks.

If you are looking for Chinese products such as ornaments, pictures, silk, chopsticks or even Chairman Mao watches, I suggest that you try *Yu Yuan Garden*, a delightful area of old-style buildings, narrow streets, alleys and courtyards with a central water garden sadly contrasted with the out-of-place branches of MacDonald's, KFC and Starbucks. Here you can find virtually anything that is typically Chinese; big scroll paintings, painted figures, pottery, silks, wood carvings, musical instruments, inside painted glassware and Chinese calligraphy. Again you have to bargain and bargain really hard, the initial asking price will be at least double the going rate and do not listen to your Chinese guide either. I actually enjoy browsing around Yu Yuan the atmosphere is buzzing and most streets are closed to cars so the environment is pleasant. Once when there with my wife, one of the shop keepers approached her and, not knowing that we were 'an item' offered her some commission for persuading me to buy certain items at certain prices!

Real China

Behind each of these smiling oriental faces is a shark that makes the Great White look like a goldfish. Also to be found in Yu Yuan, are several local food outlets, one of them is a dumpling shop where you can buy for take away all sorts of boiled and steamed buns. You will notice that the queue is always very long here giving the impression that the food must be really something special; don't be fooled, many people in the queue are paid to stand there in order to give the misconception that the food is something out of the ordinary. This is related to the Chinese way of thinking that if a restaurant is full, the food must be good, whereas if the restaurant is empty there must be something wrong. The truth is it all seems to taste the same whether you spend 30 Yuan or 300.

The subway in Shanghai is the best way to get around but it is crowded. It comprises nine principle lines that stop virtually everywhere that is interesting and interchange in the middle at *Renmin Guang Chang* or Peoples Square. A ride on the subway is only 3 to 5 Yuan to go to most places. The trouble is that it is not very foreigner friendly until you get past the ticket barrier and into the station, so buying a ticket and knowing where to go is tricky. Once you get into the subway, the trains have announcements in English and the signs use *pinyin* (a Romanisation of Chinese) as well as *hanzi* (Chinese characters). When buying a ticket, you have to look at the map and locate where you are heading which tells you the price of the journey, the station names are all in characters so it is really difficult for a foreigner but new bi-lingual machines are now being installed. You then buy a ticket for that amount and use the automatic barriers to descend to the platforms. The subway staff do not speak English either so check your guide book carefully and learn to pronounce two, three and four yuan (*er yuan, san yuan or si yuan*) in order to buy the ticket. If you have some coins then use the ticket machines which are pure simplicity, if you know the Chinese name of your destination!

In my experience, most Chinese museums and tourist attractions are tacky and poor, don't bother with the Tourist Tunnel at WaiTan it is just a laser light show. The science museum, housed in an amazing building, is aimed at kids, overcrowded and expensive, even the fish in the tank were plastic. The art museum on Peoples Square is poor and the staff are rude, the main interest is the painting section. Some of the parks are nice and *Shi Ji Gong Yuan* (Century Park) in Pu Dong is a really big place with a huge lake, a wide variety of plants and an excellent network of footpaths. It is next to the science museum. If you like temples then visit *Jing An* Temple but there are finer examples elsewhere in China.

Around Shanghai, there are several towns that are built on networks of waterways; *Suzhou*, which the guidebooks bizarrely describe as 'Venice of the East' is a fairly pleasant place to visit with many of these canal streets. You can get to Suzhou easily from Shanghai by bus or train and it takes about 2 hours by bus or only 40 minutes on the new express train. You will notice when you get there that the prices for virtually everything are substantially cheaper than in Shanghai, especially Chinese gifts, art, silks and pottery. The nicest thing about Suzhou is the large number of ornamental gardens that are open to the public, some have music and entertainment, others are very large and take a full day to discover but if oriental gardens are your thing then Suzhou is the place to go.

Shanghai has some excellent, if expensive, nightlife and a full guide is given in the free publication 'That's Shanghai' they also have a website www.thatsshanghai.com The magazine is freely distributed and you will always find one in Starbucks when you stop for a cup of coffee that won't break the budget. For some reason, the Chinese think they can charge about three times the going rate for a cup of coffee; at many Chinese-run coffee shops as well as Beijing and Shanghai airports they will charge 50 or 60 yuan (£3-£4). It would be sufferable if it tasted good but usually they add that disgusting evaporated milk and serve it in a miniscule sized cup, it is the height of meanness. At Shenzhen airport, they have a café in the departure lounge that's called the Tea Leaf Café, selling coffee at 45 yuan per cup, the name seems appropriate and what's more they complain if you ask for a little bit of milk 'you should have ordered latte!' (60 yuan per cup). Just to rub salt in the wound they serve it in a chipped red cup, the exact same type that comes free with a jar of Nescafé. Be careful not to ask for cappuccino, it is just coffee with synthetic cream, squirted from an aerosol and floating on top, not really sure why it's there. The Chinese don't consider personal service to be of great importance; the approach is if you have to cheese a few people off, who cares! There's another 1.3 billion to work on yet.

Fortunately Starbucks is a part of American globalisation that in China I welcome with open arms, where now one can pay 20 yuan for a decent sized cup that actually tastes good too.

One of the best streets for entertainment, bars and clubs is *Heng Shan Lu* and the streets that lead to and around it. There are lots of bars, many that have live music and many with plenty of female company looking for a western boyfriend. Some of these girls are prostitutes in the sense that they want some money as well. Anyway, it won't be too difficult to find a lady in Shanghai and you should not need to part with your hard-earned to do so. If you want some more down-market but cheaper bars then try *Ju Lu Lu,* a couple of blocks away from Heng Shan Lu or *Tongren Lu* where 100% of the girls are available for after-beer recreation.

Another up-market area for bars and smart restaurants is *Xin Tian Di*, just off of Huai Hai Lu. You will see many foreigners and local ex-pats living there, some of the bars are owned and run by foreigners too. One of the annoying things in 'low cost' China and particularly cities like Beijing and Shanghai is that the price of entertainment is much higher than you would have to pay back home. If you want a western style meal the cost will be 30% higher at least, a pint of Guinness will cost you five pounds and a simple dinner of sausage and mash in a German style establishment like Paulaner House will set you back 30 pounds each. If you can survive on Chinese food and drink Chinese beer, you will find things to be a lot cheaper.

I once asked a local why for foreigners things are so expensive in China, I was told that when Chinese people go overseas things are much more expensive for them so when foreigners come to China they should also pay much more than they do at home. It is a poor argument but really it boils down to a very simple set of values that says screwing foreigners is perfectly acceptable and common-place and should be carried out where ever possible. Cheating the 'laowai', as you will often here yourself called, is programmed into them and you have to be on your guard for it all the time. Back home, when you do a good deed such as help an old lady across the road or give up your seat on the tube to a pregnant lady, you get that nice warm feeling that you have done something kind or charitable, well, sadly many

Real China

Chinese get exactly the same feeling when they have cheated a foreigner!

One thing though, they are seldom violent. Mostly the streets are safe, the main crime is petty theft and pick pocketing which is no different to Paris or London. The Chinese do not like confrontation, the usual guide books such as *Lonely Planet* always tell you to be calm and polite when attempting to resolve disputes; it is utter bullshit, they are so stubborn that they can argue all day, however, if you get angry and more important show that you are angry, they will always back down.

The best example I have of this when I returned my apartment in Shenzhen, the landlord was determined not to return my deposit, even though the place was cleaner and tidier than when I had moved in. He went on and on for at least three hours about unpaid bills, even though we went through all the receipts and totalled the sums. Eventually I cracked and showed my anger, thumping the table as I spoke, he quickly gave in.

Beijing

The trouble with any book or tourist guide to Beijing is that, like Shanghai, it changes so quickly it all gets out of date before the information reaches the shops. Therefore you must accept that this text will be a little inaccurate.

The big reason of course is the Olympic Games, awarded to Beijing on that sticky July evening in 2001 when the whole city seemed to go mad, converging on Tiananmen square in the middle of the night, waving flags, screaming out of taxi windows and being more intoxicated by the event than by any alcohol that they may have consumed.

Places Around China

Beijing was a strange choice for the Olympics, one of the most polluted cities in the world, an overcrowded airport and sports stadiums that were more notorious for executions than major events. I can only ponder over how they won and what they promised. More worrying is whether or not those promises will be kept, one article caught my eye in the papers regarding the volleyball tournament. In Beijing's proposal they affirmed that this would be played in Tiananmen square, since then they have withdrawn the commitment due to 'logistical problems' my guess is that this would be an opportunity for political protest which the whole world could sit back, relax and watch in amusement, which is why this particular pledge will not be kept. The Tiananmen incident, when those poor students were squashed by heavy tanks, is the Chinese Achilles heel, the number one embarrassment issue and it is almost criminal to even talk about it.

What the Olympics has done though, and I hope it will have the same effect upon London, is to turn the city around. All of a sudden the place is becoming much more 'user friendly' the taxi drivers are learning English, there is an explosion in the number of western restaurants and the whole city is beginning to feel cleaner, more sophisticated and civilised than it ever did before.

Beijing, like most Chinese cities, are formed around a road system, in Beijing these are a series of ring-roads. These radiate from the centre like a the ripples from a water splash, the first ring road right in the middle seems to have disappeared in name and most of the interesting parts of the city are within the second ring road. Each ring-road is, it almost goes without saying, choked with traffic. The city centre, it could be said is the long straight road that cuts

Real China

through the middle, It starts as *Jiàn gúo mén dà dào* (Jianguomen avenue) and becomes, at the very centre, *Chāng ān jiè* (Changan Street). The city does not suffer from a creeping skyscraper epidemic like Shanghai so does feel less intimidating and less crowded than its more southerly rival.

Many of the more upmarket hotels seem to appear along this street, typically four or five star and will cost around RMB700-1000 per night. I have stayed in most of them at one time or another but my favourite is the *Gui Bin Lou* (贵宾楼) or literally VIP building. The hotel has a small old fashioned lobby but as you enter the lift and rise to the second floor you are met by a splendid open inner court yard and atrium, enclosed and air conditioned yet bright and airy with a small bar and an exquisite quartet of classical musicians playing soft and relaxing harmonious music. It is just what you need after the multi-channel interference that hits your brain in any busy city and even more so in Beijing. The rooms are huge with embroidered bedspreads, crisp white sheets and, unusually for China, soft yet firm mattresses. Every other Beijing hotel is like an airport departure lounge but in this one you can really relax.

Nightlife in Beijing is pretty good, there are really two main areas which offer the same style of entertainment. First there is sān lǐ tún (三里屯) which is a bar street in the north east of the city between the second and third ring-roads, it is close to the foreign embassies and so has a good mix of local and overseas clientele. The street is about 1km long and has bars on both sides of the road. Most of the bars have restaurants and many have live music or a disco-dancing type of set-up. All kinds of food can be consumed along with the usual dazzling array of Chinese beers, all of them yellow, gassy and tasteless. This is also an area frequented by prostitutes although not as obvious as it was previously but if you are one or more single males, you will get approached soon enough. The street itself is illuminated by the bright lights of the bars that line it, interspersed with shadows from the trees that uniformly border the road. It is a very pleasant place to sip drinks outside in the spring or autumn evenings. One thing is that this place is so well known and popular that no matter how badly you mis-pronounce the name, the taxi drivers will know where you want to go.

More recently created and much more extensive than san li tun is *hōu hǎi jiǔ bā jiè* (后海酒吧街) or literally 'behind the lake bar street' This is located to the north west of the forbidden city, inside the second ring road. What hits you immediately as you enter this place is the small army of massage services on offer from elderly men and women, dressed in white coats to give them that air of credibility. If you have the need, they sit you down on a small stool and rub the parts that the normal in-room massage does not tend to reach. Mostly it is a head and shoulders style back massage, clearly encouraged by the authorities in order to create income for the majority of over 45s that are unemployed.

The next shock is that at the entrance is an attractive old-style, small Chinese building, heavily disguising its real function as a Starbucks outlet. Leaving the coffee shop to your left, though a short passage way that opens out onto a wooden type of boardwalk with a stream of different restaurants on the left and the beauty and expanse of the lake to the right.

The area has been well put together, each restaurant specializes in a particular type of Chinese cooking from south west to northeast and from Singapore to Thailand. I tried the Hunan forte with its attractively dressed waiting staff in their local apparel. The menu was in both languages so no difficulty with misunderstanding. I skipped over the Chairman Mao pork, which is just a lump of pig fat, and went for various dishes of vegetables flavoured with different types of meat. Despite asking for not too spicy, which to them must have meant spicy almost to the point of pain, all dishes were fiery which of course meant that I had to drink even more beer to cool things down. It was though very pleasant sitting outside in the warm spring evening, glancing at the lake, and dodging the determined mosquitoes.

After that I walked further around the lake, along the meandering road that goes on for a couple of kilometres, almost every lakeside space occupied by a bar, mostly with live music, not too loud and highly listenable to. The recitals of *Hotel California* (always an Asian favourite) seemed to pass from bar to bar like a Mexican wave.

A truly delightful place to spend time, any time in Beijing, I highly recommend it.

Beijing probably has the most tourist destinations and possibly all Chinese tours go there. A lot of it you can walk around for free, wander around Tiananmen square, pass through the gate, glancing at Mao's painting which they change every year and reading the big characters that were put there when the people's republic was formed. It means *the People's Republic of China ten thousand years* and *the world's people unite ten thousand years*. In the south-east corner of Tiananmen square, you actually queue up and see the mummified body of Mao himself. Even today, Chinese kids are taught that there were five great men in the world, Marx, Lenin, Trotsky, Stalin and Mao, interesting as the latter two were mass murderers and Lenin wasn't exactly inspired by Florence Nightingale down in the Crimea.

Places Around China

The Forbidden City, (called so because going there uninvited meant instant execution) or *Gù Gōng* (故宫) is behind the Heavenly Gate where you can queue up and pay to enter the rooms and chambers built originally by the Ming Emperor Zhu De in the early fifteenth century when he decided to move his palace from Nanjing to Beijing. Towards the end of his reign it was struck by lightning and a great fire destroyed much of the palace. Zhu thought that the gods were angry with him and then went into a steep decline before his eventual death.

For some reason, the entrance closes very early in the afternoon so plan to make it a morning trip. Around this area will be lots of touts offering tours to the Great Wall and other attractions.

Beijing is the staging post to the Great Wall and the same trip usually includes a visit to the Ming Tombs. Most hotels will sell this for around 500 yuan but you can get a tour outside from many minibus operators for around 100.

The Great Wall itself is impressive, an enormous structure that follows the mountain ridges as it disappears either over the horizon or into the pollution. The Ming Tombs are less likely to impress, like many Chinese tourist destinations they are poorly managed and under funded.

For shopping in Beijing, perhaps the best place to go is *Wáng Fǔ Jǐng* (王府井) which is a long street that runs perpendicular to Changan Jie right in the middle. As you enter the long pedestrian shopping avenue you will notice an art shop that never changes with three large portraits in the window of Zhou Enlai, Mao Zedong and Liu Shaoqi. This area has everything; a mixture of Chinese department stores, western style malls and smaller shops. Some of the side streets are also worth exploring as they have typical tourist type market gifts from modest stalls.

A bit further up on the left, in the evening is a night food street, a continuous line of uniformly sized stalls selling all kinds of snacks, mostly on skewers. This is clearly aimed at the tourist as everything is clean, neatly laid out and conforms to a set of rules in terms of what is on offer, the service provided and the shape, colours and size of the stalls. Some of the food on offer is a bit unusual, for example fried starfish or bull's testicles. Most worrying is how so many outlets sell fried sea horses on a wooden skewer, aren't they an endangered species?

Other markets are around that sell fake clothes, fake bags and fake antiques but these are slowly disappearing as Beijing attempts to position itself as a city on a par with New York, London or Paris.

The weather in Beijing is like most places in China, uncomfortable except for April and October. The winters are bitterly cold, often with mid-day temperatures well below zero. The summers are baking hot with numbers that soar well into the forties. On top of that, May tends to suffer from sandstorms as the winds blow great clouds of dust eastwards from the Mongolian plains, uninhibited since the Chinese have consumed most of the trees that were in the way, which in turn means more soil erosion and even more dust. These storms get worse every year, they now ground planes, make it unsafe to venture outdoors and more recently blow as fart east as the Korean peninsula.

The final thing to say about Beijing is that you cannot escape to notice how bad the air quality is. Sometimes you can hardly make out the buildings across the street. This city has had a severe clean-up operation on its hands as it does not want the embarrassing mass withdrawal of athletes due to potentially chronic respiratory problems after running the hundred metres.

Shenzhen

Somebody described Shenzhen to me as having all the hardware but no software. A reference to the many high rise shiny steel buildings with their reflective windows and visually challenging shapes yet at street level, still very much ethnic China. To most Hong Kong people it is *their* forbidden city. *Lonely Planet* probably never went there as they say some unkind things about the crime and advise you to pass on through. After the apparent organisation and comfort of Hong Kong, this does indeed, at first glance, seem like bandit country.

We need to put things in perspective, Shenzhen does, like the rest of Guangdong, has a fairly high crime rate for sure. However, China itself is an extremely safe place and non-violent, it is just that Shenzhen is slightly less safe. Most crime is petty, handbag and mobile phone snatching in particular, I have never heard of foreigners being physically attacked, raped or mugged. So ignore the rubbish in the well-known travel guides and read on, it is one of the most exciting and fun places in the country and it all comes, unlike Beijing and Shanghai, at a very fair price.

Shenzhen was founded by Deng Xiao Ping where it was one of the enterprise zones he created when he first experimented with capitalism, the city is only twenty five years old yet now has a population exceeding ten million. It's growth must be one of the most remarkable achievements of any city, anywhere on the world.

Real China

Geographically it is just north of Hong Kong and runs along an extensive piece of coastline in an east-west fashion. The city comprises five main areas that are within the enterprise zone, *Yantian* in the west, *Luohu* and *Futian* districts in the middle and *Nanshan* in the east. Just south of Nanshan is *Shekou*. Yantian has a port and the cleanest beaches but is separated, some would argue cut-off, from the rest of the city by a traffic choked tunnel. Luohu is next to Hong Kong and is where most of the crooks are! Futian is really the city centre and Nanshan is mostly residential but also houses the famous theme parks of the city. Shekou is also a port but has many foreign residents with up-market housing and international schools.

The whole city is around 45km long as it stretches along the main roadway *Shennan* Avenue. In December 2004, the Shenzhen Metro opened and effectively runs along the city underneath the Shennan highway. It is clean and fairly efficient with trains running every five or six minutes on Line 1 that is. Line 4 which runs North/South has only five stations and one of those, recently the Huang Gang border station has opened that links up with the train to Hong Kong. The trouble with Line 4, is that they treat it in the same way that they treat bus timetables, that is pay no attention to them whatsoever and wait until they, or platforms in this case, are full before the service commences.

There are three main crossing points from Hong Kong into China, by train at Luo Hu (called Lo Wu in Hong Kong) on the KCR (Kowloon Canton Railway) that starts downtown at Tsim Sha Tsui East station. The journey called be called a slow train to China as it takes about 45 minutes but only costs HK$36.

Shenzhen is the only city in China that can be arrived at without a visa. It is still necessary to buy a visa but you can do so at the Luo Hu border, it lasts five days and restricts your movements to within the economic zone of the city.

Another border crossing is at Huang Gang (now has a railway station too) and this has direct buses from Hong Kong airport at a cost of HK$100 as well as several locations all over the city, this one is open 24 hours so if arriving late, after the last bus has left, it is possible to take a taxi that will cost around HK$300, directly to the frontier. It is also possible, but not publicised, to buy a normal 30 day visa at the Huang Gang border between 9am and 5pm. When entering the Chinese checkpoint go to the office in the corner on the extreme left and apply.

The other crossing at Shekou, is undertaken by boat, again possible to buy a visa 09.00 to 17.00. If staying in this district or Nanshan then this is the way to go. Ferries leave directly from HK airport without the need to pass immigration formalities until you reach China. The check-in desk is *before* passport control at the airport and the staff there will retrieve your bags from the carousel and load them on the boat for you. The trip is relatively expensive at HK$ 230, takes about thirty five minutes and is somewhat stress-free compared to the other two methods of crossing into China. If you are heading to Futian or Luohu though, there is a 60-70 yuan taxi ride from the ferry port. There are also ferries to and from Shekou from Central on Hong Kong island and the China Ferry Terminal in Kowloon.

Both the Luo Hu and Huang Gang borders are totally inadequate for the numbers of people that use them, being overcrowded and leading to long queues. Rush hour is the worst time to cross, as so many people commute across borders, and Luo Hu is perhaps less hassle than Huang Gang. Now that Disneyland has opened, it won't be long before Mickey Mouse and friends will be at the border enticing people onto special buses that take them straight to the fun. Not sure where the fun comes from, queue for an hour, two minute thrill, queue for an hour, another two minute thrill and so on; they have to pay me to go there, not the other way around.

If you fly into Shenzhen's Bao'an airport then it is about 40km to the city downtown and will cost about 120 yuan in a taxi. The airport is outside of the city and so it is necessary to cross a controlled entry and exit point. This was put in place in the old days when the government was trying to restrict the numbers of people going to Shenzhen, fearing that they may escape into Hong Kong. Strictly speaking, Chinese need a permit to enter the city and the checkpoints are still there even though their function is redundant, closing it would mean a lot of job losses so it remains.

The best way to get to Futian centre is to take the airport bus, as you come out of either terminal, right in front is usually a large blue comfortable bus with 333 written on the side. Buy a ticket for 20 yuan from the small kiosk and the bus will take you all the way to *Ke Xue Guan* metro station in the city centre. Plenty of taxis will be waiting there to take you further. This is the safest, most comfortable and least hassle way to get to the city and it is very cheap.

Shenzhen's Nanshan district in what is known as the overseas Chinese town or *huaqiaocheng*, has three very large theme parks; Happy Valley, Windows of the World and Splendid China Culture Museum.

Happy Valley is a kind of Disneyland, a mixture of rides and attractions that appeal to the younger visitor. Extremely overcrowded at the best of times, with long queues for everything but it does have a reasonable swimming pool with slides, chutes and artificial waves.

Windows of the World is an extremely large park with a collection models or various buildings and monuments from all over the world. At its entrance is an impressive one third size model of the Eiffel Tower, for some reason, illuminated as a Christmas tree at night. If you're missing home then wander over and look at the not so inspiring recreations of Buckingham Palace, Tower Bridge and Stonehenge. They have pyramids and camels, Niagara falls and a perfect representation of the Palais de Versailles, how come they got the French bits right?

In the summer months, after 6.30pm, the park becomes a beer festival, with mostly local beers and a few equally bland international offerings. It takes place in a large hall, who's exterior is supposed to be a copy of Caesar's Palace, not the real one but the hotel in Las Vegas. There is a stage with a constant flow of entertainment including their own attempt at *Riverdance*, best described as the stiff arm floppy leg show.

Of the three parks, the best one by far is the Splendid China Folk Culture Museum. It is actually two parks in one, when you enter the left hand side there is the China part and the right hand side has the folk and culture part.

This is a huge park and you need to allow a day to see all of it. Again it covers models of virtually everywhere in China, but the models are worked into the landscape so as to make the whole place pleasant and peaceful. It is a Godsend that the Chinese don't like walking very far, they soon get tired after a couple of hundred metres then you virtually have the place to yourself. They have perfect models of palaces, mountains, scenery and monuments from across the country, even a Great

Wall that follows the peaks of the land contour around the park. It is a good place to go in order to decide as to which place you'd like to see for real.

China allegedly has some 51 different nationalities although all of them are in a tiny minority and dwarfed by the dominant Han. However, this park has a snapshot of each of these obscure races, with a small mock-up of their environment, traditional costumes and song and dance shows. There are also several stalls and shops selling related giftware and souvenirs. The only downside, and this is the same with virtually every tourist attraction nationwide, the food and beverage outlets are of poor quality, expensive and have miserable staff. The park is though highly recommended and on a daytrip to Shenzhen, perhaps the best place to go.

Please do not be tempted to go to Shenzhen zoo, it is nothing less than a freak show with, for example, monkeys dressed in silly clothes performing daft tricks. More worryingly they have a tiger that visitors can go up to and stroke. Highly dangerous you might think but no, the poor animal is drugged stupid every day for the pleasure of the zoo's customers.

The shopping outlets are in easy access of the metro and almost follow it's course from Luo Hu. At the border in Luo Hu is a large mall that houses hundreds of small stalls. This is fake city, if ever there was one. They sell and copy everything but the best bargains are to found with handbags and luggage, jewellery and watches. In order to thwart the authorities, much of what is on show is unmarked and unbranded but relatively good quality. However, step inside the shop and the assistant will get a colour brochure out from under the counter and let you choose from a range of 'designer' labels. Or you could choose a handbag and wait while they put a *Gucci* label on it for you.

Copy watches are a speciality here too, a good place to buy a *Rolex* but do not wear it too often because the jewels and gold plate soon come off, oddly the mechanisms are of high quality. Most of the shop proprietors are sharks but with a warped taste exclusively for Caucasian flesh. The price asked will always be three or four times the going rate, for an 80 yuan handbag, they will first ask 300. Just walk away until they drop the price to an acceptable level, never compare with what you would pay back home. This area is also a pickpocket feeding ground so guard belongings at all times, constantly keep a look out for characters that brush by or just stay too close.

Next stop is Dongmen district, a downmarket street of mostly clothing and shoe shops. It is just two stops on the metro from Luo Hu at *Lao Jie* station. A mostly tatty area but a great place to get bargain jeans and other denim items. There are also a couple of department stores that are reasonably priced.

Hop back on the train one more stop and you get to *Da Ju Yuan* station. Directly above is a very large shopping mall, known more by its Western name as 'The MIXc' or *wan xiang shang chang* in Chinese(万象商场) more up-market housing several designer brand shops and Chinese *almost-the-same name* pseudo-western brands. This is a big airy place, comparable to those that they have in the United States. The ground floor has lots of restaurants and coffee shops plus a couple of real bakers that bake really fresh bread. Most of the restaurants are American fast food chains such as *Pizza Hut*, *MacDonald's*, *KFC* and *Tacobell* which the *Shenzhen Daily* described as Mexican food served greasy American style.

Real China

Two stops more on the metro and you arrive at *Hua Qiang Bei*, this is really the city centre, in Futian district. A long wide, palm tree lined street with a large mixture of shopping malls, mobile phone outlets and electronics shops. The area is always crowded and busy but well worth a wander up if only because of the sheer scope of products and price ranges on offer. Whether you want cheap and cheerful products or expensive brands, you can get it all here. It is spoilt by the traffic and the fact that pedestrian crossings are not, as anywhere in this country, respected by drivers. The other problem is that so many shops have loudspeakers directed outwards onto the pavement either blaring distorted music or unintelligible sales pitches. More upsetting is the common presence of severely disabled beggars as they crawl along the street, many of them children, and get stepped over as if they weren't there.

Shenzhen should be China's gourmet capital, with the enforcement of a few hygiene rules that is. I have never seen a city, anywhere in the world, with more restaurants than this one. Just about every type of *Chinese* food is on offer, spicy, salty, sweet and always oily. They have a diner that caters for the food from virtually every city and corner of the nation. I once asked why this should be the case and the reason given is because the city has a quite high average income but it also benefits from very low living costs so people have a lot of disposable cash, so the next most common pastime after praying to become rich is to eat.

One of the best streets for this is *Hua Fa Bei Lu* and the alleyways that join it. This road is one block to the east away from Hua Qiang Bei. Seafood is a speciality and so many restaurants have their terraced displays of fish tanks at the front of the shop. Just choose what you want and they'll weigh it and cook it. If you are in a hurry and do not want to spend much, try *Mian Dian Wang* (面點王), there are outlets all over the city, the food tastes good and the hygiene levels are high. One particular advantage is that there is no need to speak Chinese, you take the card they give to you, go to the counter, point at what you want and the chef will mark the card and bring it to your table. All done, take the card to the cashier and pay. A good meal here will cost three pounds for two people.

The night life in Shenzhen is extensive as well as being very good value for money. Bars are everywhere and they are all stuffed with girls, remember this city has a female to male ratio of 7 to 1. To meet other westerners or expats, a good place to start is the Citic centre or *zhong xin guang chang* (ke xue guan metro) in Chinese, it has a really nice spread of attractive looking bars where you can sit outside and watch the world go by. A particular favourite, extremely popular with the expat community is 3D bar, also known as Beers World (their grammar), the place opens about 4pm and closes when the last person leaves, there is always someone to talk to and they sell just about every yellow, gassy and tasteless beer on the planet.

Over in Luo Hu they have several noisy music bars, each with a fair number of working girls. The best value and most downmarket is U bar (in *JinWeiDaSha*), then there is Face bar and True Colour bar; the latter have rather snooty staff and minimum spend policy if you sit close to the band.

In Nanshan, V bar on the second floor of the Crowne Plaza Hotel has a large curved bar with a dance floor in front and a band singing behind the bar. The place is always busy with lots of un-choreographed rockers prancing around and lots of cool, well-dressed whores eyeing up their prey. Here it is better to sit outside by the pool, where the music is less overpowering, and discretely observe the hovering prostitutes, trying hard not to look them in the eye which is like holding up a bar of chocolate to a hungry child.

Over in Shekou, by the sea life centre, there is a collection of really nice restaurants and bars, more pricey and mostly western. The Irish pub MaCawleys sells draft Guinness and serves excellent food. Further along is what is known as 'Chicken Street' a collection of bars, filled with scantily dressed beauties any one of which can be had for a price. There are also many of these just hanging around on the streets, I guess they have no other source of income.

It is worth pointing out the weather in Shenzhen, it is mostly tropical and pleasant with a very short winter that lasts from January through to the middle of February, the rest of the year is very warm but humid. The worst months are June, July and August where the heat and near saturated humidity make the atmosphere sticky and uncomfortable, it is even too hot to go out at midnight. With August comes the monsoon rains and spectacular thunderstorms, fascinating to watch as each tall building gets struck in turn by an army of angry gods.

Given Shenzhen's long period of hot weather, it can be worthwhile taking the time to realx on some of the nearby beaches. Very pleasant, clean and often deserted, *xichong* （西冲）just an hour's drive away makes it feel remarkable that you could be in a country with 1.3 billion people.

A lot of bad things are written and said about Shenzhen but if you want to have a lot of fun and not spend a lot of money this is the next best place to Bangkok.

Other Destinations
The truth is that most of China's cities are very similar, very few are radically different or interesting. They all, perhaps with the exception of Hainan Island, suffer from dreadful air quality, uncomfortable weather and weather extremes, too much traffic and severe overcrowding. In some ways, China suffers from the same lack of characterless monotony as the USA. If you were to be taken blindfolded to most American cities, upon seeing the light you would not have a clue where you are due to the familiar rows of fast food chains, gas stations and motels. China is the same except the picture is always choking air, grey buildings and a state of half-finished construction.

Many Chinese cities are rows and rows of square buildings, maybe five storeys high, with white tiles and blue tinted windows. Older cities tend to be similar but the buildings are worn out and grey in colour. If you go to a hotel that is higher than these box-like structures, you look down upon the flat roofs and view the decades of rubbish and debris that have been stored or discarded to the roof, a great play area for rats.

I cannot describe all of the cities here since I have not been to all of them but the following are some brief details on some of the cities that are likely to be visited, starting from the north and moving south. It needs to be said though that the three aforementioned cities, Shanghai, Beijing and Shenzhen are exceptional in that they differ greatly not only from each other but also from the rest of the country.

Harbin
This is an industrial city in the north east 'rust belt'. So called because of the large number of decaying traditional industries,

many closures and depressing environment. Due to its close proximity to the Russian (Siberian) border, the buildings are a bit different in that there is a lot of this style around.

The city does not seem as crowded as most places and the streets are wide. The centre is dominated by the large coal-fired power station that provides warmth, electricity and a nice breath of sulphur dioxide.

The summers are cool and brief, the winters are long and cold. From mid-November until the end of February the temperature stays below zero, in January it falls to -30 C typically, it is so cold the air on the face prickles as if you are rubbing a hedgehog across the skin. The moisture inside the nose freezes, picking the nose, rather than blowing it, is the only thing possible.

The upside of such a freezing environment is the ice sculpture festival that goes on throughout the winter. It is impressive, huge illuminated structures made from ice blocks, often using themes related to nationwide landmarks such as temples, pagodas, walls and bridges. The lights are inside the ice sculptures, in many colours, red, blue and green dominate. The park is very big, each ice figure can be as high as ten metres and it takes about two hours to walk around them all. Consequently the Harbin tourist season is January and February although the former is just too cold to enable walking around in any degree of comfort.

Tianjin
Only an hour by road or car from Beijing, the country's number three city and most people have not even heard of it. Tianjin is a municipality like Beijing, Chongqing and Shanghai, although it is surrounded by *Hebei* province and borders on the northeast with Beijing municipality.

This city is a very big port, anything sent to the capital will come via here.

Historically it was a stronghold for the foreign powers during the late Qing period as they either advanced or withdrew from Beijing. It follows that a lot of the buildings are of European style.

Like most cities in the People's Republic, it is in a state of construction. Some of the water sports for the Olympic Games will be held here so there is a mad panic to get the place looking more like a city and less like a construction site on time. There is a wide river that passes through the city and flows out to the sea, it is uninspiringly called the HaiHe or literally sea river. As cities develop, waterside spots become much sought after and my guess is that one day this city, only an hour from the capital, will become a desirable place to live. The Astor Hotel, a four star establishment, next to the river is an example of this, built in the nineteenth century by rich British colonialists, it is something of a Museum and art gallery with artefacts and paintings from the late Qing period. It will sound familiar to many people having a Windsor room, a Victoria room and a Gordon room, named after the General who was famous in China for assisting the defeat of the TaiPing.

Tianjin is famous for it's baozi or steamed dumplings. The most famous of all is *Goubuli*, which means that the dog wouldn't go near. A strange name but the story goes that it is named after a young man who was so hideous that he scared everyone and so they named him 'Goubuli' he did however make the tastiest baozi in the land and so he opened a restaurant which quickly became a success and even the Empress Dowager, Cixi, travelled there to sample them. Today, there is a restaurant in Tianjin's food street (*nan shi*

shi pin jie 南市食品街) actually called Goubuli but the taxi driver told me that it is not the real thing, the original restaurant is on Shandong road in an old building, on several floors. The dumplings are nice, but I wouldn't travel there especially to try them. It was a bit like the time when I had a girlfriend from Yorkshire and she encouraged me to visit the original 'Harry Ramsden's' fish and chip shop at Guiseley, before it became a marketing brand and vanished into mediocrity. I had tasted just as good in Cornwall.

Goubuli baozi are also expensive, they are steamed in individual baskets, approximately 6cm diameter and cost from seven to twenty two yuan each, which is serious money for a dumpling.

Somebody else is marketing jaozi, (boiled dumplings) and calls them '*maobuwen*' which means the cat won't smell, just to keep the originality going.

Possibly the most famous Tianjin food is *Shibajie mahua* (十八街 麻花) the deep fried crispy plaited snack that is seen at the airport and shops everywhere. Shibajie means 18 street but it does not exist, it disappeared years ago.

The weirdest snack, which I took one bite of and spat out, tasted like plasticine wrapped in deep fried blotting paper. It looks like a fritter but absorbs more oil than a Texas rancher and has red bean paste in the middle. It is called '*er duo yan zha gao*' (耳朵眼炸糕) which means ear-hole fried cake.

One thing is for sure, the people in this city have a great sense of humour and are probably the most cheerful and polite crowd that I have come across, in the whole country. They do though put on an extreme *argh* sound to what seems like the ending of every word in their highly distinguishable local accent.

Places Around China

Other Places

Chanchun is another north-east town with a long cold winter of sub-zero temperatures. They have their own ice statues here as well but not nearly as impressive as the ones in Haerbin. This city is dirty, heavily polluted and has characteristic square five-storey buildings, grey, dark and scruffy. The air smells of coal dust and cows pull carts down the street, amongst the shiny new Volkswagens that are made here.

It does have one of the biggest automobile factories in the country, a joint venture between China's First Auto Works and Volkswagen. They make the Jetta and Bora models here. Changchun also makes most of the railway rolling stock.

So many of the major provincial capitals are exactly like this, in state of construction, half falling down, half being built, too much traffic, air pollution and dust. There are some exceptions; Chengdu in Sichuan province still has the square lifeless buildings but also has wide tree-lined streets and does feel clean. Nearby Chengdu, is ChongQing, the world's biggest municipality with in excess of thirty million people, there is more interest, the city resides on either side of the deep Yangtze valley and has many hills, bendy roads and altogether a different topography.

Xiamen (previously known as Amoy) in the south, is a pleasant beachside city with the beautiful island of *Gulangyu* a short ferry hop away where vehicles are banned and the beaches are clean. There is even a hotel there, the island can be covered in a day's walking.

Guangzhou, (Canton) being in the hot and sticky Guangdong province is a lot better than it was as much of the construction is finished. However it could be a substantially nicer place, especially as the city heads the Pearl River delta. Snotty taxi drivers make the city a struggle to move around although the metro is cheap, clean and easy to use.

In the deep south, you have Hainan Island which stays hot and humid all year round. It came to fame in April 2001 when a US spy plane had to make an emergency landing after 'bumping' into a Chinese fighter jet. The island is relatively small and a couple of days are enough to see the whole of it. The southern tip has the coastal resort of Sanya with its long sandy beaches, flash hotels, endless seafood restaurants and the biggest collection of crooks and cheats I have come across in China. The annual Miss World competition is held in Sanya every year, probably the last city on earth that will have them. The principle town is Haikou, also a resort but bigger and more industrial although similar in character to Sanya with the same 'fuck the tourists' approach to welcoming visitors. Hainan is essentially run by the local Mafiosi, the taxi meters are doctored, restaurants and bars always fiddle the bill, and whores in almost every hotel. This island is simply not a pleasant place to spend your spare time.

Xi'an is one of the more famous tourist spots, it is one of the few cities left with a medieval city wall and some historical buildings of interest. The place is choked with traffic and suffers from heavy pollution and a desperately unhealthy atmosphere. It is a pleasant place though, the people are friendly and the food is cheap and plentiful although tends to be spicy. This city, formerly called Chang-an, was the capital of early dynasties and is the staging post for a trip to see Qin Shi Huang's terracotta army. In addition there are many other temples, spas and places of interest in the surrounding countryside. It also has the biggest queue outside of MacDonald's that I have ever seen in my life, at least 30 or 40 people outside on the street.

The best food to try is the leg of lamb, for about 30 Yuan a whole leg, roasted in cumin seeds is delivered to the table. It is hard to get through it but the locals will easily polish off two or three per table of four people. Xi'an also has some good dumpling shops, cheap and delicious.

China though is a big country and there are almost endless places to visit but if there is only one place in China that you can get to for some light recreation then that must be Yangshuo. Yangshuo is a small town that sits on the Li river in the northern part of Guangxi province which is supposedly one of the four autonomous regions which are represented by the four small stars on the Chinese flag.

The scenery here is, to use a well worn cliché, breathtaking. The landscape is covered with large limestone mountains that protrude up from the ground like giant mole hills, ranging from twenty or thirty metres high to several hundred. The area is a dense maze of meandering rivers, mountains, hills and fertile rice paddies. The pollution is low and the area looks and feels green and fresh. The area is what is geologically known as a *Karst* landscape, being formed by millennia of acidic rain onto a limestone base. It follows that the area also has extensive underground caves with enormous stalagmites, stalactites and thermal mud baths.

The people here are amongst some of the poorest in the whole country, they lead a simple life, have simple homes and work all day in the fields growing mostly rice but also fruit and vegetables. You can eat in restaurants where the cook pops into the garden and picks the food and kills the chicken immediately before cooking it.

The great thing about Yangshuo is that it feels relaxing, perhaps you feel intoxicated by the scenery or maybe it is the thrill of breathing clean air, after a choking visit to Beijing or Xi'an, but there is something about the place, almost magical, almost surreal. I first arrived at Guilin airport at night, following the usual three hour Air China delay. The bus trip from the airport to Yangshuo takes around ninety minutes and there is virtually no light and so the shapes and forms of the narrow peaks as they line the road can just be made out. It gives a sense of eeriness, as if being observed by giant beings from a *Lord of the Rings* scene.

Yangshuo itself is quite a busy place, something of a tourist hot spot with coaches and taxis coming and going all the time. It lies a little way along the river from the main city of Guilin. The Chinese say that the landscape of Guilin is the finest under heaven but Yangshuo feels cosier, friendlier and more fun.

As always in life, the simplest things seem to bring the most pleasure and often cost the least money, so don't go out in a taxi, don't take the river cruiser just hire a bicycle plus guide for a few pounds and spend the whole day cycling around some of the most incredible sights on earth. It is almost like a time gone by, seeing people wash their clothes in the river as well as plucking their chicken for lunch. Children run out of their house to wave and shout hello, mile upon mile of rice fields and not a tractor in sight, animals still pull the ploughs. Fishermen use cormorants to catch fish, they tie their neck so that the unfortunate bird cannot swallow its catch.

To top it all, the entertainment in Yangshuo will not leave you bored, many restaurants and lively bars, mostly open air and mostly very cheap. Souvenir shops are everywhere selling for pennies those silk and batik items that cost tens of pounds in the big cities. There is even one shop where they make silk garments, from bug to clothing, on the premises, you can see them soaking the pupae in warm water and removing the little fur jacket fibre coating. The wet silk is then collected like large wet balls of lambs wool before being dried and spun into thread manually. The silk garments are then hand made and dyed into whatever is required including complete duvets. The little bugs which must be shivering inside having had their silky coat pilfered are not wasted either, they soon get warmed up as they are dipped in a deep fryer, sprinkled with salt and eaten as a tasty (apparently) snack.

I really do not know how to recommend this place enough, less famous than the Great Wall and the Terracotta soldiers but if you do go, then all the bad experiences; countless arguments with taxi drivers, overpriced dodgy goods and uncomfortable bus rides will soon be forgotten and forgiven and don't forget the camera.

Chapter 14 – It Could All End in Tears

The Japanese
In April of 2005, there was open debate about Germany, Japan and India becoming permanent members of the UN Security Council (currently China, UK, USA, France and Russia are the only permanent members). To the Chinese, Japan is still the bogey man, to them sharing a forum with Japan would be worse than sharing the wife with a porn star. To its credit, Japan donates almost a billion US dollars in foreign aid to China each year, of this few Chinese are aware. To its demise, Japan tones down its expansionist history through inaccurate school history text books and the recent leader, Koizumi, insisted on his provocative 'private' visits to the Yasukuni war shrine.

Unfortunately, at this time, the petition to join the UN Security Council, coincided with the release of new Japanese 'ripping yarn' history books for schools. There was a lot of noise in the Chinese papers followed by student marches along the streets of major cities such as Beijing, Shanghai, Guangzhou and Shenzhen. I watched as an angry mob smashed the local Japanese *Jusco* supermarket in Shenzhen. The supermarket employed several hundred Chinese workers and sold mostly Chinese goods. Similarly, restaurants and even Japanese people were attacked. The newspapers showed nothing of the rioting, just said that the Chinese were offended by the new history books. The English language Shenzhen Daily, did not mention it at all but had a colour pull-out section with pictures of the Nanjing massacre.

Almost certainly what had happened, was that the government had ordered universities to post messages of forthcoming marches to protest about Japan's schoolbooks It would have been, I have no doubt, unpatriotic not to attend the march. These marches went on for four weekends, thousands of 'police' were drafted in. They were not real police, China does not have that many, probably civil servants ordered to attend, wearing uniforms with those just out of the packet creases. Many of these blue-uniformed recruits were filming the events with their own home movie cameras.

Eventually, Japanese protests and international comment prevailed and the marches and rioting stopped. The students who did the smashing were paraded on national TV like criminals as if they did it autonomously.

A minor event that received little international coverage yet it showed clearly how this is still a potentially dangerous country, the government remains capable of whipping up Cultural Revolution style mass hysteria and hatred. Was this really so different from the red guards persecuting the innocent, forty years ago? Propaganda can be created, spread and believed without question. There is an intense and underlying nationalism in this country, something we do not have in the UK.

I know a very sweet and polite Japanese lady, that frequents the usual expat watering holes, who was attacked during this period. The little twelve year old girl, daughter of my friend, whom I teach English to on Saturday mornings told me that one of her school chums had a Japanese digital camera, then one morning a group of other Chinese kids in the class, grabbed the camera and smashed it. Such hatred being programmed into the minds of school kids is reason for great concern.

For the Chinese it was a major own goal, it occurred just at the time the European Union was negotiating to lift the arm sales embargo that had been in place since the 1989 Tiananmen massacre. These events helped those commissioners with any doubt to make up their minds. Thank heavens the EU did not foolishly allow sales of high-tech weapons to resume.

A couple of months later, as the world celebrated the 60th anniversary of the end of World War Two, the papers and TV were filled with pictures and stories of Japanese atrocities.

These events though were significant, just as Japan was once a rapidly expanding nation that was hungry for resources to feed its industry and population, so too is China today. Japan embarked on a period of imperial expansion that was cruel and remorseless, could China possibly do the same?

Running out of Fuel

There is considerable trouble ahead, mid-summer of 2005 was extremely hot, Beijing was in the mid-forties and the south, although cooler had near 100% humidity. As a consequence, there was widespread use of air conditioners, normally they use them as a last resort as electricity is not much cheaper than in western Europe. The result was widespread power cuts. In Beijing, factories were closed on alternate weeks to save power, foreign owned enterprises were, interestingly, guaranteed continuous supply. There were widespread instructions to turn the temperature of air conditioners up to twenty six degrees centigrade, in order to save power. In Guangdong, the filling stations ran out of petrol and factories suffered frequent power cuts. Failure to set your AC unit to the directed number was widely publicised as being 'unpatriotic'.

Most of China's energy comes from coal fired power stations, and with an economy growing at ten per cent per year that means a continual increase in the country's capacity to generate power, it cannot keep up without the two new power stations per week model.

As there is now so much demand for power, lots of coal needs to be mined, more and more in fact. If you can mine it, you can sell it. As a result miners work long hours in unsafe conditions, often in illegal or unapproved facilities. Almost every week, miners are killed up and down the country due to collapse, flooding, poisoning or explosion. It is impossible to put a figure on it, since most deaths go unreported, but miners are perhaps the biggest tragedy in new China. There is so much demand for coal that new mines with little or no safety standards appear all the time. Officials are bribed to turn a blind eye, owners make fortunes from the sales of coal and week by week, month by month, men die in order to keep the air-con units going. The system needs a complete overhaul, all mines should stop work and each one should be inspected for safety but to do that would stop China. So nobody cares, except the families of the dead, the Chinese read about it almost every day but nothing is done. There are talks of having some kind of inspection system, independent and sponsored by central government but you have to be cynical and conclude that even if such a body were created, it could easily be bribed to keep its mouth shut. Where is Arthur Scargill when you really need him?

The Beijing government is aware of the problem and often mutes about how it is going to get tough on illegal and unsafe mines. According to the Hong Kong based *South China Morning Post* the government has strongly criticised regional governments for not closing down some 5,000 illegal mines, during 2005. Fujian province was especially singled out for not closing a single illegal mine. Apparently 9,000 mines have been closed and a further 12,990 have had their operations suspended. Because of the way that land is organised in China, i.e. there are no freeholds, the state owns everything, it would be impossible to open a mine illegally without the cooperation and even assistance of the provincial and/or county government. Because coal is in such demand, that means lots of money to be made all 'round. The fact that so many poor miners are killed has caused embarrassment for the central government.

Despite all this deaths rose 46 per cent in 2005 and mining accounts for 56 per cent of all industrial fatalities in China. In 2007 they claimed that the death toll had reduced by 20% which seems hard to believe since there have been no major changes and the demand for coal has increased. It is the usual propaganda machine, quote a high figure one year then show how much it has been reduced the next. Government statistics simply cannot be believed. It does though exemplify how the great Chinese economic miracle is at the expense of a large pool of 'underclass' who, in order to survive, work long hours in dangerous circumstances for little money, no benefits and sheer exploitation.

Farmers

Although China is a now seen as an industrial power house, it cannot be forgotten that there are still 800 million or so farmers. These people are not in the same sense that we imagine a farmer to be, they have a small plot of land, no tractors or any kind of mechanisation just labour hard each day manually to grow their crops and tender their animals.

A farmer's income is low, but at least they have some income and they are not starving anymore. One of Deng Xiao Ping's smart moves was to allow farmers to sell their produce onto the open market, after they have sold their mandatory quota to the government. This blossomed into the over-supply of food, and the transition from starvation to obesity, much faster than has happened in any first world nation.

But farmers are still poor, they have inadequate access to education and health care and live on less than a few dollars per day.

If China were a democracy, their situation would be a lot different as they are the overwhelming majority. Despite this they get the roughest treatment, their land is taken at will by corrupt officials to build roads, factories and other industrial or domestic buildings. The city folk talk about them as if they are an underclass, looked down upon and exploited when they come to the city to find work. Most are deeply bitter and feel left out of the 'Chinese miracle'. But wait a minute, isn't this how it all started, an over-privileged minority being overwhelmed by Mao and his mobilised mass army of peasants?

Riots in the countryside are commonplace but infrequently reported, where murderous disputes between poor farmers and industrial developers exist. Some areas are no-go for even the police.

If China cannot start to look after these people soon then maybe history will start to repeat itself. As soon as there is unrest, foreigners and their investments will make a fast exit and the country will collapse.

Polluted Chaos

And then we go back to the motor car, in an ideal world, cars would produce no pollution, sensors would be fitted that would prevent all accidents and Jeremy Clarkson could only get a job as a traffic warden. That seems a long way off, especially in China where the latest trend is to ban compact cars from cities. By compact they mean small, inexpensive fuel efficient cars. The papers have said that 84 cities have decided to ban compact cars from their roads because it would improve the cities' appearance, solve the traffic jam problem and reduce pollution.

Shenzhen is deliberating over whether or not to introduce the policy and The Shenzhen Daily then went on to quote a traffic policeman by the name of *Li Jinsen*. His remarks are pure gold, they were printed as follows:

"To be honest, compact cars do have many problems. The fuel may not burn completely as the vehicle's engine is small, which causes more pollution than bigger cars. Moreover, compact cars are slower than other vehicles, which may slow down the traffic flow".

This kind of mentality is common throughout the country, it is not just a problem with policeman Li, governments make these kind of decisions. The Chinese all think that if you go faster, there are less traffic jams (forgetting also that more accidents happen) and they just cannot understand that a three litre engine produces more pollution than a one litre model. So, the pollution will get worse, the traffic will come to a halt and more people will die on the roads.

This respect or worship of the motor car is taking priority over everything else. I often think to myself that in the future when water is rationed as it may well be due to the rate at which they increasingly consume the stuff, people will have a daily allowance of one litre for drinking, half a litre for washing the body (as many seem to do now) and twenty litres for washing the car.

It Could All End in Tears

Then there is the selfish way in which people drive, nobody ever, ever gives way to anyone else or allows somebody to pull in front with friendly wave or stops to allow small children to cross at a busy junction in safety.

Once I was driving through the city of Dongguan in southern China, stuck in a severe traffic jam. An ambulance was desperately trying to get through the traffic with its siren blaring, attempting to attend an emergency. Not a single car, bus or truck would pull over and let the ambulance pass, some deliberately cut him off, I have never seen such sheer arrogant selfish bloody mindedness anywhere else in the world.

The ultra-hot summer of 2005 saw severe fuel shortages, even petrol stations were running out, closed forecourts with no fuel signs. The government blamed the weather of course, not being able to make deliveries but it is symptomatic of a country that needs more and more energy to support its increasingly wealthy population's desire to drive a three litre.

That leads onto pollution itself. Here we have an almost insurmountable problem, one fifth of the world's people is changing from a rural backwater to an industrial power house. The first thirty percent of the country has changed already during the past twenty years, the remainder will follow in what maybe the next twenty years.

With human industrial activity comes the burning of fossil fuels, due to the energy requirements of production and the transportation of raw materials and finished goods. Further, there is the widespread use of chemicals and minerals that are used in manufactures and the associated discharge of waste products. Finally people now travel further to work where they can secure increased incomes and higher living standards. The population, with their new wealth, buys cars, air conditioners and other domestic appliances. When taking a holiday, they do not camp in the local forest or walk in the hills, they fly to an exotic foreign destination.

More fossil fuels are burned, more miners are killed digging them up, more toxic materials are discharged into rivers it is a self enhancing cycle for which China either does not have the regulations in place to stop or it wants to continue and show the world how smart it is. Even if it did attempt to change, corrupt officials could be easily bought to maintain the trends. The result will be and in many cases already is, an environmental disaster. Virtually the same thing is happening in India, another twenty per cent of the world's people.

We are all affected by high levels of pollution nowadays, be it from toxic rivers, air or food or indirectly as a result of greenhouse gas afflicted climate change.

I predict that this issue alone, be it from factories, vehicles or accidents, most likely collectively, will be the one single issue that stops China in its tracks, it has to check this ten per cent per annum growth that the government has targeted for the next twenty years. Pollution aside, where will China get all this extra energy from to fuel its annual growth? The cars get bigger, air conditioners become more normal, more power stations are built. There are tough times ahead.

The Yangtze river delta where it meets the East China Sea, leaving behind it the provinces of Jiangsu and Zhejiang on the north and south banks respectively, flows through China's most economically charged region, one that has now surpassed the Pearl river delta (in southern Guangdong). The average annual growth in this region itself has been eighteen percent, well above the ten per cent for the nation as a whole.

It Could All End in Tears

It follows that the river is now heavily polluted. Devastatingly serious although not really talked about very much, because this is also highly fertile land and an important part of feeding the 1.3 billion pairs of chopsticks.

In one county, Changxing, there are 175 battery factories, isn't one or two enough or maybe they are powering all the sex toys we read about earlier? These make sixty five per cent of the nation's vehicle batteries for use on the home market. Discharged pollutants have not only killed fish and shrimps in the river but also affected food grown in the area. The landscape surrounding the industry is a kind of toxic blotting paper as it absorbs the noxious contaminants from the factories which in turn seeps into the rivers and lakes and correspondingly is sucked-up by the roots of plants and trees.

Some areas are now completely unsuitable for growing vegetables and fruit in a region that is renowned for quality rice, peaches and plums. How much heavy metal gets into the soil is anybody's guess, the true figure would never be released, but mercury, cadmium and lead are extensively used in batteries and what's worse is that this kind of pollution is particularly persistent.

It is argued that such activity brings money into the area and offers valuable employment. The factories should clean up their act but that reduces profits in a land where Yuan worship is paramount, local governments should enforce better standards but this is a corrupt nation, officials are easily paid to turn a blind eye.

On Wednesday the 23rd November 2005, The water supply to the north-east city of Harbin 哈尔滨 was turned off. First reports were that it was due to essential emergency maintenance, the TV news showed people queuing up with dustbins for their buffer supply. The following day, the truth came out, upstream in the city of Jilin, there had been an explosion in a chemical factory. Sited very close to the Songhua river, the explosion, which also killed five people, released around one hundred tons of benzene and nitrobenzene into the river.

Benzene is a colourless chemical, derived from petroleum, and is used in various manufactures such as paint, dyes, adhesives and compact discs. It is highly carcinogenic and poisonous.

Harbin, a hundred miles or so down river, has an urban population of four million and almost ten million in the municipality. It derives it drinking water from the Songhua river, this incident could have poisoned everyone. The immediate reaction, in an area that suffers from acute winter water shortages because of the long dry season with average temperatures well below zero, was to empty two reservoirs into the river and dilute the pollutant. The flow of the water, was becoming slow at the time, due to the falling temperatures, making it even harder to flush the chemicals away, even so the toxic soup was forecasted to reach the Russian city of Khabarovsk, just over the border in less than two weeks. According to the Russians, the toxic spill affected 180km of river within their territory.

There was then some emergency drilling to find water in deep wells that is safe enough to drink, bottled water had sold out from supermarkets although more was immediately flown in. Air tickets out of the city were scarce, as were the trains fully laden. The water supply was forecast to be back on by the following Sunday. Amusingly, a certain *Ding Ning* has sued the Jilin chemical plant for 15 yuan, about £1, for the cost of a bottle of water.

It Could All End in Tears

Simultaneously, in Chongqing, another chemical explosion had also caused a benzene spill, the details of which were scanty.

These sort of stories are not surprising simply because of their frequency but China is an ecological disaster that was created in twenty years and maybe will take centuries to put right.

Bra Wars

This hit the headlines in late 2005 when shiploads of textiles were not allowed to be unloaded at European ports due to accusation, from our EU commissioner Peter Mandelson and others, of price dumping. At the same time there have been increasing calls from western nations for the Chinese to raise the allegedly undervalued Yuan's exchange rate and allow it to float openly. This is said to be the key to balancing the import deficits that most western states have with China. As usual they miss the point. Chinese companies employ cheap labour that work in lousy conditions, are not paid overtime, are entitled to few holidays and get no benefits. The businesses are probably financed by loans that never get repaid, there are no environmental controls, no product standards and no insurances and safety precautions. They have none of the overheads that western companies have. Until these are on a level footing, Chinese products, even of the highest quality, will always be cheaper. And by the way, isn't the Western World Inc rushing in their thousands to manufacture in China *because* of the cheap labour and lower costs?

Hypocrisy

It is easy for people like me to stand back and criticise China yet we in the West have perhaps even more to answer for. It is we who invented the motor car and pissed away most of the world's fossil fuel resource long before the developing world got a hunger for it. Can we really be surprised that nations such as China want some of the action too and should we not hang our heads in shame for creating the model in the first place? China now uses 6 million barrels of oil per day yet the USA with its population less than one quarter of China's uses 20 million per day.

We criticise China for its human rights record but was not bombing Iraq on the back of false, inaccurate or 'sexed-up' intelligence reports not a gross neglect of human rights? When Bush and Blair decided to drop bombs on Sadam's empire, they knew that thousands (it turned out to be tens of thousands) of innocent women, men and children would be killed, more would lose limbs or be horrifically deformed. How do they sleep at night? To rub salt in the wound our former PM is elevated to 'Middle East Peace Envoy' it's like putting the battered women's rest home under the charge of Jack the Ripper.

On the 30th November 2005 the USA executed its 1000th prisoner since the restoration of capital punishment in 1977. How can this country lecture on human rights when it unashamedly ignores the fundamental one, the right to life? It is also a racist policy, most people executed in the US are blacks who have killed whites. What's more is that Amnesty International lists the United States, along with Saudi Arabia, China, Yemen and Iran as the few countries who put to death, children under the age of 18!

Until we in the modern or western world get our own act together, there can never be a position of credibility where other nations' actions can be criticised.

It Could All End in Tears

There are also many good things to be said about China, it came from one of the darkest periods in any country's history (The Cultural Revolution) to become a stable and reasonably fair (dependent upon income) and ordered society.

Investment figures prove that China is seen as a safe place to put money, even if the returns have been poor, but the country is benefiting enormously from it.

It is fair to say that I have been very critical of Chinese customs and practises, some could argue I take a position of cultural superiority just as the Taiwan and Hong Kong people do toward their mainland cousins. It is difficult not to feel culturally superior but then following a visit to any UK city on a Saturday night, one could be forgiven for thinking that British culture has reduced to ten pints of lager, a chicken vindaloo and a punch-up. The *values* are the issue, not the culture.

It must be said though that China *is* something of a miracle; in the 1960s people barely had enough to eat, starvation in the countryside was commonplace. I can only finish on a positive note as the country displays its Olympic dream to a worldwide audience; today there is more food than anyone could possibly eat and nobody goes hungry, sure there is a wide disparage between the cities and the outside but in human history no other nation has taken so many people out of poverty, around four hundred million, in such a short space of time, less than twenty years. For that one achievement alone, today's China is a modern miracle.

Ah well, it's goodbye to China, I am now leaving, waiting at Hong Kong airport for VS201 to take me smoothly back to London; dreaming of the next day's pint of St Austell Ale, I

Real China

must however wait and sip the last local beer – yellow, gassy and tasteless.

Suggested Further Reading

Interesting books on China are surprisingly few apart from the glut of CEO style, "dare you miss out" type of management fodder. The following though cover some of the specific areas highlighted in this book, in much greater depth.

The Coming Collapse of China – Gordon Chang. He explains at length the fragility of the banking system and the way that the state owned firms are sinking the country's wealth.

The China Dream – Joe Studwell. Detailed accounts of how so many large corporations have put so much money into China with very poor returns.

Mr China – Tim Clissold. Accounts from an investment banker on specific cases of losing loads of cash in China for various reasons.

Mao A Life – Philip Short. A superbly detailed biography of Chairman Mao.

1421 The Year China Discovered the World – Gavin Menzies. A well argued book suggesting that China's early technological achievements led to discovering the Americas and Australia long before explorers such as Magellan, Columbus and the great Captain James Cooke.

To The Edge of the Sky – Gao Anhua. A heartbreaking account of how Mao's China tore a family to pieces and against each other, covering the early thirties until the Author's emigration to England in 1994.

The China Daily – A good source of what is happening in China now, although the statistics can usually be disproved with a few simple calculations.